The Hawk's Gray Feather

Volume I of
The Tales of Arthur

The Hawk's Gray Feather

A Book of The Keltiad

Patricia Kennealy

ROC

A ROC BOOK

5F

5-90 BT 1900

ROC
Published by the Penguin Group
Penguin Books USA Inc., 375 Hudson Street, New York, New York 10014, U.S.A.
Penguin Books Ltd, 27 Wrights Lane, London W8 5TZ, England
Penguin Books Australia Ltd, Ringwood, Victoria, Australia
Penguin Books Canada Ltd, 2801 John Street, Markham, Ontario, Canada L3R 1B4
Penguin Books (N.Z.) Ltd, 182–190 Wairau Road, Auckland 10, New Zealand

Penguin Books Ltd, Registered Offices:
Harmondsworth, Middlesex, England

First published by Roc, an imprint of Penguin Books USA Inc.
Published simultaneously in Canada.

First Printing, May 1990
10 9 8 7 6 5 4 3 2 1

 ROC is a trademark of Penguin Books USA Inc.

LIBRARY OF CONGRESS CATALOGING IN PUBLICATION DATA
Kennealy, Patricia.
   The hawk's gray feather: a book of the Keltiad / Patricia
Kennealy.
      p.   cm.—(The Tales of Arthur)
   ISBN 0-451-45005-1
   1. Arthurian romances—Adaptations.   I. Title.   II. Series:
Kennealy, Patricia. Tales of Arthur.
PS3561.E42465H39   1990
813'.54—dc20   89-38574
                                                           CIP

Printed in the United States of America
Set in Times Roman
Designed by Nissa Knuth

Acknowledgments

My thanks to some longtime heroes of mine: T. E. Lawrence (of Arabia) and James Graham, first Marquess of Montrose; for all-purpose inspiration, and from whom I stole most of my (well, Arthur's) battle plans.

Thanks too to heroes of another order: Henry Morrison, my agent; John Silbersack and Christopher Schelling, my editors, and the other good folk at NAL—all for conspicuous valor in the face of heavy fire (mine, alas!)—and the late Eileen Campbell Gordon of the late Rivendell Bookshop, for the unfailing supply of encouragement, friendship and world-class Celtic sourcebooks.

And thanks beyond thanking to Arthur—or Ambrosius, or Riothamus, or Macsen Wledig—Celtic emperor or British king or Romanized warlord: Whatever name he may have called himself, or may have been called by others, he set it in letters of flame on the walls of legend, and without him this tale and many others could never have been told.

For my sister, Regina

*I*n the Earth year 453 by the Common Reckoning, a small fleet of ships left Ireland, carrying emigrants seeking a new home in a new land. But the ships were not the leather-hulled boats of later legend, and though the great exodus was indeed led by a man called Brendan, he was not the Christian navigator-monk who later chroniclers would claim had discovered a New World across the western ocean.

These ships were starships; their passengers the Danaans, descendants of—and heirs to the secrets of—Atlantis, that they themselves called Atland. The new world they sought was a distant double-ringed planet, itself unknown and half legend; and he who led them in that seeking would come to be known as Saint Brendan the Astrogator.

Fleeing persecutions and a world that was no longer home to their ancient magics, the Danaans, who long ages since had come to Earth in flight from a dying sun's agonies, now went back to those far stars, and after two years' desperate wandering they found their promised haven. They named it Keltia, and Brendan, though he refused to call himself its king, ruled there long and well.

In all the centuries that followed, Keltia grew and prospered. The kings and queens who were Brendan's heirs, whatever else they did, kept unbroken his great command: that, until the time was right, Keltia should not for peril of its very existence reveal itself to the Earth that its folk had fled from; nor forget, for like peril, those other children of Atland who had followed them into the stars—the Telchines, close kin and mortal foes, who became the Coranians as the Danaans had become the Kelts.

*   *   *

Brendan had been twelve centuries in his grave when a time fell upon Keltia at which the Kelts still weep: a reign of blood and sorcerous violence, civil war and the toppling of the Throne of Scone itself; and all at the hand of Edeyrn the Archdruid, known ever after as Marbh-draoi—"Death-druid"—and rightly so.

Edeyrn fastened round Keltia's throat the iron collar of the Druid Theocracy and Interregnum, and, with the help of traitor Druids and the terrible enforcers called Ravens, kept it locked there for two hundred terrible years. The royal house of Dôn—such of it as did survive the Marbh-draoi's slaughter— was forced into hiding, while a great resistance movement, known as the Counterinsurgency, was formed to fight against the Theocracy's forces.

Yet even iron collars may be broken by a single sword-stroke, so that the arm behind the sword be strong enough— or so fated . . .

*T*his tale takes place fifteen hundred years before the reign of Aeron Queen of Kelts, as recounted in *The Silver Branch, The Copper Crown* and *The Throne of Scone.*

The year of its telling is approximately 2100 AD by Earth Reckoning, and when it begins the year by that count is 1952.

Twelve musics we learn in the Star of Bards, and these
the twelve:

Geantraí, the joy-song,
whose color is gold and whose shout creation;
whose number is one, and one is the number of birth.

Gráightraí, the heart-lilt,
whose color is green and whose descant rapture;
whose number is two, and two is the number of love.

Bethtraí, the fate-rann,
whose color is white and whose charge endurance;
whose number is three, and three is the number of life.

Goltraí, the grief-keen,
whose color is red and whose cadence sorrow;
whose num ber is four, and four is the number of death.

Galtraí, the sword-dance,
whose color is black and whose blazon challenge;
whose number is five, and five is the number of war.

Suantraí, the sleep-strain,
whose color is gray and whose murmur calmness;
whose number is six, and six is the number of peace.

Saíochtrai, the mage-word,
whose color is blue and whose guerdon wisdom;
whose number is seven, and seven is the number of lore.

Créachtraí, the wound-weird,
whose color is brown and whose burden anguish;
whose number is eight, and eight is the number of pain.

Fíortraí, the honor-hymn,
whose color is purple and whose banner justice;
whose number is nine, and nine is the number of truth.

Neartraí, the triumph-march,
whose color is crimson and whose anthem valor;
whose number is ten, and ten is the number of strength.

Dóchtraí, the faith-chaunt,
whose color is silver and whose crown transcendence;
whose number is eleven, and eleven is the number of hope.

Diachtraí, the soul-rune, sum of all before it,
whose color is all colors and whose end perfection;
whose number is twelve, and twelve is the number of God.

—Taliesin ap Gwyddno

FORETALE

*S*ay of the brightness: that gladness that is of a summer day, sky like blue cream, thick and deep and calm, wind warm and strong on a hill high above the plain, you lying bone-idle beside me on stubbled grass in the sun.

Such a day it was that day I met my friend. 'Friend'! So small a word for so large a force as he was to be in all my lives: Arthur. In Keltia we say it better: 'anama-chara,' soul-friend, true-friend, the friend of the heart; that one out of all your comrades who can know you better than the love of your life. Sometimes the one who stands back to back with you in the fight, or shoulder to shoulder with you in the peace, is more a part of your deepest being than the one who sleeps side by side with you in the night. The face of a friend is ever the most accurate mirror, and so it was with us.

Here now, so many years after that day in the sun on the hill, in Seren Beirdd—Star of the Bards, our college from ancient days at Caerdroia itself—I can remember such things better than I recall what passed here last week. And rightly so, for Star of the Bards is a star of memories; a fitting name for such a place, where memory is all and all alive, realer than the deeds recalled; for even the light of the stars we see is but a memory. We have never seen a star, only space's memory of its light, itself as it was ages since in time's long

1

mirror; and maybe even that is a lie, a tale we tell to ourselves for comfort. Though I have been myself out among those stars, that light, I cannot even now say for sure.

And maybe even this is a lie—perhaps I never knew him at all, not the friend, not the brother, not the King; never saw Arthur any more than I have seen a star. All I knew of him was what touched me, and maybe I made it up for comfort.

I can comfort myself here well enough, remembering now what light was then: the hero-light that shone round Arthur, so bright and clear that I can still recall my astonishment that not everyone could see it even in the end; the lynx-light that lanced from Gweniver's eyes, that spark of cold clear intelligence that was her best grace and first defense; the werelight that Morgan made from the power of her mind, to be a shield and a shadow—if light can be a shadow—for all Keltia, from now until such day as that light must fall on other worlds than ours.

But beyond these walls the light is real enough. It is spring again here at Caerdroia; the wind out of the east down the Strath carries greenness behind the snow-smell, and before high summer comes in I would set down that which I myself was witness to: I, Taliesin called Pen-bardd, son of Gwyddno and Medeni, of the name of Glyndour, born in Gwaelod drowned, foster-brother to Arthur the King, mate to Morgan Magistra.

I have outlived them all now, as I had never thought to do: my King, my Queen, my lady, my sibs, my teachers; even my Companions, most of them, are gone before me. I write this account for myself, therefore, and a little for my son and his daughter; but mostly I write it for you and whoever else may come to read it. Whether foreign lands and after times will believe what is here set down I know not—that shall be a matter between my skill at telling and yours at hearing—but I am bard, not historian. There will be places where I shall set my word against that of the recorders, and who may say which of us has the right of it? All I can say to you is how it was for me.

This place where bards have been made for a thousand

years—though I myself was never schooled here as should have been, as now the young folk are free to be—has become my home, more truly home than any other place. They are most kind and caring of me, if now and again they treat me overmuch as a living treasure or sacred relic, especially those young ones; though they are a little frightened of me as well, and it is good they should be so. The young should always be a little—a very little—feared of those from whom they learn.

Mostly they learn such things as I can teach them, and ever they will try to tease from me such things as are not scribed down in the histories and cast already in legend's daunting stone: the little things, the comic tales and tender moments, the fits of error into which those who are not gods and legends—and especially those who are—can often fall. It would make a cat laugh—it would make Arthur shout with mirth—to hear what the years have made of us, he and Gwen and Morgan and I and the others, each of us in a different way. But there is naught a poor bard can do to change it now, and I think I would not if I could. For that is the way of legends, they so often have so little to do with the truth—and no more should they, for they serve a different purpose. Some say a higher one.

I have spoken to you here as I would were you sitting by me in this chamber, our toes to the hearth and full methers to our hands. But the tale I tell now I tell as a bard must tell it, for I am nothing if not bard; and, not bard, I am nothing in truth . . .

For it all happened long since, and those who cast the longest shadows are vanished now into that fierce and burning Light. As for my own part in it, it seems that it happened to someone else, and not to me at all.

And perhaps that is right and as it should be; any road, it seems to make the best tale so, and what true bard could wish it other?

Book I:

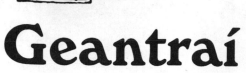

Geantraí

Chapter 1

$\mathcal{T}$he planet Gwynedd is a fair world, mountainous for the most part, roofed and ribbed with stone, some of the toughest stone in all Keltia—hard and strong and close-grained and fine. Of stone too are its people: Kymry of the truest Kymry, and of those the folk of Arvon in the west are truer still.

They have much cause to be: Arvon, lapped by the sea on three sides, walled by mountain fences from the rest of the continent, breeds them so, and has done for ages past.

I speak not to vaunt, for I myself was born on the borders of that land of sea and stone: I Taliesin, youngest child of Gwyddno, lord of Cantred Gwaelod, and Medeni his wife, who died of some plague when I was yet too young to know her. There were often plagues in those times, many said sent by Edeyrn the Marbh-draoi, to chasten the race of Kymry, that if he could not bend their stiff necks then by gods he would break them.

But for us as for the rest of Keltia, the chiefest plague was the Marbh-draoi himself. Edeyrn, onetime Archdruid of Keltia: It seemed that never had there been a time when he had not been sitting at Caerdroia, in Turusachan, seat of our rulers since the days of Brendan. Once, though, he had been a loyal servant of the Copper Crown, counselor and friend to Alawn Last-king—until he overthrew him.

In truth, Edeyrn had been Theocrat, magical dictator, usurping overlord—call him what you will, it does not alter the evil fact of him—for near two hundred years. And though we Kelts are a long-lived folk—not a few of us complete two centuries in full health and wits—the Marbh-draoi (as all in Keltia called him, though never to his face—it means 'Death-druid', and it was full-earned) was not too far off that age when first he came to power. Therefore it is most unnatural, this span of his; none can say why such a gift of years should be granted to so bent a one, and some even mutter darkly that he is some alien changeling come amongst us from outside. They are wrong who say so: Evil as he is, Edeyrn is beyond question Kelt, and his powers Keltic beyond question—and we will find in time an answer to both him and them.

Yet that answer has been long in coming. Kelts are independent souls, and we do not suffer gladly the rule of such a master. Almost since the day Edeyrn took power for himself, breaking the ancient rule of Ard-tiarnas and Fainne and Senate and Assembly and House of Peers that has served us so well and so long, there has been a resistance.

We call it the Counterinsurgency, for most of Keltia, save for certain gross opportunists and treasonous rabble, regard the Marbh-draoi as the true insurgent. Still, he carried many with him in those first victories, to our sorrow and everlasting shame: Druids of his own order; certain of the lesser ruling families, such as thought to profit by the event (and aye and alas, some of the greater ones as well); upstarts too, who lost no time in tying themselves into his cloak-fringe.

But many more loyal ones stood away: the great orders of the Ban-draoi and the Fianna and the bards; many even of Edeyrn's own Druids; most of the highest kindreds on all the worlds; and were forced into hiding for it, or done to death where they could be caught. As for the common folk of Keltia, they chose much as common folk, or indeed any folk, anywhere, would choose: to be left alone to live their lives as best they might; with honor if it could be managed, with the least degree of dishonor if not. Though not to be greatly praised, neither are they to be greatly blamed; they helped where and when and as they could, and if they could not help then at least they did not often hinder. They wished only to survive, and sometimes—oftentimes—even that poor grace was not to be given them.

By the time I was born—in the year 1946 of the Common Reckoning, but in our Keltic numbering 1493 Anno Brendani—the Counterinsurgency, whose fortunes in war had been somewhat in eclipse of late, was once more rising to another great wave of rebellion. The backwash of that wave, though it was to swamp many a coast, would in time rear a crest that would break in thunder, and the flood of that following tide would swirl even to the gates of Caerdroia, and beyond.

On the northwest coast of Arvon, in the sea-province of Gwaelod, stood the castle of Tair Rhamant, 'Three Romances' —named so by the grateful bard who had told three splendid tales to a prince of Gwynedd, and who had had for reward both castle and province. Whatever else those marvellous tales may have been (besides most persuasive), they are long forgotten; castle and province too are gone now, and all the folk with them, but in those days Tair Rhamant was a wondrous place for a growing child.

I was the youngest of my family. There were seven of us—four brothers and three sisters, all of us dark-haired and blue-eyed: Tegau, the eldest daughter, my father's heir; then three boys born of one birth, Elwyn, Cadreth and Adaon; then two girls two years apart, Shelia and Rainild; and then, a score of years after, myself.

I spent those early years at Tair Rhamant seemingly as an only child, for the others were nearly always from home, serving in the hidden hunted armies of the outlawed Counterinsurgency, and they came and went upon the orders of the secret commanders. I was in deep awe of them all, of course, chiefly because they were older and a child so very much younger than its sibs cannot but admire and envy their advanced years for those years' sake alone; but also because even to my child's mind it was plain that what they did—

what small part I could understand from the very little that was told me—was a goal and a glory. And my eldest sister, Tegau, seemed to me the most glorious of them all.

Everyone in Keltia—and many beyond, even, now—knows the story of Tegau Goldbreast: how, losing her right breast in battle with the forces of Owein Rheged, Edeyrn's arm on Gwynedd, of whom I shall have much to say later on, she scorned to have the healers regenerate it—my folk have long since mastered such techniques—but instead replaced the lost breast with one fashioned of pure gold, vowing to keep it so until such time as Keltia was once again free. I have been told that outworlders often find this tale strange and troubling; though I can see where they might find it so, it never seemed that way to me, even as a lad of five, nor I think to any other of our folk. Perhaps it takes a Kelt truly to understand her reasons—and a Kelt to have had such reasons in the first place.

There were few shadows on those years at Tair Rhamant. It seems forever summer as I look back, and near forever as well; but it was five years only, and then all was changed, never to be the same again.

But while my paradise lasted, I rode, and swam in summer in the shallow blue waters of the great bay, and began to learn bardery from my father's house ollave, Benesek, a dour black-browed Kernishman who brightened like the sunrise whenever he settled his harp in his lap to play.

Of my father, Gwyddno, the lord of Cantred Gwaelod, I saw but little; he was unceasingly busy with the governing of the province. Or perhaps it was that he busied himself deliberately, so that he might not have to busy himself growing close to me, who was not only his last child at home but perhaps an unbearably vivid reminder of his dead wife—for I have been told by many who knew her that I have such a look of my mother as to seem Medeni ferch Elain returned in man's guise. If my father took that likeness as salt in his wounds, I took it as her gift to me, and hugged that poor shred of comfort to me often in the dark nights, trying to remember her, what she had been like—she herself, for of course I knew her face and voice well from the holograph messages and portrait-prisms she had left her children as legacy. But it troubled me deeply that I had no real memory of my mother, her arms and love and comfort, and that none spoke of her to me; and doubtless I troubled my father, for whom I see now I must have been a living memory, too deeply for his peace—or my own.

There was one other at Tair Rhamant who was there from my earliest years, one of the first faces in my memory; and it dishonors no one to say now that he was more my father than Gwyddno ever was or could be. He was known as Ailithir in that time, which is to say 'wanderer' in the Vallican dialect that we use in our part of Arvon. If his true-name was known to any in Gwaelod, it was never spoken, or even thought on for all I knew, and it was not until many years later, and far from Tair Rhamant, that I came to know it for myself.

But however he may have been called, he was a Druid, of course, though this knowledge too was kept secret for long, and therefore I shall call him so in these pages; and if I thought of him as any one particular thing it was as a mere sorcerer—Druids, true Druids, were not thick on the ground then, but sorcerers were ever among us. A man in late years, full in power and the wisdom of his hidden order, he was no native of Arvon, or even Gwynedd, and his parentage, like his name, was knowledge I did not come by for long. But I have ever thought of him as having sprung from the earth itself, or the sea, or the stars, or the sacred stones: It seemed presumption to suppose a mundane father and mother for such a one as he, and he for his own part never spoke of any kindred— a rare sort of omission indeed for a Kelt, for to us kindred is all.

My father may have known the truth of Ailithir—I think, now, that he must have done—but if he did he told no other. It was commonly supposed by the castle folk that Ailithir's family had perished at the hands of Edeyrn, and that this added to all the other evils had sufficed to turn him against his onetime Archdruid and the rest of his order (or at least against the spoiled ones); and, thinking so, they treated him with gentleness as well as with fearing respect. But none knew for certain, and to the best of my own knowing, few know now.

Looking back, I marvel that the five-year-old Taliesin was not frightened out of his wits by this forceful, majestic presence; for power was palpable where Ailithir walked, going before and behind him like that carpet of snowflowers which sprang up where Olwen White-track stepped, in the old tales Benesek was beginning to teach me. But I was never afraid, and when he began to teach me magic—child's magic only to begin with, to conjure the tinna-galach or shape the clouds for play—I was afraid still less.

Which was well for me: alone, shy, loving only Benesek and the harp, and Ailithir and the magic, and my dashing brothers and sisters when they came home on their swift, secret visits. I knew nothing in those days, nor for long thereafter, of my father's steadfast refusal to bow the knee to Edeyrn, as my grandmother and great-grandsirs had done before him. Now of course I know that far from distancing himself from me out of pain and bitterness, he did so out of love, and out of hope that I might be saved in the end. And so I was, but not by his sad, noble, ultimately vain sacrifice.

It was a calm bright summer, that year that I was five. A promise of fine harvest in the fields of the cantred; rumor of a visit from my brothers, who had been fighting far in the east, in the cantred of Sarre that lay near Gwynedd's royal capital of Caer Dathyl; new learning from Ailithir and Benesek. Then one night in late summer I was shaken awake by my nurse, Halwynna, Benesek's wife . . .

"Master Talyn, your lord father would see you."

And indeed Gwyddno stood there beside my bed, turning something over and over in his hands, then thrusting it unseen into the pocket of his tunic.

There was a note of fear in my nurse's voice plain even to

my sleepy senses; it spoke of concealment also, the sort that a grown person will put on for a child when there is troublous change afoot. A noble attempt, but foolish, for the child will ever see through it with a child's cold clear sharp little eyes, and I did so then.

"What is wrong, Wynna?"

"Naught wrong; but let your father tell you how all is well." With a gentle push she landed me in my father's arms, for one of the first times I could remember; and then he was telling me, with such a gravity as he would have used to a retainer lord, that he must go to Tara, to the Throneworld itself, there to speak face to face with Edeyrn the Marbh-draoi.

"The Lord Edeyrn summons me to Turusachan, Tal-bach; or rather, to Ratherne, his tower in the valley of Nandruidion. It is but to speak of matters of state; there is naught for any of us to fear."

But there for the first time did he lie to me; for I could sense his fear, sensed it in the arms which held me now so tightly; fear for me, fear for the folk he left behind, but not one fearful thought for himself.

"Tasyk—"

"Nay, cariadol; you will be lord here in my absence, you must learn to carry yourself like one. Ailithir will guide you"—or had he said 'guard'? Even now I cannot say for sure—"until my return. I have sent word to your brothers to delay their visit a while yet, and that their sisters should not come either. I do not want to miss seeing them after so long a time apart."

I could sense that that too was fear speaking, that he wished my sisters and brothers to stay far from Tair Rhamant just now; and his fear, and the love I sensed behind it, bade me as no command of his could have done, to hold my tongue and question him no more.

He held me close awhile in silence, then drew back a little and took something from within his tunic breast: the thing he had had in his hands when first I woke to see him.

"Your mother"—my eyes shot to his face—"gave me this on the day she told me she carried you beneath her heart;

she had found it, she said, walking in the Canterfells up
behind our castle. It had fallen out of the sky right at her feet,
and she took it up from where it lay. Do you know what
it is?''

''It is a hawk's feather,'' I said, proud of my knowledge.
''Coll the huntmaster has been teaching me.''

''Aye so; and does Benesek teach you, too, what the
hawk's gray feather may mean?''

When I was silent, he smiled, and taking my hand he laid the
slim silver plume across my palm, and closed my fingers
gently over it.

''In the bardic speech it signifies courage, and far seeing,
and swift striking, and high soaring beyond the flight of
common wings. This is what your mother Saw for you,
cariadol, and she gave me the feather to give to you when you
were of an age to understand. I do not know if you have
reached that age and that understanding, and now perhaps I
never shall, but I think it well for you to have this, now. Do
you know what I say to you, Talyn?''

I made no answer to my father, only smoothed the feather's
tiny barbs with my fingers, over and over again. This had
been in my mother's hands; my mother had found this and
had known it was for me, had found a meaning in it that
reached back and forward as far as Sight might See. She had
taken the omen where it was offered and had made from it a
gift for me, perhaps knowing even then that she would not
live to give it me from her own hand—as it seemed my father
knew something now. But still it was her gift, and his through
her: And as I touched the feather it seemed that I had sudden
wings to fly with, and wind under them, and was hovering as
the hawks did high above Tair Rhamant, riding the pillars of
air that rose where the hills called Canterfells ran down to the
sea. All at once my father, and this chamber, and even my
own body, seemed very far away.

''Taliesin?''

I came all at once back to earth, looking up into my
father's face, seeing the love and the sadness, and the resolve;

and even then I think I understood that I should not see him again.

"Aye, tasyk," I said, and threw myself into his arms, speaking muffled against his neck. "Aye, I know."

He dropped a kiss on my hair, and then he was gone. I sat back in the bed, drawing the feather through my fingers, pressing it to my lips. A tall shadow stirred beside the door: Ailithir, who had come in with my father and had been silent witness to our farewell.

He came forward now, and in my sudden passion of fear and pain and uncertainty that was certainty in itself—my first adult emotion—I held out my arms to him sobbing. With a tenderness I had never before seen in him—and was to see in him but seldom after—he held me and soothed my sobs and tucked me back again among the quilts and pillows. That done, he sat on the edge of the bed as my father had done, looking soberly down upon me, it seemed as from the same strange distance as that from which I had looked down upon my father. After a few moments of this steady regard, he reached out a hand to touch my forehead.

"Sleep, Taliesin."

I heard the sleep-magic in his voice—the suantraí, we bards call it when we set it in song—and knew it was useless to fight it. It came to me then that of all those closest to me, he alone never called me by aught but my full and proper name.

"My father—"

The crags of Ailithir's face seemed to sharpen. "Your father the Lord Gwyddno spoke to you as to one of his counselors, young master; therefore shall I do no less." He made no move of the body, but all at once the sleepiness fell away from me, and I sat up in the bed again, hugging my knees, as if listening rapt to one of Benesek's night-tales.

"Your father has been lord of Cantred Gwaelod since the death of your grandmother who ruled it before him. In the ordinary way, your sister Tegau, as firstborn, would come to rule it in her turn."

"Tasyk has explained this to me," I said, not understanding why he chose to speak now of the succession to the provincial lordship.

"Well, as you know, Tegau and the rest of your brothers and sisters are away fighting against the Marbh-draoi Edeyrn; and your father too fights against him. This is why he has been summoned to Tara: He has held Gwaelod free of the armies of Owein—free even of the presence of Ravens, those minions who work Edeyrn's evil will upon us all—and he has kept the folk free of demands that other folk in Keltia have had to suffer. So far, he has done all this and yet remained within the law, or such law as Edeyrn still deigns to obey."

"And now?" I was not understanding much of this, save that my father had apparently done something for which he might be punished.

And indeed, Ailithir's next words confirmed this: "And now Edeyrn has called him to give account of himself, for what is seen to be his—disobedience. You understand that, Taliesin?"

"When *I* am disobedient, I am punished," I muttered; resentfully, for I was beginning to feel sleep lap round the corners of my consciousness once more, and guessed that my teacher was sending me into the safety of its remove. But I managed one more question. "Will tasyk be punished too, do you think, athro? I should not want him to be punished."

But Ailithir said only, "You too, Taliesin, must fight against the Marbh-draoi, in your way; and in your time."

The last thing I remember of that night was the feel of his hand upon my head, set there briefly and gently, in blessing or in binding I could not tell, and sleep claimed me before I could puzzle it out to my satisfaction.

Yet when I awoke early in the dawn, my father gone from Tair Rhamant, the hawk's feather lay beneath my pillow.

Chapter 2

*T*hough logic tells me now that there must surely have been a span of days, perhaps many days, between then and the searing memory that follows so hard upon it, it seems to me no time at all, that scarce had I fallen asleep when again there came an awakening in darkness.

This time a tall figure stood beside the bed, holding a shielded lanthorn. I knuckled the sleep out of my eyes to see that it was Ailithir, and that he looked a touch grimmer even than usual.

"Make no sound, lad, and no delay. Dress yourself for travel, and take with you what small things you would."

Unquestioningly obedient—what cause had I to doubt *him*?—I swung my feet to the cold floor. A pair of leather trews pulled on—my feet pushed into the boots that Ailithir held for me—the points fastened; then a thick warm gwlan leinna and overtunic and laced leather doublet: It was summer no longer at Tair Rhamant but full autumn, as it comes betimes to that part of Arvon, and the fields lay already under frost of a morning.

When it came to choosing remembrances, there was not so much of real value to choose from; our house was not one of the great wealthy kindreds of Keltia such as Clann Douglas or the Chyvellans of Kernow or the Aoibhells of Thomond. But there were things I would not leave behind, for something in my teacher's manner told me more, and graver, than his few words.

So I took from their wooden case the paired cloak-brooches of wrought silver that had belonged to my great-grandfather, given to me by my own father on my last birthday; two rings left me by my mother, a heavy gold ring with a topaz and a sapphire set in findruinna; the little book with a clasped cover that Benesek had made for me, to write down such things as I was beginning to wish to—and to need to; the hawk's feather that had rested so short a time among these treasures. And of course my harp; 'Frame of Harmony,' I had rather grandiloquently called it. It too had been a birthday gift, from Tegau; gods knew how she had managed to send it, or had remembered —had even known—that it was what I had been pining for all that year past. But it was a proper harp, the telyn of our Gwynedd mountains, and a handsome one, with devices of our house carved along its flange and forepost, and my name done in runes of gold upon the harmonic curve.

As I lifted it, still in its soft leather wrappings, I looked up at Ailithir in sudden fear, that perhaps he might think it too large or awkward or frivolous a burden on our flight—for flight I now knew it must be—but he shook his head as if he knew my fearing thought, and himself hoisted the pack to his shoulders.

When we emerged from the castle, by a postern gate that gave onto the screes leading up onto the Canterfells, I was surprised to see that it was still dark, though far in the east, behind the greater mountains that fenced Arvon like a triple wall, I could see the faintest touch of gray light.

That light had long broadened and brightened by the time we came over the crest of the fells. We had passed some hours since out of sight of Tair Rhamant—I had turned to bid it farewell with a wave and a word, though Ailithir had kept his face forward and his back to the castle—and now, safe among the high crags, we paused to rest a little. Ailithir set me down in the concealment of a granite overhang; though he had borne me in his arms for the last stiff upward pull of our long slow ascent, he showed no sign of weariness.

I saw now, as I had not noticed before, that he was dressed as I had never before seen him, in the dark supple leathers of a warrior; and though his great ashwood staff was bound across his back, there was a shortsword in the boot-sheath and a glaive at his belt. For the first time I began to wonder what had in truth befallen, and what of my father, and where were we bound; but looking at Ailithir's face I knew it would not be good just now to ask.

But he seemed to hear my questions all the same, for after a moment he turned to me and smiled.

"All is by command of your father, bach. He will be delayed a while on Tara, and has bidden me take you from Gwaelod. Time it is you began your fostering—you are near a year past the age—and it is to your new home that we are bound."

A sense that he himself had awakened in me caught at what lay behind his words. "Why then do we go alone, athro? At least Benesek should come too? And Fannir and Conn, they were set to look after me?" I caught at his cloak. "Where *do* we go, who *are* to be my foster-parents?"

Ailithir had been looking back along the way we had come, the first time that day I had seen him give a backward glance; as he turned again to me his face was cheerful, but I had the feeling that that was not how he had looked a moment since.

"Well, your father may not have spoken of them to you, but he did so often enough to *me* . . . They are the Lord and Lady of Daars, Gorlas Penarvon and Ygrawn Tregaron his wife. They were your mother's dear friends, and later your father too came to know and love them. So that when the matter of your fostering was considered, they were the ones your mother would have, and she had her way."

I mouthed the names to myself: *Gorlas and Ygrawn.* Though like every other Keltic child I had always known I must be fostered from my fifth birthday, I had not given it much thought, and could not recall any mention of who my foster-kin might be.

"And it is to Daars that we are going now?"

Some of my apprehension must have showed, in spite of my best efforts, for Ailithir ruffled my hair and laughed.

"It is, young sir. On foot it shall take us rather longer than it might have done in another time, but on foot it must be." And in spite of the laughter in his voice I did not dare question him as to why it must be so.

We had been perhaps a fortnight on our way when the weather changed, and my guide changed with it. Cautious he had ever been as we crept slowly southward, keeping always to the high hills and the trackless uplands, giving a wide pass to such few townlands as there were in that rough country. Yet now, as the sky grew strange above us and clouds streamed from west to east on a wind of portent, Ailithir seemed to snuff that wind what way a hound will scent of danger; but whatever he read in the sky he kept to himself.

That night we slept in a high corrie, out of reach of the wind's fingers. We had eaten a spare meal, as was our custom, and few words had been exchanged between us. Ailithir seemed lost in some far place, as if he listened to words he alone could hear; we had done more miles that day than had been our wont, and I was weary, so when the meal was done I wrapped myself in my cloak and tucked myself into a little hollow of the rocks.

I do not know what awakened me first—the light or the voice or the wind now risen to a gale—all I remember is that I was suddenly full awake, and shaking with a fear whose source I could not place. Then I looked up, and I knew.

Ailithir was standing atop the great granite outcropping that guarded the mouth of the corrie. His arms were uplifted under the blazing stars, his cloak cracked in the wind, and the moonlight fell over him like poured silver. He was speaking, not to me, in a voice I had never before heard him use—but then I had never before seen him in the fullness of his power, at full stretch as Druid. And though to see him revealed in his strength should have comforted me, perversely I was not comforted but terrified; I wanted him to stop, I wanted to be miles from him and from that place, safe behind stone walls and bolted doors and bars and moats and fences.

But I was there, and all I could do was what I did: buried my face in my cloak and pulled the hood over my head and clapped my hands to my ears. And still the terrible boneshaking thunder of his voice went on . . .

At last there was silence on the hilltop, and the wind had died away, and I ventured to peek out from the shelter of my cloak. What I saw made me gasp: Ailithir still stood upon the rock, but the light was gone and he looked—dwindled; small and spent and unspeakably ancient. I found myself wondering things I had never thought to think of: who was this man who called himself 'Wanderer,' what place had he come from, why was he here with me . . .

"Taliesin." The deep voice had lost none of its command, I must have been mistaken about the diminishment. Nor was there any question of its not being obeyed: I threw off the covering cloak and went forward to him.

He had stepped down from the rock as I came, and now he knelt to bring himself down to my own level. As he took my hands in his I looked into his face. Something of the druid-power still glowed in his eyes, but now it was nothing near so fearful; still of course a thing to be respected, but I felt nothing of the terror that had gripped me earlier, and I met his gaze with trust and confidence.

He did not speak until we were again down in the corrie, not in our little sleeping hollow but on the cliff's edge, looking down into the dark valley that fell away before our feet.

"Until tonight I have had no clear Sight of what was toward; only the warning—I fear not from your father, lad—that I must take you and flee Gwaelod for both our lives, and more besides. But by Hu himself I swear that had I had the smallest glimpse of what I have seen come this night, I had commanded all Gwaelod to flee . . ."

The terror was beginning to seep back into my bones. "What has happened, athro? What have you seen?"

Ailithir turned me gently to face the valley below; the ground-mist that rises in autumn was beginning to drift along the slopes, and I was somehow enthralled by those slow rippling veils.

"And dost think thou art strong enough to see, then, lad?" His voice murmured now in the High Gaeloch, the great formal tongue that I had heard only a few times in my young life. "Well enough; it is a thing must be seen, for none would else believe . . ."

I looked where he bade me, or rather where his thought bade me, for he spoke no word more aloud; into the white mist, until my sight began to swim, or perhaps it was the clouds that swam. All at once the swirling curtain was pulled aside, and I saw not the valley floor below the clouds, but Gwaelod itself, and Tair Rhamant on the edge of the sea.

How the magic was made I did not know—even now I am less than certain—but it was real enough: I was high above Tair Rhamant, above even the Canterfells, yet I could see with a strange sharpness all that passed so far below, even to the folk abroad in the twilight, and the beasts in meadow and lane.

The sun was on the point of setting, and darkness was beginning to engulf Gwaelod. Yet somehow it seemed strangely and terribly wrong, and as I leaned forward, puzzled by the wrongness, I saw with horror that the darkness came from the *west*, not the east, and that it was no darkness but a monstrous towering wave.

I must have cried out, for I felt Ailithir's hands seize my shoulders in an iron grip, but I did not look away; I think I could not have even had I tried, and certainly I wished to . . . Tair Rhamant the waters took first, that bright happy place gone in an eyeblink, vanished under the green wall. The wave must have been of colossal height, unnatural height, or else the land was sinking, or both together, for the water rolled on across the Canterfells as if the hills had been emmet-heaps, and burst down upon the lands that lay behind. Even from my vantage-point I could see the folk running wildly now, dashing out of their housen, running anywhere, anyhow, in a desperate vain attempt to escape the death that poured down upon them; then they too were gone, folk and beasts and buildings all alike, and still the water swept inland.

Inland—there *was* no more 'inland,' not now, only the sea, foaming furiously around the feet of the Spindles themselves, the mountain wall too high for even that towering wave to breach. All Gwaelod lay beneath the heaving waters, everything and everyone I had known . . .

I felt myself shaking—I had been until that instant unaware of my own body, still on the corrie's edge—and I clung to Ailithir's arms as he held me. "The hawks—the hawks—" I repeated over and over, not knowing if he understood my meaning or even my words. I could form no more coherent lament than that, seeing over and over in my mind's eye not the utter devastation I had just witnessed, that my mind, wiser than I, knew I could not survive with intact sanity the sight of, but a smaller grief: the flights of gray hawks, circling above Tair Rhamant as they and their breed had ever done, circling now over the sheets of sea that covered Gwaelod forever, circling and circling, until at last they plunged exhausted into the gray water.

Gradually I came back into myself, calmed enough to speak. "My father—the Marbh-draoi—"

I knew even then in my deepest heart that my father was dead, killed on Tara by the Marbh-draoi's word as surely as Gwaelod had been drowned by the Marbh-draoi's hand; but before I could bring this knowledge to light Ailithir had lifted his own hand and thrust it away for a time, knowing that to face it now would destroy my already wounded soul.

"The Marbh-draoi cannot endure forever, Taliesin." Ailithir's eyes were seeing something years and distances from this moment. "For his dán comes now upon him, and by the grace of Malen and Mihangel he shall be cast down; you yourself shall be among the ones who help to do so. But for now—"

He raised his hand again, and when it had passed before my eyes I looked up at him in puzzlement.

"Athro? I have had such a *dream*—why can I not remember?"

In the mercy of the rann of forgetfulness he had placed upon me, I did not understand the look that crossed his countenance: sorrow, and hope, and love, and a far triumph.

"*Shall* I remember?" I persisted.

And still I did not understand when he smiled and answered. "When there is need, son of Gwyddno; when there is need."

Chapter 3

*W*hatever the necessity of our flight may have been, for me it was no hardship to be travelling through that fair wild country, in what has ever since been my favorite season of the year.

It had been cool and bright for most of our march, with a few blowy days of wind and shower-squalls; on the slopes the trees were already well into their turning, though in the valleys the leaves were still showing some green. Above us, the geese were going, as they did all down the Arvon flyways in autumn, their thin skeins black across pale skies; their far music, half-remembered and never forgotten, still haunts my dreams, and whenever I hear it in these latter days, I am back on those long-ago autumn hills.

This particular day was a glancing back to high summer, clear and bright and hot. The sun had burned off the morning mists, and now it brought out the fugitive hay-scent in the stubbled fields, so that when I closed my eyes and breathed deep of the warm fragrant air, it was August I breathed, not mid-October.

We had been journeying nearly a month now; already it was a full fortnight since that memorable night of vision I could still, most maddeningly, not remember. We had left north Arvon long since, striking inland now through the high hills, a little east of south. Ailithir, after a silent day or two, had put his somber mood behind him, as resolutely as he had turned his back upon Tair Rhamant, and for the days that followed he had been a cheerful companion.

It may seem strange that I accepted all this upheaval so calmly; but remember that I was yet only a month or so short of six years, and resilient as only a child can be. To me, a great journey south, sleeping out, in the company of the person I loved and trusted more than any other, was no bad thing at all; and the horror I had Seen had been mercifully masked from my memory—at least for a time. It could not, of course, be forever denied; but Ailithir, even as he had thought it best that I behold it, was to shield me from it for as long as he deemed that shielding best.

One thing he did not spare me was lessons: Even under the open sky, he drilled me while we walked in such lore as I had been studying at home, under his tutelage and Benesek's, and I was happy to be instructed—in languages (a Kelt's chiefest love and first learning; tongues are a thing innate with us, we seem to acquire them almost without being taught), and basic principles of music and bardery and history, and even some sword-drill and practice with bow and spear, though martial disciplines were not his best skill. But never once, during all that southward slog, did he impart to me magic—not the least littlest rann or rune or pishogue.

Informing all he did teach me was a loving reverence for the natural world, for the many realms of living things, that I have never seen equalled in any other, man or woman: To Ailithir all was truly one creation, the grass underfoot and the earth beneath the grass and the rock beneath the earth and the fires at the planet's heart; the waters that coursed and the winds that blew above them and the heavens that arched above the winds; and every creature that lived in and on and amid it all. Partly I think this came from his Druidry and the teachings of his order, but mostly I think it was something in him; and more than anything else it was this that I learned best on that long road into Arvon.

* * *

I was walking with my eyes closed, trying to do as Ailithir had been teaching me, to sense through other means than eyes alone. "When the eyes of the body are shut, the body becomes itself an eye; then you can see with your skin": It sounded simple enough when he explained it, as most of his precepts usually did—but, also as usual, I was finding it rather less simple in the doing.

I had succeeded so far, though, in that I could tell when clouds were passing far overhead even if they cast no shadow upon me, and when some bird of the meadow called away to my left I could follow its movement by the spacing of its cries and even the faint flap of its wings. But though at first I was most occupied with simply keeping my footing on the rough sheeptrack we were walking, after a time it did seem that my feet could see for themselves, and could be trusted to pick out the path most likely to keep me upright.

Alive so to the myriad sensations round me, I should not have been surprised that I felt the thing before I saw it, and before Ailithir quietly warned me of it: It rose up before my closed eyes and open senses like some great warning hand, as chill and palpable as the cloudshadows on my sun-hot skin, and my eyes flew open.

The landscape and sky seemed blinding white for an instant, bleached and leached of tint; then my colorsight returned, and I stared up at the tall gray sentinel stone rising out of the grasses, as if it had grown there since Keltia began—as perhaps it had, or very near. But Ailithir went up to the carved bluestone pillar, and laid his hand upon it as in greeting.

"This is the border-stone of Gorlas's lands; beyond this begins the maigen of the Lord of Daars. We are safe now." And that was the closest he was ever to come to admitting that we had not been safe before . . .

"We have but a league more to go, bach," he added then. "The lands of your new fosterers lay less wide to the north than to the other airts. If we do not tarry, we shall come to Daars in time for the noonmeal."

So we did not tarry, and coming over a heather-clad ridge,

the hills blazing purple as far as I could see, we halted. Daars lay below us, the Caer-in-Arvon, small and neat and bright in its little valley. In truth it was not so small, either; larger by far than Tair Rhamant with its three straggling villages, and I began to feel a little out of countenance, like some country-boy, a keeraun faced with his first sight of Caerdroia.

No need to feel so, as I was soon to learn: Daars, no Caerdroia, was one of those places that welcome one home though one has never before passed their gates. On a rise of its own in the valley, facing south into the sun's full warmth, it was a proper town, with winding streets around a central square and broad fortified walls of cream-colored stone. Its castle loomed above the other dwellings, built on a cliff above the little river that bisected the glen. Prosperous Daars looked, too: I could make out even from our present distance the colorful signs swinging outside the shops, the merchants' devices plain upon them, and judging by the activity in the square it was market-day.

Seeing all this, my spirits rocketed up like a groundlark startled upon the nest. All at once there seemed to be lifted the strange weight like a restraining hand that had lain upon my heart for days; and there came to me at the same moment that warm smiling certainty that sometimes, if one is very favored, will come upon one all unlooked-for: the unsought sense, the found knowledge that a door stands ready to swing open into a time of change, upon a great and lasting happiness.

It swung sooner than I could have thought: We were not alone, Ailithir and I, in the high field. Perhaps twenty yards away, a boy stood watching us, his face alive with eager curiosity. At first he seemed but one with sun and sky and heather; then I touched Ailithir's hand and pointed. But he had already seen.

To my open-mouthed astonishment, he waved and the boy came running; it would seem they knew each other, for there had been gladness in that salute, and no surprise either side. Now that he approached, I could see him clear, as I see him still: a lad of my own age, give or take a year either way, tall for that age, and sturdily made, with hair as red-brown as a

castaun and eyes the color of a peaty stream. His dress gave
no clue as to his rank; it was the garb of any active child out
for a day on the hill, tunic and trews and boots of good plain
quality, having seen hard use and much wear. Though all my
instincts were pushing me forward, shyness took me then,
and I held back.

He conquered that with one look; young as he was, he
knew already how to win hearts to him. He came toward me
and held out his hand, and without thinking I put out my own
to clasp it. From a distance, I heard Ailithir speaking, and his
deep voice held warm satisfaction.

"Taliesin ap Gwyddno, be known to your foster-brother—
Arthur of Arvon."

I remember very little of the rest of that day: Surely we
must have all three of us gone down into Daars—Arthur
would never have been so discourteous as to remain at his
skylarking when there were guests in the gate, and there was
no cause for us to linger on the hill—and presented ourselves
before Gorlas, Lord of Daars, and been welcomed with due
honor and ceremony. Surely all this must have happened, but it
is vanished now beyond recall.

What will never vanish is my memory of what came next:
of how, having been taken to a chamber that someone told me
was to be my own, I saw a lady come into that chamber and
kneel down beside me; and my memory tells me too that
never before, and but once after, had I seen anyone of such
perfection of face and form. And then she spoke to me.

"Taliesin"—her voice was deep and furry, the kind of
voice a cat might have if it were to choose to speak, and I
thought the voice as fair as the face—"I am Ygrawn, Taliesin.
I was your mother's friend, and I loved her dearly, and it is
by her wish that I am to be your foster-mother. I know we
shall be great friends, you and I." She took my hand, and I
dared to look up into her eyes: Violet they were, not the
vivid purple of heather but the pale cool lilac of amethysts,
set off by two shining wings of blue-black hair.

Many there were who found Ygrawn Tregaron, daughter of

the Duke of Kernow, a hard and proud and waspish woman; and doubtless they were right who found her so, for so had she proved to them. But if she had shown herself hard or vengeful, then just as doubtless had she been right to do so. I was to learn that never did Ygrawn strike or snap or chasten where it was not richly deserved, and even when she did so, seldom indeed did she act from her full strength. That strength would be seen later in its true light and measure; but I have ever thought Ygrawn to be among the most just judgers I knew, and I never saw cause to change my view.

And, at that moment, nor did I find her either hard or cold; one look from those brimming eyes, a few words more of my mother, murmured for my ear alone, and I was in her arms, my own thin arms wound tight around her neck.

But if I recall so little else of that momentous firstday, above all I remember Arthur. We had sat at the high table for the nightmeal in hall, he and I facing each other at the table's ends, with Gorlas and Ygrawn and Ailithir and several others of our elders taking the places between, beneath the canopy of state that hung along the wall.

I had been seized a while since by a notable hunger, having only just remembered that for the past four weeks I had walked long and far on scant commons; Druids are not known for their cookery, especially over a quartz-hearth on the march.

So I ate everything that was put before me, and asked as politely as I could for extra helpings, and stuffed those too as quickly as they came to my plate, aware of Gorlas's indulgent eye on me, and Ygrawn's smile—as warm as before, though now with a touch of sadness too, as if she were seeing someone else in my face, and perhaps she was—and ever conscious of Ailithir at Gorlas's left hand.

But Arthur and I smiled into each other's eyes as if already we shared a secret, though I doubt we had so far managed to exchange more than a score of words, and most of those had been part of the fostern-rite. We had stood side by side before Gorlas and Ygrawn and Ailithir and Gorlas's Druid Dylan— and this I do remember—had flinched only a little as Ailithir and Dylan gently made the tiny cuts, the second of the Three Cuts of ritual, in the side of our wrists, and caught the drop or two of blood in the great silver graal. I remember that we drank the drink of fosterage, he and I, and spoke the words of pledging, and gave each other the kiss of brothers. The rite need not have been so speedily performed, I suppose, now I look back on it; but perhaps it was in Gorlas's mind to get me safe under his lawful protection as soon as might be done. For Arthur and me it made no slightest differ, I think we had done our own rite up there on the hill, in that moment when we first laid eyes on each other; our brotherhood was made in that moment, and not oath nor blood nor bond could seal it firmer.

At last the meal was over, and we were free to retire. All at once I was desperately tired, and I looked round for Ailithir, my only familiar anchor in these strange new seas. But he had gone out with Ygrawn, the two of them deep in talk; so I was borne up to my bed by Gorlas himself, with Arthur, full of good-natured chatter, running along after like an eager hound puppy, anxious not to be left out. After I was bathed and brushed and dried, Ailithir came in alone to see me safe settled, with a kiss and a blessing and a few words of comfort for the morrow. Of our journey, and the still unspoken reason for it, we said no word, and presently, bidding me sleep, he quitted the chamber.

But I could not sleep, not straightway, and lying there in the big fourposted bed so like my own at Tair Rhamant I cast my memory back over the days that had taken me from there to here, and jabbed futilely as ever at that wall in my mind that seemed to be sealing off some terrible secret.

The rigors of the journey, and the relief of its ending, and perhaps most of all the richness and sheer volume of my dinner, all took their inevitable toll, and in spite of my best efforts I soon drifted off. Having succumbed I must have slept heavily for some hours, for when I awoke with a terrible wrenching shudder, my heart pounding and a cry on my lips that I caught back before it could be uttered, it was still dark.

When I was calmer, I could tell a little by the texture of the air and the quality of the silence that it was nowhere near dawn but deep night still, perhaps not more than an hour either side of middlenight.

Looking round the room, I told myself fiercely that all was *well*: I was safe at Daars, I had a fostern now, and foster-parents, and above all I had Ailithir still; I was here in this spacious, pleasant chamber, in this supremely comfortable bed, beneath thick feather quilts and upon soft pillows. Even the furnishings were like to those I had left behind: carved cupboards and presses against the walls; fair hangings, intricately woven tapestries; a very workmanlike desk with inlaid computer pads; and, standing in splendor in a wall-niche to itself, my own beloved harp, free now of its wraps and glowing in the firelight.

Almost I managed to quiet myself and turn again to the pillows; but the feeling of terrible wrongness that had thrown me from sleep now invaded me again, stronger and darker and colder than before. In my unthinking terror I jumped down from the bed, caught up a chamber-robe and threw it about me, and ran out of the room in my bare feet, down to where I might find the comforting reassurance of voices and lights and people.

No one was about in the castle's silent upper halls; it must have been later than I had thought, in my state I was no fit judge of time. Or even place: In my confusion and desperation I kept turning as if the halls I wandered were those of Tair Rhamant, not Daars, and only grew the more panicked when rooms and towers were not where I thought to find them.

At last, more by chance than intent, I came across a part of the castle that seemed to show signs of life: I heard voices—servitors clearing away for the morning, most like—and passed lighted chambers, but found no sign of anyone I sought. In the end it was Berain, a warrior in Ygrawn's service, who found me wandering weeping in the maze of corridors, and who bore me in her arms to where Gorlas and

Ailithir and Ygrawn sat late awake in Ygrawn's own grianán, the three of them deep in talk.

They all three leaped to their feet when they saw me tear-stained and wretched in Berain's arms, and each reached out eagerly to relieve Berain of her burden. But Ygrawn was quickest, and herself carried me to the deep comfortable chair beside the fire where she had been sitting, and settled me in her lap.

By this time I was almost past the reach of reason, or even words; I was shivering uncontrollably, as with high fever, though my skin was ice to the touch, and Ygrawn wrapped me in the fur throw that had been warming her own knees. I did not understand what they had been saying to each other—I had caught a few exchanges before they were aware that Berain and I had come into the darkened room—and I did not understand now what Gorlas demanded of Ailithir, nor the urgency of his tone.

"How could he know? You put the forgetting-rann on him, did you not, and I take oath no one here told him—" He fell silent at a look from Ailithir, and Ygrawn glanced up and shook her head in a warning of her own.

Lulled in the warmth of fire and fur and breast, I ceased to tremble, but only the edge of my terror was dulled. As soon as I felt more myself again, I struggled to sit up in Ygrawn's encircling arms—strange that I should struggle, it was the first time I could remember that I had been held so, in a mother's embrace—and gazed imploringly at Ailithir.

"Athro—"

He came and knelt before Ygrawn's knees, and I was struck afresh with terror at the new grimness that hardened his face. I could feel in my mind the crumbling of that wall which had been protecting me somehow from a dreadful memory. But he was speaking now, and with all my might I willed myself to listen.

"Taliesin, hear me. Your father is dead; he has been slain on Tara by the Marbh-draoi Edeyrn."

It seems strange to say so now, but through the sudden lancing sorrow I heard his words with a kind of relief. I had feared and expected to hear gods knew what unimaginable tidings; to hear Ailithir tell me, with unspeakable gentleness, of my father's death seemed almost a disburdening. My father had been dead in my child's mind since the night he left Tair Rhamant; to be told of it now, though the grief I felt was no less the real for it, was only to be told of a thing already accepted.

"I woke up—there was something I felt—it was then that the news came, athro?"

Ailithir and Ygrawn exchanged a swift look. But he said only, "Aye, child, it was."

And as if those words had been a trigger, suddenly the wall in my mind, that had been slowly fracturing, breaking up like ice in the spring, was breached entirely, and memory poured flooding back, inexorable as those waters I now remembered, the waters that had rolled over Gwaelod, and I cried out then in the mingling of the two griefs.

"Tasyk—the wave—" And I wept in Ygrawn's arms as Gorlas and Ailithir took it in turns to tell me: how my father had challenged the Marbh-draoi, there in the Archdruid's very stronghold of Ratherne; had challenged him to his face, cursing him and his usurping ways, and Edeyrn had destroyed him. They spoke too of how it had been Ailithir's Sight that had saved the two of us: Edeyrn's plan had been to strike when my brothers were home on their secret visit—not so secret after all, it seemed; perhaps someone had indiscreetly gossiped, or there may have been a traitor—and my father was to have been forced to witness the destruction of his cantred and his family, and then to have been slain himself. But he had thwarted that, to save at least his family: Gwyddno had called his own death to him at Ratherne, and Edeyrn in his fury had drowned the cantred all the same.

We were to learn later that a few hundred folk had managed by various miraculous means to escape the whelming of Gwaelod: hundreds, out of tens of thousands. . . One even, a Trevelyan, a worthy son of that bold wild clann, had actually ridden his white mare to safety ahead of the wave. Had the water been only a little higher or stronger at the time he could not have done it; but it had broken, and though it was still running swift the mare proved swifter, and showed her heels to the flood. That wild gallop was by decree of her grateful master the last time she would bear any greater burden upon her back than her own shining coat, and both master and mare found their way to Daars not long after we did.

But that was later: Now I wept for Gwaelod, and for my father, and for myself; and all the while I wept Ygrawn rocked me on her breast, and her own tears fell upon my head.

But my new foster-mother was not the last comforter I was to have that terrible night . . .

After I had been borne once again to my bed, and the door had shut behind Ygrawn and Gorlas and Ailithir, a shadow stirred in the dark corner beyond the big carved press. Even before the fire glinted on his hair I knew who must be hiding there, and it came to me that Ailithir too, and perhaps Ygrawn, must surely have sensed his presence; but if they had, they must also have thought it good for him to be there, for no word was spoken to command his return to his own chamber.

He came forward to stand beside the bed, and I sat up to meet him. His face was grave, as I was to learn it seldom was, and the brown eyes seemed to look beyond me to some other time and place, as I was to learn they so often did.

"My father is dead," I heard myself explaining. "And my mother—now I have no one."

I had not said it to be pitied, but as simple statement of fact; that is the bard's great curse and greater gift—that whatever befalls one, it seems to be happening to someone else and not to oneself at all—and already it had begun its long work.

But Arthur shook his head. "Nay," he said. "Not so; now you have me."

Chapter 4

Gorlas himself came to me that next morning, before I had been awake long enough to do much more than bathe and dress and say the short prayers I had been taught by Ailithir with which to begin the day.

My new foster-father was a man in his early prime, no more than eighty at the time, not tall but strongly built, with black hair and the same deepset dark eyes to be seen in Arthur. Like my own father, he was not one of the great lords of Keltia; both were chiefs of minor houses, ruling over minor provinces of little political importance and less wealth. And again like my father, Gorlas was well pleased to have it so; he was perfectly content in his Caer-in-Arvon, and had not wish nor will to rule anything more.

Nor was he a man of subtlety, and he came at once to his topic.

"Taliesin, Ailithir tells me I may speak to you as I would to one of my own lords or chiefs, and so I shall. You are my son now, as lawfully as Arthur; but you are still Gwyddno's son, and it is as your father's son that Edeyrn will be seeking you. We have heard that he has learned of your escape with Ailithir, and though I do not wish to frighten you overmuch, you must know that he will hunt you down if he can the way he hunts your sisters and brothers. —Nay, do not fear, they are all safe, by the best intelligence we have—and our intelligence is usually the best.'' He settled himself in the chair by the window. ''What I wish to suggest to you is this: that we give out to folk that you are my nephew, the son of my dead sister Teleri, who was killed last year in a fall. We shall say that she had made a brehon marriage with a lord of whom her family did not approve, and that you were the result; so that when she died, we could do naught else but take you in and raise you as our own. Thus, if any Ravens or other of Edeyrn's creatures come seeking you, they cannot name you as Gwyddno's.''

He paused expectantly, perhaps a little disconcerted by my calm acceptance. But what was I to say? I was six years old, and it sounded a fine plan to me. So I spoke the first thing that came into my head.

''And Ailithir? How shall we hide *him*?''

Gorlas laughed, clearly relieved. ''Oh, never fear, that one is able to hide in an open field! It would take the Marbh-draoi himself to winkle him out, and I doubt not but that Edeyrn will keep well off from Gwynedd for some time to come.''

''And my—and methryn?'' It came hard to my lips at first, the word for 'foster-mother,' but then it seemed the finest thing in the world to say, and I said it again. ''What does methryn say?''

''All this is her thought,'' said Gorlas. ''She spoke of it to me this morning, and there is one thing more that she did think of: that while you are here you should be called by some other name. I fear that even a Raven might have no doubts as to the true identity of a surprising new fostern at Daars, Taliesin by name.''

''What shall I be called, then?'' Unexpectedly, I was delighted by the idea of a new name, and the romance of being in hiding.

''Let him be known as Gwion.''

Both Gorlas and I looked up in surprise, for the voice was Ailithir's, and neither of us had marked his entrance. He came forward now to join us, his hair and beard whiter than ever against the blue robe he wore.

"Is that not perhaps too near his father's name to be a safe choice?" asked Gorlas a little doubtfully.

"A common enough name in this part of Gwynedd." Ailithir stretched out comfortably in the window-seat, one elbow on the deep sill, looking down over Daars and the river. "Any road, it is one of the names his mother gave him at his saining. It will serve well enough."

'Gwion,' I thought. *How strange to have a new name* . . . Still, it had been mine all along: Taliesin Gwion Idris Glyndour, son of Gwyddno. My forenames had always felt far too grand for the likes of me—names of kings and gods and wizards— and I wondered now what my mother had Seen, to give such names of power to her youngest child.

But the kindred-name of Glyndour had ever been a source of shy pride: Though it was one of the very last names to come to Keltia from Earth, five hundred years since, he who bore it first had been himself a true Terran, born on Earth, one of the last to make the great immram. He had been a mighty lord of the Kymry in that time, a period of war and civil strife; then he had lost his war, and simply and suddenly he had vanished away—taken by *us* to Keltia to live out his days in honor and in peace. I often wondered what folk of Earth had made of his going, both then and in later years; it must have been a marvel and a mystery. Owein, he had been called, a prince of our folk . . .

But they were both looking at me expectantly now, my foster-father and my teacher, and I hastened to answer the question I guessed one or both must have asked.

"It will serve very well."

We settled in at Daars, Ailithir and myself, more swiftly than I would have thought possible. Within a fortnight, already I had near forgot that I had ever known another home than the comfortable old castle on the river-cliff. I had made a private fortress of the room I had been given that first night, and I supposed Ailithir found as congenial to his own particular tastes and needs the isolated tower-chambers he had chosen for his use.

Nor had our coming stirred so much as a ripple of curiosity amongst the castle folk. As I had suspected from the moment of our meeting with Arthur, Ailithir had been often in Daars; indeed, he had spent some years here before coming to us at Tair Rhamant, and whenever he could spare the time he had made return visits since—which was why Arthur did not find him a stranger. And since I had always thought Ailithir had been at Tair Rhamant from the beginning of time, if not before, this new knowledge came as somewhat of a surprise.

But if Ailithir's return to Daars were no surprise to its folk, by any reckoning my own advent upon the scene should have been rather more of one. Yet my presence was scarce remarked upon: Gorlas and Ygrawn were casually commended, when the matter was mentioned at all, for taking in the poor orphaned sister-son whose own father's clann would not have him. This tale gave me a strange feeling whenever I heard it, and I confess many times I longed to declare the truth; but even a six-year-old understood the need for concealment, and I gradually grew to accept it without a second thought, even to the point where I must set myself to conscious recall of the truth. It never occurred to me until much later that perhaps Ailithir might have had a hand—or more than a hand—in the folk's easy acceptance of the story.

Or perhaps even in *my* acceptance of it: I learned to answer to 'Gwion' as readily as I had to 'Taliesin,' and only Ailithir and Arthur, and sometimes Ygrawn, still called me by my old name; and then never but in private, lest ears should hear that ought not to.

Nor did it take long for my old routine to be reestablished: Lessons at Daars were as necessary as lessons had been at Tair Rhamant, and I was at my studies again before I had been more than a sevennight in my new home.

I was not the only student in the castle schoolroom: Arthur shared my lessons with me. Though I pined at first for Benesek, I was soon too busy even to mourn him, as my new instructors began the courses of study that were to have so great a weight in all our lives after.

Those teachers were chosen by Ygrawn herself, she not wishing to leave so important a choosing to her husband's more casual and less careful nature. In the old days, the days before Edeyrn, after our fostering was at an end Arthur and I would have been sent to study at one of the great centers that had flourished in Keltia since the beginning. Kelts are passionately fond of learning, prizing knowledge and those who can impart it above all other things, and we have schools for every trade and craft and art: for bardery and battle, for magic and music and all manner of making.

But Edeyrn had dissolved all such places long years since, in his panicked fear of what might not be taught there; and of course the bards and Druids and Ban-draoi and Fianna were his chiefest foes. Even I knew how among the leaders of the Counterinsurgency were some of the cleverest minds in Keltia; and so they would have had to be, to keep the resistance alight so long, flaming so strong in the face of all Edeyrn could send against them. Edeyrn was right to fear learning: Knowledge has ever been a sword to cut down tyranny, be that tyranny the work of an evil overlord or an unjust monarch or an overbearing religion.

Yet, though the schools were closed, folk must still be taught such useful things as reading and ciphering and tongues, or what use could they be to the Theocracy? Therefore Edeyrn permitted a sort of instruction to be put forth by a sort of bard: a sanctioned bard, controlled and managed and ever under the eye and hand of the Ravens. For all his rules and safeguards and vigilance, though, the Marbh-draoi never knew how subtly—and flagrantly—his tame bards did violence to his intent; never knew until later, and by then it was too late. But it was not only bards who were the secret enemies of the Marbh-draoi and his works . . .

Among the others who were so, in Daars at least, were our teachers of record: Ailithir, of course; for as few folk, and no Ravens, yet knew him for a Druid, he was free to teach us as he—and Ygrawn—saw fit to.

But we had two other teachers, Arthur and I: One of them, Elphin Carannoc, was one of those subverter-bards I have just now spoken of. A master-bard too, if anyone in those degenerate days could be said to be a master at all; and to his everlasting honor Elphin never called himself so. But he was a bard if ever bard there were: a bard in his soul; and after all is said and sung, that is where bards are made. So he taught us both: history and tongues and mathematicals and enginery, philosophy and astrography and rhyme; taught us well, if I may say so.

Our third teacher— Since the closing of the Fianna academies and the great War College on Erinna, the soldier's art had fallen off in Keltia. Though Edeyrn indeed had need of bully-boys to enforce his will on the folk, it was *not* his will that highly trained warriors should ever again be raised up in a body, as formerly, lest they should unite to depose him; and so his own troops were given but minimal instruction in special garrisons, under the gentle tutelage of Ravens.

But there were still true-trained Fians in Keltia all the same—my own sister Tegau, I would later learn, was herself one of them, and one of the finest—and whether by Ygrawn's contrivance or some other's, we had a secret Fian for our tutor in war.

"Hold! Wrong! Again!"

The shout rang like a bell through the faha, and as regularly as a bell did it seem to sound these days. We had learned to obey it, Arthur and I, and to disobey it at our sore cost: We heard its iron tongue even in our dreams.

Scathach crossed the faha and stood before us, surveying our flushed and chagrined faces. I myself had less far to look up these days—I had been at Daars more than two years, and had grown near a hand and a half, though for speed of growing I could not match Arthur, who was shooting up like a young red birch—and now I lifted my eyes to my teacher's.

She was herself not overly tall for a woman of the Kelts, nor more than averagely fair to look upon; but even then I thought Scathach Aodann beautiful, for when she was lost in her art, when that thing that speaks the same to all of us blessed with the gift of a calling was speaking to her—when it had caught her up in its grip as it would later have me in my bardcraft, and Arthur in his artistry, and others in music or magic or feats of skill and strength—she was in those moments fairer than Ygrawn herself.

But this was not one of those moments, and if Scathach was caught up in anything just now, it was annoyance with her two pupils—my sorrow to say her wrath was not often misplaced; though to my guilty relief it was Arthur, not I, who seemed to be the offender on this particular occasion.

"Well then? What do you say for yourself?" She pulled off her leather practice helm, ran her fingers through the straight shoulder-length dark crop and fixed him with her eye.

Arthur breathlessly launched into a spirited defense of the maneuvers he had employed in the sword-drill we had just been engaged in. Much to my surprise, Scathach, who had at first been listening to him with that ages-old expression with which a teacher will hear a clever pupil's inventive excuses, suddenly began to look interested, then genuinely interested, and at last somewhat taken aback; amused, even, and admiring, in a grudging kind of way. Abruptly she gave him a brief nod and an unreadable smile, cuffed him lightly on the ear and walked away; and I wished I had been paying attention to what my fostern had been telling her.

I taxed him with it later. "What did you *say* to her, I have never seen the old she-bear look so confounded!"

Arthur shrugged happily and thrashed bare tanned legs in the water; we were in the pool-baths after our bout's conclusion—the customary soak that followed exercise and preceded the nightmeal.

"Something she was not thinking to hear. I have been reading and studying a little on my own—it was but an idea that came from it."

"Oh aye! It surely seemed to be a plausible one."

He grinned. "It did seem so, did it not . . . Well, you know how it is for you, Talyn, when you have the need to put something into words?"

I nodded my understanding, for I knew very well: The little bound book given me by Benesek was long since filled with my scribblings, and now had half a dozen fellows beside it on a secret shelf in my cupboard.

"For you, it is feeling," Arthur was saying, addressing the vaulted tiled ceiling as he floated on his back in the warm water. "For me, it is—well, *doing*. I know not how to say it better: It can be sword-drill, or bowcraft, or the spear-toss, but more than any it is the planning of such things, to bring them together and make of them a pattern—to wield them together as one weapon."

"If that is how you see things," I said judicially, "you should go to train for a Fian."

He rolled over onto his front, gave me a strange look. "That is what I have said to my father, and to Ailithir."

"And what do they say in answer?"

"Oh, what *can* they say—that Fianship is dead in Keltia, and any lass or lad who showed promise of being such a warrior would quickly be reived away by Ravens, to train for Edeyrn's service. And since I would sooner be dead in a ditch than serve *that* one—"

He shrugged again and splashed away down the pool with a strong stroke. The dull burning loathing I had never been able to overcome seized me once again at sound of Edeyrn's name, and I spoke what came to my lips, though Arthur did not hear.

"That will never be *your* fate—you shall be all you wish to be, and more besides: to bring the Marbh-draoi down, and all his creatures with him; to restore to the throne its rightful blood."

But that was an aisling if ever there was one, a vain and waking dream, and well I knew it: The House of Dôn, Keltia's royal house for the past five hundred years, was all but dead, and some even held that it had perished utterly. When Ederyn had overthrown his friend and master, Alawn, last king of the Dôniaid to rule, he had ordered not only Alawn but his queen Breila Douglas and every other living member of that line to be put to the sword—men, women, children, all—any with a blood-link however distant to the rightful rígh-domhna.

But one there was the sword had missed: Within a year of the slaughter of her kindred, a new Queen of the House of Dôn had been proclaimed. Queen in hiding, queen in exile, queen with a price on her head, but Queen of Kelts all the same: Seirith, who struck back hard; and after her, her son Elgan, and his daughter Darowen. A slender thread to hang a royal house upon, but soon the thread thickened: Darowen and her consort Gwain produced three sons, and two of them became king.

Even I, as a babe at Tair Rhamant, had heard of the first of those: Leowyn, called the Sun Lord, as much for his blazing temperament as his golden hair. He had become his mother's heir on the mysterious death of his brother Amris; had wed a princess of Galloway; and had been cried ten years since as lawful King of Kelts; a meaningless title even so, as Edeyrn still held the Ard-tiarnas, and his Ravens still held the sword-hand uppermost.

Yet even Edeyrn, for all his evil, had never dared put on the Copper Crown, nor wield the Silver Branch nor sit upon the Throne of Scone. Perhaps some lingering inhibition from his days long past as a true and faithful Druid forbade it; perhaps the crown and throne and scepter carried some arcane protection of their own, an innate menace that warned him away. Whatever the reason, Edeyrn had never claimed these royal symbols, or the name of King, for himself; though all else in Keltia lay trodden deep beneath his boot . . .

A splash beside me brought me out of the aisling, and I was looking into Arthur's damp and grinning face.

"Where have *you* been?" he asked. Any other lad would have ducked me under for such woolgathering; but he knew how I still woke in terror from dreams of Gwaelod, walls of water roaring through my sleep.

I smiled back, and began to paddle toward the pool's edge. "Nowhere in especial—nowhere at all."

It was about that time that Ailithir began to claim more and more of our time for special schooling, though we did not notice at first the direction this schooling was taking.

To us, it was dull and unexciting: meditations, mainly—exercises in visualization, training in focusing, disciplines of stillness of body and mind. Even the simple magics I had learned from Ailithir at Tair Rhamant—to shape the clouds or call the tinna-galach—were forbidden us now, and any greater magic was denied us.

Or so at least we thought then: We were too young, and too new to the ways of magic, to see what Ailithir was doing—how he was preparing the ground for the greater seed that would fall, and letting the bearing earth of our souls lie fallow until that seed-time should come. We were only lads, and impatient as lads and lasses will be, and too clever for our own weal; and so we deserved what our insistence earned for us . . .

"Show us some magic, athro."

Arthur, bored as usual with the lesson—as these days he was with anything that did not require him to have a sword in his hand—looked up at Ailithir from under the red-brown glib, straight brows lifted with a hopeful, artless look that nearly made me choke.

But Ailithir did not seem annoyed at our unwillingness to concentrate on the lesson; only gave us both an indulgent glance that had some kind of measuring behind it that I had not seen before, and which should have warned me right then that a new sort of lesson was about to be taught.

"So you two heroes would see magic—what was it you had in mind to see?"

"Oh, I know not!" Arthur could scarcely believe our teacher's apparent concession. "Something greater than pishogues, any road."

Ailithir raised his own brows at that. But his voice stayed mild. "And are you both such masters of lore that you judge it time to move on? Well, perhaps you have the right of it: Sit there, then, and let us see what may be seen."

Except for our certain knowing that we were still seated on our cushioned stools, in our own schoolroom, the afternoon sun still streaming in at the windows, it was all at once as it had been that moon-silvered midnight in the Arvon hills, when

I had sat beside Ailithir on a granite knob and looked to see visions in the rolling clouds. My heart began suddenly a slow pounding as the room darkened around us, and I could not feel my own body or the seat beneath me. Though I could not see him sitting beside me, I knew it must be the same for Arthur, for I heard him gasp as the darkness took him.

Then the dark lifted and lightened, but when I could see again it was not the familiar schoolroom that I saw: A long blue inland sea rimmed with mountains lay below me now—I say 'below' because I seemed to be hanging motionless in the air high above it, as if I sat astride a falair. Far distant, along the line of a trail through a pass, five horsemen were making their slow way across the mountain's green breast. It was the distance that made their pace seem so stately, for I sensed a desperate urgency in their errand, whatever it might have been, and when I strained my sight for a closer look I could see that they were riding hard.

Try as I might, the only thing else vouchsafed to me was the color of their mounts—two white horses, two black, one bay—and a glimpse of the golden hair of the one who seemed to be leader. Whether that one was man or woman, I could not even tell so much, for darkness swept down again, to veil all the bright picture, and when it lifted once more I was back in my chair in the schoolroom, shivering a little with the mystery of it and staring at Ailithir; for I knew that never would he have allowed us such a Seeing without some great reason.

He, however, was watching Arthur, and when I too turned to look at my fostern I realized that whatever he had seen, it was not what I myself had beheld. Arthur said nothing to either of us, though, and it was not until Ailithir, with an enigmatic smile, had quitted the room that Arthur spoke.

"What did you see, Talyn?"—and listened, strangely subdued, as I recounted my vision.

"And you?" I pressed, when he seemed to forget that he owed me a telling in return.

Arthur started a little. "Oh aye, I was forgetting . . . Well, it was a far place—not in Keltia, I think—a strange hot dry world. There was a hard black plain, and mountains like stone knives edging it, and fire-mounts in full eruption, two of them, like twin horns of flame. And the sky—it was not blue, but dull red.''

There was a long silence in the room. Just when I had decided to speak again, he continued.

''And there was a ship—dark green of hull—a starship, a ship of war, such as I have never seen in Keltia; a ship such as the ones we had before Edeyrn came. It was falling like a meteor, straight for one of the mountains of fire.'' He looked sidewise at me then, visibly shaking off the magic and the mood as a dog will shake off rain, and managed a fair imitation of his usual care-naught grin. ''Well, I asked for magic, did I not? But next time, Talyn—next time you have leave to cut my tongue out before I so ask again.''

Chapter 5

*T*hat cautionary lesson of Ailithir's—if indeed caution was all there was to it, and I have never for an instant believed *that*—accomplished such purpose all the same: Arthur, though soon his cheerful self again, displayed a new thoughtfulness, and a marked willingness to accept his teacher's pace and not force a swifter. As for me—well, let us say that Ailithir was pleasantly surprised to find both his pupils less reluctant to practice those disciplines they had previously so chafed at.

But time passed no matter who was pacemaster. Five years now since my coming to Daars: half a lifetime to an eleven-year-old. A summer at that age is near a year, a year seems near eternity; while to me now—as must have been to Ailithir then—a year spins by like a month. Rising twelve, I had about the weight and inches that were usual for one of my age, coupled with a gravity that I suspect would have better befit someone ten times my years. I knew every inch of my beloved Caer-in-Arvon, from the castle down to Stanestreets, the ancient quarter of twisting wynds and lanes and alleys that made a quaint muddle-maze behind the city walls. I had a horse of my own, a sturdy dun garron with black points, whom I called Faor, and a half-share, as it were, in Luath, a tall gray-brindle staghound whose only love was the chase and whose only gods were Arthur and myself.

The nightmares of Gwaelod were all but gone now. Five years of continuing love and protection had taken away the terror, though the memory would never leave me; and never even in that terror's tightest grip had I prayed that it should, some calamities are better remembered than not. Ygrawn and Gorlas had well fulfilled the trust placed in them: If Ygrawn was perhaps a little overwhelming at times, or Gorlas less effective than he might be, I knew they loved me as they loved Arthur, and I had come to love them as devotedly as if they had been my birth-parents. And many times there were—and are even now—when I was obliged to set myself to remember that they were not.

Not that I forgot Gwyddno, or Medeni whom I had never even known: They lived forever for me in memory, and in more than memory once I began to master the framing of my feelings in words. My notebooks were filled with reflections on them, and those others I loved, or would come to love; and the skill to craft those reflections was being shaped by a master hand indeed.

I have said before that Keltia's ancient arts of Druidry and bardcraft and Fianship were quashed by Edeyrn's policies. But though this was for the most part true, it had come slowly clear to Arthur and to me that true bards and true Druids and true Fians yet existed; and that, by dán or by design, we had all three for teachers. As I say, it took some time for this knowledge to come upon us; indeed I do not recall even now being told straight out, as a child, that Ailithir was Druid, or Scathach a Fian. Such dangerous secrets, with their counterpoint of life and death, were not to be entrusted to twelve-year-olds, though I think that we could well have kept counsel on the matter. For we were learning concealment of mightier secrets yet in those days, learning in great gulps and leaps, as the ground Ailithir had taken such pains to prepare drew near at last to sending up its first green shoots.

But if our studies in Druidry were much of a match, Arthur and I had outdistanced each other in our other trainings, the ones that were to set the pattern for the rest of our lives: he as warrior, I as bard. So while he was off with Scathach, refighting historic battles or planning future ones, I spent my days with one who was to have as great a part to play as any in the dán for which we were all preparing—or for which we were being prepared.

If I have not yet spoken as much of Elphin Carannoc as I have of Ailithir or even of Scathach, it is by no means out of slighting or spiting. On the contrary: Elphin was one of those teachers that a gifted student, if fortunate, will come by earlier in life rather than later; not to form or force the untaught talent, but to clear the way for it to move and grow of itself. And for me there in Daars, hungering for words and the lessoning to use them, Elphin seemed sent by the Holy Awen Itself.

Though music has ever played its rightful part in bardery, in the very earliest days of Keltia to be a bard was to be one for words alone. And such words: aers and scriptals and saltars and ranns, the Stories Great and Stories Minor, the epics and annals, the tales and the triads, the chaunts and the colloquies, all the lovely treasure a bard is heir to. Oh, mistake me not, the music is no less fair or mighty, and I pride myself more than perhaps I should that since my time—and in large part because of me—it has become so important in a bard's training, though it was chance first made it so. Still, Frame of Harmony is by my side even now, and I can hear pipe and harp and fidil from morn to middlenight here at Seren Beirdd . . .

But words were wingèd in those days, and it was Elphin taught me first how they might let me soar.

Yet before the soaring must come the slogging: I was bent over my copying one afternoon—a particularly hellish passage from an old Erinnach text—when Ygrawn came into the room. This was of itself by no means unusual; the lady of Daars often came to look in on her son and foster-son in the schoolroom or on the practice-field—though I do not recall Gorlas ever doing the same—and our teachers were no more troubled by her presence than were we.

I glanced up at her with a quick smile and a look of amused despair for the heavy weather I was making of my copying. She answered with a smile of her own, but only after the smallest of hesitations, as if some distracting thought or mood had caught her up. But then she took her customary seat by the windows, and so quiet was she that after a very short while I forgot she was even there.

All the same, some message must have passed between teacher and mistress, for when I glanced up again Elphin had gone, and Ygrawn was watching me in steady silence. My apprehension must have shown on my face, for I saw her expression change at once.

"Ah, Tal-bach, I am sorry! Go on with your work—"

I put down the light-pen, grateful for the excuse to leave off, and set aside the much-mauled text. "Nay, it is done; or as done as I shall make it today. . . Is aught wrong, methryn? Just now you looked—well, I have never seen you look so, and though I would not pry—"

Again the lovely face shimmered with change. "Between Elphin and Ailithir, you are learning to look far and deep! A Sight to serve a Druid, and words to put point to your Seeing—" There was true-praise in her voice, and I flushed to hear it; not often did Ygrawn commend, and never but for cause.

She leaned back in her chair, putting her two cupped palms together in a gesture full of grace—and one habitual with her when she would speak of serious matters. But when she spoke, it was on a topic I had not expected.

"Talyn, have you been happy here with us? I have ever thought you have, to be sure, but perhaps it is not so after all."

My store of words, so lately commended, seemed to rush and stumble over itself in its haste to reach my lips. "So happy—I cannot say how happy—you and Gorlas-maeth—Ailithir—Elphin—Scathach—"

"And Arthur?" came the cool quiet voice.

"*Arthur!*" The words went up like fountains. "He is my

brother, my comrade, my anama-chara—if I had not had
him to my side these years—"

"Yet you have true brothers and sisters of your own."

"Oh aye; but save for a few brief messages I have heard
naught of any of them since—since Gwaelod."

Ygrawn was watching me even more closely than before.
"There is word now," she said after a while. "From your
sister Tegau."

Cold blankness closed round me, and for an instant I could
not speak nor move nor breathe. Then:

"She is not—none of them is—they are all—" Words
failed again, and I could only stare in mute imploring, arming
my soul against what she might now say.

Suddenly it seemed to dawn on her what I had asked. "Oh,
nay, Talynno, my sorrow to fright you! Stupid and cruel of
me—nay, they are all well; at least they were when Tegau
last had word of them."

"What then?" My heart began to settle back into its place
behind my ribs.

Ygrawn leaned forward, a look of grave purpose on her
face. "I must share this with one of my sons, Taliesin, and
when you hear you will know why Arthur cannot be the one
. . . Tegau sends to let me know that the Marbh-draoi turns
his attention toward Daars."

I must have made some small protesting sound, for she
smiled grimly. "Aye, it was of that I too thought: Gwyddno,
and what befell him and his province alike when *he* came to
Edeyrn's notice."

I found my voice again. "But my father was a partisan of
the Counterinsurgency, it was well known—Ailithir has told
me—more, he had six children enrolled in its ranks. Gorlas-
maeth—"

"—supports the Counterinsurgency no less than did Gwyddno
his friend," she said evenly. "We have never spoken of this
to you or Arthur because we thought it best you did not yet
know. But now Edeyrn's eye is upon Daars, and Gorlas may
be called to account. This is what Tegau wishes us to be
prepared to face."

"Surely my foster-father—"

Ygrawn sighed, and took my hands in hers. "Your foster-father is not a politic man, Taliesin; I would be untrue to what is yet between us did I not recognize that in him . . . He is not even so politic as Gwyddno was, and look what befell *him* in the end. Gorlas will not silver-tongue his way along for years, what way your father did; he will confront, not conciliate, and never dream he might do other." For a moment a strange smile lighted her face—composed of rue and pride and affection and exasperation, it seemed to have the measure of Ygrawn and Gorlas both in it, and I stared, for it was the first time she had let me see as an equal into her heart. Then the smile faded, and fear and care were plain in its place; but her voice was steady still, as if she spoke of some lord who was a stranger to us both.

"But all of dúchas rank are suspect these days," she said then. "The Marbh-draoi fears—rightly fears—that one, or many, may rise up against him out of one of the old houses that have never truly accepted his rule. Still, he cannot replace all such chiefs with his own creatures; therefore does he suffer such as my lord, and your father, to go on—until such time as it no longer suits him."

"Why do you tell this to me, methryn, and not to Arthur?"

There was no mirth in the laugh Ygrawn gave. "I cannot say for certain. Perhaps because the word came from Tegau, and she is your sister; perhaps because this—forgive me, bach—is a thing not unfamiliar to you; perhaps because I know too well how my son would answer it." At that the laugh became true-mirth, and I joined in it. "Aye, truly! Yet even so, Arthur is already better able to subdue his feelings and master himself to his own ends than ever Gorlas was. He will never be a trimmer the match of, say, his uncle Marc'h, my brother who is Duke of Kernow; but nor do I think he will himself ever come to face a summons to Ratherne. Other things, aye; but never that. At least, may the Mother make it so . . ."

Ygrawn rose to leave, and I rose too for courtesy. "I know you will say no word of this to Arthur, Tal-bach, and so I need not offend you by begging your silence. But I *would* ask you to speak of it with Ailithir: I have myself told him of Tegau's warning, and it seems he has had warning of his own, so that you need not fear to break confidence. It may be you and he together will see a thing that I have not.''

"There is not much Ygrawn fails of seeing,'' remarked Ailithir when I recounted all this to him later that same day, up in the tower chamber with its long views down the glen. He looked for a moment as if he were about to say more—something to do with Ygrawn's powers of perception, or something else entirely—then just as visibly he changed his mind. "Your own Sight grows sharper these days—what do you See in this?''

Before I could think I had spoken. "That Ygrawn fears I might be discovered, or else that the Marbh-draoi already knows that I am here.'' The words shocked me, for I had not thought any such thing with my conscious mind, but Ailithir only nodded, as if that were what he had thought himself, and my saying it but confirmed his thinking.

He said no word on it, though, and I began to consider the implications of what I had just pronounced. What if Edeyrn did indeed know that Daars had sheltered the last of Gwaelod? There were other survivors of the wave in Daars this very hour; I was by no means the only waif that Gorlas had taken into sanctuary. Would Edeyrn in his vengeance bring upon the Caer-in-Arvon the same death that he had sent upon Tair Rhamant?

It seems strange to say it now, but for myself I had no fears whatsoever. Perhaps my Sight saw dimly even then the glow of that unimaginable future, already blazing below time's horizon like a yet unrisen sun; perhaps I had simply not the traha to think that the Marbh-draoi would destroy Daars on the odd chance that Gwyddno's son might perish in the ruins. It might have been better for us all had I thought so . . .

Ailithir had fixed me with his eye, as if he knew my thought—as very likely he did. "What must be shall be; but let not your love for Gorlas, or for Arthur, keep you from

Seeing when seeing most is needed . . . even if that Seeing be a thing you would rather not have seen.''

"I would never do so," I said, a little hurt that he should think I needed such a cautioning.

He saw the sudden stiffness in my manner, laid a gentle hand on my shoulder. "I know, bach; but Sight may be our saving. These days, none of us can afford to blink.''

For all my resolution to keep this new care out of my face, something plainly yelled itself aloud to Arthur, for I caught him observing me during the nightmeal, a quizzical gleam in his brown eyes; more than once I felt the touch of his mind on mine, as his loving concern tried to sound my defenses. But I was as skilled by now as he in such matters, so that my will garrisoned the walls of my mind against him, and after a while he withdrew the touch.

I was relieved that he did so, for I knew well that his inborn good manners would forbid him to inquire outright. Having been put off, however gently, Arthur would not attempt my mind again, and so Ygrawn's confidence was safe—at least for some while longer. But I had reckoned without my fostern's persistence, that to the end of his days was never to let him leave a thing unresolved or a question unanswered; which was Keltia's great gain, and in the end her greatest loss . . .

It had become our custom to pass the hours between nightmeal and sleeptime in our grianán—what had once been known as the nursery and was still on occasion of our forgetting our new dignity referred to as such—in study or relaxation or plain bone-idleness, according to our mood. Sometimes we talked, but mostly this time was our quiet time, which I preferred to spend with book or harp, and which Arthur most often used these days to make something.

A little in envy, I think, of my bent for words and music, he had sought for something creative of his own, and found it too, in a great and genuine gift for artificing. It did not seem to matter much what he put his hand to, the skill served him well for all: painting or carving or the crafting of things of beauty—jewels, daggers, one time a tiny gold falair with ruby eyes, as gift for his mother. Arthur used his talent to escape into himself from the demands of the day; my talent was no escape but only another demand, and in the end it took me out of myself altogether. Yet each of us created truly in his own way.

Tonight, though, there was no making of any sort. Foremost for us were the staggering tidings announced by Gorlas at the nightmeal: Leowyn King of Kelts, rightful ruler of the Six Nations, prince of the House of Dôn, was dead. The bright Sun Lord had perished without point, in a dreary nighttime roadside brawl, casually killed by drunken Ravens who did not know whom they had slain.

Well, no doubt they knew now, and much to their regretting: Edeyrn could not have been pleased that Leowyn Pendreic should die at any man's hand save his, and the Ravens had paid for their offhand murder. It was some small consolation to those loyal to the true Ard-rígh that his slayers were now themselves slain, and neither swiftly nor pleasantly. But for the most part, Leowyn's death, without meaning and without hope, came but as one more grief to a folk already near foundered with despair.

It did not occur to any of us at Daars—not even Ailithir—to wonder at the timing of the day's two events. Edeyrn had long since closed his fist upon any widespread transmission of news in Keltia—save what he wished us to hear—and Leowyn might have been a year dead, or an hour, and we would know it not if the Marbh-draoi wished us not to know it. So we had of force developed an informal net of whispers—true ones— that stretched from planet to planet. It was this word-web that Tegau had touched, to bring warning to Ygrawn; and later it had carried word of the King's murder.

But Tegau's warning and Leowyn's slaying were unrelated in our minds at that hour, and stayed so for long after—to our very great sorrow. Perhaps if we had thought to link the two— But we did not, and the mistake was to cost much for many folk.

Now, though, we sat in our grianán, as people were doing

all across Keltia, and thought on this Ard-rígh we had never known.

Arthur stirred where he sat brooding before the fire. "Still," he said, "though the King be slain, there is yet a King of Kelts."

He looked as doubtful at that as I did feel: The dead King's successor was his brother Uthyr, about whom little was known, save that he had a name for gentleness and rare scholar's gifts, and was thought to abhor battle; not perhaps the likeliest of rulers in such a time.

"We would have a High Queen instead," I said in answer, "were she not too young in years to claim her rights."

Arthur's whole being seemed to spark at that, and had I been Ailithir in that moment, or even Ygrawn, I might have seen that spark for the fire-seed it truly was. But I was only a lad myself, as oddly intrigued as my fostern at the thought of a princess no more than a year or so younger than were we.

"Gweniver," said Arthur, and I wonder now that the very night outside did not shiver at the saying. "She is Uthyr's heir-apparent, by her right from Leowyn her father. Do you know, Talyn, she shall be Ard-rían even in despite of any children Uthyr may come to have of his own; such is our succession law."

I knew it as well as did he, Elphin had drilled it deep enough. But it is law from our most ancient days in Keltia, and Earth before that, and maybe even from somewhere else before Earth, if the old tales are true, and there is no reason to think they are not: Should a monarch die, that monarch's successor is the next nearest in blood who is of age to rule; a son or daughter, of course, if one or the other should be to hand; a brother or sister, aunt or uncle, niece or nephew or cousin if not. Few Kelts, and no royalty, lack at least one or two of these.

As King Leowyn's only child, therefore, Gweniver had been Tanista since her birth. Had Leowyn died before becoming King, Uthyr would have succeeded Darowen their mother; but in any case Gweniver would have been heir. Now Uthyr was King because of his niece's lack of years—our law also provides that none may wear the Copper Crown, or claim it, who has not reached thirty-three years of age. So Uthyr was King in exile, but it would be Queen Gweniver to follow him, and no heir of his body.

"They say Uthyr would sooner be a Druid scholar-monk—if any such still were—than hold his place as King," I said after a while. "For all that, Arthur, you and I or the sheepkeeper could be cried as sovereign tonight and it would make the same differ—which is to say no differ at all. If there is any king in Keltia it is Edeyrn, and it has always *been* Edeyrn, and it will most like always *be* Edeyrn. Uthyr and Gweniver are maybe themselves as dead as Leowyn, and there will come no savior for Keltia out of the House of Dôn."

Arthur shook his head impatiently and rolled over to stare into the flames. "They live—*where*, I cannot say; but I am sure they live. As for Edeyrn, no tyrant yet has lasted, in Keltia or beyond. And if we speak of saviors, did not Athyn herself prove that saviors may come of humble houses as well as mighty ones?"

I smiled and said nothing, knowing his secret dreams. Athyn Anfa, that indomitable one who had risen from simple Erinnach horsegirl to Queen of Kelts, Ard-rían by acclamation, was one of Arthur's great heroes; ever in his mind was the hope that as she had once done, so too might he one day do. Athyn's modest origins were comfort and goad alike to him: Although never a glozer or worshipper of rank for rank's sake—what I have since heard outworlders call a snob—Arthur sometimes lamented a little, I think, that his house was not a grander one.

Not, I hasten to add, for any vain pride of name or mere self-glory—Kelts are among the most democratic peoples in the galaxy; we are more impressed with persons than with pedigrees, and for all our reverence for our rulers, in the end it is the aristocracy of soul that matters most with us; and all his life to Arthur it mattered more even than that—but simply because Arthur could not conceive of such deeds as he felt it in him to do being done by one who was no heir to kingdoms but only to a minor dúchas on a minor world. Like Arthur,

Gwynedd was as yet but poor in power; at the time of which I am telling, the great worlds of Keltia were Erinna, Kernow, and, then as ever, Tara herself; and in Gwynedd, Arvon was the beggarly cousin of fat and important provinces like Berwyn and Sarre.

So I looked at my fostern's face in the firelight, that face I have never ceased to love: thin, eager, fine-featured, the chestnut hair a tangled curling thatch to his shoulders, the clear dark eyes shining with possibility. Looked at him, and thought again of Athyn . . .

But however removed she might have been from the direct succession, Athyn Cahanagh had at least been of the rígh-domhna. To the best of my then knowing, Arthur's claim to any such lineage was a poor and stretched one—though every Kelt alive, or dead for that matter, can boast royal, even divine, blood, if one goes back far enough. Ygrawn of course was of high descent, but of ducal rank, not royal or even princely, and in any case not of the House of Dôn. Gorlas, surprisingly, did have some link to that all but vanished kindred, but by no herald's tricks of tracing could his claim be seen as a close one, and there must have been many hundreds in Keltia at that time who stood nearer the Copper Crown than did the blood of Daars; if not near enough for Edeyrn to think to slay.

Nay, for the folk only the true blood of the Dôniaid would suffice; and that, now, meant two persons only: Uthyr and Gweniver, wherever they might be hiding, and if they yet lived. It seemed to me a hope vanishingly small, either way, and the Crown restored the most vanished hope of all, and I listened with only half an ear to Arthur muttering over the names of the Pendreic rulers-in-exile, like some failed or forgotten rann: Alawn, Seirith, Elgan, Darowen, Leowyn, Uthyr; and Gweniver that would be.

But then, for all Ailithir's fond hopes, I was a most erratic seer.

Chapter 6

𝔉or all its high far tragedy, the death of King Leowyn was to Arthur but a false drag across the scent he followed: that seeming mysterious secret he knew I was keeping from him. For my part, I knew he would have it out of me in the end—not even Luath was keener or steadier or more untiring in the hunt—but I was hoping to keep the thing my own a while yet. Obedient to Ygrawn's wish, I said no word to anyone of my sister's warning. If Gorlas knew, he was not saying either, and Ailithir, who *did* know, was for his part silent too.

But though all was silence, all at Daars was not well; and nor did I cheat or cozen myself into thinking it so. Naught to name or note, only a certain, or uncertain, feeling: watching Berain, Ygrawn's guard-captain, putting an extra edge on her weapons; listening to the undertones in Elphin's chaunting every night in hall; sensing the spring-steel tension in Ygrawn's whole body when she would embrace Arthur and me and brush a light kiss over our foreheads and give us goodnight. From Gorlas, yet nothing; he was as calm and unrufflcd as he had always been, so that I, looking to find in his face or voice or mien something of the stern secret rebellion of which Ygrawn had told me, grew only the more baffled the more I found nothing like, and wondered if it were there at all, or indeed had ever been.

But it had, and it was; and soon it was made plain to me in no controvertible manner.

It was a rain-filled afternoon in early spring, too late for snow and too soon for greening. Arthur and I, released betimes from our lessons by Ailithir's ill humor, were too delighted with our unexpected gift of freedom to quarrel with or question its cause: Pausing only to catch up our cloaks and call Luath from his doze before the fire, we pelted past the guards at the castle gate and headed down into the town.

Despite the rain and chill, the streets of Daars were far from empty: not thronged but modestly thick with townspeople, and a fair sprinkling of folk in from the outlying glens and townlands, come to do their marketing or visit friends or attend to tasks or truancies of their own.

We spent an idle hour or two wandering through the Stanestreets, our favorite quarter of the city, with its cobbled alleys and tall narrow houses and lanes leading into tiny squares lined with shops. It was a craftsmen's quarter: leatherworkers and potters and jewelsmiths and the like, all of whom knew us well and most of whom had enjoyed our modest custom. But my favorite shop of all, and the one that by tacit agreement we ever left for last, was the luthiers' workshop in Swan Street—the place where harps were made. On other visits I had hung round the artisans like a bee sipping from a flower, and they for their part had seemed pleased to share their joy in the work.

Today, though, the luthiers seemed to have no time for us. Perhaps the weather had got into the wood, and made them cross; save for a brief greeting they said little, and their mood seemed one of distraction. Though they would never have shown us open discourtesy—more for that we were their friends than that we were their lord's sons—still there was a palpable coolness, and after a brief five minutes Arthur gave them a rather short good-day and dragged me with him back into the street.

The rain was moving off now and the day brightening, so we strolled back leisurely through the main market-square, thinking to buy a pastai or two, or perhaps a sweet, to hold us until supper. We had not been paying much mind to how we went, and so when we found ourselves in one of the blindstreets that ran off the city walls, we turned round with a laugh and a groan for our inattention, to find our way back to our route.

To our surprise, the street was not empty behind us. A man stood upon the rain-slick cobbles, effectively barring the path, and though he was dressed in the Arvon fashion, we somehow knew him to be no man of the district. Another shared our doubt: Luath had bounded forward, every hackle lifted on his massive neck and the tips of his gleaming fangs just showing under a curled lip. He was growling, very softly, though it came to me that the growl was more the one that a dog will use to discourage an enemy when he himself is afraid, rather than one of challenge or confident hostility. Arthur hastily hooked him by his studded collar, lest the stranger take offense, or worse.

But when the man spoke, his voice was pleasant and his words unexceptionable. "Hail, young masters! Where to on so dour a day?"

We returned the greeting, though how he had known to call us so—he had used the word in local dialect which translates as 'young lords' and is reserved for the children of chiefs—we could not guess. Certain it was he had not twigged us from our attire: As usual in our leisure hours, Arthur and I wore garb that would have disgraced ragpickers' brats—muddy boots drooping and half unsoled, threadbare tunics, trews with the knees worn through and leinnas out at the elbows— and we bore no badge or device that might have made our rank apparent to a stranger.

So while Arthur, ever my master in politesse, engaged the man in small chat, I withdrew a little, and studied the stranger with the wiles Ailithir had been at such pains of late to teach me. It was immediately plain to my kenning that this man wore concealment as casually as he wore his raincloak. Yet it seemed too that there was about him naught worthy of hiding: He was tall, but no more than the average; dark, but so were most Kymry in the west of Arvon; neither over-graced nor ill-favored of face. Nor was there any trace of accent to his speech: He seemed a man who belonged it might be anywhere, and yet he seemed also to have come from nowhere.

Whatever, clearly he did not belong in Daars, and stealing a sidewise glance at Arthur I could see that my fostern thought so too—though all the stranger would have seen in his manner was the courtesy any Kelt would have shown. Still and all, it was with a sudden thrill of trepidation, and a greater of astonishment, that I heard Arthur inviting him up to the castle for the nightmeal and lodging till morning.

It was not the invitation of itself that caused my wariness and surprise; that was law and custom in Keltia, bred into our very bones—we would no more think or study to do such than we would think to breathe, so instinctive a matter is it with us. Indeed, Arthur and even I had offered hospitality on other occasions, to other strangers, in the name of Gorlas and Ygrawn . . . But this particular stranger was not as those others had been; everything about him seemed just that least littlest bit wrong. He was just that one word too glib, the encounter had been just that minutest fraction too casual, the man himself the tiniest shade too eager to take up Arthur's invitation.

So I hung back a pace or two as we walked up to the castle, though the stranger repeatedly turned round to include me in converse, and I kept my thoughts shielded from anyone who might be trying to read them. For the one first thing that had struck me, a warning that had blazed like a fireflaw from the stranger's eyes to mine the instant our glances had met, was the certain knowledge that he knew me.

Knew me for who I was: Not some bedraggled street-waif, nor yet the lord's nephew of my masquerading, but Taliesin Glyndour, son of Gwyddno, escape of Gwaelod, brother to six troublesome thorns in the Marbh-draoi's foot. And running in tandem with this sensing was another, darker and more dire knowledge: This man, whatever he feigned to be, was almost certainly one of Owein's Ravens.

*   *   *

"Well of *course* he is a Raven!" said Arthur, rolling up his eyes at my obtuseness. "I confess I did not see it until that we had spoken for a time—certainly not until after you had kenned it—do you think I had asked him to supper else?"

I stared at him. We were in Arthur's chamber, where he was changing his clothes for something more befitting his father's high table; I had already attended to my own attire in my rooms down the hall.

"You *know* he is a Raven, and yet you invite him to take hospitality of us!" I threw an exasperated look of my own at Ailithir, who was sitting in the window seat, and did not see it. "Athro?"

At that he looked round at me, answering my glance with an uplifted brow. "Adhalta?" he replied, echoing my tone and overlaying it with a faint touch of surprise and reproof: Clearly I had not shone so brightly here as I had thought. He saw this, too. "*Think*, Taliesin," he added in a kindlier voice.

I thought, and blushed. "Ah. For that it would be best to keep an eye on him ourselves, whilst he is in Daars."

"Aye so," said Arthur, lacing up his points. "And no bad thing would it be, either, for my mother and Scathach and Elphin to take their own measure of him. And you above all, far-eolas," he said to Ailithir, using the term of most respect— 'man of knowledge'—from pupil to teacher.

Ailithir bowed where he sat. "My thanks for the name! Now I bid you listen both, and listen well"—here his whole being seemed to somehow hush—"This stranger in the gate is an enemy to us all; not to us of Daars only but to all in Keltia. The master whom he serves serves a darker master still—keep this well in mind. Taliesin, I doubt not but that your kenning is a right one: that Owein, having heard rumors, sends his Raven here to ferret you out. You did well to ken him so swiftly; and you, Arthur, did as well to think quick enough to offer him our board. See you do as well to guard your minds and your tongues during the nightmeal and after, and if you can do so without discourtesy, keep away from him entirely. We do not know as yet what skill he might have, and others better used to it will take up the kenning for you.''

He rose then, and I saw that he was dressed for once as a lord of Gorlas's court, in paper-fine sith-silk and a floor-length robe of dark red velvet, a chain of pearls and rubies round his neck.

''Come, my lords; let us go down.''

We were the last to arrive in the Great Hall; ordinarily this would have annoyed my foster-father, but I saw at once that he was taken up with the guest. Out of the tail of my eye I caught Ygrawn's quick unsmiling glance, and from over against the wall Elphin gave me the smallest of nods. My relief was intense—*So, then, they had all been warned*—and I spared a moment to study my fostern.

In the years I had been at Daars, Arthur had gone from a sturdy lad to a tall and well-grown youth. Fourteen years old next Wolf-moon, he was already taller than his mother, who by no means lacked inches, and like a staghound puppy not yet grown into its paws and bones, he was still a little stiff-limbed when he moved. But as the hunting-dog is seen in the puppy, so the warrior that would be was seen in Arthur even now; promise too of rare good looks—the chestnut hair and oakleaf eyes, the pale Kymric coloring, owing neither to Ygrawn nor Gorlas but to some other forebear; near or far as may be, but in no case of the line of Daars.

He crossed the hall now to lead his mother up to the high table at the room's eastern end, and I followed with Ailithir. Gorlas himself escorted the stranger guest, whom by now we had been let to know was called Perran, though I doubted even then that it was his truename, and later—much later—I knew that it was not. But the story he gave Gorlas now was that he was a traveller from Vangor in the southeast, passing through Arvon on a holiday journey. The tale was *just* plausible—even in those days of Edeyrn pleasure journeys were not entirely forbidden—but to my prejudging ear it seemed unlikely, and it seemed I was not the only one who thought so.

"From Vangor, is it?" murmured Scathach as she passed me on her way to her own place at the high table.

"Where is the wrong there?"

"Oh, very like none, to be sure; Vangor is a fine place. It would be finer still did it not lie within a few hours' ride of Caer Dathyl—and those who rule at Caer Dathyl these days."

And it was not the House of Dôn that did so . . . I watched Perran take the guest-place a little ways down the table's length. Caer Dathyl, the ancient seat of the princes of Gwynedd since the planet was first peopled, was now unwilling homeplace to Edeyrn's sword-arm—Owein Rheged. Stupid it was of Perran, or whatever his name was, to claim residence in Vangor—a place long under Owein's yoke and sway. It served only to focus attention on what had shouted itself from the first: that here was one of Owein's trained and trusted killers—one of his blood-beaked Ravens.

There would be direr dinners to come, but at that point in my young life that meal was the worst I had ever endured. To sit there, in sight of all in hall, choking down the odd mouthful of food, and more ale and usqua than I had any business drinking at my age, knowing all the while that not seven seats away sat a man who sought my name and life, and perhaps the lives of my foster-kin as well— It did not make for the pleasantest of evenings, and more than once I caught concerned glances from Arthur, Elphin and Ygrawn.

But all things end at last, though the evil ones seem to take so much longer to do so, and after a while I heard from a very long way off Gorlas calling the tune for the dancing that followed the feast. By now the drink had worked most powerfully upon me, and I was, not to put too high a gloss on it, just at that point of cupshot truthfulness where anything might be said—and too often is. Luckily, others had seen this too; and while Arthur, Scathach and Elphin were all casually converging on me with intent from separate corners of the hall, Ailithir got there first, and lost no time haling me out onto the broad terrace that hangs above the river.

The cool damp night air flowed over my burning skin and

cleared some of the ale-fumes away; when I could see again I looked up at Ailithir, and quickly lowered my head again.

"I am sorry! But he might have—"

"He might have been the one to give order for the death of Gwaelod, think you? And because you thought him so, is that good reason to give him cause to slay you too, or at the least deliver you over to Owein? Idiot boy!" He cuffed my ear, not gently, and my mind cleared wonderfully. "No Raven killed Gwaelod; that took a stronger hand than some hireling's. Nor do I think Owein himself did so. As for the other thing—" He paused for a few moments, that distant listening look coming over his face; then he was back. "I do not think he knows you," said Ailithir at last. "He may have come here under orders to seek you out, that is probably true enough. But I and others were kenning him close the whole night, and unless he is exceptionally skilled at hiding his thought, he has accepted the tale that you are Gorlas's poor sister's boy, hidden away for shame and pity. We are safe enough, maybe, for the time being."

I lowered myself carefully onto a stone bench, for the lights of Daars below were beginning to go in and out in a manner I cared for not at all.

"But?"

"But the fact that he has come here at all—that someone in power, Owein, or whoever, has seen fit to send in spies—*that* is what mislikes me so about it."

"It will be as my sister Tegau said, then," I muttered. "The Marbh-draoi turns his eyes to Daars."

"It seems so, and that is all we shall say of it here and tonight. Bed, you; and not so much as one finger do I lift to ease your potsickness."

"But I am not—" And then, my sorrow to say, I was.

Chapter 7

When I opened my eyes next morning—at least I *thought* it was the next morning; to judge by how I felt it could more plausibly have been the middle of next week—the dreadful spinning giddiness was gone, and the sick spasms at the back of my sand-dry throat gone too. And so, I sensed at once, was Perran . . .

After a while it seemed to me that I might safely sit up; but the instant I did so, I fell back into the pillows with a piteous groan.

"Bad head?" came the mock-sympathetic question.

I stopped whimpering at the altogether impossible pain in my head—there never *was* such a headache, my very hair hurt—long enough to squint muzzily at the indeterminate blob in the chair by the bed. The blob resolved into Arthur; he was holding something in his hands, and on his face was a smile to match his tone.

"Go away." I pulled the pillow over my head, rolling over as I did so, and was instantly sorry I had moved.

"Drink this," said Arthur when I had stopped making the pathetic sounds that seemed the only right response to how I felt. He was holding out to me the thing he had had in his hands: a mether half-full of some dark noxious-looking herbal swill.

"Never." He continued to look down at me, and after a moment I sighed and capitulated, gagging as I tried not to taste the mether's contents. "Done. Now go away."

"Not until you eat this." When I jibbed, Arthur added coolly, "Not one word do you get of what news I have this morning heard unless you do."

It was only some dry oat-cake, and out of my shame I tried to hide how sublimely good I found it; my body craved the salt and sugar, and I gobbled up without further protest each farl that Arthur so inexorably held out. Not only that, but the vile-tasting drench he had all but poured down my throat seemed to work with the short crumbly cake to restore me to human state; already the punishing headache was fading to a more bearable throb.

"Better?" he asked.

"Much. Now what news?"

"Ah, that . . ." Suddenly he was drifting toward the door. "Well, there is no news. I lied so that you would eat, the herbs in the drench work better on a full stomach—" Before I could marshal brain and arm to let me throw something at him he was gone.

Well for me that I threw nothing after all, for almost before Arthur was through the door from the one side Elphin Carannoc was coming in from the other. At sight of my teacher I sat up in the bed and ran my fingers through my elf-locked hair—so much better did I feel that I could perform even that rough grooming without undue discomfort—then looked up at Elphin with a face as near to guileless as I could that moment make it.

Not near enough, it seemed. There was a silence of perhaps five seconds' duration, and then Elphin and I both burst into laughter. He recovered himself first.

"I promise you it is no laughing matter, master Gwion." He laid the slightest glassy edge on the name, and the smile vanished from my face.

"I am well reproved," I said humbly, and the penitence was genuine. "Last night—"

"Last night you might well have ruined all, were it not for

Ailithir's hauling you so timely off. You are well repaid for your foolishness." The glint then of a green eye. "If it is drowning you are after, do not torment yourself with shallow water."

The double edge of the old saw sobered me instantly. "I will not, then . . . And from now on ale and usqua meet not in any mether of mine."

"Good. What more do you think can be learned from this?"

He was watching me with that same measuring look that Ailithir so often used upon me, and almost as often upon Arthur. Under the impassive green stare I began to fidget a little, desperately afraid that that seeking eye should find a flaw; and in my fear I began to babble.

"I think I have learned—learned that I know nothing? And that I can learn *how* to learn." Miraculously, it was the right answer: Elphin's dark handsome face split in a grin. I added cautiously, lest I might ruin my success, "Though I do not yet know, athro, what it is you would wish that I learn?"

He said nothing, but let his glance wander over to rest upon Frame of Harmony, my beloved harp, where it stood in its accustomed wall-niche. When he spoke it was with sudden decision, as if some question long thought-on had been just now settled in his mind.

"If bardic colleges still existed in Keltia, would you now be thinking of going off to one of them to study?" Seeing the blank astonishment, he smiled. "What I mean to say, Talyn"— and that was cause for further astonishment, almost never did he call me by my truename—"is only this: Is it your wish to become bard? For if not, a true gift has been wasted on you."

" 'A true gift'? You mean—*me*? Mine? *My* gift?" In my excitement and sudden shyness, my voice went squealing out of control, as it did now it was breaking. Chagrined, I relaxed my throat muscles to recover the new baritone deepness. "You can offer this to me? I thought you were not—I mean to say—" It seemed my manners had gone the way of my voice, and again I was silent, reddening at my lapses.

But Elphin only laughed, and slouched down luxuriously in

the chair Arthur had vacated. "Oh aye," he said. "I know very well what you thought I was not—a bard trained. It has been better that folk should think so—well, at least most folk. But now there is need for you to know differently, so listen and I shall tell you: I *am* a true bard, an ollave, trained in the true schools. Not at Seren Beirdd, to be sure, as I would have liked, and as you should be; but—in secrecy—brought up through the degrees in the ancient way."

I stared at him, too confounded by what I was hearing—both the words and the unimagined implications—to think of myself or my ale-head or anything else save what I had just learned: Elphin my teacher was a true bard, and he had said that I might be one too.

"How can this be?" I asked after a while, out of all the whirling welter of questions that filled my brain.

"Well, your sister Tegau is a Fian, is she not, and Fians are every bit as proscribed as bards. Not to mention Druids, whom we had better not mention— It should not come as such surprise: Ederyn may have forbidden the schools, but he cannot forbid the knowledge."

"But—where can such things be learned? Who is there to teach them? How long has it been so? When can I—" In my bubbling excitement I had bounced forward on my knees in the bed, and now almost fell out of it altogether.

"In good time," said Elphin, catching me before I went over the side. Turning the topic: "Yesterday, down in Stanestreets—Arthur tells me you knew this Perran was a Raven, come to Daars to seek you. You knew this before Arthur did?"

I nodded. "It came to me as soon as we turned round and saw him there blocking our path. It was—it was the way it *felt*; had it been only some old far-a-tigh doing the marketing it should have felt very different . . . But it was Arthur thought quicker than I, and acted on it, praying him come take the nightmeal here in the castle."

"Yet it was you saw him first for what he was." Elphin tapped his chin thoughtfully with the edge of his closed fist. It seemed to me, watching him with all my yearning soul in my eyes, that he had come to yet another decision, akin to that one he had earlier made—and it seemed also that this new one would not have been shared with me, as was about to happen, had I answered differently the questions he had been asking.

"You know how Edeyrn does permit tame bards, of a sort, in Keltia?" he said then. "Bards he thinks have been force-formed into his own pet drones?"

"Aye, else how would children be taught even such simple skills as ciphering and mathematicals? An ignorant population is less use to him than even a half-educated one. But I have wondered often as to those bards."

"Well you might," said Elphin, "for they are not all they seem, any more than I am. A great part of their number—I should put it at one of every three, and most like more even than that—are in fact no bards of Edeyrn's making, but of ours."

The room had gone very still. " 'Ours'?" I repeated blankly. "Well—*whose*?"

Elphin rolled up his eyes. "And this is the same lad can sniff out a spying Raven in a public street! The Counterinsurgency's, bach; whose else?"

Now it was said I only wondered that I had not guessed before. Vague clouded pieces of the hitherto unsuspected puzzle suddenly shifted into place, the whole great and beautiful picture beginning to form before my dazzled eyes.

"All this time—secret bards, and so of course secret Fians, and secret Druids as well. The old way is not dead after all."

"It never even fell gravely ill," said Elphin with a smile. "Oh, to be sure, we had to scurry in the early years, to save the records and the skills and those who carried the secret of both." The smile had ghosts behind it now, and the room seemed thick with presences: It had not been so easy after all; the measure of the suffering was to be seen in the gallant gaiety of the smile. "Aye," he said briefly, "and many, many were lost. . . But for long now the learnings have been safe in place, and we who have been trained in the crafts are forever seeking out those we may ourselves train up, that the knowledge does not die as did those whose deaths saved it. And, Taliesin Glyndour ap Gwyddno''—he used my name gravely and deliberately, and it sounded in my ear like some high and proud title of old Keltia—"I think I have found one such in you."

I sat for a while in perfect stillness, and Elphin respected it. Within, I was anything but still: My young soul felt as some small mountain lochan into which the hand of a god had suddenly cast a giant boulder. The ripples were dashing back and forth and the countercurrents clashing; all I could do was wait out the turmoil, until my being like the lochan's surface once again cleared to calm.

"You know that it is what I have ever wanted," I said then, still uncertain if I could trust my voice; both of us heard the tears that stood behind it—I think it is the hardest thing there is, to get what one has wanted. Lack is ever easier to deal with than gift . . . "And if you offer it I accept most gladly. But also I have been thinking to train as a sorcerer—Ailithir has been directing our steps that way, both Arthur's and mine—"

"And nothing to keep either of you off that path; in fact, from what I hear, both of you are well along it. But the one training does not of necessity preclude the other. Arthur, as you may by now have guessed, is being taught also as a Fian—by a Fian."

"Scathach!"

"And Berain," said Elphin composedly. "And there are others in this very castle who have been walking other paths, other ways— But it will be for them to tell you when they judge it best, not for me to do so now."

I leaned back against my pillows with a long, happy, heartfelt sigh. "You have told me already more than I think I can quite encompass."

"Then let me tell you but one thing more, and we will speak no more of it today." Elphin leaned forward in the chair, his hands clasped in front of him and his elbows on his knees. All the smiling was gone now from him: Face and body alike were suddenly taut and focused, and I felt myself going very still and small to hear what he would tell me.

"It was your sister Tegau sent warning to the Lady Ygrawn, that the Marbh-draoi's attention might be turning to Daars; and now we see the proof of that in Perran's visit. How think you that warning was passed on?"

"I had not thought—some secret messenger?"

"It came from Tegau's lips to Ygrawn's ear through a chain of bards."

And then of course it was all there for me, the last puzzle piece dropped into place. In a blaze of clarity I saw it all: The bards that Edeyrn thought to be his own tools were instead the tools of his downfall, and the tools of the re-making of Keltia. In his blind arrogant traha he had thought them his, and so gave them freedom to roam the worlds. Some in fact *were* his; they had taken the Marbh-draoi's coin, had been bought for gold as no true bard could ever be. But those were few, and in the end they would not matter; they would fall with their master and be swept aside, and his hand would not be strong enough on that day to save either them or himself.

Elphin had quietly watched the revelation blazon itself upon my face, and now he spoke again. "One day, Talyn, I promise you it will be so; and I think not long now. We shall both live to see it, as so many of our dear ones did not, and if the Mother allows we shall have a hand in it yet. Not bards alone will do it but Druids and Ban-draoi and Fians and brehons, and the plain folk of Keltia who have naught to throw against Edeyrn but their lives. It shall be done."

"And I may help! I will put my life and skill and strength—"

"I doubt it not," said Elphin, and reached out to ruffle my hair. "Not yet a while, though, young Gwion"—and I knew from the name that our secret conclave was over—"and I think not from here; not from Daars. But we shall see. In the meantime"—he took up one of my copying-books from the table and tossed it at me—"I suggest a review of the secondary precepts of meter. Your lines yesterday had more extra feet in them than a céadchosach."

Alone, I sat in bed hugging my copybook and my new staggering knowledge both alike, my potsickness utterly vanished and forgotten. It did not occur to me to wonder that

Elphin should choose to impart all this to me *now*, nor that he had given me not even the most cursory cautioning against speaking of it—and, no mistaking, this was the sort of knowledge that one might, quite literally, die for. Indeed, as Elphin had said, many already had . . . and if I accepted the knowledge, with its price, I myself might yet.

But the other side of that coin was the realization that Elphin would never have told me had he not thought I could grow to the size of the knowing. I was thirteen; not yet a man, certainly, but as certainly no longer a child. I had seen Tair Rhamant. I could keep my counsel.

"A true bard," I said aloud, testing the sound of the words on the air, on my lips, in my soul. It had been promised; and when I had won it, I would make Gwaelod—and Gwyddno—the lament their deaths had earned them. That too was promised.

But first must come the learning, and so I opened my book.

In the wake of Perran's spying visit, all we in Daars were more alert, more aware, more watchful even than usual, as a warrior will be when he knows battle is imminent, but not from what quarter, or even in what guise, it will present itself. All he knows is that it *will* come, and that he must meet it; and so it was with us.

Arthur and I stood somewhat apart from this: Our lessons continued unchanging, no added content or altered tack to reflect the new knowledge we had been given of our part in both present and future. Even that knowledge, though, was an equivocal gift at best: We had been thought grown enough to be told, yet still too young to be given aught real to *do* . . . We understood the reasons for this very well, but—as had been declared—we were still children and so we fretted a little (in truth, more than a little, and more than we should have done) that for us it was still the schoolroom and not yet the battlefield. But we spoke of it to each other whenever we had need of comfort, to reassure ourselves that it *was* true, what we had been told, and not some aisling one or the other of us had woven out of dreams and hope and air.

"So you will be a Fian after all, then, as you have longed

to be.'' I was talking to Arthur one night, as he lay with his head pillowed on Luath's flank, both of them looking well content.

Arthur's dark eyes lighted. ''It seems so—and you to be a bard, and a *spy* . . . Did I not tell you it should be so, that we should be permitted to do what we might for the Counterinsurgency?''

''Hush,'' said Ailithir, not lifting his eyes from his texts. ''Do not speak that name aloud, even here to me.''

''Why not? Is not our own home safe enough from Edeyrn's ears?''

''Safe? Maybe; but no place in all Keltia is safe these days. Daars, it is true, has been safer than many, but as your sister Tegau has told us, Taliesin, it is now less safe than most. We would all do well to guard our tongues—and our thoughts— more even than formerly.''

''Well,'' I said, determined not to be quashed overmuch by our teacher's dour uncheer, ''when you have taught us to be sorcerers, Druids such as you yourself are, that will be easier. We shall but summon our magic, and the thing will be done.''

At that Ailithir did look up, his glance moving from me to Arthur and back down to his book. ''And who is it has told you I am Druid?''

''Why—no one *told* me—us—I but thought—'' I stammered in my shock. ''Athro . . . are you *not* then Druid?''

He threw back his head and laughed, a full warm laugh such as we had never heard him give before.

''Aye, lad, I am Druid right enough! And doubtless I should not have said *that* aloud either . . . But since all round me are owning up to their hidden ranks—Elphin and Scathach and Berain and the rest—I warrant it was time I did so too. Much good the knowing will do you both though,'' he added darkly, ''for you will not be able to speak of it.''

''You mean we must not speak,'' said Arthur, his chin now on Luath's back so that he might watch Ailithir.

''Nay, I mean that you *will* not speak,'' said Ailithir evenly. ''There is compulsion on you both that you may not.''

"A spell!" Arthur shot up in his excitement, all but over-turning Luath. "You mean you have put some rann on us, athro, and we never even knew it?"

"Something of the sort." He saw our dazzled faces. "It is no great sorcery," he assured us. "Nor is it that I felt I could not trust you to keep silence on your own. But with Perran here in Daars, and perhaps others about, it seemed best to take precautions. When you are Druids yourselves, you will understand."

But Arthur had in the midst of all this heard something more, and with his usual straightforwardness went to the heart of his fears.

"Will the Marbh-draoi slay my father, athro, as he did Talyn's?"

Gone were the days when the mention of my murdered parent brought me to tears; I felt a twinge of distant sorrow pinch at my heart, but after eight years of warm and abiding love from Ygrawn and Gorlas, the memory of Gwyddno had receded, and with it my sense of loss. So it was that I could consider Arthur's question almost as equably as could Ailithir; and looking at him, I could see also that he had not been surprised that Arthur had asked it. But his answer was a brief one.

"As to that, I have not Seen, one way or another."

Not good enough, plainly; now Arthur swung that devasta-ting dark glance on me. "This, then, is what you have been trying to hide from me, Talyn, for the fortnight past; not so?"

No use to try to lie; even then he could read truth in face and voice—more than that: He could read it in hearts.

"Aye, braud, it was," I admitted miserably. "It was your mother asked me to keep silent on it. My sorrow but I could not go against her wish: yet I promise there is naught known. Only a word from my sister, passed on by the bards to the Lady Ygrawn."

Arthur seemed surprised that I should apologize. "How could you do other than keep it hid, if she did order you to do so? But listen now: If my mother fears this, then it is truly a thing to be feared, and no mere saulth or half-taish." He leaped up, and Luath sensing his mood rose too, stiff-legged as if for battle, hackles half-lifted. "Is there naught we can *do* then, athro? To save my father? Or Daars?"

The anguish in the question throbbed in the air of the room. Ailithir put down his book and came round the desk to stand before Arthur, his hands on the boy's straight shoulders and his eyes upon the flushed and frustrated face.

"Listen well, Arthur of Arvon," he said slowly, and I felt the hair on the back of my neck stirring like Luath's hackles at the power that was now in my teacher's voice. And hearing it, I wondered if all along I had not known what he truly was—more than Druid, even, though that I was not to learn until later . . . He was speaking again to Arthur, and to something, or someone, beyond Arthur and me and the room in which we stood; and he was heard.

"What must be, shall be; even I cannot See it, not just yet. There are greater things moving than this of Daars alone, and you shall come to stand among their chiefest motivers. You also, Taliesin, and others . . . and if Gorlas must perish for it, or Daars, or Gwynedd itself, that were small price to pay for what will be bought by such a spending." He lowered his hands then, and Arthur shook himself all over, one great convulsive shudder from head to foot, still staring up at Ailithir.

I did not wonder, for I could not take my eyes from Ailithir myself: I seemed to be seeing him truly for the first time in long—seeing *him*, not merely the outward seeming of him: the tall spare figure in blue robes, the iron-gray hair and high-bridged jutting nose and clear-cut chin, and above all the eyes . . . And my thought went back to that night in the hills between Gwaelod and Daars, when I, tired and terrified and not quite six years old, had awakened to see my beloved teacher transformed to a being of terrible and near godlike powers: Ailithir standing upon a high rock in a howling wind, lightning leaping from his upflung hands.

Then Ailithir smiled upon us both, a smile of great sweetness that was blessing and banishing both together: blessing for us whom he loved and banishing for the fear he knew he had set within us. He made a small gesture, and the room seemed to breathe again; indeed it seemed that all Daars had held its breath while he had spoken.

Still, try as I might—and Arthur too, for we compared notes on that moment often enough after—I could for all my soul recall no word of what Ailithir had said. And I say now, as I would have then had I only been able to remember, that in truth it was best we should *not* recall his words, lest sheer terror should have frozen us where we stood. All came to pass as he had said, and more, and greater beside; but had we known that too, the terror would have been all the sooner.

It came soon enough as it was.

Book II:

Bethtraí

Chapter 8

*I*t was nothing like Gwaelod, the death of Daars. For one thing, I it was who Saw it coming—though I did not come by this vision far enough in advance of the event for it to do much good. Even now I cannot say if the Seeing made it any easier for me—certainly it made no differ to the dead—as a thing dán had decreed, and no act of man or woman; or if it was all the harder to bear for having been Seen . . .

The Druids and the Ban-draoi say that great changes cast long shadows, and that to See such a future requires only that one stand where the shadow may fall across one's soul. They say never a word of how one's soul will shiver in that shade—and perhaps it is as well that they do not. It is a hard gift, the Sight: Never does it come to order, when one would wish to See at least not without some grave and goodly price being paid. It has rules and laws all its own, and because we on this side cannot perceive them we say that Sight has no master.

But for myself I think it has a Master we know naught of, and that Master it is who sets the laws of Sight and the rules that bound it: who shall See and what it is that shall be Seen. All we know for certain is what we may be shown; and even *that* we do not always recognize—not until the thing is full upon us.

*   *   *

I was lost in a dream of Tair Rhamant, such a dream as I had not suffered for years now. Yet it was not Rhamant, nor Daars even, nor any other place I knew; it was only that the water made me think it.

An unknown strand, then, and out between beach and horizon great waves rearing themselves up; giant waves, that hung in place and did not move but only stood, rooted in the deeps, growing taller and thicker every moment. And every moment more and more were forming, in ranks behind the ones nearest shore; until at last their foaming furrows, hill-high and glass-green, reached the horizon itself, and maybe beyond. But no crest toppled and fell, not so much as a fleck of foam, and I awoke from the dream sweating, in the most profound terror I have ever known.

Strangely, it was not the terror that freezes one where one may stand, for before my eyes were full open I had flung on my chamber-robe and was out into the corridor, dashing barefoot up the winding stair to Ailithir's chambers, where I had seldom gone unless summoned.

Yet I knew this *was* a summons—though scarcely one of his making—and when I staggered panting to the top of the stair the door swung open before I could lift my hand to knock.

Ailithir stood there, and caught me as I tumbled through into the room. He had been reading, it seemed, for a book lay open on the table and the fire still burned low, but he was clad as I in a chamber-robe; perhaps he had himself awakened from a restless sleep, perhaps he had never yet that night been to bed. Any road, he sat me down in a chair across from his—neither of us had as yet spoken a word aloud—and in the way he had taught me I stilled my mind and let my eyes become as windows, that he might 'look-past' to see what I had seen.

He needed to look neither long nor far. *So it has begun,* I heard him say; then realized he had spoken with the inner voice, as he had seen my vision with the inner eye. Doubtless he read in those images of motionless waves—waves that had seemed to rise forever, hanging back before they crest and fall—far more than had I, for all at once he broke the link and stood up, his face expressionless, his voice quietly commanding.

"Now it has been for you to See first what comes upon us. Go and wake your brother, and make ready to depart."

I was never to remember afterwards just how I had done all that—warned Arthur, gotten back to my own rooms, begun packing; all I can recall is that I did so. Indeed, it was becoming terrible custom: another escape in danger and the dark, though this time danger would prove far closer than before. I had gathered together warm clothing, my precious copying-books, the treasures that had come with me out of Gwaelod and those I had come by while in Daars, and was strapping my harp to my back when Arthur appeared in the door.

Desperate moments have often a power all their own to focus our minds and awarenesses on utterly trivial, and utterly true, aspects of things we have gone on blithely unseeing of for weeks or months or years even. As I glanced up to see Arthur standing there, I suddenly seemed to *see* him: not him as he was then, or as I had known him, but as he was to be. Saw all the glory begin to gather round him—the laeth-fraoch, the hero-light—saw him taller, older, stronger, surer; in love and in pain; saw for the first time the king he would become, and the legend after.

Only for a moment: As I drew in my breath at the beauty and the terror of it, it was gone, and he was again only Arthur, my foster-brother, dressed as I was dressed for a journey, with a bundle much like mine and Luath dancing beside him. We exchanged silent looks, and then we were out again in the corridor that ran down that wing of the castle parallel to the walls outside.

But now it was not as it had been before, a place known to us filled with the comfortable secure silence of night and sleep. Above our heads we heard the sound—unmistakable, though never before heard by either of us in life—of laser fire from low-flying attack craft. We heard too the cries of the folk in the city below, the curses of the castle warriors as they struggled to defend their trust against an enemy they could not reach. That it was Edeyrn, striking at Daars and Gorlas through his Ravens, none could have doubted; that simple slaughter was all he had in mind, none was yet sure.

At a sudden turn in the hallway we cannoned into Elphin and Berain. Ailithir must have used methods swifter than speech to rouse them, for they too were clad for flight, their faces grim in the sconcelight. And as we, they too were silent, but taking some of our gear from us they shouldered it with their own. Then all four of us were running hard, Luath bounding ahead, as we were dragged along at speed through a part of the castle I had never known was there.

I dared a question in between puffing strides. "Where are we?"

"An old tunnel beneath the river," said Elphin, throwing the answer over his shoulder. "Be silent now, and run, if you would live."

So we ran until I thought I should die of the running, and not at the Ravens' hands at all; then a door swung, a wall moved silently aside, a gate opened. I felt on my prickling skin a cold electric sparkle that I later learned was a restraint field lifting, and then I was breathing great gulps of fresh night air, the smell of hills in darkness all round me.

We were high on the side of the valley across the river from Daars, near to that same place in the open fields where Arthur and I had met that first fateful morning. Instinctively I turned to look back at the city, but Elphin moved with sudden swiftness to block my view. I opened my mouth to question, but then came a voice cutting down sharp from above us.

"Nay, let him see! Let them both see!"

The voice was Ygrawn's; I stared as she came toward us out of the dark. She was clad as a warrior, her black hair bound up in the mionn, the braided wreath-like arrangement worn by Fians in the field, and in her hand was a bare gleaming shortsword. I had never seen her so before, but it was more than surprise that now made me gasp: Her face was a warrior's face to match her bearing, but tears stood upon her cheek.

I looked back then at Daars, where Ygrawn's eyes were turned, and myself wept at the sight: The little city seemed laced with light, abloom with it like some exotic nightflower. But it was the light of death that burned now over Daars— corpse-candles, not the Solas Sidhe. Killing bolts from above were ripping seams of fire along the streets, the dust and smoke plain to be seen rising in the rainbow laser glow. We could hear the screams even from here, even above the roar of the attacking ships—sleek black engines of destruction, killer hawks flown by Ravens, and not a one of our own did we have to fly against them.

Or so at least I thought, until I turned once more to my foster-mother. And gasped again, for there behind her, gleaming in the tunnel-shaft that had hidden it, was a starship, a personal craft the like of which I had not thought still existed in Keltia. Edeyrn had forbidden them more than a century since, fearing lest his unquiet and unwilling subjects should become perhaps too mobile, to threaten his sway with unsanctioned goings and comings. Ravens had gone through the worlds destroying any ship they came across, and it had been commonly believed that none had survived.

"No time, Taliesin!" snapped Berain as I stood open-mouthed and staring. "Get in, for all our sakes! Arthur, inside! *Now*!"

Arthur leaped for the door in the shining black hull, and I but a half-step behind him; Luath too scratched and scrabbled in, and then Scathach, who had been guarding Ygrawn and the ship both, slammed the door to. I stumbled forward through the dim companionway, then all but fell over my own feet into an open space: the main cabin. As the engines began to shake the ship beneath us, and the hill itself, I threw myself against the wall of the cabin, to huddle there beside Arthur, staring dully at the score of others present: Elphin, Ailithir, Scathach among them.

And as I stared, something dark and terrible, something that had been growing silently for the past hour, suddenly burst into the light, even as the ship did burst from the concealment of the hill.

"Athra-maeth! *Gorlas*! Where is my father?"

The cry cut like a sgian through the cabin, hanging in the air; I saw Scathach's face crumple like a child's—aye, even she—and then I realized that the cry had been my own.

Beside me, Arthur gave one convulsive move, as if a spear had gone into his guts; then he had seized me by the shoulder, and those unfathomable dark eyes were holding mine.

"Talyn, hear me. He stayed behind."

I stared at him uncomprehendingly; he might have been speaking in some galláin tongue. Then: "Ah, nay, he would not, he did *not*—we must wait for him, he will surely come to us here. Athro—" My words had tumbled all together in my haste to deny what I knew to be true; this last plea was addressed to Ailithir, who had crossed the cabin and now stood over us. His voice came down as from the top of a mountain, heavy and passionless as some brehon's pronouncing a sentence all know to be warranted.

"It was not his choice to leave Daars, Taliesin," he said quietly, and even in that moment a small part of me found itself able to wonder how came it that I was so suddenly 'Taliesin' to all: 'Gwion', it seemed, was as dead as Daars—as dead as Gorlas.

With a whimper that would have better become Luath I curled up into myself; Arthur beside me, whom one would have thought to have greater cause for grief, made no move and said no word. The ship was high above Daars now, banking steeply to avoid the Raven ships still swooping upon the burning town. The attackers did not seem to be aware of us, and in my daze I wondered incuriously at that; surely we must have made some trail or trace in our lifting out of the hill? But my mind could not hold the thought, and then all at once there was no longer a sensation of motion beneath me. The ship grew level and solid, and it seemed that we hung there unmoving between earth and stars. I did not know then, never having been in such a craft—or even dreamed it possible—in all my life, that we had gone into true-flight; that Daars, indeed all Arvon, was now far below and far behind.

I do not know how long I huddled there, silently grieving with a kind of terrible inward keen; I doubt it was very long, for Ygrawn would not have left Arthur and me alone in our pain any longer than she must. But all at once she was there; she had turned over the piloting to Berain, and, ignoring the others, came straight now to us, kneeling before us and taking my hand and Arthur's in her own.

Mother and son looked long and deep and calm into each other's eyes, and I watching noted with a strange detachment that for the first time since I had known them, their faces bore each the stamp of the other.

"He is dead then?"

I could not believe that that cold clear voice was Arthur's; could not believe that he had managed to speak at all. My own throat felt as if a sword-edge were pressed against it, and I could not have spoken just then had my continued life depended on my speech.

Ygrawn nodded once; a nod that was less affirmation than the salute of formal greeting and parting, or the inclination of the head one will use to a king.

"He chose to stay, amhic; his choice too that I should go, for I had never left him else." The amethyst eyes moved sidewise to rest on me; I saw where tears had made her black lashes into starry points. "And so you have lost another father, Talyn . . . All is dán; he said it himself before we parted. His to stay and die with Daars; mine—and yours, both of you—to go, and to go on." She gestured round the cabin at the others, who had in decency turned away to give her some shred of privacy while she spoke with us, and raised her voice for them to hear her. "This is Gorlas's last bidding to us all; we here, we that are the last of Daars."

Scathach stirred. "Some others may yet have escaped, lady."

"May the Mother make it so; but we cannot tarry to search for them. We must go north."

"North!" In my startlement I got a word past the sword-

edge: Even after all these years, north to me yet meant
Gwaelod.

Ygrawn saw and smiled; a kind, tired smile. "Nay, norther
still. There is a place where we shall be welcome, and safe
too—as safe as any can be, in a haven where others are who
have fled as we flee now."

Whatever she must have felt in that terrible moment—alone,
her lord dead behind her, her home destroyed, herself left
with two children to protect and a hunt upon her heels—it
was the measure of Ygrawn Tregaron that she kept it to
herself. The only unbending she permitted herself was a
sudden quick fierce embracing of Arthur and me together—
for a few moments our three heads bent as one—and a kiss
upon the brow for each of us. Then she stood up, brushing
the last of her tears from her face as she did so. Save but
thrice only, in all her life and mine thereafter I was never to
see her weep again.

After Ygrawn had whispered a few brief words to Ailithir
and to Scathach, she went back to the command cabin; only
then did I dare to lift my gaze to look round at the faces of the
others. I was not yet daring enough to look upon the face of
Arthur who sat beside me, his arm firm and warm and strong
pressed against my own. From his place crouched at our feet,
Luath looked up at us both, his face as desperate and pleading
as only a dog's can be, his soul in his eyes and a low anxious
whimper in his throat. Then I saw Arthur's hand go out to
ruffle Luath's ears in reassurance—the only reassurance any
of us had to give just then. But the hand shook, and then
being withdrawn closed at once to a fist, knuckles showing
pale against the tan with the force of the grip.

And looking now upon Arthur's face I felt as Luath had
felt: I understood what had made the hound afraid to raise his
eyes to his own beloved master's. If my grief was composed
of abandonment and sorrow, and Ygrawn's of sorrow and
resolve, Arthur's was of resolve and vengeance. There might
be sorrow in it as well—undoubtedly there was, he had loved
Gorlas dearly, though he knew well his father's faults—but it

was not yet to be seen, for he did not choose that any should see it.

But I saw in my brother's face what I had long ago felt in my own heart, when first I came to comprehend why it was my own father had been murdered, my own home destroyed. And now it was Arthur's father, Arthur's city, butchered by the Marbh-draoi's will . . . *Ah gods,* I cried out in my heart to whoever might hear me, *is there no safe place for anyone anywhere? No safe place for* me?

No answer came; not then, not eight years earlier. Not for many decades would my cry be answered; and by then I would be asking other questions. But for now, though I had wept for my father and for Gwaelod, my farewell to Gorlas and to Daars was other wise: Arthur had not wept, and therefore if not he, then not I; but I had now another lament to be made, and yet another reason for me to become bard enough to make it.

Chapter 9

Grief is a wearying thing; but, fueled by your anguish and your anger alike, in the midst of your grieving you think that you will never sleep again. To you in your sorrow sleep itself becomes a small death, though you would a thousand times sooner welcome its sister, and in your desperate need to cling in thought to your loved lost you begrudge any time spent in unconsciousness. It is as if sleep is but another remove, and your lost one is too far removed already. Reason is nowhere near it; your entire being has become a burning-glass of mood. You may be exhausted, you may even yourself be wounded bodily; in your new single-eyed focus on sorrow it makes no differ. Yet your body knows better than your brain what must be done to begin to heal you; and, sooner rather than later, will you or nill you it betrays you into sleep.

When I opened my eyes I was lying in one of the wall-beds—tiered blastcouches set into the cabin's inside walls—with a blanket over me and my boots and gear all piled into the little store-hold at the bed's foot. Someone must have carried me there and tucked me in to uneasy rest, for I had no memory of coming there under my own power. But save for Ailithir, who sat unmoving by the viewports, all the others seemed to be sleeping as I had been—either themselves squirreled away in one of the other wall-beds or curled in nests of blankets on the cabin floor.

Suddenly wary, I drew back beneath the bed's sheltering overhang like a snail into its shell; but Ailithir was beckoning me with a smile and a lifted hand.

I slipped out of the wall-bed, taking care not to tread upon any of the sleepers underfoot, and went gingerly across to him: gingerly chiefly for that I still could not quite believe that I was in truth aboard a starship, and feared to step firmly lest I should somehow cause us all to plunge straight down to earth. Ailithir watched me come, and when I reached his side, and the ship was still flying true on course, he put an arm around me and drew me closer to the port.

"It *is* a wonder, is it not? We are not 'customed these days to see in Keltia such scope of science and artifice and art." He ran an appreciative hand along the port's gleaming bubble curve. "Once though, Talyn—and gods willing, once again soon—ships such as these, and more intricate enginery beside, were common as grass among us. It was the Marbh-draoi deemed skill and science too dangerous for the folk to continue to practice and enjoy—too dangerous for *him*. So it is that we have lost part of our ancient heritage from Earth: the tools and knowledge that gave us freedom from slavish toil, so that now we must take hours and days to do in sweating effort what drudgery could one time be done in minutes with no more than a lifted finger, and we free for kindlier tasks. Such is the high solicitude of Edeyrn, to ease the lot and labor of the folk . . ." The bitterness in his voice was savage; sensing my bewilderment, he smiled again and shook his head.

"Well, even so, all such knowledge is not lost forever—no more than your bardery—we will give it all back to Keltia when we have driven out the Marbh-draoi and his creatures and his ways. But look now, Talyn, see where we do go."

I craned past him to peer out the bubble, looking up to orient myself by the visible stars. And I frowned, puzzled, for according to the positions of the great constellations—Caomai, the Armed King; Camcheachta, the Plough; Inion Rían na Reanna, the Daughter of the Queen of the Stars; Llenaur, the Lady of Heaven's Mantle, that great sweep of frostfire in the northwest—we were flying *south*, though we had all heard Ygrawn declare that our refuge lay to the north. When I looked from the stars to the earth below, I gasped: The great mountain range of the Spindles, that runs from east to west across the top of the continent, was rising up white-fanged across our path.

"We came round and over the pole from the other side of the planet," said Ailithir behind me. "All to shake off pursuit, though I think there was none even at first, and certainly there has been none all these hours since."

"How can that be?" I was staring rapt at the cold comb of peaks below. "Did they not see us in flight?"

"Do you know, I rather think that they did not," he answered after a pause. "And the reason they did not shall be explained to you later on—though you shall see it proved even more plainly before we come again to earth."

"And where and when shall that be?"

Arthur had come up to stand with us; it was he who had spoken, and his voice carried no stresses other than the everyday. He met my eyes then, and gave me a curt nod which conveyed, Aye, I know your pain, and Aye, I admit to mine, and Nay, we shall not speak of it yet awhile.

To my surprise, Ailithir did not answer Arthur's inquiry. In that same instant I had other things to think about, for the ship dropped beneath us in a sudden sickening movement, that vertiginous lurch and shudder of a horse going down on its knees; Arthur reached out a hand to steady me as I swayed unbalanced. I had one brief swift thought as to how unsurprised he seemed—far more off-hand than I—to be on a starship amid all these marvels of artificing. Then I realized to my chagrin that he must have known all along; had most like been taken into the confidence of Scathach and Berain and the other warriors who must surely have shared the secret; and I felt a twinge of hurt at the seeming exclusion.

"We are coming out of true-flight and beginning our approach," said Ailithir, by way of explanation for the ship's sudden drop. "That vale below is Nordereys—Coldgates. These are the End-lands; but though they be the edge and end of the habitable places, they are far from empty. There is a secret among them that the Marbh-draoi would give half his magic to uncover, and all these years he has not dreamed of what—and whom—these hills have sheltered.'' He straightened in his seat. "And now they will open their gates to shelter a few more lost ones . . . Go you both and wake the others. We are nearing our new home.''

In a very few minutes after Ailithir had warned us, the ship began a long lazy spiraling descent, dropping like a hunting snow-owl down toward the glacier-fields into the perpetual winter of the great hills.

Strapped in my seat for the landing—well, not strapped, precisely; a thing I had never heard of held me in place, a force-field like an invisible hand—I glanced round at the others. Their faces were all calm and assured, as if they had done this sort of thing many times before; as perhaps they had. For me it was breathstoppingly exciting, as I could see through the port the ship's passage spinning up veils of snow on either side. But though I strained my eyes until the sun on the white expanses made them dazzle and water, I could see no sign of the promised refuge. Until—

A flash of blue-white lightning seemed to engulf us, and the ship gave a soft, heavy shiver all down its length. I looked quickly at Ailithir, who smiled, and at Scathach, who nodded; but no explanation seemed forthcoming from either. And then I was not wanting words, for beyond the port I saw before us a great mountain that had not been there even seconds before, tucked in among taller, snowier sisters; and as I looked I saw that it was opening for us—a vast black gate yawning in its frosted flank.

So wide was that portal that, as we passed in, I could not see where its bounds might be; the edges were lost in the dimness within the mountain's heart. But I *could* see that the entire peak was hollowed out like a summer gourd, and rank upon rank of ships like to the one we now were in stretched away in the secret vault under the snows.

The vast chamber beneath the mountain was like to a

shieling, one of the caverns used in high country for the warm stabling of stock in winter and their cool comfort in the hot season; and so, with a certain grim irony, this place was called. But by merit of its sheer size—and by reason of its grave purpose—it was like to no shieling known before, and I began to believe, as I think I had not before no matter how desperately I had wished to, in the reality of the Counterinsurgency, and its strength to set against Edeyrn.

When at last we settled to the ground, I did not even feel the jar; I was too caught up in wonder. Ever since we had passed through that strange barrier of blue fire— But Ygrawn was in the cabin now, and all round me the others were making ready to leave the ship.

She came to me as I stood a little apart, put her hand on my arm. "My sorrow I had so little time to be with you," she said in that rippling low voice of hers. "That will change from now, I promise; you and Arthur and I, aye, and the rest too, will be safe here in the shieling—and there are other folk . . . But enough."

Something in my silence must have spoken to her, for she all at once broke off her reassurances, and simply smiled and kissed me. Then unsealing the main hatch of the ship she stepped through, and we were close after.

We stood in the tremendous cavern hollowed from the mountain's stone heart. The chill of the place struck to the bone, and as I trudged blindly along behind Ygrawn and Ailithir, who seemed to know how to go and where in this strange unthought-of haven, I felt my mind begin to dim to a kind of unquestioning acceptance, all dull and sleepy and perversely acquiescent. It was at last too much for me—all of it, Gorlas and Daars and our flight and this place—and in my owlish daze I trod upon Berain's heels who walked in front of me, and who had suddenly halted.

Before us was a blank rock face, in the dim sconcelight gleaming with frost that had formed in the stone's veins and crevices. Ygrawn was speaking, but I could not understand a word of what she said. And as I stood there before the granite wall, dazed and sad as only a child can be with cold and weariness and the utter incomprehensibility of it all, the rock opened before us.

On the rock's far side was the shieling proper—warmth and light and many folk to welcome us. I was no less confused in that moment than I had been a moment since, standing stupefied and frozen in the dark; but though I shrank back, I could sense that the crowd pressing forward was a friendly one. Then all at once the throng parted, and my sister Tegau was bending over me, chafing my stiff fingers in hers and scanning my face anxiously for recognition, out of eyes that were the color of my own.

"Do you remember me, Tal-bach?"—gently, as if I might *not* remember (as if I could ever forget!), and she not wishing to fright me. She gathered my hands then to her heart, and I felt through her gwlan tunic the smooth hard curve of the breast of gold.

And then, stern hard warrior of fourteen as I thought myself, I was in her arms, my face buried in the warm soft breast, and she was ruffling my hair as she had always used to do.

The chamber she took me to was small, carved from the rock by some means I did not know, with a tiny air-shaft that wound up through the stone to pull in cold fresh air from outside and heat it on its way down. Crystals stood in niches, to give light and more warmth, and their glow fell in pleasing patterns on the rough walls and uneven floor. On a wide bed against one wall were strewn thick furs—ice-bear, red lynx, silver wolf, even a pelt of the great northern snow-lion. I was by now too weary of body and spirit even to spare a thought for my companions, where they might be or how they were faring: I threw myself down into the furry herb-scented softness and knew no more until Tegau set down a small tray beside me.

The delicious scent of breakfast wound into my dreams, and all at once I woke ravenous.

"Is it morning then? I must have slept for hours." In my

haste I burned my mouth on the hot shakla, and puffed in air
to cool it.

"Some hours," said Tegau smiling. "But as for morning—
not for you. You are to eat, and then you must sleep again."
At the protest forming on my lips: "It is not my order,
Talyn—though I do agree—but Ailithir's. Arthur too is to
spend the time as you will spend it, so you need not think you
are being unfairly dealt with."

I sipped more cautiously at the shakla, uncaring of my
knowledge that the drink had more in it than met the eye or
even the tongue, and then applied myself to the pastai and
chunk of cheese that lay on the plate.

"How did you come here?" I asked through the mouthful
of gravied meat and crust. "Are the rest of the family here as
well?"

"They come and go," said Tegau, "and they are all hale
and happy. I am here more or less on fixed post . . . But the
others know of your coming and are glad; you will see them
when next they are here. As for your first question, I came
here long before Gwaelod was lost—long before mamaith had
died."

I looked up at the mention of my mother—*our* mother,
wondering suddenly if the tale of plague my father had told
me had not been just that, a mere tale; if Medeni ferch Elain
had perhaps died instead of something quite different . . .

Tegau saw the questions forming, and sidestepped them as
neatly as ever did Ailithir. "Later, braud; later you will know
all. I promise! Now you must sleep again."

"Will *not*," I said with great spirit, but a warm, exquisite
slumbrousness was blooming through me: Whatever sedative
had been in the shakla had worked quick and well, and I was
away.

Neither Arthur nor I was permitted to spend much of the
next twenty-four hours in a waking state—unfair as we both
thought it, when at last we were awake to think so. The
combined wisdom of Ygrawn, Ailithir and whoever commanded in the shieling seemed to hold that such grief and

terror as we had endured could be best healed from unconsciousness, and I think our own bodies concurred, however mutinous our minds might be, with that judgment. Any road, none in the shieling was like to dispute them, and Arthur and I—sleeping away for a night and a day and a night again, like a pair of wintering hedgepigs—*could* not dispute them.

And yet even when I woke at last—was permitted to awaken—I could not say that our elders had been in error, for the events of Daars had magically receded far enough for me to begin to contemplate them in calm—if not in freedom from pain. That last, I knew even then, would never wholly be mine when I thought of Gorlas and Daars, but at least now I could look back and face it fairly.

On opening my eyes, then, I sensed that it was day; though how precisely I knew it remained a mystery, for my inner clock had been turned all throughother, and no light seeped down through the shieling's rock roof. But it *felt* like daytime, perhaps because of the activity I sensed beyond the chamber door—many people, awake and bustling; so after bathing in the small pool-bath that gave on the sleeping-room, and dressing in fresh clothes from my pack, I opened the door and ventured out into the corridor.

And fell back against the door, eyes wide and jaw agape with staggerment. Half-dead with sorrow and fatigue as I had been on our arrival two nights since, I had not really registered the true size and scope of our new home. The huge chamber we had passed through—where the ships were kept and cosseted, like prized bloodstock in the most incredible of stables—was but one part of a vast underground complex.

From my chamber door I looked down through a gallery rail, two stories down, to the floor of an enormous cavern where scores of folk hurried busily about; glancing up, I saw that there were more tiers of galleries above mine—I counted ten before the helical rows were lost in the darkness of the cave roof. At intervals round the walls, under the overhang of the gallery rows, were heavy doors of bronze or copper that apparently led into other, similar caverns on various levels, or perhaps into the great ship-cave itself; and through those doors passed a constant stream of people.

I have no idea how long I simply stood there staring, watching the folk below. How many from how many places in Keltia had found their way here? How many Daarses had there been, how many Gwaelods, on how many other worlds? Were all these folk, like me, like Arthur, waifs of Edeyrn's making; or had some come here out of other reasons, out of anger or duty or love? And where in all this vast hidden city would I find those I knew—Tegau, or Ygrawn, Arthur or Ailithir or any of those who had come with me from Daars?

In the end I did not have to search far; indeed not so much as a step, for just as I began to panic a cold wet nose pushed at my fingers, and I looked down with joy to see Luath. His tail was whipping back and forth in his ecstasy at having found me, and I take no shame in admitting now (indeed, I took none then) that my joy was no whit less than his.

I was down on my knees kissing him back when I felt his delight redouble, and I knew by that that Arthur had found us. Fending off Luath's renewed attentions, I turned and stood, and he was there.

"You are a lazy poor slob," he said with great affection. "Now *I* have been up and doing these three hours since. Come now and I will get you something to eat, though your sloth does not deserve it, and then we will go to my mother. She sent me to find you; it seems she has a thing to tell us both."

All at once I was aware of the chasm of hunger that split my middle; a pastai or two and some drugged shakla go not very far, even to fuel sleep, and I eagerly followed Arthur down to the cavern floor.

An hour later, having been stuffed to bursting by the solicitous and sainted folk who ran the cookplace—crisp brown sausages, fresh greens (with all that snow outside!), hot soup so thick it would scarcely pour, a kind of folded panbread filled with all manner of savory bits; my sorrow to say I gobbled like a week-old bonnive—when I rolled away from the table at last, it was to trudge after an increasingly impatient Arthur through one of the big doors into an adjoining cavern.

This one seemed to be devoted to offices, as the one we had just left was a place of living-quarters. Here there were banks of equipment blinking ominously, vast screens that showed the views in all directions outside the mountain in which we were hidden, hologram displays whose purpose was a mystery. Like almost everyone else in Keltia at that time, I had been deprived of access to any real technology, and the sudden revelation of such richness of enginery made me feel ignorant and poor.

Not so my foster-brother: Arthur seemed to know his way about already, and strode through this impressive array of wonders with scarcely a second glance, and again it was borne home to me that he must have been receiving such training as I knew naught of . . . But I kept on at his heels, considerably more daunted, wondering very privately as to his state of mind and heart, how he was feeling Gorlas's death and his own plight. Strangely, it never occurred to me to apply that thought to myself: I was in just exactly the same situation as Arthur, but somehow I did not think of it so. Perhaps the fact that I had been through it once before—the bereavement, the sudden upheaval of my entire life—made it seem less terrifying now that I was encountering it for a second time. Or perhaps I was for once simply concerned with someone else's feelings before my own, that his pain mattered more to me than mine.

Whatever the truth might have been, the speculations occupied my mind and I paid no heed to how we went or where. I came all at once to myself: We were in yet another living-cavern; Arthur had paused before a door and was setting his hand to the touchplate. He spoke his name and mine into the voice-lock next the frame, and then the door swung silently open and I followed him through.

The chamber was rather more spacious than my own, though just as simple in its furnishings; but already it bore the mark of its occupant. Ygrawn had ever had that knack, to make a place her own however briefly she had been there; and she had applied that knack here—naught overmuch, just touches here and there, for she had brought little enough gear with her from Daars. Yet even so the chamber seemed to have been hers for years if not for always, and I sank down into a pile of pillows and raised my eyes to her face.

"How is it with you, amhic?" She bent to kiss my cheek, and I inhaled the lily-oak fragrance that ever clung about her. The amethyst eyes held mine. "Are you well settled, Talyn?"

So of course I said aye, and then I was telling her more of my meeting with Tegau, for she had seen only our first moments of reunion; told her too of my enforced and pro-tested slumbers, and my discovery of Luath and Arthur, and my gluttonous breakfast. Her delighted laugh pealed out, and I looked at her in wonder, for I had not thought to hear her laugh so soon.

"Ah, Talyn, you are surprised that I can laugh? Well, it is not that my sorrow for my lord is any the less for it; he himself would be the first to bid me merry."

Which was surely truth; but of how she herself had wept for her lost lord, and would again, she said no word—not then, not ever. Her grief was deep and true and lasting, and she held it no one's concern but hers alone. Though I know now that there are many kinds of love and loving, and that what she had felt for Gorlas was not the love of which we bards like best to chaunt, still she mourned him honestly and well. But just then I knew none of this, and so I was still surprised.

If she saw she gave no sign. "Come," said Ygrawn instead, and as she rose from her seat I saw that she was clad rather more elegantly than either Arthur or myself: more for the halls of her own palace than the depths of the shieling.

"We are summoned to audience," she added from the doorway, "and we must not be tardy in our coming."

"Audience?" Arthur, who had been silent all this while, now looked up with interest. "Who gives us audience in such a place?"

But Ygrawn only smiled, and lengthened her step, so that we had fairly to trot to keep pace behind her.

We walked clear round the gallery onto which Ygrawn's rooms opened, and through yet another set of doors into yet another living-cavern. I would later learn that there were near a hundred of such caves all told, most lying deep beneath the great peak Sulven, but others stretching away under the mountains to the east and south—living-caves and storage-caves and caves for every purpose imaginable. Coldgates gave shelter in all to more than a thousandscore folk, and it was by no means the only shieling, or even the largest; the Counterinsurgency had learned from bitter lessons to build well and far-flung and strong, to protect its people that were its future.

Now our destination was plain even to Arthur and me. Across the floor of the new cavern, two warriors stood guard either side of double doors made of findruinna and gold. As we drew nearer, I saw that one of the guards was my sister Tegau, and I began to greet her with delight. But my smile died half-born, for she looked straight and stern before her, a glance cold as the bare sword she bore, and never looked at me at all; and I realized that she *was* a guard, and that therefore within the chamber beyond the golden doors must be something—or someone—worthy of such guarding.

I had no more time to ponder this, for in crisp unison Tegau and her fellow pulled back the doors for us to enter. My eyes adjusted sharply to the light within—dimmer than any light I had yet encountered in any room of the shieling, indeed all other rooms and caves seemed more than usually well-litten—and when I stopped blinking I jibbed a little in surprise as I saw what charge my sister guarded.

On the other side of the chamber—as its light was lower, so the chamber's size was larger than any other I had yet been in—a man sat in a plain high-backed chair on dark green cushions. He was perhaps ten or twenty years Gorlas's senior, no more, and perhaps not even that; as I approached him I could see that he was aged more with cares than with years.

He was not overly tall, had not the build of a warrior, nor did he possess fairness of feature beyond the common run.

Yet despite this there was about him something that made all else unimportant and vain; and as this grew plainer to me with each instant I stared, until in the end it seemed to shout to shake the mountain above us, without one word spoken by any in that silent room I bowed my head, and placed fist to heart, and made the bent-knee reverence to royalty that I had never before made in my life, nor had ever hoped or dreamed to make.

Ailithir's voice rang now rich and deep through the silence; in it I heard his pleased approval of me, and something I had never before heard from him: I heard deference, and it was not to me that he deferred.

"So see the eye and heart of a true bard, they will pierce all disguise and concealments . . . I present now the Lady Ygrawn Tregaron, daughter of Bregon Duke of Kernow, latterly Lady of Daars; Arthur Penarvon, Lord of Daars, son of Lady Ygrawn and the Lord Gorlas ap Kynvelyn; and the Lord Taliesin Glyndour ap Gwyddno, youngest of Gwaelod and brother to the Lady Tegau Goldbreast."

Never in all my fourteen years had I heard myself announced so: It was a formal presentation to a royal presence; and slanting my glance sidewise, past Ygrawn who had made a curtsy that was a graceful subsidence to the very floor, I saw where Arthur had followed my lead and made the same bent knee as I. And though I saw too that he had not the slightest idea why I had done so, I knew my instinct had not failed me, and that I had been correct in both my reverence and my first assessment. It was a bard's judgment I had made, and I had judged aright.

"Rise, dear friends." The voice was gentle, clear, cultivated yet strong; the voice of a scholar or diplomatist or brehon, and the voice of no weakling. No more than that did it say, and we rose from our reverences.

Then Ailithir spoke again, and now he spoke straight to the man in the high seat, and he spoke the words I had known he would speak.

"Gods save Uthyr, King of Kelts."

Chapter 10

I felt rather than heard Arthur's indrawn breath of astonishment; it carried not only shock that he had not known, but chagrin that he *should* have known, and as Uthyr Pendreic pushed himself stiffly up from his high seat, to descend the single step to where Ygrawn still stood with bowed head and to take both her hands in his, Ygrawn's son gazed upon his King with eyes that seemed to drink his presence.

My own eyes were busy with another sight entirely: The room's dimness was thickest in the corners of the dais, and as I had straightened from my reverence I had gradually become aware that someone else had been there all along, in the shadows behind Uthyr's chair.

A girl stood there, watching Arthur as steadily and openly as Arthur was watching Uthyr. Tall she was, with a grace of carriage and a straight-shouldered posture that not even Ygrawn could match. Her hair was black, not Ygrawn's blue-black nor even the usual Kymric brown-black but a true ebony; it stood out from the ivory skin like a stormcloud round a snow-peak. Her eyes were gray with gold flecks, black-lashed, with straight brows drawn out like wings above them, and her mouth was full and firm and clearly cut, near as pale as her skin.

So it was that I looked for the first time on Gweniver, and

thought her fair and brave, with a kind of defiant pride that masked a desperate shyness. But Arthur too was looking at her now as she stepped down from the dais, and with a tremor of foreboding I saw that he saw only the arrogance.

But he had plainly also seen who she must be, for after the smallest of hesitations on both their parts he was bowing to kiss the hand she held out to him, and after the briefest of murmured courtesies he stood back for her to pass.

When she moved from him to me, I saluted her as he had done, proud that I was not too ill-turned-out that day to greet a princess. If my garb was perhaps less elegant than it might have been, it was certainly several cuts above my usual attire, and I was thankful for my afterthought decision to wear some of the few jewels I owned: the two rings my mother had left me, a gold torc set with seastones that had been a gift from Gorlas, a small pendant pearl in my left ear, such as Fian warriors wore of old. It was chance and vanity that had clad me even that impressively—my gear was not yet unpacked, and these things, the most precious and costly I had, had all been carried by hand in the one bundle I had refused to part with—but still I was proud.

Gweniver seemed to have read the thought, for she smiled—not unkindly, but tentatively, the diffidence in her bearing not what I had thought to find in a Tanista of Keltia. Now that she stood close to me, I could see more than surface beauty in her face. The set of the mouth told of strength of character, and humor, and implacability; and there was a lancepoint intelligence in the gray eyes, keen enough and sharp enough to make me resolve then and there never to allow myself to be its target.

As she had done with Arthur, Gweniver addressed herself briefly (and bravely, for the shyness was still uppermost) to me—I have not the least recollection of what she said, or what I answered—then she moved away with a half-curtsy as her uncle the King approached.

Uthyr had all this while been talking with Ygrawn and Ailithir, and none present—ourselves least of all—expected him to spare time and attention for a pair of greenstruck lads.

But that was not Uthyr's way, as we were to find, and now he stood before us, his assessing glance tempered by a smile warmer and more practiced far than his niece's. He spoke first to me, which surprised not me alone.

"The Lady Ygrawn tells me you are training for a bard, young Glyndour," he said, in a light pleasant tenor voice. "We have ever a need for all the bards we can come by; I know you will make us a good one."

I bowed before replying. "I thank you, Lord, for your confidence; gods willing it shall not be misplaced."

"Never that . . . I knew your father well in our youth, and your mother also, and I grieved to hear of their passing. I know the rest of your family even better, for they have been here often in service of the Counterinsurgency, and they serve it most well and bravely. Glad are we all to have you too safe here at last." He clapped hand to my shoulder, and through the long slim fingers I felt the strength of him; not a physical toughness—though his very survival showed he did not lack there either—but a strength of the inner self, a core and soul spun tough and fine as findruinna wire.

But he had turned his attention now to Arthur, and for no reason that I could put in words, either then or later, it came to me that Uthyr had deliberately saved this encounter for last. Yet his words when he spoke were unexceptional, and I wondered if I had been mistaken; a moment later I knew I had not been.

"Welcome, Lord of Daars," said the King, and Arthur snapped at once to respectful attention, fist to breast as Scathach had been at pains to teach us both. "A Fian to be, as your fostern will be bard . . . but no ceremony, amhic. I knew *your* father too."

And then came the most extraordinary moment of all that extraordinary meeting: Uthyr as he spoke had been searching Arthur's face with something that to me at least looked very like a hungry eagerness, and then it struck me that he had said no word of Gorlas by name. Before I could puzzle on this further, the King had lifted his arms and drawn Arthur to him in a paternal embrace.

As he did so, my eyes flew from Arthur, his face showing only carefully controlled surprise, to learn the reaction of two others in that room. Over her son's shoulder, Ygrawn was watching Uthyr, and I had not a hope of reading the thought behind her face. Her look was one of perfect composure, seemingly compounded of many other things: frankness and satisfaction and challenge, and strangest of all a smile. And Uthyr was looking back at her; still on his countenance was the eagerness of before, but now there was a different shade to it, as if some most desperate question he had not dared to ask had been answered, and answered beyond his hopes.

Yet Uthyr's was not the other face I sought . . . Turning my head, I found the one I looked for: Gweniver, standing by the throne and watching her uncle, tall and motionless as a young birch in that breathless quiet that comes before the blast. But though there was stillness upon her body, there was none in her face; it was alive with reflecting of the storm within. Curiosity I saw, as fierce and focused as a laser; and uncertainty, and astonishment, and jealousy, and protectiveness; and to me as I watched these play across her face the sum of them was fear.

Then she drew her glance away from her uncle and brought it up to cross my own, so hard and quick and challenging that almost I thought to hear the chime of steel on steel. I was unprepared to face *that* blade, and so I bowed instead, and with a nod she swung her gaze from me and leveled it at Arthur.

He did not even feel its touch. Through all this, I think, he had been aware of none save Uthyr; after the unexpected salute he and the King had made a few exchanges of converse, commonplace enough to us who were eavesdropping shamelessly, and no more than that. But now Uthyr was giving that particular inclination of the head that royalty uses to signify 'you may withdraw.' We bowed again all of us, and did so; and as the doors began to close behind us the last glimpse I caught of those within was Gweniver assisting her uncle back to his chair.

Yet not quite the last: Through the narrowing crack of

light, just before the doors swung to, I felt the swift touch of
a pair of glances. One was Uthyr's, and even I could sense
the yearning in it; the other was Gweniver's, and even Arthur, I think, could sense the threat.

No need to say how I was bursting with questions; but one
look at Ygrawn told me there would be no answers for me in
that quarter. Ailithir, then? I craned to look beyond Ygrawn's
cold profile to see if questions would fall upon any kindlier
earth there; but he seemed preoccupied with his own thought,
and did not respond to my hopeful inquiring glance.

Well, if there were to be no answers just yet, perhaps
somewhat could be learned by more questions—but not here.
I caught Arthur's eye, jerked my head in the direction of our
rooms, then listened as he made our excuses to Ygrawn. He
need scarce have bothered, for she seemed as distracted as
Ailithir in the audience's aftermath, so not half a minute later
we were hastening back to the cavern where our day had
begun—it seemed to me days since.

I was surprised to see by the chronodials in my chamber
that I had been awake a bare three hours; those hours had
been wearying enough for a full day. Closing the door behind
us, I leaned back against its comforting steel thickness, and
blew out my breath in a long, heartfelt sigh. Only then did I
look at my companion.

He was sitting before the quartz-hearth—open fires were of
course not possible, here in the mountain's depths—staring at
some point upon the stone floor just past his boot-tips, as if it
were showing him prodigies in the plain rock. Had I known
him less well, I should not have seen the cloud that was on
him; knowing him better, I should have known well enough
not to ask . . .

"So that then is the King of Kelts! What did you think,
braud? Of all us present, he greeted you the most fair."

Arthur stirred where he sat, mechanically reaching out a
foot to scrummage Luath's underbelly, which the hound had
presented in hopes of such attention.

"I did not think ever to come before him," he said simply. "Least and last of all here in this place—"

"Well, if naught else, it proves that Coldgates is safe. They would scarce have hidden the King here else, nor his heir with him, if it were not so."

At mention of Gweniver Arthur seemed suddenly to come to life, though it was by no means admiration that sparked him, and withdrew his foot; Luath looked up indignantly, then flumped down before the hearth and went promptly to sleep.

"Oh aye, *her* . . . Did you see, Talyn, when he greeted me with the annerch"—the word meant the formal embrace exchanged between lord and liege—"how darkly she looked upon us? It was not for me, that salute, but for my father; and yet still she grudged it me." He shook his head, and I closed my lips on what I had been at point of speaking: Uthyr's strangeness of manner, and his omission of Gorlas's name. "Tanista she is, Talyn," he continued, "and as such I shall honor her. But on my soul there shall never be more between us than that."

Well, oaths have been broken ere now, and will be again after . . . But this was the first time since our flight from Daars that Arthur had spoken of his father, and I reached out gently with mind and heart to coax the moment along, for I thought it good that he should come openly to terms at last with his grief.

"He went most well, braud—Gorlas-maeth. It was his choice to do as he did, and by so doing he saved our freedom."

Only the corners of his mouth moved, and that but briefly; the rest of his body—and being—was better controlled. "Aye, he did so; and true it is that he did choose; even in the end Edeyrn could not command him. That, surely, is something."

"Much." I leaned forward to look more closely at him, for I had heard something—or to be more correct, had *not* heard something—that gave me pause. "What then? You must speak of it to *someone*, soon or late; can you, will you, not tell *me*?"

The tone was a triumph for me: I had put into the final question all the bardic tricks at my poor command—the low undemanding pitch, the gentle unheard persuaders, the coaxing that was almost a purring seduction—all only to get him to speak.

Whether he responded to my still fledgling bardcraft or his own overwhelming need must remain forever unknown; but Arthur turned to me with all his unhappy soul bare upon his face, and spoke to me from the depths of his pain.

"Then why can I not weep for him? I have tried, Talyn. I have no tears for my father."

Whatever I had been expecting to hear, surely it was never this. It did not even seem a thing I could hope to comfort; but all my love and all my instincts told me I must try.

"It is early days yet, Artos"—the childhood name came naturally to my lips—"Sorrow is not a thing can be commanded."

"*I say I cannot weep!*" The violence of the cry shook the room; Luath's head came sharply up, keen hound's eyes seeking enemies. "Gods but have I not wished to? My eyes have burned with wanting tears to come to them. But I cannot, Talyn, and I do not know why. *You* had tears for him, there in the ship," he went on more calmly. "Elphin, Berain, Scathach even—but not I."

"Tears are not always the first answer, especially for those whose loss is the greatest." I did not know how to speak to this, could only reach back into memory for griefs long healed. . . "When I lost my own father, when I lost all Gwaelod—I could not grieve for him, or them, straightway. It took time to make it real, and at first it was simply too vast a thing, my mind blanked it out so that I might stay sane until I could deal with it—"

Arthur gave a short laugh. "Would I *might* go mad for it; even that would be far to the fore of this—this *un*feeling. Almost it is as if—as if my father had not died."

The words were like a whip across my face. I think now that I knew in that instant the whole truth of it; it needed only another word or two, another link of logic, another— But no more came, and it slipped by me, and a different thought came instead.

"Do you speak to your mother, then. *She* will tell you, as it seems that I cannot, that you will grieve for Gorlas in your own time, and no less deeply or less lovingly for the lateness of it. Besides, she too has griefs might be made easier for the sharing with her son."

He looked at me, all his defenses down, and I could see the terrible conflict that was being fought behind his eyes—saw too the mastery he was bringing to bear on it.

"Aye, then," he said, and in his voice was only weariness. "I will speak to my mother." The voice hardened. "But not, I think, just yet."

Oh aye, he spoke to her in the end; he could not have held off from it very much longer and still have kept his reason. But he managed to hold off for a good few weeks; *I* had need to speak to someone, too, and I did not hold off anywhere near so long . . . As soon as Arthur had left the room with Luath, I went to find my sister Tegau.

She was free from her guard's duties for some hours, and had in fact been just on the point of coming to seek me out. So we went back together to her own chambers, in a cavern I had not yet seen; it seemed to be a garrison cave, quarters for the military members of the shieling's population, and on my asking Tegau confirmed this.

"Full half those dwelling here are Fians or other ranks of warrior class: kerns, galloglasses, even cavalry—though just now horseless! But that is not all we are: Most of us have another edge to our swords. We are scientists, or artificers, or even farmers; *someone* has to tend the ships and make the tools and grow the food. Here and in the other shielings we all turn a hand to whatever needs doing; so will you do, once you are better settled." She paused then and looked at me for the space of ten or so heartbeats; her face changed, growing gentler, warmer, and all at once I could see our father Gwyddno in her eyes.

She for her part saw the myriad questions in mine, and so

for the next hour and more, family was all we talked of: the whereabouts and welfare of our five siblings (most of them in the east of Gwynedd just now, fighting Owein); how Gwaelod had perished; my safekeeping at Daars; how Gorlas and his city had been destroyed; the flight here to Coldgates.

And Tegau told me what I had never yet heard: how Edeyrn had killed our father; how the Marbh-draoi had been called tyrant and necromancer to his face and before all his court, by Gwyddno in anger, knowing full well that he would die for his defiance.

"He was slain by sorcery, Talynno; never let you forget it, and learn all you can so that one day you may defeat it . . ."

But that was not all we spoke of, sorrow and loss, not unseasoned by tears, Tegau's and mine alike; there was love and even laughter to offset the sorrow, and very soon indeed it seemed that we, who had been strangers these ten or so years past, had never been apart. Yet for all that, not one word of our mother: Tegau did not offer, and somehow I did sense it was not yet time to ask.

I had, however, many other questions. . . "Tell me of this place, this shieling."

"What would you know?"

"Well, everything! Who built it, and when, and how, and whyfor, and how came the folk to live here, and—"

"Enough, enough!" laughed my sister. "I have a duty-shift I must soon return to . . . For the most part, you will find your questions better answered in the libraries than by any answers I might have; you have only to ask one of the recordkeepers to help you. They are all bards, and will be pleased to assist one of their own."

"Bard only by courtesy," I said, for honesty compelled me. "Many years and much to be learned before I may be truly called so . . ." Then I saw the indulgent affection in her eyes, and was abashed, for I was unused to the teasing give-and-take that can be between a brother and sister; though in truth I rather liked it. "Tell me this only now: What defends the shieling against the eyes of the Marbh-draoi? Surely his Ravens, or he himself, must notice the comings and goings in so desolate a place? Or the energy traces, which must be vast?''

Tegau sat back again in her chair. ''I will answer this, and then truly I must be gone— Do you remember, when you were coming in to land, a kind of blue fire through which your ship did pass?''

I stared at her. ''I could never forget it! It shook the ship as we passed; I thought perhaps it was some kind of lightning, or other pulse-charge.''

''Not a bad guess.'' Tegau paused a little, considering how best to explain, while all the time I leaned forward like a hunt-rider in my seat, so eager was I for the knowledge. ''In all the years of Edeyrn's rule,'' she said presently, ''though on the outside scientific exploration has been forbidden on pain of death, in the shielings and other hidden sanctuaries it has gone on apace. And one of the first things our necessity forced us to learn was how to conceal—and defend—ourselves with light itself.''

''So the blue light I saw—''

''—was a kind of shield. It can be cast round a place like a magical circle, and it protects that place and all within just as surely as any riomhall. It hides everything within its bounds; it is as if that within does not exist. And not places only: It hid your ship from the Ravens' notice—that is why there was no pursuit. That is also why you could not see Sulven until you were past the barrier—we call it a pale. Light itself bends around it, and only those ships—or persons—holding keys to the defense may pass through unharmed.''

Even in my wonder that last caught my especial note. ''But if a ship not keyed tried to pass? Or a person? Would they be—''

Tegau's face was both hard and gentle as she answered: hard for the unalterable necessity of it, gentle for that she was, after all, trying to explain that necessity to a lad of fourteen, and he her brother from whom she had long been parted.

''Aye, Talyn, they would be destroyed. We have not yet reached the selective capability of merely shunting inoffensive intruders away, and nor have we reached the point where we can afford to take the chance. Any ship, any person, who comes unbidden within range of our shield, must be our enemy, and must be dealt with so.''

"But innocent folk—''

"—may be slain in error. Aye. I know. My sorrow for it . . . Perhaps some time soon one may come to us with the knowledge to change this; I pray it may be, and so do all of us who live each day only by grace of the shield's protection. Think how it might be if that shield did not exist: the Counterinsurgency laid bare to Edeyrn's sight and slaying, Keltia's hopes for a fairer future destroyed for all time to come, the last of the House of Dôn put to the sword . . .''

When I made no reply, Tegau sighed and rose from her seat, and laid a hand upon my shoulder; I did not see the sad gentle smile, but I heard it in her voice.

"Hard it is, Talyn, to come to grips with cold needfulness. All we here have done it, and so now must you. But I think you have done so before now—twice at least—and will again. You must.''

After she had gone, I sat on alone awhile, there in a warrior's chamber, thinking on all that she had said and not said; and knew, gods help us all, that she was right.

Chapter 11

*T*he very deeps of winter now at Coldgates: Outside, the air was chill and sparkling, snow lay upon the ground to the thickness of a spear's height and more, winds raged around the peaks and down the ice-choked valleys. Only the mountain's own hollow body protected us from the white beast that was winter in the End-lands; like babes before birthing we huddled in our granite womb.

The which could as easily be our tomb, if the shield failed, if systems broke down, if supply lines were severed; the refuge had been made as self-sufficient as possible—we produced our own food and light and air and water, did all our own artificing, cared for our sick and wounded, maintained the health of the rest in body and in mind, made provision for our continued—and, aye, ultimate—defense. Yet the chance of disaster was ever present, like a shadow in far corners; all in the shieling knew it, and all had learned to live with it.

And as Tegau had promised, I learned too. Perhaps the simplest fear—the day-to-day fear, that of mere survival—was less simple for me for a stranger reason. To me, all the wonders of artifice that maintained the shieling—the sheer power and diversity of an unfamiliar and unimaginable science—seemed unknowable and perverse. I have said how Edeyrn denied such wonders to the common run of folk, and

116

by that denial had invested them with high glamourie. Even I felt some of that awe and mystery, and I, as the child of one chief and foster-child of another, had seen more of such contrivances in my fourteen years than most Kelts would these days see in a lifetime.

But, now here in Coldgates, living among more science and magic than I had dreamed possible, I saw that these things were not wonders at all, but plain tools like any other; and those who worked with them in service of the Counterinsurgency worked with them as casually as a man outside might work with a loom, or a woman with a plow. Such technologies as were commonplace here would seem the veriest aisling to that woman or that man, and all the others like them: They lamented the loss of science, but they had never even known it; they yearned for its return, but they never hoped to live themselves long enough to see it. For to possess once again such powers would mean of force the overthrow of the Marbh-draoi, *by* force, and such a thing was dreamed of only in the hidden sanctuaries; and even there it was as yet but a dream.

No dreaming, however, for me . . . As the days passed, I bloomed. There were plenty of other young folk at Coldgates, lads and lasses of my own age to be my friends—a thing I had never before really known. All I had had was Arthur, and all he had had was me; we had so grown into each other's souls that by now it was not like having a friend or even a fostern, but another self. We were no longer companions for each other; we had all but *become* each other.

Not that either of us held this to be any bad thing; though I think Ygrawn and Ailithir both were somewhat concerned, foreseeing a time when we would not be together, and worrying lest our closeness should make that separation, when it should come—and come it did—more painful than it might otherwise be. Arthur and I thought only that we should go on forever so—who thinks different at fourteen?—and in the end we came as near to it as any might.

Yet sometimes I confess it could make things difficult:

when one of us, say, had somewhat he would conceal from the other, and could not; or when one had a thing to share, and could not, finding that the choice, the volition, of offering was diminished. We could not hide such things because naught was hidden; we could not share because all was shared already—at times the involuntary union of spirits can be most inconvenient, if not even tiresome.

But chiefly we cherished our nearness and our bond, and met many down the years who envied us that closeness— envied *me* the more, for that it was Arthur with whom I shared such links—and who would have given much to have such a bond, with Arthur by choice, but failing that with anyone, in their own lives.

And then one day of days a truth was told to test its holding . . .

That afternoon I was in the grianán used in leisure hours by Arthur and myself and some other of the young folk quartered on our cavern level. Deep in the rock as it was, the chamber would never in ten million years know the touch of the sun, and so the name was purely symbolic; but it was convenient, and we used it without a second thought.

By chance—or dán—I was alone when Arthur came to find me. I looked up from my reading to greet him with a smile, and then I saw his eyes.

People speak idly of a smile that freezes upon one's face; they have no idea, and for myself I had not thought until that moment how such a thing might feel. Now I knew.

"Arthur?"

He looked blankly at me as if I had been some importunate stranger, then shook his head and dropped heavily into the facing chair.

"I have been to see my mother," he said presently, after the silence had grown intolerable. "*You* know—for that I could not grieve for Gorlas. Until now I had not been able to bring myself to speak to her of it."

"Well, then," I said, hoping to cheer and encourage. "What does methryn say?"

Arthur gave a short indescribable laugh: In that one harsh wordless syllable spoke despair, and betrayal, and confoundment, and something that seemed very near derangement, and bitter, blinding pain.

"Well, for one thing, she says Gorlas was not my father."

The room spun about me. "Ah, nay, Artos, do not even in jest—"

"*He was not my father!*" shouted Arthur, and I shrank back in terror at the fury that blazed from him. He took a deep shuddering breath to master himself, and went on in a cold clear deadly voice. "It was not possible, do you see, that he could sire any child; and this my mother knew before they were wedded . . . by which time I was full two years old."

I scarcely dared to raise my voice above a breath. "Then—"

Again the desperate, half-mad laugh. "Whose son am I? Well, I myself asked that very question, and thus did my mother answer: I am the son of Ygrawn Tregaron and Prince Amris Pendreic, eldest child of Darowen Ard-rían and her consort Gwain of Kells."

The silence was white and taut and neverending. I dared not look at Arthur, but all I could see before me was a face. One face: not Arthur's, not Ygrawn's, not even Gorlas's (ah, Gorlas-maeth!)—but the face of Uthyr Pendreic, King of Kelts, as he looked upon Arthur in the presence chamber when they had met those few weeks since. And all I could think was one thought only: that the King had been seeing then for the first time his own nephew, his eldest brother's only son; and that Uthyr had known very well who Arthur was.

But now Arthur was speaking again, and my glance flew to him. He was ashen-pale, but calm of countenance: I knew that calm of old, however, knew well how he ever used it to conceal anguish and anger; and so I kept my eyes close upon him, watching him as if he had been a fevered child.

"It was all a secret union, for that their kindreds did not approve, and sought some better match for each of them." Now his voice sounded less cold than casual—another bad sign.

"What match could be better found than the Tanist and a

duke's daughter?'' I had not meant to speak, lest I break that carefully bridled calm—his grip on its reins was barely there—but the words came forth, and he spoke to them as if they named a thought of his own.

"Many, if the Tanist in question is but a prince in name only, and the duke is not beloved by that Tanist's mother . . . Bregon my grandfather, who was Kernow's duke at that time, wanted better for my mother than a life in hiding and a hunted lord, and spoke against the match. Darowen''—no 'Ard-rían', I noted, and certainly no 'grandmother'—"for her own part took offense, and so forbade it.''

Arthur's hands, that had been gripping the arms of his chair, began to tremble, until I thought the wood would crack and splinter beneath the convulsive spasms of his fingers. I poured out a measure of usqua to the depth of a handspan and held it out to him; his hands shook so as he drank that he spilled near half the cupful, but the rest flowed down his throat like water, and the terrible trembling ceased.

"He was killed, my—Amris—four months after my birth. I am to the best of anyone's knowing his only child; he it was who named me Arthur. So much, at least, did he give me.''

I have ever been more than commonly quick to grasp nuance—perhaps it was simple shock that had slowed me here—but all at once it broke upon my dazed wits like an exploding star.

"Then—it is YOU who are heir to Keltia! Not Gweniver, but you! Amris was eldest of the three brothers, and so now it comes to you!''

The color was beginning to leach back into Arthur's face now; but before answering my astonished outcry—though to him the thing had been self-evident long since—he held out the mether. I refilled it to the brim, and held my breath and my peace alike while he drained it; this time the golden-brown drink went down unspilled.

His words came cool, if a little too precisely clipped. "As to that, not so. The succession law as it now stands provides that an heir born of an oathfast marriage—as was the Princess

Gweniver—takes precedence of an heir born of a union with a ban-charach—as was I.''

'Ban-charach'—literally, 'the loved woman'—is a title used for one who is a man's pledged lover (though not pledged to wed), or one who is accepted in place of a wife, or one who is partner to a man in addition to a wife. Not mistress nor concubine nor courtesan nor lennaun: To be ban-charach—or far-charach for that matter, it is a state for a man as well as for a woman—is as honorable as to be wife, and has by law most specific rights and privileges. But Arthur knew all this as well as any Kelt . . .

"That may be,'' I said then. ''But still Amris was senior of Darowen's sons. Leowyn the Princess's father was her secondborn, and Uthyr who now reigns is but third. By descent of line—''

"No matter. Leowyn and Seren were wed at the stones, and my—and Ygrawn and Amris were not. So though I am the firstborn of Darowen's firstborn, Gweniver must still come before me.''

I leaned back, studying him in silence as he toyed with the empty mether. ''Many will not see it so,'' I said at last. ''When word of this gets out—and it will—I think you will find more than a few folk more than willing to set you first in the succession—as your father's son.''

He flinched as if I had struck him upon a bleeding wound—as indeed I had, and had meant to, though it tore my own heart to do so. But better it was he heard it first from someone who loved him, who had naught to gain by suggesting the possibility—though Ygrawn must have said somewhat to him very much like to what I had just spoken, for I saw by his eyes that the wound was not a new one. But his tone kept its even calm.

"It is not within their choice—nor yet within mine—to do so. Keltia is in desperate straits enough without a battle over meaningless rights to a nonexistent crown. Any road, Uthyr remains King no matter who be named his heir, and neither the Princess Gweniver nor I will be of age to rule for full twenty years to come, nor could rule even then save on Uthyr's death.''

This was of course truth uncontrovertible, and I said naught in answer for naught could be said. Arthur too fell silent; I watched him covertly, then reached out in gentleness, almost in stealth, to touch both his hand and his thought. But he was far distant, and felt neither touch, and I withdrew as quietly to a distance of my own.

What must it be *like*! Suddenly to find yourself not only not the son of the man whom all your life you have loved as your father, but the son of a prince of Keltia whom you never knew—a man who, had he lived, would have been King of Kelts reigning this day, and you his firstborn and only heir . . .

His sudden change of birth status would be the least of Arthur's concerns just now: There is no bastardy in Keltia, and never has been among the Keltic nations from our days on Earth and earlier. Brehon law, renowned throughout the galaxy for fairness and compassion, holds every child to be true-born. Any differences in birthright and birthrank—and there are many, subtle ones as well as great—come about solely according to the relationship of the child's parents. For not only do we have no baseborn in Keltia, we have ten different sorts of marriage—every one of them most legal and all equally honorable—and, needless to add, goleor of brehons and jurisconsults to sort it all out.

I began, slowly and laboriously, to untangle it in my mind. Had Amris and Ygrawn chosen to wed, they might have contracted for a night or a month or a year or for life; so long as the term was clearly stated, the contract witnessed, the thing was lawful. Even though they had chosen instead the céile-charach union, Arthur was still heir by law to his father's name and rank and estate as well as to his mother's. He was sole and chief heir only for that Amris had fathered no others, and so his right in the royal succession could not be denied; but if Amris Pendreic had had ten wives and had had ten children by each of them, still would Arthur have held place among them as the firstborn of his father.

So. Knowing all this, then, Uthyr was not likely to attempt to have his new-found nephew set aside; remembering how the King had looked upon him, embracing him for all to see, I concluded it was most unlikely Uthyr would even wish to try. Which meant—

But I was not ready to face that fence just yet. All in all, a thorny matter, the more so since it concerned a throne—even a fallen throne. Whatever the outcome, no shame attached to any of the principals in this, and my fostern would be feeling none now, only . . . Arthur knew himself now to be royal, to have that highest blood he had always yearned after; and not just royal of the rígh-domhna, one of many kinsmen in vague orbit round the throne, but heir of line to the Copper Crown itself. And what in the name of all gods did he think now to know it?

And Ygrawn . . . I almost groaned aloud, for in my boggled daze at Arthur's revelation I had forgotten entirely that the revelation had been in fact hers. Ah methryn, dearest mathra-chairda, what a secret for you to have kept all that time— Knowing that any breach of that secrecy would mean her son's death, and very like hers as well, she had kept it—and them—safely hidden, but only by means of a lie. And knowing Ygrawn as I did, I knew that for her that part had rankled the deepest.

A plain lesson in necessity, as Tegau would say who had been teaching it me. Edeyrn and his creatures would have been relentless in their hunt for Amris Pendreic's heir and lady. He would have seen in them what I had already seen: a new hope for the resistance, a banner to rally the Counterinsurgency, blood of the House of Dôn to secure the Throne of Scone.

My thought turned then to Gorlas, and the love and admiration I had ever felt for him grew tenfold. He had known all, had sought to protect his wife and her son by making Arthur the heir he himself could never have. By so doing he had earned his own measure of glory; he had done a thing for Keltia that would live forever, and he with it. He had dared greatly, and had succeeded beyond all imagining: Never in all my years at Daars had I heard a breath of intimation that Arthur Penarvon was anything but Gorlas's own child.

It seemed that Arthur had been following my track of thought. "I could not weep when my—when Gorlas—when *my father* died," he said, voice firm and clear on the title he would ever give Gorlas in his heart. "I did him, and myself, no honor thereby—though now at least I know whyfor. But neither can I rejoice in that knowing: It seems my father died long since, Talyn; before ever yours did. And there is more—"

I closed my eyes. "Artos, I do not think I can *stand* any more."

"You must," he said evenly. "For it concerns you as well as me— I have said that I was two years old before I became by law the son of Gorlas. For those two years it was Ailithir who stood as father to me, and protector to my mother. She had been turned out by her own kindred, and denied by Darowen—though, to his everlasting honor, Uthyr helped her as much as he might—and after Amris was gone she was alone, with few resources of her own and an infant son to tend."

In spite of myself, I laughed. " 'Few resources' if they be Ygrawn's outmeasure a planet's resources for anyone else."

Arthur's old charming grin flashed then, and my heart soared to see it. "Oh aye, she managed well enough, as they both tell it— I forgot to mention that Ailithir .me to confirm this, once my mother had finished her tale."

"And he did so?"

"He did, and told me more beside . . . Any road"—he resumed the telling much as a bard might have done—"I was two years of age when my mother wed Gorlas—who knew all the truth from the first, by the way—and took me to live at Daars as his son and heir."

I had been calculating under my breath, tallying dates and years, and now I sat up in surprise.

"And it was then, once you were safe hid at Daars—"

Arthur nodded. "It was then that Ailithir came to you at Tair Rhamant. It seems that he has been a prime mover of all this coil, to what end I know not—and he will not say—and just now I think I never wish to know.''

Yet even as he claimed not to wish the knowledge, both he and I knew well that he did wish it, if perhaps not yet awhile; but as for me—

"If I leave you for a little, braud? You will be well enough alone?''

The laugh this time was gentle and weary and sad, as if all the white fire of emotion had been reduced to grieshoch by the fierce passions of the hour past.

"I will be well enough . . . You would speak with our mother, then? That is kindly thought of; she will be needing comforting just now. Go to her, and I will be here when you return.''

I hesitated, then went to the door. As I coded the touchplate so that none else might enter until I did return, I sensed the exhausted peace that clung round him and was glad. A poor substitute for his usual cheer, but by the Mother it would do for now . . . I looked up at a sudden movement from his direction, and for the first time in all this hour tears came burning to my eyes.

The movement had been Arthur burying his face in his hands and bowing his head to his knees, and I quickly shut the door behind me lest I should see any more.

Chapter 12

*F*or all my words to Arthur, strangely enough it was not Ygrawn to whom my steps first led me, but Ailithir.

Plainly, by some magical means or other, he had been expecting me, for he was in his chair by the window when I entered the chamber. By some other equally plain magic—as tribute to his rank as Druid, or perhaps simply as tribute to his powers of persuasion—Ailithir had acquired for himself one of the very few windowed chambers in all Coldgates. A tiny window, true, deep-silled and field-shielded and tucked well back beneath an overhanging brow of solid rock, but a window all the same, that looked down over the snowy sides of Sulven. He sat in his chair, outlined by the diffuse blue of the reflected snowlight, and he did not look at all surprised to see me. Then he lifted a hand, and I came obediently forward.

On my way here I had resolved that I should not speak first, that it was I who was owed the explanation: I was feeling vaguely insulted, and I was very angry indeed on Arthur's behalf, and I had also a half-formed sense of having been somehow *managed*—chivied and channeled into some predetermined course, all for some great purpose not my own. So I stood on the other side of the window-nook from my teacher, and did not take the indicated chair but only stood and glowered.

"Sit, Taliesin," said Ailithir at length, his voice mild as but seldom I had heard it. "We have much to discuss, and you will be more comfortable in a chair than not," he added, and with a sulky flump I obeyed.

But no sooner had my rump touched the cushion than I flung myself forward, all my questions battling to be first upon my lips, all my angry pain plain upon my face. Again Ailithir lifted his hand, and my questions quieted, and even the pain eased away into a kind of half-pleasurable sadness.

"It is true," said Ailithir calmly. "My greatest sorrow is that he could not have been told before. But we dared not tell him, not before we had him safe at Coldgates, nor before his uncle had seen him and approved. Not wise, that he should have been told sooner."

"You might have given some—"

"You think so? Listen, then: My charge in this, sole and sacred and laid upon me by my masters, was to save his life; and that I have done. Everything that his mother did, she did according to my counsel and her own judgment. Would you then blame her? Or Gorlas? If your wrath needs to fix blame on someone, Taliesin, I am very much at your service to accept it."

At that my anger left me, and I shook my head. "Nay . . . But from what I have heard, perhaps I should rather be blaming Amris Pendreic. His late Highness cuts not so brave a figure in all this: To leave his ban-charach and their baby not yet a half-year old—"

"—to go on an errand of danger and darkness, in the service of the Counterinsurgency, and to die thereon. Is it for such that you would blame him? Amris was a brave and bonny lord; I looked on him almost as my own son, and surely Ygrawn would not have loved him had he been any less worthy than he was. But since you are longing so to hand blame around, perhaps you would blame Darowen Ard-rían?"

All my rage came rushing back. "I might!" I snapped. "And now I think of it, I *do*; and I blame Bregon Duke of Kernow right along with her."

Ailithir said nothing, did not even look at me; only waited

in patience—a half-understanding, half-disappointed kind of patience—for my anger to cool once again. Presently he rose and went to the window, leaning against the stone sill and staring down over the bone-white valley below.

"I know it must seem to you and to Arthur that your lives have been intolerably meddled with," he said after a while. "And you hold me to be the chiefest meddler . . . And in many ways you are right: I contrived to leave Ygrawn and Arthur in safety in Daars, and then having managed that to my satisfaction I went on to Tair Rhamant to begin managing *your* life . . . That is what you think, and I say freely that that is how it must now be looking to me, were I in your boots. Yet I say also that I had a charge as well where *you* were concerned, to save *you*; but I could not save your father and Gwaelod any more than I could have saved Gorlas and Daars. All I can offer you by way of reason or motive is that it has been Seen, by those whose Sight in such matters is the longest and most to be trusted. You have been saved for a purpose: Arthur, you, Uthyr, Ygrawn, Gweniver, all of us here in the shieling even—all part of a vast and varied plan; and the plan is not mine, nor yet my masters'."

I glanced up, but his back was still turned to me. "That is the second time you have made mention of your 'masters'. I did not know you had any."

At that Ailithir gave a bark of laughter and spun on his heel to face me. "Meaning, I suppose, that I have not seemed to behave as anyone's humble and obedient servant . . . Well, that may be, but I have masters all the same; though by another reckoning it could be said that I am one of those masters myself." He pushed his heavy chair a little closer to mine, and before seating himself again he faced the door and murmured somewhat under his breath. Instantly a sparkling wall sprang up, a barrier of dancing light between us and the rest of the room, and he looked at me unapologetically.

"A precaution only, against listening ears or uninvited guests—for what I shall tell you now is for you alone to hear."

"Then I may not tell Arthur, even?"

"I will myself tell him, when the time is right for telling; he has greater things to think on just now . . ." Ailithir put the tips of his long thin fingers together, tapped them several times thoughtfully, as if he were weighing between them the right words to frame that which he would impart.

"You have known for some years now that I am Druid," he said at last. "What you have not known is just what kind of Druid I am . . . I spoke of masters: These masters are called the Pheryllt, and I am of high rank among them—nay, not the highest! That burden falls upon another . . ." A smile had lighted his face like sudden sun on snow, but now it passed, and it was winter again in his eyes, and I wondered briefly who that other might be.

"We are the most secret of Druids," he went on. "Teachers for the most part, whose duty and joy it is to raise up certain of our Brothers to be masters themselves. But sometimes it falls to us in very special case to take on pupils from an early age, and school them from the first in the way that they must go—gifted pupils, blessed with talents seen perhaps once in a hundred years. Two such are you and Arthur, and I was the one given the charge over you, for this great reason of dán I just now spoke of."

I accepted this in silence, only hitched my chair closer still; he saw, and smiled.

"We of the Pheryllt are not teachers only, Taliesin; also we are custodians of the highest and holiest truths of Druidry, come down to us from the sainted Brendan himself—such things as are known to few even among Druids. And I say now, son of Gwyddno, that in time these things will be not unknown to you."

I had been hanging upon his words and mien and countenance —my eyes must have been by then as round and bright and spinning as two tiny moons—and in my wonder I questioned him as simply and openly as a child.

"Who are you, athro?"

And Ailithir—for the last time now 'Ailithir' in my life and in these pages—put by his grand and weighty words, turning upon me a smile of beauty and loving

sweetness, and answered me as gently and softly as a
father.

"I am your teacher, Taliesin, and my name is Merlynn
Llwyd."

In the hush that followed his words, as if with the speaking
of them all thought and movement in the chamber were
suspended by force, one thought alone was left to me, rever-
berant in the stillness: This day must from all time have been
destined to be a day of revelations. For first my fostern had
been revealed to be a prince of Keltia, and now had my tutor
been revealed to be a Druid of Druids. Even I had heard
rumor of Merlynn Llwyd—rumor that would be better described as legend and fable; had heard those tales as of some
mighty hero of the past by chance living in our time, such a
lord of magic as I in my humble estate might never hope to
know. For the tales said many things, and most perhaps were
myth, but on one thing all tales agreed: Merlynn Llwyd was
the Marbh-draoi's chiefest adversary, all but his equal—and
perhaps even that—in sorcery and strength.

And now, as I had earlier with Arthur, I wondered only
that I had not known all along: In the strong clear light of
retrospect both truths seemed so plain that the blindest talpa
in earth might have read them. It seemed that for years I had
had a prince for my brother and a wizard-lord for my teacher,
and I had lacked the sense and sight to discern either one.

"Nay, Taliesin, that is one thing you must never think."
So sunk was I in my self-pitying gloom that I had forgotten
Merlynn still seated not three feet away. *Merlynn* . . . I tried
the name out silently, and it fitted well—both the man there
present and the image of him in my mind; but it comforted
me that his look was still that of Ailithir who was no more.

"Do not blame yourself for not seeing; there was greater
magic at work to veil both truths from you, and from all the
worlds beside, than you shall ever know. Nay," he said
then, catching himself up sharp, as a rider will snatch at the
reins to steady a horse that has stumbled, "there shall come
one to command greater magics still, and you shall know her

well, for she too is part of the pattern; indeed, you and she together shall weave much of it ere the end."

His eyes had taken on a look of distance as he spoke; with a shiver I knew that what he was Seeing was not in this room to be seen. But now he came back into his eyes, and smiled, and I knew that whatever or whoever else he might be, though the name so long familiar be never said again, to me he would be, still and always, Ailithir.

I was about to say as much when the door opened behind us: Ygrawn stood there, beyond the sparkling veil of power that was still thrown up like a curtain-wall across the room. She was grave of face, but her head was high and her eyes steady as she glanced from me to Merlynn and back again. Then she smiled, and I could not keep back my gasp of surprise as she lifted her hand, fingers close and stiff as a blade-edge, and cleaved a pathway through the magic barrier as if it had not been there.

"And that, Talyn," she said, still with a smile, "is the *last* surprise for you this day; I so promise!"

Merlynn's deep voice cut an explanation across my bemusement. "The Lady Ygrawn, Taliesin, is long time a Domina of the order of the Ban-draoi."

Had he said she was in truth not my foster-mother at all but the Queen of the Sidhe, I would have been no more surprised; it seemed I had lost all capacity to feel astonishment, and cared not a jot that it should be so. So although I had fully intended to be as angry with Ygrawn as I had earlier been with Merlynn, instead I found myself on my feet making her the reverence due to a high priestess of the Mother; and she for her part returned my salute as solemnly.

I was only vaguely aware of Merlynn—strange how swiftly that name had replaced the other in my mind and heart; I had heard the one since I had been a five-year-old at Tair Rhamant, had known the other for but the past quarter-hour, yet already it was as if Ailithir had never been and Merlynn had been always—leaving us alone together, striding through the veil and sealing it behind him as he left the room.

Not knowing how to begin, for my heart was very full and

my brain most muddled, I stared piteously into Ygrawn's violet eyes, and, as she had ever done when I had had need of comforting, she took both my hands in hers.

"Do you hate me then, Talynno?" she asked quietly. "I would well understand if you did so."

I could only shake my head. "Not that ever; but—ah, methryn, how could you *bear* it, all those years . . ."

Ygrawn smiled at that, but the smile was that one which makes light of past pain, dismissing it as a thing of no importance; and I saw well by that very dismissal how important, and how painful, that past had been.

"Such things look ever worse at a distance, and over someone else's shoulder; had it been yourself back then, and I asking of you now, doubtless you would be saying much the same . . . though I will admit it was no revel! When such dán comes upon you, Talyn—and it will—you will find that there is a kind of peace in perfect inevitability. Each choice you make denies forever all the other choices, until at last there is no choice left for you at all, and you but follow the path that is the only one your choosings have left you; and that path is the path of dán."

"And it was so for you and—and Prince Amris?"

Her whole face lighted with a gentle warm remembering. "You would have liked him well, Talyn; he was gifted as are you, with the bard's gifts of words and irony. He saw through all, and laughed at most; but never unkindly, and malice was to him a thing unknown. Arthur is sometimes so like to him it makes my heart turn over; and yet not entirely like, for Arthur knows how to hate."

I was careful not even in my deep mind to frame my instant thought: that after this day Arthur would know perhaps even better how to hate . . . But it seemed Ygrawn did not need my thought to know it.

"I should be surprised if he is *not* hating me just now, and more than a little, for that I have so long kept the truth from him, thus keeping him from his heritage and his rank and his place as Amris's heir. But keeping him in ignorance meant keeping him in safety; that secrecy was the only choice I could make, that last path of choosing all other choices did lead to. Amris was dead, and both his kin and mine had turned us away, and I had a son at my breast whose dán mattered more than all other dáns together.''

I stared at her, thinking of Arthur as I had glimpsed him the night of our escape from Daars: not the Arthur of now, but the Arthur who would be—the future King.

"Did you See, then, methryn?"

Ygrawn shook her head. "Not then I, but Merlynn; though later, even I— When first I knew I was to bear a son to Amris, I was of two minds as to whether I should choose to bear the child at all. We were homeless then and all but friendless, moving like fudirs from shieling to shieling—such ones as would even shelter us, for few places dared defy Darowen's edict. She had in her wrath against us commanded none to lift a hand in our aid, not to give us so much as a farl of bread or cup of water. Yet for all that, we *were* helped, generously and often . . . Any road, it seemed the purest selfishness to bring a child into so hard a life, for no better reason than that we both so dearly wished one. Well, merely to want a child is not enough: There must be safety and security and the promise of a good and happy future for a child to be born to; else the child is better off if it never comes to be born at all.''

"But can such things be ruled?'' I asked shyly. "Oh aye,'' I quickly added, blushing as I saw her smile, "I know how it is that folk may choose that a child should not be conceived, but—''

"It is the Goddess's gift to all women,'' said Ygrawn, and now she was not smiling, "that any child for whom life would be less than—less than kind may be embraced again into its mother's body. Better for all three souls, child's and parents' alike, that a fitter housing should be found for the returning spirit. It is no great tragedy for a soul to wait a little time in the timelessness between turns of the Wheel, and in such case the lords of dán will never fail to find that soul a better vehicle in which to make life's journey. All women know this, and as Ban-draoi, I knew it more throughly than most: that it was for me to decide this for my child. And yet in the end it was not I who decided.''

"Amris, then?" I breathed, awed at her words. This was a great mystery of which Ygrawn was speaking; it seemed to me then—as indeed it does still—to be the greatest proof of love that a woman may show for her child. For in the end it is solely the woman's choice: She is the child's mother, and she alone knows what will be best for her child. But it is the hardest of choosings: To consider only what is best for the babe and the person it will be, not merely what she might selfishly wish for herself; to love a child enough not to let it come into a harsh and hungry world, but to give it back into the keeping of the lords of the Wheel, in the certain faith and knowledge that they will find the soul another, safer, home, even though it be not with her . . . "Amris?" I asked again.

"Nay," said Ygrawn, seeming to wonder yet again at the high strangeness of it. "It was not Amris but Ailithir—Merlynn. He spoke from Sight, said that though the child were born to grief and hardship, yet would he be High King in the end, to overthrow Edeyrn, and bring back to Keltia all that had been lost.'' She gave me a sidewise glance out of brimming eyes, and laughed. "Oh aye, I know what you are thinking! That Ygrawn Tregaron had delusions of grandeur, wild aislings puffed up by her vaunting vanity to appear as prophecy. Indeed, there were many times I thought so myself—it was Amris alone kept me grounded in the real. And then he was gone . . .''

"But Arthur was come.''

The look she gave me then dazzled with wonder and joy and gratitude, and I had to lower my eyes. "He was; and however bitter and grievous and unconformable the manner of his coming, he is here, and he is uncontrovertibly blood of the House of Dôn.''

"A prince," I said, and even in my own ears my voice sounded flat and strangled. "To be King in time, as Merlynn has Seen and you have said; never have I known him See awry, or you decree in vain.''

Again Ygrawn took my hands in hers. "It changes naught,''

she said softly. "He will need you more than ever now—aye, and in that time to come. From the very first day I met you, Talyn—nay, even before, from the hour your mother told me of your coming—I knew you would be first to stand by Arthur's side and last to leave him. Would you leave him now, before he has even begun to think of beginning his great task?"

I looked down at the slim, strong-fingered hands, cool and pale, that held mine. Fifteen years since, those hands had held the dán of all Keltia; had proved strong enough to grasp that flaming future, for duty and for love—should mine now prove any less strong than hers? I had the same reasons and none of the risks—only my own silly pride, to think that aught was changed between Arthur and me save the name of his father . . .

Without conscious willing my fingers tightened on Ygrawn's, and I looked up into her sad, loving, questioning eyes; and in my eyes she saw my answer.

Chapter 13

*B*efore leaving me to my thoughts and new resolve, Ygrawn had mentioned that Uthyr wished to make Arthur known as his nephew to the folk of the shieling, and as soon as might be; and too, though not just yet, to all the rest of Keltia. To that end, he would be calling a general aonach, perhaps even that very night: This was not the sort of news could long be kept a secret, even behind the stone walls of the shieling; and once known there, it would not long remain unbruited beyond. Best therefore to come out with it at once.

I had my doubts. Angry and hurt as he had been when I had left him, Arthur would be in no accommodating mood, even though the one he was being asked to accommodate was not only his King but his uncle. Or so at least I thought: When I returned to the grianán, I found an empty room and a scrawled note coded for me upon the touchpad, to the effect that he was well enough but wished to be alone for a while longer.

Yet in my own chamber, when I went there to change for the nightmeal, I found another message, this one from Ygrawn and of very different burden. It seemed that Uthyr was resolved to proclaim Arthur that same evening; the aonach had already been called, and my attendance upon my foster-brother was commanded by the King himself. I was therefore to attire myself suitably, and go straight to the place of assembly.

What magic had been wrought, to turn Arthur so suddenly compliant, I could not guess. But with a kind of angry rebellious obedience, I dressed 'suitably'—a new blue velvet tunic and trews, white sith-silk leinna, boots of soft embroidered leather, and every jewel I possessed. If my fostern was to be declared a prince of Keltia before the leaders of the Counterinsurgency, I reflected sourly, far from me to disgrace him by looking like a peasant. I rammed one last ring onto my finger and went out.

"No magic at all," said Arthur in answer to my question. "I but sat and thought while you were gone, and then Merlynn came to speak with me." He grinned at the look on my face. "Oh aye, he has told me; in fact, he came straight to me from telling *you*. That is goleor of owning up, all in one day . . . And before you ask, nay, *I* had not guessed either who he truly was, so you need not call hard upon yourself for not knowing."

He spoke lightly, but I could see his glance running nervously over the curious faces turned our way, and wondered again at how quickly he seemed to be accepting this vast alteration of his entire life, past, present and to come. True, there are probably few pleasanter things than suddenly finding yourself to be of royal birth; but I had seen the shock and anger that had been his first, instinctive, reaction, and I knew well that this new and rather impressive calm was a product of sheer strength of will. Knew too that it was but a leash cast round a thunderstorm; a most temporary measure indeed.

Still, there was no sign just now of the leash's breaking: Arthur was certainly paler than usual, a little more distracted, a little less attentive; but otherwise the only outward sign of his inner conflict was a restive reflex gesture he had had since childhood—a flexing of the fingers of his sword-hand, in an unconscious rippling motion from smallfinger to thumb and back again. He made it now, twice, and saw me watching; though he flushed a little, he said no word but looked out again over the hall.

We were standing just within the entrance of the immense cavern that served as a great hall in quiet times, and as an adjunct ship-bay and even field-hospital in times of more urgency. Save for the main ship-cave itself, it was the only place in the shieling of a size to hold a gathering of all the folk together.

And gathering they were: From every cavern of Coldgates people were streaming past us into the assembly-hall, had been for a half-hour past, their faces uniformly alive with curiosity, their voices making a low thrum of expectation. Such a summoning of all the shieling's inhabitants was all but unprecedented, and though there was much speculation as to the reason, by Uthyr's command no explanation had been given out, and so they wondered.

I had had shameful thoughts of losing myself in the throng once the thing was well under way; but Arthur had grimly advised me to think again, saying with point and fervor that if he had to be the unwilling chief actor in this unlikeliest of masques, then by all gods I was going to stand beside him and give him countenance, and if I tried to do aught else he would break both my legs for me. I heard beneath the jesting threat the terror flare out for an instant that he had been at such pains to conceal; and though to amuse and distract him a little I made comic pretense of escaping, I would sooner have broken my legs myself than left his side.

So it was that I was there to see it when the two royal cousins, both of them grandchildren of Darowen Ard-rían, met as kin for the first time.

I marvel now that Gweniver and I began so badly with each other; but in those days she was so with everyone, thrawn and waspish, cross-grained and froward with even the friendliest folk. Even with Arthur. With Arthur in especial . . .

She entered the great cavern unattended—Uthyr kept no state to speak of at Coldgates, deeming it vain and silly, and doubtless he would have kept little enough even had he been Ard-rígh at Turusachan; Gweniver merely disliked having folk around her—and stopped in front of us, running a very cold, very gray gaze over us both. Plainly Uthyr had told her

of her new-found cousin, and just as plainly she was far from
pleased to learn of him.

She was tall for a lass of her years, taller than I; even
Arthur did not have to look down more than a half-hand to
meet those frosty eyes. That night she was wearing a most
becoming gúna of green and gold, with a chain of dark
emeralds straining back the hair from her forehead and diamonds glittering in her ears.

Easy to see she had had already far more practice than ever
Arthur would at being royal. *She* would never have to bid
folk remember that she was a princess born; her royal bearing
was innate, she could no more have set it aside than she could
have stopped breathing—and were she ever faced with such a
choice I had no doubt but that she would have far preferred
the latter.

Tonight's encounter was by no means like to the last time
we three had met together, in Uthyr's presence chamber,
when Arthur and I were but newly arrived at Coldgates.
Then, at least, for a moment I had sensed some faint friendli-
ness in her; today there was not a glimmer of it. She stood a
few feet off, her face a mask and her eyes cold as a piast's. It
was for royalty to speak first, and so both Arthur and I
remained respectfully silent—until all at once it dawned on
him that he was now as royal as she, and that perhaps it
would be the diplomatic thing for him to initiate their converse.

But Gweniver had noted both his lapse and his blushing
recovery, and just as he opened his mouth to speak, she
disdainfully slid in the first word—clearly wishing it had been
no word at all but a sgian between his ribs. Even so it was
every bit as pointed . . .

"Greeting to you—cousin," she said, the brief pause before the appellation perfectly timed to convey both reluctant
acceptance of fact and grim resistance unto death. She turned
then on me: "*And* to you, my cousin's fostern. You must
then be my cousin too, for that you are his foster-brother."

I looked at her and met the full blast of her loathing, as she
had not dared to loose it on Arthur—whose name you will
note she had still not spoken, nor mine neither. Presumably

she felt freer, or safer, to vent her displeasure on me, who was after all only there that night as adjunct to my fostern. For my part, I cared not at all, thinking it better far that she take out her wrath on me than on Arthur, who had already quite enough with which to deal this night. Still, I was surprised that she should allow her enmity to show, and I murmured some banality in answer.

Which seemed only to enrage her further, or perhaps it was simply that she was bent on taking offense and would have done so regardless. All at once she extended a hand for us to kiss—we could scarce refuse—and then withdrew it sharply, as if she had by accident touched some noisome slimy dead thing and it was only her perfect mannerliness that kept her from wiping clean her fingers then and there.

After that Gweniver seemed to tire of the exercise, for she ignored us altogether; but her mood, evil enough already, was surely not improved a few moments later, when Uthyr entered the now-packed cavern. Ygrawn and Merlynn and some others accompanied him, but all his attention was for his nephew and not his niece. And however uncivil Gweniver's bearing had been to us thus far, I suddenly knew it for that self-defensive combativeness I had noted in her from the first; and was sorry for her, though she would surely have hated that still more had she but known.

And yet I felt the pain she now was feeling: All her life Gweniver had been first her father's, then her uncle's, pet and pride. The one she had lost, and now it must surely seem to her that she was losing the other. Worse, she was being forced to watch her loss, and *smile*, as Uthyr took to himself his brother's long-lost son. I say all this not to fault her; indeed, I think there are very few in Keltia, or anywhere else, would *not* have been in as towering a fury to be so treated, and in public too. Even I—and I have always counted myself a placid person—would have been by now fairly choking on my wrath. I was only surprised that Gweniver could discipline hers so well. But then she was a princess.

Uthyr I *did* fault: Though he had not set out a-purpose to humiliate his niece before her future subjects, in his eagerness to welcome his nephew he was doing just that. And though I also believed that with only a little thought he might have managed it all far better—thus averting many future sorrows—so caught up was he with Arthur that I doubt he even noticed how his lack of tact was working upon Gweniver.

Which of course only made things worse. Impossible for her to withdraw to save face; she had to sit there on the dais, in the heir's traditional place on the monarch's left, while Uthyr gave the right-hand place to Arthur. Who, I must say (and it is the bard and not the brother who says it), bore himself most well, though he flushed to the very roots of his hair as he took the seat, giving a half-bow to the King, and to Gweniver who sat with face averted as far as she dared, and to his mother, and to the assembled inhabitants of Coldgates.

I was watching all this from my own seat some few places away—Arthur had thrown me a glance of pure terror when he realized we were to be separated, but there was no help for it—with Ygrawn on the one side of me and my sister Tegau on the other. I could not see Merlynn without discourteously craning my neck, but I knew he was there on Arthur's right, and I was heartened to know it; he would not let Arthur's nerves get the better of him. The rest of the row of chairs on the dais held folk I knew only vaguely: those high in Uthyr's councils and the shieling's governance.

Strangely enough, we were not there to dine; that would come later. This was an aonach, not a feast; its sole purpose was to present Arthur to the people, and as Uthyr was not one for much ceremonial, that purpose was quickly achieved.

Rising from his chair between Arthur and Gweniver, Uthyr stood a few moments in silence, as a king should; then he began to speak. His light clear voice was given weight and depth by the cave's granite walls, and the throng fell hushed on the instant to hear his simple words.

"My friends," said Uthyr, "I present to you Arthur Pendreic, son and heir of Amris, eldest son of Darowen Ard-rían and Gwain King of Keltia." He turned to his right, gesturing Arthur to rise, and upon Uthyr's worn, tired face was a look of such joy as I had not thought him capable of showing.

Yet it was not altogether to be wondered at: Uthyr, the gentlest and most sensitive of Darowen's three sons, had been greatly troubled at her treatment of Amris and Ygrawn; more troubled even than that, at the Queen's denial of her firstborn grandchild. Trained as a brehon and scholar, in character Uthyr was vastly different from his brothers: Where Amris was ruled by love of lore, and Leowyn by love of war, Uthyr was ever ruled by love of justice. To his mind, Darowen, High Queen though she had been, had set herself in the law's reverence when she forced outlawry upon her son and his ban-charach; and when she pronounced their child to be no blood of the House of Dôn, in the eyes of that child's uncle she had pronounced herself a tyrant.

But now, as by some great gift of the gods, it had come within Uthyr's powers to set right this vast unjustice. No wonder he rejoiced; as I looked on him in that moment, I saw that to him this was the best deed he had ever done or ever would hope to do. In the end it was to prove not so; but just then to him at least it seemed so, and he was glad beyond all measure.

But the folk to whom he had made this ringing pronounce-ment had so far received it in absolute silence, and for one terrible moment I thought that perhaps they would refuse to accept Arthur as prince. I glanced at Ygrawn, but she was watching Uthyr and did not see my look, or sense the fear that prompted it.

I glared out over the hall, in some insane thought of shaming them, and saw as I did so that I had been mistaken: The silence had not been the silence of denial, but the silence of those too greatly moved to make response. Many of those present had known and loved Amris well, and, far from rejecting his son, they were looking on the boy and seeing, through their tears, his father whom they had lost.

Then like a slow-building earthquake came at last that which I had waited to hear: a rustle that grew to a murmur that grew to a shout that shook the stone of the cavern and the hearts of all within—shouts of "Arthur!" and "Amris!" and "Uthyr!" and other cries of approval and delight. It seemed that the folk of Keltia—at least those few thousands of them here in Coldgates—rejoiced as greatly as did their King to find another and unexpected branch of the Dôniaid, and were no more reluctant than he to show their joy.

Uthyr had been gesturing vainly for silence again and order, but only after many minutes did the delirium subside so that he might be heard.

"I know you have many questions, and in the next days I promise that they shall be answered every one of them. For now, I have but two things more to say: First, that I honor the Lady Ygrawn Tregaron, daughter of Bregon Duke of Kernow, as ban-charach to my brother and mother to my nephew, and therefore do name her second lady in the land by right of that, to give place only to the Princess Gweniver"—Ygrawn, whom very little ever took by surprise, was surprised, but recovered herself at once and bowed gracefully to Uthyr from her chair—"and second, that before all here assembled I raise my nephew to the rank of heir-presumptive to the Throne of Scone: Arthur Pendreic, Prince of the Name, to follow in the line of right succession the Tanista Gweniver, daughter of Leowyn King of Kelts and Seren his Queen. So say I, Uthyr King of Kelts."

And saying so, Uthyr took Arthur's hand and set upon the midfinger the seal-ring of Amris Pendreic: a great balas ruby with the stag of the Dôniaid carved inghearrad into its polished table.

If the cavern had been silent following Uthyr's first pronouncement, that silence had been the din of war-horns by compare to what hush now fell; I have never heard, before or since, so swift and heavy and complete a quietness. It choked the chamber like a sudden fall of snow, thick and settled, muffling movement as well as sound. Clearly the raising of this newfound royal kinsman to the rank of Prince of the Name—two places from the throne itself—was a rather different matter from his mere proclaiming as one born of the rígh-domhna.

For my part I was not much distressed by the general reaction—they would all come round in time, once they had thought on it awhile—but Arthur's response was to leave me as staggered as his naming had left the crowd.

I have not yet said how he looked that night. Oh, he was dressed princely enough—velvets and leathers and a heavy gold torc—and certainly his bearing was that of a prince; but then it had always been. He was handsome as ever, eyes bright, hair thick and shining to his shoulders, and all at once I could trace in his face the bones and lineaments that had never come to him from Gorlas. Though I had never seen Amris Pendreic—not so much as a hologram portrait of him—I suddenly knew his features as they blended with Ygrawn's there on Arthur's countenance; Uthyr I saw there too, and Darowen Ard-rían, and even Gweniver's likeness showed plain in his face.

But chiefly I saw Arthur, who was all and none of those; and on that face I knew better than my own I read many things: pride, aye, and excitement, he would not have been human had he felt any less. I do not know what others may have discerned there—Merlynn and Ygrawn would not be seeing the same things as Uthyr or I—but what I saw now shining from Arthur's face like the light from the sacred stones was something just as ancient and every bit as holy.

It was his acceptance of that mystic compact that is between prince and people, that unspoken mutual oath sealing ruler and realm. Not enough to be born to it: The thing must be made in full knowing and by free choosing; without it, all the royal blood in all the worlds may course through one's veins, and it will make no smallest differ that it does so. And though a king or queen be crowned ten times over, it is this first, deepest, acceptance that is the true sacring, and in the end the only one that matters.

So I watched Arthur as in silence he covenanted himself to his people, and saw that they had not yet decided that they should likewise bind themselves to him; and still I was not troubled. Now, however, Arthur had risen to his feet, and in the throbbing hush he bowed to Uthyr and to Gweniver and to his mother, and turned, head held high, to face the folk.

They had not been expecting him to speak, and as he

looked out upon them to command their attention, they stared
back at him with something approaching hostility, as if it
were some obscure outrage that he should dare address them.

He ignored it, and, hand clenched shut upon his father's
ring, he began to speak. If his words were less brief than his
uncle's, his voice was deeper and stronger, riding easily over
the low murmurous undercurrent of comment that was running through the cavern.

"I presume to address you by right of the blood of the
House of Dôn my lord uncle the Ard-rígh has just now by his
grace acknowledged." His voice grew more confident as he
relaxed into the moment, sensing his power to control them,
and the note of challenge lessened.

"Until today I had not known the truth of my birth. Those
who are wiser far than I deemed it best kept secret, as they
have now deemed it better that I—and you—should learn
otherwise. Yet that secrecy did save my life; without its long
shelter I should not now be standing here among you. But I
am here"—his voice rang out in the perfect silence, like the
hai atton that rallies the hosts—"and by grace of the Highest
God I will use my poor gifts to do honor to that House of
which I am sprung, or perish in the trying. Yet I wish also to
do honor to him whose love and protection preserved me
these fifteen years past"—here Ygrawn sat up very straight in
her seat, and Gweniver for the first time lifted her gaze to
look at him—"And so I say that although Uthyr Ard-rígh has
given me to bear the name of Pendreic, and I thank him for
that as for all things, I remain Arthur Penarvon and will be
called so, by right of the man who will ever stand to me as
the only father I have known—Gorlas, Lord of Daars."

He ceased speaking, and his eyes went at once to Ygrawn.
He had won his gamble—I had felt the instant when the
hearts of the folk had changed, when they reached out and
took the covenant that he had made with them, and pledged it
back again—but neither he nor Ygrawn heeded it, looking
only upon each other; he a little hesitant, as if wondering had
he done aright, she triumphant, tears on her cheek but her
smile brilliant with love and pride.

Then Arthur's gaze moved on to me, and I knew by the sudden softening round his mouth, and the sudden crinkling round his eyes, that he saw in my face what I had meant for him to see: indeed, all there was to be seen just then—pride and love as had been in Ygrawn's eyes, but added to those a brother's respect and a bard's approval.

His glance went then to Uthyr, with a subtle new deference and dawning affection, and already a prince's distance seemed drawing in around him. And Arthur looked then at Merlynn, and though I could not see my fostern's face, I could see our teacher's; and I looked away, for what I saw there was not for me to see.

And last of all Arthur looked at Gweniver. So did I, to see the Princess's answering look, and for the second time in that day that had been one long astonishment I was astonished at the unguarded truth that stood upon her face.

She was staring at Arthur as though seeing in him something she had never imagined possible—much as a hawkmaster who has found an eagle chick in a nest of partridges, or a huntsman seeing a wolf cub suckling amongst a lapdog litter. And though she plainly hated what she was seeing, she was honest enough to respect it and brave enough to show that respect; and I think I never in all our lives after had greater admiration for the Princess Gweniver than I had that night.

And so I was astonished for the third time, as Gweniver rose from her chair and reached her hand to Arthur, and Uthyr stepped back a little that they might meet the closer. Then Arthur bowed deeply to her and kissed her hand, and in front of all that company Gweniver the Tanista curtsied to the Prince of the Name of Dôn.

Chapter 14

I know what you are already thinking; and be very sure that the rest of Coldgates, once the thunderclap surprise of Arthur's naming had ceased reverberating in the stone, was not far behind you in thinking it.

It was in all truth too perfect *not* to be thought of: Here were a princess and a prince both of the ancient line of Dôn, scarce a year apart in age, both healthy and handsome and quick of mind and tongue. What could be more fitting than that they should wed when they had reached an age for it, and so seal the bloodline and unite the claim each might otherwise make in the other's despite upon the Crown?

Well, it is not so wild a thought, and you need not blush for having it. Crowns, and lesser things beside, have been saved before now by just such managed measures. Though it is not usual in Keltia for first cousins to wed, neither is it unknown; nor by any means forbidden, or even too much frowned upon when it does occur. Of course the perils of inbreeding are well understood, but there are in the event precautions that can be taken to mitigate those. Any road, the general opinion was that a single close match would not unduly endanger the royal gene pool, and this particular match, close though it might be, would solve a good many problems. Perhaps even as many as it would make . . .

The one problem no one seemed able to solve was that of bringing the two principals together in the first place. Despite that pretty show in the great hall, neither Arthur nor Gweniver could abide the other for more than five minutes running. The apparent truce between the Princess and the new Prince had barely lasted through the feast that had followed the aonach—a most discomfortable meal—and since that night hostilities had flared out into open warfare more often than peace had prevailed.

Oh, they were skilled enough at covering their dislike, particularly in the presence of the King; indeed, so much so that Uthyr was the first to begin speculating on a possible future match. The rest of the shieling, with perhaps more opportunity than the King of observing matters first-hand, kept a more judicious perspective—though of course hoping passionately that all might work out to the general will. Folk are such sentimentalists at heart, even—especially—in the teeth of the facts . . . Ygrawn, who knew best of any, confined herself for the moment to remarking only that Amris would have seen straight through it, Leowyn would have forbidden it, but Uthyr had ever loved happy endings.

A dangerous indulgence, as would in time be shown; but just now it did no great harm, and it made him happy. Gods knew little enough else did . . .

As I had expected, and had gone so far as boastfully to predict to a disbelieving Arthur, it took hardly any time at all before he had become the darling of the shieling. Partly this swift and sweeping acceptance was due to Uthyr's determination that Arthur should have his rightful place; and though the King's resolve was no small factor, in the end it was Arthur's own determination that he should rather *earn* that place which made him so soon a part of the people's hearts.

All the same, some there were in Coldgates who were not above some mean-spirited gibing; taunts that were meant to reach Arthur's ear, and did, to the effect that he was already a prince proclaimed, so why bestir himself to make show of substance.

But that was not Arthur's way, not then, not ever; and as for the gibes he paid not the least attention. At Daars he had forced folk to judge him on his merits and his faults, as anyone should be judged, and had asked allowance for neither birth nor title. How much more so now, here: He would prove himself *as* himself, not as Amris's son or Uthyr's nephew or Darowen's grandson; and those who sought to test him, thinking to find a soft princeling and a cheap victory, learned otherwise to their extreme, and immediate, sorrow.

Despite the trials of Arthur's new position, or mine as his foster-brother—as such I came in for my fair share of scuffles defending his honor or my own—our new life swiftly swung into a pleasant daily routine very much like to the one we had known at Daars.

Our lessons continued as before, with Merlynn and Elphin and Scathach; but now we had access to other teachers, and resources undreamed of, and fellow students to challenge us and chaff us. And in those classes and friendly competitions, and most particularly in those contests that were not so friendly, we learned much, and met many who would suffer with us a long and harsher schooling still: friends like Tarian Douglas, future Princess of Scots; or Grehan Aoibhell, heir to the Prince of Thomond; or Elen Llydaw, whose mother owned half the planet Arvor. Friends of humbler estate as well, I hasten to add; Arthur was throughout his life the last person in Keltia to hold high birth as requisite for his friendship, and as for me—well, no bard ever born was a respecter of rank. We had many friends, and dearly loved ones, whose nobility lay only in their hearts. It was simply that as Coldgates was the most secure of the Counterinsurgency's strongholds, here had been sent for safekeeping many heirs of high and wealthy kindreds—even as Arthur and I had been sent—and out of sheer proximity those furnished our first friends, though scarce the last; or the only.

Others Arthur soon met who would stand to him in vastly different aspect: Uthyr was wasting no time in acquainting his nephew with the business of statecraft, and not a week after

Arthur's creation as Prince of the Name, he was introduced to some of those who helped that business to be conducted.

It may sound strange to say it, but even a throne in exile and eclipse must be served and maintained by courtiers: As Uthyr was a shadow High King, there were also in the shieling, and elsewhere, those who constituted what might be likewise termed a shadow Council.

These were the mighty among the Counterinsurgency, those who had thrown their lives and fates and fortunes in with the House of Dôn, for good or for ill. For the most part they were not soldiers, but neither were they courtiers for empty show: Though a king in exile may need fewer advisors round him than one who is safe enthroned, by dint of his doubtfuller position he needs far better ones, and beyond most monarchs Uthyr had an unerring gift for choosing the best.

Chief among those, as with any ruler, were the planners of policy and of war: Marigh Aberdaron, Uthyr's Taoiseach or First Minister, plotter for the Restoration; and Keils Rathen, Uthyr's war-leader, architect of the means by which that Restoration was hoped to be effected—military victory over Edeyrn. Neither of them noble, their places coveted by those of lesser ability if higher rank, Keils and Marigh had been with Uthyr since his accession; they had served Leowyn before him, had been in their youth friends of Amris. They knew Ygrawn and respected her greatly, and though they loved Arthur for his father's sake as well as his own, they were full ready to be as severe taskmasters to him as ever they could be, and so they proved.

Even Arthur saw the justice in that, though it did not stop him bitterly lamenting it. "It is training, Talyn," he said defensively one day, when I had rebuked Keils—in the war-lord's absence, you may be sure—for some more than usually harsh assignment. "I must learn, and quickly too; and if I fail, they will have failed."

"Maybe so," I said, unimpressed. "But I wonder does the Princess Gweniver—the *Tanista* Gweniver—work twenty hours and more at a stretch, as I see by your eyes that you have been doing?"

Arthur murmured some dark oath under his breath and knuckled his tired eyes. "She does not have to, does she . . . She has been royal fifteen years longer than I; presumably she has learned a thing or two along the way."

"Oh aye, doubtless she has; what way even a blind horse will pick up the odd mouthful of hay . . ." I put my fingers on the top edge of the scroll he was studying and walked them up the paper, pulling it out from under his hands. "Leave it awhile. Statecraft is not well learned by weary princes."

He laughed, but gently tugged at the scroll, and I allowed him to pull it back again. "That sounds a thing a bard might say—if there were a bard around to say it," he added wickedly.

I sighed, less for the taunt than for his tiredness, but knew he could not be persuaded to rest, and much against my judgment left him still at work. On my way to my own rooms it came to me that I might profit by some counsel, and I turned in my steps, back the way I had come, to seek it in the usual place.

He was of course awake when I came to his door—in all the years of our association I do not think I ever once found Merlynn asleep, perhaps he did not trouble to do so; though I *do* recall seeing him eat and drink, at least once or twice at any rate—and he greeted me as brightly as if it had been three hours past high twelve and not three past middlenight. I pulled a chair from the tableside and sat on it back to front, my chin resting on its carved top.

"Why is he so set on learning in a year everything Gweniver has learned in fifteen times that?"

Merlynn marked his place in his reading and considered my question, if not perhaps the tone in which it had been couched, with due gravity.

"As to that, he is but doing as he has ever done. Has he not always been first to finish a task or read a book or learn a new thing? It angers and troubles him to be ignorant, and he loves to learn for the learning's own sake; what wonder that he should be eager for this new knowledge? Besides, he needs to know, and knows he needs: Uthyr comes to rely on him more and more, as you have seen.''

I had seen; I liked it but little, and I said as much now. "And any road," I added, "he will never be King, so why does he tax himself so?''

Merlynn gave me that very particular glance of his—the one that is perfectly without expression yet still seems somehow to suggest that you have been very stupid indeed—but said nothing, and after a moment or two I capitulated to the glance as I always did.

"Very well! I know better! We all know better! You know best of all! But does *he* know?''

"Ah. Now that is the only thing of sense you have so far said.'' Merlynn closed the book and leaned back with a discursive air. "Time, I think, for a small lecture to refresh your memory of the law. When a royal heir, man or woman, dies before becoming monarch yet leaves a minor child behind, that child does not become its parent's heir directly. The dead heir's siblings, if any, move up in the succession in turn to become heirs to their dead brother or sister, and the child is for the moment displaced.''

"I *know* this," I said crossly. "And it is most unfair.''

"No matter. Now when the new heir becomes monarch, that displaced child then becomes *first* in the succession, ahead of all the new ruler's own children—if children there are, or if later there come to be. Therefore did Uthyr become Ard-rígh after Leowyn's death, as his next heir of line; only if Gweniver had been of full legal age on her father's death would she have followed him directly as sovereign.''

"It is just as Leowyn became heir on Amris's—oh.'' Too late I saw it yawn before me like a ditch before a jump, and like an unwary hunter I was in and floundering before I could pull up.

Merlynn smiled. "Just so. Aye, Arthur was passed over as his own father's successor, just as was the Princess as hers. Of course none knew Arthur's whereabouts at that time— well, none that would have spoken up—and few even knew he existed at all. But even had Arthur been a prince proclaimed what time his father died, still would he have been passed over, and still would Leowyn have been named Tanist to follow his dead brother.''

I was concentrating so hard I almost missed it again; then it all fell into place.

''But—*that* means Arthur should on Amris's death have been set first after Leowyn; ahead even of Leowyn's own child, as you have just said. Arthur should all these years have been first heir to Keltia, not Gweniver at all—''

''Now you have put your finger on a thorn that troubles many: *Certainly* he should have been set ahead; that is why Uthyr labors so now to make up to him for that slighting. It is only because of Darowen's spite that Arthur is not now Tanist; his father was Tanist, followed by two brothers who ruled, and the Tanistry should now belong to Arthur—Tanistry only, for that he is still too young to rule, any road, and Uthyr still lives. It is all perfectly plain in law.''

''Then why is Gweniver still Tanista? Surely she should be set aside, and Arthur named in her place?''

''Not so easy, I fear,'' answered Merlynn. ''For one thing, Gweniver is still the child of an oathfast marriage—though her father was a second son—and Arthur is still the child of a céile-charach union, though his father was the elder son. His claim is held by most to be as good as hers even so, and many hold it better: He is senior heir, she is more conventional heir. To those whose opinions in such things matter most—the Chief Brehon of Keltia, for one—their claims are of exactly equal weight and validity before the law.''

''Which means?''

''Well, they could fight it out; it has been done before.'' Seeing my exasperated look, Merlynn apologized with a gesture. ''Nay, perhaps not . . . Given then that each wishes to avoid the bitterness of a disputed Crown, and the putting down by force of the other's partisans, there is but one way.''

I knew we should have had to come round to that, soon or late . . . ''They must wed each other.''

''Aye, but that is not the whole of it. They must wed *and*

share the sovereignty equally between them. He must be Ard-rígh and she Ard-rían, to rule jointly.''

I gaped at him, but he did not *seem* to have all at once lost his wits . . . ''We have never had such a thing in Keltia,'' I said tentatively.

''No.''

''Few other kingdoms that I know of have had such a thing?''

''They have not.''

''It would be something new, then.''

''It would.''

Well, much help *he* was; I thought on it awhile. ''Given then that it would be a thing untried, and given also that those two are who and what they are—what chance such an arrangement might work?''

''Not much chance. But what is their alternative, or ours? To raise civil war for the sake of the Crown, split Keltia like halves of an apple, take the field against each other? All while Edeyrn sits back and watches and laughs, and we do his work for him . . .''

''They will not like it much.''

He stood up, went to the window; but it was night outside, naught there that even he could see.

''What care what they may or may not like? It will be their duty, and they will do it like it or loathe it. In the end neither will fail to see that it must be done. Think again, bach,'' he added in a kinder voice. ''There is no other way. If one of them takes the Crown over the other, it will mean certain death for the one who does not rule, certain disaster for the one who does and no hope forever for Keltia of freedom from the Marbh-draoi. Those are not happy choices; but what is their own private happiness to set against that?''

I went away uncomforted back to my rooms. Merlynn was right, of course, as he ever was; it was my own fond foolish fault that I had not seen it so before. I had thought only of the two persons, Arthur and Gweniver—and of the two I had chiefly thought of Arthur—and the cost to them both should they be forced into a political match. I had never considered what the cost might be to all Keltia if they were not.

But before I went to my bed I looked in again on Arthur. He had fallen asleep over his books; carefully I eased his scrolls and pen and computer-pad out from beneath his head, and dimmed the lights with a whispered word. He would have a stiff neck in the morning, but I had neither the strength to move him unaided to his couch nor the heart to wake him.

Besides, I thought as I closed the door behind me, if all that Merlynn had said were true, the unyielding, uncomfortable table was at least as felicitous a bed as any Arthur was like to find in his future, and I left him to it.

Others, though, were happier in heart-matters . . . The first to notice that Uthyr and Ygrawn were falling in love with each other were not they themselves but their children.

For Arthur's part he was delighted; in the months we had now been at Coldgates he had come to care for his gentle uncle as deeply as ever he had cared for Gorlas. It was as if he was offering Uthyr the affection and respect he could never now in life offer his true father; and it gladdened me to see that Uthyr paid his nephew back in kind.

As to Uthyr's niece—well, as Uthyr was not quite High King (save only in law), Gweniver was not quite his child; but her possessive jealousy would have done credit to the most father-besotted daughter in all history. As bards we learn tales of such, all most unfortunate of ending; but Gweniver would have made those daughters of old to look as uncaring streppochs. She detested the thought of her uncle marrying Ygrawn, and spoke against it night and day to anyone unwise enough to listen.

It was not for that she did dislike Ygrawn; indeed, she stood rather in some awe of her, Ygrawn being an accomplished Ban-draoi Domina and Gweniver even now in the midst of her own studies for the Sisterhood. She was even being tutored by Ygrawn's own old preceptress, the Ban-draoi Reverend Mother Ildana Parogan. It was simply that

Gweniver feared and resented anyone—woman *or* man—taking first place over herself in Uthyr's heart.

Since her father's death—Seren her mother had died long since—Gweniver had had for family only Uthyr. He had been more than uncle and father-surrogate: He had been friend and confidant and mentor and advisor. Never had he refused to help or comfort or cosset her; he had praised her when she did well and scolded her when she was waspish, and she thought more of him than of any other person alive. Small wonder she would resent an interloper; how much more so one who was her loathed rival's own mother.

And what did I myself think of the intended marriage? I thought it was a miracle of dán, and praised all gods for the granting. Ygrawn would never love another as she had loved her dead prince; she had found protection and true companionship with Gorlas; but now with Uthyr she had a thing she had never before known—freedom, and the chance for real work. Ygrawn was one of those who are born for great doings; she had been wasted at Daars, it was like keeping a sun-shark in a garden pool, or a falair in a cellarage. Like them she needed scope and light and liberty, and as Queen—Queen! I had not thought of it until that moment—she would have all those things.

Duties she would have too, of course; and if to be Queen in exile was to be confined somewhat, nevertheless it was still to be Queen. And though she would never have wedded Uthyr for that title's sake alone, the knowledge that she would soon become Queen of Keltia worked upon her; so much so that she sought counsel of me . . .

"You are my son, Talyn," she said simply. "Have you no bard's advice for your foster-mother?"

All I had for her was my loving blessing, and I gave it unstinting. But even as I embraced her I sensed her unnatural constraint, and sensed too what caused it. Still, I waited for her to tell me.

She did so without reserve. "They say I wed him only to be Queen; that I wed Uthyr only for that Amris and I never wed, that I care not which brother it is so long as I get a crown out of it.''

Gods, jealous folk will put all manner of muck in their mouths and think it pearls of truth. . . "What do *you* say?''

She looked up at me under her lashes, the old wicked judgmental glance. "*I* say plague take them all.''

"That is what I like to hear." I sat down again and smiled at her. "Folk will say what they please in any case—you yourself taught me that; nor have you ever cared what the common run did mouth on about.''

"No more do I now," said Ygrawn. "It is only for his sake—for I do love him, Talyn, and crown or no crown I would wed him all the same. Yet I cannot say that the thought of being Queen much displeases me.''

"Why should it? It is a worthy and worshipful thing, to be Queen.''

"Not that . . . But I shall be able to do such *good*, Talyn; it is duty and fulfillment and my delight in both, to serve Uthyr and Keltia and myself all in doing what I wish most to do. Do the folk then blame me aright?''

"Not to my mind, methryn," I told her, adding with a grin, "So I may tell the folk it is purely a political thing?''

Ygrawn matched my smile, and the violet eyes sparkled. "Ah well, I have ever been a creature of politics; too late, I think, for me to change.''

The plans for the wedding—a quiet one, just close kin and friends and Uthyr's Councillors in attendance, with Merlynn and Ildana to preside over the rite—went forward, and all seemed calm. Too calm, perhaps; even the spiteful gossip had blown away like some evil miasm of the swamps, and nothing else had been stirred up to take its place.

I should have been grateful, for Ygrawn's and Uthyr's and Arthur's sakes, and I suppose I was; but also I felt intolerably pressed upon, hedged round with unseen briars, and not wishing to darken anyone's joy just now I dealt with it as best I might.

Which mostly entailed solitude, a thing difficult to come by in Coldgates. But in my needy straits I had managed better than I hoped: I had found a place where no one else ever seemed to come, a tiny watchpost high up in the shieling's roof, a low-ceilinged chamber hardly bigger than a press, with one of the precious windows set deep in the stone embrasure. Long unused by sentinels now that the pale protected our refuge, it had become *my* refuge in my strange new mood, and as the days drew on to the wedding I daresay I spent more time there than I should.

One afternoon perhaps a fortnight before the ceremony I found myself possessed of a splendid fit of bad temper, and selfishly I resolved not to share it with others but to keep it all for me. So I climbed to my tower, like a little black cloud growing surlier with every step, longing only to be alone in my retreat and enjoy my mood in peace.

As I came up the last flight of the steep twisting stair I heard soft scuffling sounds above me. My hand went to the sgian at my belt—spies? assassins? rats?—then as I came round the final turn I saw, and took my hand from my knife.

"Highness? Is all well?"

Clearly not, if the furious glance from behind the tangled dark hair spoke true. Gweniver had been weeping long enough to blotch her face with it, but she was still proud enough and angry enough for it to matter greatly that I should not see. Once she saw I *had* seen, she threw back her hair from her face with a fierce defiance, and looked me straight in the eyes.

"Nay, my lord, all is *not* well! How should all be well—how should—how—" Her voice broke and choked with tears, and the mobile face quivered like a shiver-oak in storm; without regard for my watching she threw herself down again on the seat beneath the window and wept as if her heart would break.

I stood there at considerable loss, my own evil mood utterly forgotten. It seemed that I should do something, but what? Gweniver cared for me near as little as she did for Arthur, what comfort could I be to her here?

On the other hand, I myself had known loss and sorrow,

and I was ever deep afflicted by others' suffering. It is the empathy that lies the other side of the bard's remove: A bard may dispassionately observe, so that he may write of a thing; but that dispassion only cloaks an empathic union with the sufferer that none save another bard can truly comprehend. One is removed from emotion, but one is at the same time inside the emotion; it is a hard thing to explain. Bards will know.

At such times, though, instinct is all we have to go on, bard or no: So I sat beside Gweniver on the stone bench, and took her hand in mine, a little fearful that she would throw it off if not break my arm altogether. But astonishingly she crumpled slowly against my side, still heedlessly weeping, and I put an awkward arm round her shoulders.

After a while the sobbing eased, and she began to speak, and what emerged then was a long and broken tale that came near to breaking me as I did listen: She spoke of how her family had lived in hiding for their lives, for near two hundred years, since first the Marbh-draoi came to power; how as a child she had been forced to flee with her parents every few months, sometimes oftener still, from one hiding-place to another, many times just barely ahead of hunting Ravens. Then one day had come the crushing weight of the knowledge that she would be Queen herself one day, the struggle hers to carry forward; and the added burden of knowing that she must not fail, on her all depended—else the sacrifices of the past two centuries were wasted and vain.

Her mother, she said without a tremor, had died young, of the loneliness and the terror; she herself had never had a real home or a true friend—her only family had been her father and her uncle, and then her father too was gone . . . And more, until I thought I would die of the hearing; yet who was I to give way under a mere telling, when she who was telling it had endured fifteen years unyielding until now?

"—and Goddess forgive me but from the first I was sick with jealousy of Arthur." Gweniver's voice had taken on a kind of sibylline inevitability, emotionless and clear. Indeed I think that by now she no longer even remembered that she was speaking aloud at all; it was to her as if she spoke in sleep, or to her own soul, and to no human ear; and if she did remember, she no longer cared.

"*He* had had a happy childhood," that low cool voice continued. "And I could not begin to imagine how that must have been. Gorlas may not have been his true father, but he was more a father to Arthur than ever my father was to me, and I envied that so sore I could not speak."

I found my own voice. "But your own father—King Leowyn lived until you were, what, ten years or so?"

Gweniver's laugh was frightening in its bitter brittle bite. "King Leowyn! Do you know, Taliesin, that is how *I* ever thought of him too? Never as my father, never 'athra' or 'tasyk' but always to me 'King Leowyn' . . . That should tell you much right there."

It told me more even than she knew, for that was the first time she had ever called me by my name to my face . . . But she was speaking again.

"I think that for his part he mostly forgot he even had a daughter at all. He was ever on the move, never there when I needed him, and when at last my mother needed him more than ever she had needed him before, he was not there either. Save for my uncle and me, she died alone." Something flickered in the gray eyes, something cold and old and far away. "And then he was killed—so stupid, so wasteful; and I had no one left but my uncle."

I said nothing for a little time, then: "I was orphaned myself before I was six years old; though I at least had brothers and sisters, they too were never there. I had only Merlynn and Gorlas and Ygrawn—and Arthur."

I had said his name a-purpose, to test what she might do. Though she did not answer that, still her answer surprised me: Tears came again to her eyes, and this time not for her own sorrows but for mine.

"I know," said Gweniver. Haltingly, as if it were not a thing she had often had occasion to practice, she reached out in sympathy to touch my arm. No great distance, as I still sat close beside her on the bench; but too great a distance for her even so: Her hand closed on air and fell away. But her words could be a bridge though her touch as yet could not.

"I have heard of Gwaelod," she said softly, "and how your father did stand against Edeyrn in Ratherne itself. A thing to be most proud of, Taliesin; he went out by his own choice with honor, and even Leowyn Ard-rígh cannot say as much. But I have so pitied myself I have forgotten that others too merit pity . . ."

It was a brave soul's leap in darkness: Never until this hour had Gweniver spoken so to another; she did so now knowing that she spoke to one with whom she had ever been at odds, and that by so open offering she risked rebuff. Yet she risked it all the same; and yet not all, for though I waited a few moments, she said no word of Arthur. It seemed that as yet her pity could reach no farther than to me, who had sat and listened and wept with her this hour past.

Even so I was much moved, impressed by the courage she had shown, not disheartened by the falling short, knowing that all would come in time. It was a high fence she had set herself to; but she had proved just now that she could clear any barrier she chose—that last wall too would be leaped, if not just yet. But until then—

I came to myself with a start. While I had been thinking all this, Gweniver had been setting herself to rights, smoothing her hair, cooling her burning cheeks with snow scooped from the drift just inside the window. Now she stood up, straightening her shoulders as she did so, and I saw that once again she was the Tanista as before. But it was not all as before, and as we went together down the long stair, I knew she knew it as well as did I.

I cannot say we were never again to disagree in all the years that were to come: We had bitter differences, and often, and the last of those was the bitterest of them all, and not for us two alone. But from that hour on, Gweniver and I were unfriends no longer, and that just then was enough.

Book III:

Saíochtraí

Chapter 15

So Uthyr and Ygrawn were wedded, and once more Keltia had a queen. And within the year had also two new princesses, for in the spring following the marriage Ygrawn gave birth to twin daughters. Uthyr, wild with joy, commanded the infants to be named after two great royal ladies of the House of Dôn: Marguessan the firstborn; and, her junior by a half-hour, Morguenna—never to be known by any other name than Morgan.

Neither Arthur nor Gweniver was present for the birth, or for the saining held three months later; had it not been for the combined order of King and Queen-to-be, they would not even have attended the wedding itself. As it was, none of the three of us was to see the babies, or their parents, for almost a year after their arrival, though that was due more to distance than to disinclination—well, at least it was so for *my* part, but then I had no real stake in it.

By 'distance' I mean only that we three were no longer in permanent residence at Coldgates. The first to depart was Gweniver, who went with Ildana, the Ban-draoi Reverend Mother, to a hidden college of the Sisterhood on Vannin—travelling as befit the Tanista in one of the Counterinsurgency's treasured starships. She would remain there for the next three years, being trained as a sorceress—for which calling, so went the general opinion in which even Arthur and I concurred, she had a real and considerable talent.

She went to our not-so-secret relief, and I think to Uthyr's also, if one were to judge by how she had been dealing with the fact of her uncle's marriage—not well—and by what sort of niece she was proving to Ygrawn—grudging. Oh, Gweniver was never openly uncivil to either her uncle or her new aunt—Arthur and I, alas, were not so fortunate—indeed, to give her her due, she was invariably scrupulously polite. But there is in that kind of courtesy a discourtesy that is like a slap in the face: Though Ygrawn for the most part ignored it, I know there were times when she longed dearly and deeply to box the Princess's ears, and restrained herself from so doing only for that such an action, however satisfying she might find it, would pain Uthyr far more than it would his niece. Uthyr, no fool, saw well the difficulty, and though Gweniver would soon have gone in any case, the King arranged that she should go sooner than she might have done otherwise.

Though our own departure a month or two after took place under no such cloud, Arthur and I also were sent out from the shieling—though sent nowhere near so far as Gweniver—on a secret and shadowed journey to the east.

We were more than a little fearful to leave the solid protection of Sulven's flanks, for since Daars had been destroyed we had known no other home, and if truth be known did not much wish for one now. No help for it, though, and we did not go alone: Our companions were true and trusted ones—Merlynn himself, who was to be both guide on the journey and tutor once we had come to our still unknown destination; and lads who had become our friends in Coldgates, and were like us being sent to train away from home—Grehan Aoibhell; the young Dyvetian Kei ap Rhydir; Arthur's cousin Tryffin, son of Ygrawn's brother Marc'h who was now the new Duke of Kernow; some three or four others beside.

Our journey was very much to the same purpose as the Princess's: For just as there were secret schools where lasses learn to be Ban-draoi, so too were there places for lads to become Druids, and the place we now went to was where we would begin to become.

After a fortnight's hard faring—much of it on foot, I am sorry to recall, for even on such a worthy errand we dared not take one of the precious ships to convey us—we came in sight of our new home.

Our journey had taken us almost due east from Coldgates, through the trackless wastes round the great inland freshwater Sea of Glora; but before we had come within sight of those shores we had turned sharp north, then east again and south, and it was a strange and scareful region into which we crossed at last.

Once, long ages since, all these lands had been the cauldron-floors of a chain of giant volcanoes, basins of liquid fire, each of them so wide that Caerdroia itself could have fit inside with room to spare.

For tens of thousands of years, the firemounts had slumbered; then one day, long before ever a Kelt had come to Gwynedd, they had roared awake, tearing their guts out in what our scientists hold to be the greatest natural explosion Keltia has ever seen. The very floors of the chain of craters buckled and collapsed one after another into the empty magma chambers below; then the rains and winds of countless millennia had worn down the walls, leaving a wide, hollow plain ringed by remnants of the mountains' flanks: Glenfhada, the Long Valley.

That was not all that was left: The firemounts, nameless forever, had perished, but the forces that had fed them were still moving, far below the valley's twisted floor—even after all these centuries too hot in places to cross on foot. There were sheets of black glass sloping into shining dunes, obsidian plains like miles of shattered lacquer, fissures that seemed to drop away bottomless down to the planet's core. The valley's length was alight with steam-vents and fumaroles; with scaldings, those evil bubbling pots of molten sulphurous stone, whose exhalations made your breath catch clawing in your throat; geisyrs too, splendid exploding fountains of superheated water—everywhere smokes and fumes and sub-terrene thunder.

Ever had folk shunned those lands for pure prudence's sake: the Long Valley was no place in which one might safely dwell. But that made it all the safer for us; Ravens called it Uffern, and avoided it like grim death—the which it had been in truth, not so many years ago, for an entire cohort of Owein's enforcers. They had been ill-advised enough to pursue a fleeing band of loyalists into the valley, and came never out of it alive; though their would-be quarry, I am most pleased to report, escaped and thrived thereafter.

And we hoped to do likewise, we who came there now, as we looked from across the valley's width at our new refuge. Called Bargodion, for it stood on the very edge of the ancient caldera rim, it was in fact the rim itself: A sharp narrow ridge of rough dark stone rose up like a ship's keel above a chain of scald-pools, and carved into the ridge's thickness was a Druid stronghold.

We were by no means the only ones to come here to study, though by compare to nowadays the college was no larger than a hedge-school. But the days I speak of were dangerous days, different days; and so that neither learning nor learner might be lost, the Druids scattered both: few students in each place, and many places, each of those places as remote and strangely defended as Bargodion.

Here it was, then, that Arthur and I, so at least we hoped, would become Druids made. We had been learning magic and lore all along, of course, in Daars and then after at Coldgates, taught by Merlynn chiefly and by others as we did progress. Having begun as most boys do who show magical promise, as sizars, or postulants, at the age of twelve, we were seventeen now, and had both just been advanced with our fellows to the rank of sophister. In the next year or two, according to our speed and scope, and if the Druid preceptors found us worthy of it, we would take our first initiation, in a rite that would be our first true encounter with the soul and heart of our Keltic heritage.

Though we covered up with a fine casualness, I think we

were all equally feared of the unknown rite to come. And rightly, for it is a fearsome thing; I know now too that women face a ritual just as much to be feared, when they come to be made sorceress and priestess according to the way of Nia. Perhaps their road is even more perilous—though all Paths are paved with danger for the frivoler, or the malcontent, or the idler, or the halfhearted—simply for that it *is* the way of Nia. She was of the ancientest Dânai, that race from the stars who settled Atland on Earth of old, there to build great cities and greater edifices of the spirit, and to flee—and many of them to perish—when by the working of their enemies they were whelmed in the waves. (Strange how often our bane has come upon us from the sea, and yet we cannot seem to thrive but near its shores . . .)

But Nia would surely have passed on to her daughters of the spirit many learnings lost to the rest of Keltia, even to Druids, whose Order her own son did found at her command. Brendan, mighty Astrogator though he was, had learned much from his mother; but he was still a mortal Kelt, and the knowledge he had sent down the years was mortal knowledge— or at least the most of it was, where Nia's legacy may have been far other. But whether it be science at heart, or magic in soul, or some blend of the best of both, it matters little: What counts for all in the end is how one may use what one is given; and that, here in this place perched on the edge of cataclysm, was what we had come to learn.

"And learn we must," lamented Grehan one day some months later, "else Merlynn will doubtless throw us over the cliff's edge; why else build this place overlooking a hell-pit?"

From where he sat with his books strewn like leaves about him, Arthur looked up and laughed. "All for convenience's sake in neatly disposing of failed Druids? Could be!" He turned again to the day's lesson. "Now the rann Thair is to call rain and mist in time of frost, while the rann Bith may be used for summer rain, and the rann Plenn is not to be spoken for a sevennight either side of the Sunstandings. Should rain be needed in such times, the rann Quyl—"

Kei and Tryffin groaned as one, but Arthur continued inexorably on, until we had been reminded of how we might summon rain any day of any year on any world of Keltia. Usually he was the one to rebel against the rote-work that was so much a part of this stage of our learning, but today it seemed he could not get enough of it, though the rest of us rebelled in our turn.

We had formed the pleasant and useful custom of studying as a group, the five of us who still remained of the company that had come from Coldgates a year ago. Arthur, Grehan, Tryffin, Kei, myself: We had been joined just recently by some new recruits, among whom one Betwyr ap Benoic seemed most of like mind with us, and as far as we were able we had admitted him to our circle.

Bargodion itself was oddly conducive to the study of sorcery: A year since, had any told me I would be learning my magic on the rim of a dead volcano, I would have laughed that one to scorn. Yet somehow the harshness of the lands about, and the knowledge of the limitless power that lay beneath them, seemed to underscore all that was taught us, a childish but effective demonstration of relative strengths. Today, beyond the window where Arthur sat amid his books, the vast vale was golden with smoke from one of the perpetually active fumaroles; not dangerous to us—there were sorcerers here at Bargodion could command the earthquake, hold the very lightning in leash if need arose; certain sure they could control an infant volcano—but impressive all the same.

Though I sought just now, had in fact been trying for some minutes, to command something perhaps just as impressive a natural force—Arthur's undivided attention—I paused a moment to look out over that view that never failed to enthrall. Far south and west of the golden haze that drifted over Glenfhada, a distant spur of the Spindles split, holding in its granite arms the Sea of Glora. If rumor spoke true, that sapphire sheet of water was not all those mountains held: A dún, a great hall of the Aes Sidhe, the Shining Ones, was said to be hidden somewhere among those pathless wilds. Not so ancient or mighty perhaps as Dún Aengus on Tara the throneworld, where Nudd the faerie King held court in splendor beneath the hollow hill, but a fair and high hall even so—though none I knew had ever been there, or beheld it, or could even say who was lord there, or lady.

I glanced again at Arthur where he sat so apparently absorbed in his studies; though I could tell from the set of his head and shoulders that he was well aware of my gaze, he would not look up to meet it. And just as well I knew why he would not: He did not wish to hear the rest of my news, and thought I would be too polite to interrupt his work and force it on him. *After all these years, how little he sometimes knows me . . .*

I had been gone from Bargodion this fortnight past, on a flying visit back to Coldgates, the first time I had returned there, and I the only boy so far to do so. But my brother Cadreth had been wounded in a battle with Owein's forces, far in the east in the province of Raen, and Tegau had summoned me back to the shieling, that I might be at hand should he not survive. Indeed, they had even sent an aircar for me, so grave had his condition been thought—though in that kindness I saw Uthyr's hand. His compassion would have insisted on the concession: He had ever been most fond of me, as I of him; too, he had done it to please his queen—and Ygrawn, of course, was still my foster-mother.

Whatever, I had been very grateful; happily, Cadreth was soon recovered, thanks to some skilled work by the healers and sorcerers, and the remainder of my visit was of pleasanter stamp. And *that* was what I wished to tell Arthur, and had been so far balked: I had given him news first of all of his mothcr, and of Uthyr his stepfather—lasathair we call it in the Gaeloch, 'half-father'; it seems a kinder and truer way to call such a one—and he had listened eagerly enough. But whenever I tried to speak of his new sisters he had all at once found urgent need to attend once more to his books.

Well, he would hear, will he or nill he . . . "I have seen your sisters, Artos, you know. You must return yourself to meet them before they are much older—they are the fairest little lasses I have ever set eyes on. I have never had younger

sibs—no more have you, now I think on it—and it was the
grandest fun to play with them, the King himself was creep-
ing on the floor with us . . .'' I had not been watching to see
the effect of my speech, dared a quick glance now. Still the
chestnut head was bent to the book—I sighed and continued
doggedly. "They are not much alike: Marguessan is lighter of
hair and of eye, and though they are both lively Morgan
is the quieter—''

Oft enough in our years together I had run up against that
unexpected stubbornness of Arthur's that was like no other's:
as contrary as a gauran, as adamantine as a findruinna wall.
No one could get other of him in such mood, and I but lost
my labor to try now. But what was the difficulty? He had
genuinely rejoiced for Ygrawn and Uthyr when word had
come of the birth of his half-sisters—his cousins too, come to
it. Perhaps that was it there? I glanced sidewise at Grehan; he
shook his dark blond head and shrugged, as baffled as I, so
that was where I left it, and left Arthur too.

But I put the problem to Merlynn later that night, after the
evening meal. Whatever demons had got into Arthur seemed
to be afflicting the Druid master also, for he was in a mood to
be as uncommunicative as only he could be. I tried vainly to
get him to speculate on my fostern's mood and mind, and the
more I asked the shorter grew his answers. At last in my
passion of annoyance I asked something I was instantly to
regret.

"Well, if you will tell me naught about Arthur, tell me this
then: Have you Seen for the babes yet?''

To my astonishment he answered me swift and straight. "I
have Seen; two dáns for two princesses. One I will not speak,
not now, not yet . . .''

"Then speak what one you would, or may.''

Unexpectedly Merlynn smiled, a warm, benevolent light in
his face. "I think I need not tell you; have you not Seen it for
yourself?''

I blushed. "Aye, well, as to that—I have Seen *somewhat*;
but I thought I must have read it amiss . . .''

He shook his head, still smiling. "Nay, you Saw true. You

and Morgan will be beloved of each other; you will wed in
time, and Geraint shall come of it, and he shall find that
which has long been lost.''

As he spoke I had been staring at him, jaw agape, my head
slowly moving from side to side in my wonderment; for all
that he had just spoken, I had Seen this fortnight past, and in
that wonder's grip I dared ask further.

''And she? What of *her* dán?''

''Morgan? She shall make for Keltia a greater protection
than all your swords together, though it shall not come save
through the bitterest loss in all our years.'' Merlynn shook
himself, or something shook him; I could not tell just which,
but he trembled violently from head to foot, and at once was
calm again. ''It takes me so,'' he said crossly, ''as if I were
only far-labhartha, the tonguetalker's manikin, and it speaking through me will I or nill I . . . But as to Arthur, let him
come round in his own time and do not plague him. We
cannot force his heart, and would not wish to try.''

I nodded, and rose to go, for by now the hour of curfew
was on us and my chamber was not close by; I would have to
scurry if I were to make it to my bed before the bell went. But,
my hand upon the hasp, I remembered something, and turned
again to him.

''You said you had Seen two dáns, athro—two dáns for
two princesses. Can you not say what dán is Marguessan's?''

Merlynn looked at me then. Perhaps it was merely a trick of
the light, perhaps it was truly that I saw that unspoken dán reflected in his eyes—but whatever it may have been, I drew myself up and bowed hastily and pulled the door closed behind me.
And once safe in the hallway outside, no matter the nearness of
the curfew-bell, I leaned against the rough stone wall and shook,
for what I had seen just then in Merlynn's eyes was death.

Not my own death—that would have troubled me not in the
slightest; as Druids we are taught how death is not the end but
merely a way-station for the voyaging soul, a bruidean or traveller's halt between the worlds. Nay—the death I had glimpsed
in Merlynn's eyes was Arthur's. And for all my learning, and
all my faith, I could not keep myself from terror and dread.

Chapter 16

*W*hatever I had seen, or thought I had seen, it was not a thing to speak of—one's dán is after all one's own, and though by chance it might be glimpsed by another still it is not something to be spoken aloud. Indeed, after a while, I had succeeded in convincing myself that I had been mistaken, conveniently ignoring the corollary: I had accepted the Seeing of my fate and Morgan's, therefore I should accept the Seeing of that which would be Arthur's.

Well, I could not, and did not, at least not so that I would admit; but it had lodged somewhere deep within, beside that other glimpse of Arthur's future I had had on that long-ago night when Daars had perished, and grief and glory ran on together like two yoked stallions, unchecked, unchallenged.

How even the glory was to come to pass was as yet a mystery, to Arthur as much as to me: But to their everlasting honor, neither Arthur nor Gweniver, so far as I or any knew, ever had any dark or jealous thought as to their infant kins-women; to fear that Uthyr's daughters might seek someday to supplant their cousins as the King's first heirs of line. Marguessan was elder by a full half-hour, and so she was her father's firstborn; but the law so laboriously explained to me by Merlynn still held, and neither Marguessan nor her sister could alter it even if they would. Gweniver remained Tanista

174

by decree, Arthur Prince of the Name; since the senior titles
were already held, the baby princesses had been created
instead royal duchesses—Marguessan as Duchess of Eildon,
Morgan Duchess of Ys. Ancient titles of the House of Dôn,
and grand enough, but in the end as insubstantial as all the
other titles, even—nay, especially—Uthyr's own; for as Arthur himself had so rightly remarked, what point to squabble
over the succession to a vacant throne and usurped Ard-
tiarnas, when the shadow of Edeyrn still stood between in any
case?

So the time passed at Bargodion, ever to our profit though
perhaps we did not always see it straightway. After a time of
settling in, we had found our footing among the Druid masters and the other lads, and after our first year there I am
happy to say that our missteps were few and not overfar from
the Path. To no one's great surprise save, I think, his own,
Arthur was proving to be a gifted sorcerer; if not so gifted in
magic as the Fians at Coldgates had thought him gifted in
generalship. For myself, though I yearned for the years of
bard-school that would follow after this time in Glenfhada, I
was not far behind Arthur in magic, and in some disciplines
fairly surpassed him.

But the rivalry, though real, was friendly always; whether
between us two, or among Grehan and Betwyr and Tryffin
and Kei and the rest of our yearmates. I had not thought,
before coming here, how vast and varied the scope of Druid
learning was in truth. At Daars, and even at Tair Rhamant
long since, Merlynn had begun our teaching long before we
were even aware that we were being taught: the little cantrips
and the smaller divinings, such things as children might learn
without fear, though not as games nor playing neither.

Those pishogues made a firm seating for the real learning
that was now upon us: the greater divinings, like the
neladoracht, the cloud-vision, by which so long ago I had
seen Tair Rhamant destroyed, or the divinings by stone or fire
or nicksticks. And the great ranns also: the snaim-draoi, the
druid's knot, for binding without cords; the arva-draoi, the

druid's fence, for barring without bolt; ranns for healing and ranns for harm, for seeking and for finding, for blessing or for bane.

We learned too—at least we were taught, which is not always the same thing—the judgment that must ever go with such power; or rather the beginnings of judgment, for that is a thing that one never ceases to learn, Druid or no, from one's first conscious act as a child to one's life's end; and we all of us learn it even better thereafter.

I would not have you think that we were such marvels of students that our three years at Bargodion were one long road of glory. By no means: To be in pupilage is never easy or simple, and as we advanced from sophisters to the rank of inceptor—the highest and last before our initiation—our struggles grew with our knowledge, as we fought to bring learning into line with aptitude and will.

"Who would have thought magic to be such a slog?" demanded Tryffin, at the end of one more than usually trying, and tiring, session under Merlynn's goad. "Better I liked it when I knew nothing, and could do everything—or so at least I thought."

Rueful laughs, small and shamefaced, answered him; all of us had thought his thought, now and formerly. It is so with any skill, I think: Certain it is I have seen it so with bardery, whether another's or my own, or watching Arthur craft some delicate fair thing of silver or gold, or seeing Scathach move through a Fian sword-drill. The more a skill is studied, the less its natural ease and grace can show. Oh, the basic competences must ever be learned, how else can flair become more than mere sleight or facile smoothness? But once the ground-learning is well mastered, 'how' should never be thought on again. Who in first infancy considers the skills of muscle and balance needed simply to walk upright, or, later, what child thinks on the intricate combining of finger-play and mind-play that allows it to scribe words on paper? In my own craft, once the notes and strings and times and voices are learned, bards strive their best to forget them; for in that forgetting lies true mastery, when art is as unthought-of by the artist as breathing is by the body.

However, first must come the rules, whether they be rules of music or rules of magic or rules by which a babe comes to know that putting one foot before the other is the best way to get where it wishes to go. And for all his good-humored complaints, Tryffin knew it as well as the rest of us—which was to say by now very well indeed.

"Say you so, Tryff?"

Arthur had come up behind us all unnoticed; he had been detained some moments by Merlynn after the rest of us were dismissed, and though I shot him a questioning look, I saw naught on his face save his customary composure. But there was something more even so, and before I could open my mouth to ask, or even send my thought to probe his, he was speaking again.

"Well, however much or little my worthy cousin thinks he may know or can do, I have somewhat to tell you all from one who knows rather better: Merlynn bids me say that all we here have passed and have been found acceptable for initiation." After the instant glad noisy clamor had subsided a little, he added warningly, "That is not *all* his word: Also Merlynn bids us remember that how acceptable we shall be found in the end depends all on how we face the rite itself."

Yet even Merlynn's characteristic cautioning could not douse the excitement his other words had kindled, and we carried it with us through the nightmeal and our study-period after. But when I was at last in my own room, preparing myself for sleep, a tap came at the door and I looked up, unsurprised, to see Arthur. His face was clouded, and I thought I knew why . . .

"You are feared of the Speiring, now it is upon us, and of what comes after," I said, and after a moment he nodded once sheepishly. Well, and why should he not be; I too was feared of the rite that was, please gods, to make Druids of us. We had learned, in the course of our own studies, that the Ban-draoi rite of first initiation is in form of an immram, a sacred voyage, and the Fianna too, and the bards, have particular rites of their own; but just then it was enough for us that we were asked to face the Speiring—an ancient word meaning asking or questioning—and its sequels.

"More what comes after the asking, I think," said Arthur after another long pause.

"We have studied these three years past for just this end," I said, not knowing what he wished to hear me answer. "We are sorcerers in all but the final sealing."

"Yet still we might fail at that final test."

Ah . . . "Undoubtedly some will fail," I agreed. "But why in all the hells do you have this sudden thought that you might be among them? You have been high in the estimations of the masters, and yourself have been master of all the rest of us in almost every discipline and learning. Merlynn himself has spoken often of your gift . . . Artos, what is *on* you? Tell me."

It was not so creditable an effort as others I had put forth what time Arthur had been too shy or too sulky to speak out, but to my surprise—his too—it worked as well as ever, for he turned to me with a look as straight as a sword.

"Two things, then. The first—well, I have ever seen myself as a warrior more than a wizard, and this you know from of old, Taliesin," he added quickly, as if I might try to gainsay him. "And if I am for war, how can I be certain that magic is not for me simply one more weapon, a little more exotic than most?"

"You can be certain because it is both true and not true," I answered at once. "True because magic *is* a weapon, and has ever been; no shame in using it so. And not true because even a talpa could see that for you magic is far more than a simple tool; and not true still more because you will never wield it as a weapon unless you must—not until a day when it is the only choice left to you."

Arthur's head, that had been lowered as he listened, came up at that, and his grin flashed then.

"Therefore let us all hope that day is long in coming . . . but first let us answer this Asking."

*   *   *

I did not feel the hood being lifted from my face, only stood there stupid as an ulagaun in the glow of the torches, though the chamber in which I stood was by no means brightly litten.

Merlynn and other teachers had described this chamber to us many times, so that as I now looked upon it for the first time I felt that I had been here often before. Here were the tall crystal pillars that betokened the Airts, the four sacred quarters; there ran the inlaid ring of gold that marked the riomhall, the magic circle, upon the slated floor; and everywhere the sigil of Druidry—the double shields and the broken rod. I stared at it now as if I had never beheld it: a strange device, the rod passing between the paired shields like the letter Z or a levin-bolt . . .

I shook myself a little to clear and focus my mind, spoke to myself as to a fractious colt: *Taliesin ap Gwyddno, you are come here before the gods and the Brotherhood to be made Druid. Try then to comport yourself as the child of a chief and fostern to the King that will be* . . . The severity was more in the inner voice than in the words; whatever was wherever, though, it worked well enough—my trembling eased, and I dared to run one quick glance from one side to the other of the place in which I stood.

It was a great vaulted chamber upon the topmost peak of Bargodion's serrate ridge; for as the Ban-draoi have their holy halls deep beneath the earth, so the Druids build theirs next the sky, or as near as may be. Therefore was it called Ard-na-draoichta, Magic's Height; it was walled and roofed, not open to the heavens as are the ancient nemetons, and, save for the sacred sigil, its polished walls were bare of ornament.

As in all such places, a bench or low altar stood in the North. Before it now were gathered the senior priests, all white-robed and gold-collared as befitted their rank, while the newest Druids of all, those fellows of mine who had preceded me here this night, were huddled in a little knot in the riomhall's Eastern quarter. Arthur and some others of our friends had all gone before me to their tests, so presumably they were watching now from that Airt, and sending me all the help they could, or dared. But keeping my eyes resolutely averted from them, I drew a deep breath and began.

First came the nine-times'-measure: I paced round the circle's gold rim three times sunwise, three times widder-shins, three times again to sunwise, each pace stepped off to a beat of my own heart.

When I halted, it was in the North. A senior master, one Tannian by name, stepped forward to face me; he was high among the Pheryllt, and the collar gleamed gold at his throat. Though he made no move, I suddenly found myself unable to stir, every joint and bone and muscle and tendon turned to frozen stone.

"Hear thou the Seven Questions that the holy Brendan hath ordained thou shouldst answer, sith that thou be Draoicht in truth."

The ancient sonorous words of the High Gaeloch rolled out above my bowed head; when the questions came, they came from all quarters and all Airts, and not from one throat alone.

A voice first out of the East: *"What is the highest wisdom of man?"*

And with the greatest effort of my life I lifted my head, and strove to make tongue and lips and throat frame the seven answers.

"To be able to work evil, and not to work it."

From the West: *"What is the greatest folly of man?"*

"To wish a common evil, which he cannot work."

Out of the South: *"What is the worst principle of man?"*

"Falsehood."

A voice in the North: *"What is the best principle of man?"*

"Correctness."

From above me: *"Who is the poorest man?"*

"He who is not content with his own soul."

From beneath me: *"Who is the richest man?"*

"He who grudges not greatness in others."

And last a voice that seemed to come from within me, from all Airts at once: *"What is the noblest goodness of man?"*

And I whispered, "Justice."

And the voices were silent, and asked no question more.

And in the silence I stood shivering again. Though I had been drilled long and hard and often on those ritual answers, at the first word of the first question it seemed to me that my memory had been wiped clean, as a chalkboard may be by a pass of an arm. And in that sudden blankness it seemed too that I had had to pull the words up from a deep well, and I was cold and tired and a little short of breath. But the thing had barely begun, and the Speiring was the least of the trials I would face here . . .

My answers had won me a supporter: Tannian took his place at my left side, and walked beside me to the South, where the second part of the rite would be faced—the Seachtanna, the seven tests. As there had been seven questions, and seven answers, so now would there be seven tests, and if I failed at any I failed all.

I do not recall much of this ordeal; for ordeal it was and no mistake, to prove both body and soul. There was the Collar of Morin, that would tighten and choke the false swearer; the Adze of Mochta, that would burn the tongue of the false speaker; the Coire-fíor, the Cauldron of Truth, whose boiling waters would strip the flesh from the bones of the unworthy candidate.

I know now that no such tortures or cruelties would have befallen, save in the candidate's mind only; the Brotherhood is not barbarous, to cause to suffer or maim, and though at the moment of testing the pains seem most grievously real and terrible, they are but glamourie. But in those moments—as the Collar closed around my throat, as the tip of my tongue touched the Adze, as my hand went into the Cauldron's seething water—I thought very much otherwise.

Still, I felt a flush of relief when those first three tests were past—and passed; and I faced the remaining four with confidence renewed. Next came the Tre-Lia Mothair, the Three Dark Stones—though truth to tell only one of the three was black. The way of it was this: A small keeve was brought of fine sooty ash from one of the nearby fumaroles, and three small stones—one white, one black, one speckled—were buried deep within. I thrust my hand into the gritty ash, felt the three stones; felt one leap and quiver under the touch of my fingers, and withdrew it, and that stone was the white stone.

The Crannchur, the Lot-casting, was a like test with wood and water, and the Iarn-Luchta, the Iron of Luchta, was a third. Last of all came the Arisem-ac-allawr, the Waiting by the Altar: nine times round the black basalt altar-stone, then a draught of Cormac's Cup, that held the sacred water over which mighty ranns had been spoken. So I paced round the stone to stand in the West, and Tannian held the cup to my lips while I drank, and I was not dead having done so.

But nor was I done, not yet: There was yet a journey to be gone, and though it was not so far a faring as the Ban-draoi immram, nor so fearsome as the Fian's test of soul, it carried its own fears and perils, in a different place, in the lands of Dobhar and Iar-Dobhar.

Come with me if you come at all: Come first then to the Bridge of Dread; cross the sword-edge though it slice your feet to the bone and you walk bleeding in your own steps. But if ever you have given hosc or shoon, sit you down and put them on, and cross the bridge as you will for you may pass.

From Bridge of Dread when you have passed, come next to Tippermuir, the Plain of the Well; stand at the well's lip and see the water as it rises close and falls away just as you would drink, for you are parched from your journey. But if ever you have given drink to those who thirsted, the water will never shrink from your cupped hands but leap as a fountain to fill them.

From Tippermuir when you have passed, come next to the Dismal Plain, one half of which is so cold that a traveller's feet will freeze to the ground, and the other half the ground thereof grows grass like spears, to prick you to the bare bone. But if ever you have given meat to those who hungered, a friendly stranger will give you there an apple and a wheel, and following these across that plain you will strike a fair broad road, and that road will lead you home.

It takes longer to tell of it than to tread it, that Path: Before

I knew the time had passed, I was back among my white-robed Brothers in Ard-na-draoichta. And now I had two supporters: As Tannian stood on my left, so Merlynn himself stood now upon my right.

They were there to stand with me in the North for the thing I had dared and fared and fought to win: the oath-taking. It is not something I can speak of even here, even now. If you yourself have taken initiation in any Mystery School—and all Mysteries are the same Mysteries, on all and any worlds; that is the greatest Mystery of all—you will know, and remember, and understand. If not yet, then you will come to know in time, so be content . . . Thus I vowed, and was stripped of my candidate's gown, and the white robe placed upon me. I took then my place in the quarter where stood the new Brothers, beside Arthur and Grehan and Betwyr who had been made Druid before me, and together we watched Kei and Tryffin and the others who came after.

The initiations past, the next days were filled with leave-takings: The very school itself was taking leave of its students and its own location. It had been decided by the senior Pheryllt that sixty years in Glenfhada was long enough, and it might be unwise to press our luck any longer. Though there had come no word from the spies or even a thought or dream or Seeing that our secret place had been discovered, the masters did not care to chance it; Edeyrn had strange ways of learning secrets, and not all his informers were so easy to spot as were his Ravens.

For myself I was greatly sorry; I would be leaving in any case, now that my studies as Druid were done for the time being, and I would go to the bards with Elphin as had long since been decided. But in three years I had grown to love the Long Valley, and I had learned much here. Even so, before I came to leave it I was fated to learn one thing more, and it more staggering than aught else I had learned, then or ever.

The night before our departure, Merlynn called me to his chambers—a summons not unusual with him, he often did so, though never for any reason graver than this summoning would prove. When I reached his rooms I saw that Arthur too was there—again no very uncommon thing, we had often been instructed together, or reprimanded together—and I assumed, as I saw Arthur had already done, that we had been called by our teacher for a last private farewell. We would be returning to Coldgates, but Merlynn was to stay on here awhile, for purposes of his own.

I should have been more surprised had Merlynn *not* wished to see us again before we left: This would be the first time that the three of us had been parted. We had been together since Arthur and I were six years old; and save for those years at Tair Rhamant with me, Merlynn had been with Arthur since before his birth. For our part, we were well pleased of the chance to bid him a loving farewell away from the rest of our classmates: Here at Bargodion he may have been among the most terrifying of our tutors, but to us he was forever Ailithir, and we loved him more than we loved our blood kin.

Now he looked upon each of us as we came near, deep into our eyes and beyond, and for the first time since I had known him I found I could keep my gaze strong and steady looking into his. It was not defiance, but strength earned and strength learned, speaking without words to a strength greater and older by far. But I too was Druid now, and though I could not face Merlynn Llwyd as an equal, then or ever, I could face him as a Brother now always . . .

Merlynn saw this as he saw everything, and I felt the answering warmth of his emotion as he released me from his gaze and trained it in turn on Arthur. What he saw there must have pleased him as well, for he seemed to make a decision in that moment that he had not yet made when we entered the room; and, had he seen other in our faces than he had seen, would have decided very differently.

"I have a thing to say to you two that is not for the others to hear," he said abruptly. "Time is now that you must know who it is you shall face—"

Arthur and I exchanged a swift touch of mind on mind:

This was what we had waited to hear, had feared we should never know . . .

Merlynn looked from one to the other of us, spoke in a clear and terrible voice. "It is your dán to overthrow Edeyrn. I have Seen it long since, and as I have Seen so now do I say. The Marbh-draoi will be cast down by you two together, and by your comrades from this place, and by Companions you will have after—the Princess Gweniver shall be among them."

I felt Arthur's surprise and tiny flare of anger at that, though it did not shock me greatly to hear it, and it was almost at once forgotten in the blazing wonder of what came next.

Merlynn smiled; a strange, sad, tired, extraordinary smile. "You remember, Taliesin, you once wondered who it was that were my masters?"

"Indeed," I said. "I was surprised to learn even that you had any; and then you told me that those masters were the Pheryllt, and that you yourself were one of them."

"Aye so, and it was truth—if not perhaps all the truth. Though you did not then say, you wondered too, did you not, who was it that was chief among those same Pheryllt."

"I did so—" I began to answer, and then the answer answered me. "*Edeyrn!* It is Edeyrn was, or is, that chief!"

"And you claim you have no Sight to speak of!" For a moment Merlynn looked on me with fond indulgent pride, then he grew grave again. "Aye, it is Edeyrn, right enough . . . The Pheryllt have been since the days of the holy Brendan the highest of Druids, the teachers and trainers of those who would themselves be Druids, the keepers of the deepest knowledge. And of the Pheryllt the Ro-sai, the Great Teacher, is the highest and wisest of all. So Edeyrn was, before his error—"

"Error!" gasped Arthur. "Do you call it so?"

Merlynn nodded once. "I did then, and I do now; a greater and ghastlier error than most, for which in time he will answer, and his correction—which he shall judge upon himself, as does any soul before Kelu—shall be the match of that failing. For when any sorcerer, man or woman, turns entirely

to the Darkness it is an evil day; when one of such excellence
does so, how much worse for all . . . You will see now why
our task to unseat him has been so long and bloody a battle;
and also we had not the needed tools to our hand, not until
now. But there is one thing more: Have you never wondered,
either of you, how comes it that the Marbh-draoi has ruled
Keltia for nigh on two hundred years, and yet has aged in
bodily appearance perhaps two decades only, still seeming as
a man of sevenscore years or nearabouts?''

"All Keltia has wondered," said Arthur. "It cannot be a
fith-fath."

"It is no fith-fath. Listen while I tell you: Edeyrn is
human, right enough, but half his blood is the blood of the
Sidhe."

I heard Arthur's long catch of indrawn breath; for myself,
as Merlynn spoke I think I had begun to guess a little what
the truth might be—but I was still shocked to my bones to
hear it said.

"Of the *Sidhe*!" said Arthur. "But *how*?"

"His father was Rhûn, as he gives out; that part of it is
true. A mortal Kelt, a worthy enough man; lord of a small
dúchas in Moymore on Tara, far from the Hollow Mountains
whence *she* came: the Queen Seli, wife to Nudd that reigns as
King from his throne in Dún Aengus beneath the Hill of Fare.
She it is who is mother to Edeyrn."

The silence in the chamber was profound, and after a
moment Merlynn continued.

"The Shining Folk are not so unlike to us after all, it
seems; they too grow bored with duty, and quarrel with their
mates, and run away from home, and do the wrong thing—
Seli did all these, and when at last she repented of her
wildness and returned to Dún Aengus where Nudd took her
gladly back again, she brought with her another son—Rhûn's
son—a boy called Edeyrn. This then is how he can grow
older and yet not grow old—because of his half-faerie blood.
And that blood too has made him privy to magics even we of
the Pheryllt know naught of—"

"Then if he is brother to the Sidhe, and has magics we may

not master," cried Arthur, "how may it be that he can be brought down?"

"*You* shall bring him down," said Merlynn, his dark eyes alight now and burning into Arthur's; I was for the moment forgotten, and very glad I was to be so. "You shall be High King in the end; but first you shall learn war with the Fianna, and when the time comes for it you shall go to Loch Bel Draccon, to the Forest in the Sea, and there take the sword Llacharn from the hand of the Lady of the Loch. It will not be the sword to destroy the Marbh-draoi—that task is for another, greater Weapon—but it will serve to begin the work. It will serve."

And Arthur looked back at him unflinching and undoubting, and I saw the fire pass from Merlynn's eyes to his.

Chapter 17

Whether it was that Merlynn had set some sort of unperceived rann upon us to rein our tongues, or simply that we were too shy or too awed to speak of it even between ourselves, neither Arthur nor I, for long thereafter, uttered so much as a syllable of comment as to that fate of his Merlynn declared that night.

At least part of our awe and hesitance surely came from the fact that, to my best knowing, it was the first time that any in place to know *had* said as much to him it concerned most closely: that Arthur Penarvon would one day be Ard-rígh of Keltia. Oh aye, it had been hinted at and muttered of and decreed in clouded pronouncements, to me and to others; but until that last night in Bargodion, none before had ever said it straight out to that future King himself.

But if we did not speak of it, then surely we thought of it: At least I know I did, and knowing Arthur I have no doubt but that he thought much upon it. It bore upon him more than anyone—though I daresay that by now he was growing used to grand destinies being surprisingly revealed—and he would be less than himself did he not think on it, and what it meant for him as well as for Keltia.

But, as I said, we said naught of it; and by the next morning we were on our way back to Coldgates, for the most part the same small band that had come thence three years since. For now would come that time for which Ygrawn and Gorlas and Merlynn had begun long since to prepare us: that time when Arthur and I must be apart.

We had known of course that such a time must come, but the knowing would not make it any the less painful at parting. He would go to the Fians with Scathach and Berain, and I to the bards with Elphin, and save by purest chance we would not see each other for some years. Then he should be a Fian, and I a true bard; and together we would return, later, to the sorcerers—to the Pheryllt—to study for the rank of master-Druid. Cold comfort: But we clung to that future as to a talisman or sacred relic; in the days that followed, very often it would be all we each of us had to hearten us.

For the moment, there was the reprieve of time at Coldgates: time in which I met for the first occasion since my childhood my sisters Shelia and Rainild, renowned warriors in the fight against Owein. Time too in which Arthur met for the first time ever his sister-cousins Marguessan and Morgan, now well-grown three-year-olds, merry and handsome and clever as otters.

We greeted again with joy Uthyr and Ygrawn, and received their royal blessings; the Princess Gweniver was not in the shieling, but still studying with the Ban-draoi preceptresses on Vannin. Such had her talent proved for sorcery that it had been decided, with Uthyr's consent, to keep her on for one more year after her initiation, so that she might take then the Domina year that was usually put off until later. When she did return to Coldgates, she would return as a high priestess of her order; a distinction of achievement that would not fall to Arthur and myself in our own order for some years yet. We were both a little pricked in our vanity, I think, but mostly we were relieved; any cause that kept Gweniver out of Arthur's path was cause for delight for both of us—and doubtless for Gweniver herself as well.

Any road, three months later—though it seemed a bare three weeks—we departed Coldgates on our separate paths, to learn of life beyond the shelterings of shieling and Druid-school, in the other Keltia, that secret Keltia that flourished in Edeyrn's despite.

Arthur was first to leave, gone one morning of late summer to a hidden Fian camp far to the south in the mountains of central Arvon, a bare fifty lai from the ruins of Daars, deep in the Grain Valley Range. And I myself went off only a day or two later, companioned by my much-loved Elphin, to a bardic hedge-school that had survived two centuries of the Marbh-draoi's seeking to destroy it.

Elphin himself had been trained there, though it did not stand now where it did then, or where it would next year. For only by sheer mobility had the bard-school lasted those two hundred years: Bargodion, safe hid in the sulphurous wastes of the Long Valley, had been untroubled for six decades, and would most like have been as safe for sixty decades more. But Tinnavardan, House of Bards, had enjoyed no such permanence.

Its very name reflected its rootlessness: Usually such training schools are called after some natural feature of the land surrounding—Bargodion, named for the volcanic ridges of Glenfhada; or Scartanore, the ancient Ban-draoi mother-house on Erinna, long since closed by Edeyrn, that is called 'Thicket of Gold' for the stands of goldenbirches that grow upon its hill; and so on. The one constant Tinnavardan could claim was that still it survived and thrived, despite all Edeyrn's grim seeking; and despite its perpetual wanderings—it changed its hidden location on average every two years or so—still it managed to turn out trained bards to meet all the Counterin-surgency's needs.

For bards in these days were not only reciters of lore but keepers of records and teachers of the ancient ways of Keltia; and, aye, spies—and the secret schools must produce men and women who could do all with equal ease.

Bards too that would pass Edeyrn's scrutineers: And that was no small or easy matter. For one thing, one must appear less learned than was in fact the case; and must conceal one's loyalties to the Counterinsurgency above all, for another—many lives were the stake played for here. But only by passing such scrutiny could one be licensed to practice openly as a bard, and for most of us that was the desired end.

Coming and going freely throughout Keltia, as almost no others were permitted to do these days save Ravens and Edeyrn's own bent Druids—bards were the lifeline of the Counterinsurgency, passing information from world to world. But whether one aimed to take a place as house poet with a noble family, or to be a journeyman teacher of children, or an anruth—a wandering bard playing for hire in the halls of the mighty—one was required to withstand examination by the Raven commander of the district, and after that a testing by one of Edeyrn's pet Druids.

A fairly daunting prospect: But thanks to the training I had just completed at Bargodion, I had less fear of facing that Druid, whoever he might be, than by all rights I should have had; it would be a simple matter—or so I prided myself—to hoodwink some creature of Edeyrn's. After all, was I not a *true* Druid? And my inquisitor, chosen by random chance, whoever was available and at hand, was most surely not . . . And as to fooling a Raven, well, how hard could *that* be?

"I will tell you how hard," said Elphin severely, having heard me boast one time too often. "Do not ever again make the mistake of thinking Edeyrn's servants to be poor stupid spaniels, easily duped by any plausible lie. Many of them may well be, and perhaps even most are; that does not mean that in your labors for the Counterinsurgency you shall always be fortunate enough to encounter only the stupid ones. Edeyrn would not have so tight a grip on Keltia's throat without strong help: Very many of those who are loyal to him, whatever their personal motive, are cunning ambitious coggers, and cleverer folk than you have been caught ere now." He gave me a reinforcing stare. "I mean this, Taliesin: Never underestimate our enemy, or overestimate your own ability to outfox him."

Chastened, I muttered some sort of apology, and Elphin nodded acceptance. We had been travelling from Coldgates for many days now, moving mostly by night through the Mains of Gwynedd, those wide, unpeopled lands that lie west of the Sea of Glora. Though my companion had still not divulged to me the precise present location of Tinnavardan, I had guessed, from the general heading of our course, that it was sited just now in the great woods that cover most of the province of Sarre. Too close to Owein's westermost strongholds for my liking; but the Raven forces seemed to have no wish to clear out the forests—having learned through prior ventures the cost of such undertaking—and so the school was just now safe, or as safe as any other place on the planet.

It was also near to Arthur's new home—two hundred or so miles east—but my secret, cherished hopes of visiting my fostern were dashed early on.

"Out of the question," said Elphin when I put forth my first shy suggestion, hoping against hope, that I might do so; or even, failing that, that Arthur might some time come to Tinnavardan. Seeing the stricken look that must have been on my face, he relented a little—but only a little.

"It is truly not possible, Talyn, do you see," explained Elphin kindly. "He will be far too taken up with his Fian training to be stravaiging round the countryside on visits. Come to that, so will you be busy. This is no game-time for either of you: Arthur now is receiving the kind of training that his talents merit, and that training and those talents together may prove in time to be the saving of Keltia. Would you endanger that simply to see him?"

"He is not like others, I know that; who knows it better? I would not distract him from his labors." I was a little stung that Elphin should think me ignorant of my fostern's gifts and dán, though I spoke nothing more than that.

But Elphin smiled as if he knew all the truth. "I know well you know it; and does Arthur in the end come to be Keltia's savior, he will not become so without you by him."

At that my patience broke, and I snapped out the words in anger and annoyance.

"Say you so? I have been hearing this from Merlynn and Ygrawn and Scathach and, aye, yourself, and gods know who else—for *years* have I been hearing it, and no one can give me the smallest scrappet of base for it other than 'it has been Seen' or 'it is dán' or any of a halfscore other reasons just as air-drawn and foam-founded as those.''

Elphin drew his fingers over his bearded chin. "You have true doubts, then, as to either—your dán or Arthur's?''

The tone, and the implied judging that lay behind it, shamed me, and after a moment I shook my head. "Nay—not *doubts*, just so, athro, but—''

"—but questionings, and wonderings, and the need for assurances that are not mere words alone.'' He did not seem troubled, nor did he speak to mock my doubts. "Well, Talyn, I cannot give you those, nor can anyone among us, not even Merlynn himself. But perhaps you may find Edeyrn a solider source for belief than any of us you rail against.''

I stared at him, as he sat on the other side of the little quartz-fire on which we had cooked our meal, and which we now huddled near for warmth in the chill evening.

"Edeyrn!'' I said at last. "How could he be—''

"Because if *he* believes, then must not you believe also? Consider: He murdered your father and destroyed Gwaelod, for many reasons but among them the hope to drown you along with the province; he sent Ravens—aye, Ravens, I said; Perran was not the only one by any means—to search you out all over Gwynedd. Once your survival was confirmed, he gave orders that Daars too should be destroyed, thinking to kill two whelps with the same spear, before they should be sufficiently grown to cause him trouble. And not you and Arthur only: Though he has long known of your hands in his downfall, he has Seen others' also—why think you that Leowyn, and Amris before him, died as they did?''

"King Leowyn's death was sheer mischance, Gweniver herself told me so,'' I stammered, my mind reeling. "Was it not, then? And Prince Amris—Merlynn said that he was slain while on some mission for the Counterinsurgency.''

"True enough, as far as it goes.'' Elphin put his hands behind his head and leaned back against his pack. Above him the cloudy sky began to darken with the setting of the unseen sun. We were sleeping rough for the third night straight, there being few loyalists in these parts to give shelter to a pair of travelling rebels—few folk of any sort, which was why Elphin had chosen this route.

"Leowyn's death was mischance only for that Edeyrn did not know of it when it happened, nor had he ordered it just then," he said after a pause. "But Edeyrn *had* ordered it, make no mistake, aye, and Amris's death as well. And both deaths were of a piece with Gwaelod, and your father's slaying, and Perran's coming to Daars, and the hunt for you and Arthur—oh aye, the Marbh-draoi knows you both well! Understand then, Talyn: All our lives are at risk in this, that is the choice we make; but *we* are hunted only as renegades to the Marbh-draoi's rule. You and Arthur—aye, and Gweniver, and Morgan and Marguessan now too—are hunted because you are who you are.

"Edeyrn knew *you* yet lived in spite of his efforts, and he would rather have you taken or slain than all six of your sibs. Gweniver—well, she is acknowledged heir to Uthyr, and that is cause enough right there; the same too for the lasses. As for Arthur, Edeyrn knew that Amris had fathered a son, and that that son lived and prospered. But he did not know where that boy might be, or even who was his mother; and Merlynn so managed it that all Gwynedd, and even the Marbh-draoi for many years, believed Arthur to be Gorlas's son. Though he might have suspected otherwise, Ederyn could prove naught; and so we were safe in Daars for as long as we were."

I stirred in my cloak. "Then how came it that Daars fell and Gorlas was killed? Did Edeyrn learn he had been cozened all those years?"

"We still do not know," admitted Elphin with a sigh. "There must surely have been some treachery in it—at least Scathach and I have ever thought so, though we had no proof then and none now—but it may be simply that as Arthur and you became presences more easily discerned by magical Sight, Edeyrn was able to see you more and more clearly."

This was no comforting news, and I pondered it awhile in

silence. "If that is how he found us out," I began, then hesitated. "Then by logic we should be hidden from him again, now we are both Druids and well able to shield ourselves, as we could not before."

Unexpectedly Elphin laughed, but not at my words or at me. "I should say so! At the least let the old bodach run his nose up against it, does he try to sniff you out again . . . and I daresay Merlynn will have arranged somewhat as well."

"And if it was not Sight but treachery after all?"

This time there was an edge of ice to my teacher's laugh. "Then let the traitor run up against our swords, Scathach's and mine and some others' . . . But enough of talk for now. Smoor the fire, and get what rest more you can. We must be afoot again before middlenight, and we have still a long way to go."

At dawn one day in our fourth week of journeying, we sighted a dark smudge on the horizon to the south, on the edge of the endless plain. Far to the west the Arvon mountains stood grape-blue in the dawnlight, save where the sun's rays touched their tips with gold, and between us and that sun stood the lowering black bulk of the lone mountain Cruach Agned, its three horns sharp against the brightening sky.

Elphin paused, and took a flask from his pack to drink and fill again from the stream that ran by our feet. I did the same, and putting my own flask away I pointed southward.

"What is that lies there?"

"That is where we are bound: Corva Wood, present home of Tinnavardan and still a day's march off. But we are near enough to dare travel by daylight in these parts, so what say you? Do we sleep now and go on again by night as usual, or walk on and come to Corva in time for a late supper?"

I instantly elected to go on now, as I was not in the slightest sleepy and heartily bored with nightmarches; and Elphin was pleased with my willingness to continue. Doubtless he was right about us being safe in travelling by day hereabouts: The land that lay between Agned and the first fences of Arvon was open but much broken—rolling uplands crossed by three major rivers and a myriad of feeder streams, all racing down to the plain from the heights to east and west. Few Ravens ever bothered to patrol here; it was thought in Coldgates that Owein's strategists trusted on the rough terrain, boglands and many watercrosses to keep any Counterinsurgency troops from passing this way.

Still, the region was not left all ungarrisoned: The great stronghold of Ravens' Rift stood on the far side of Agned, a good fifty miles from where we now walked. Guarding the main pass that led like a narrowing funnel down out of the central plains, Ravens' Rift held the main road—the only real road, all others were mere tracks—stretching southeastward to Caer Dathyl, and the other towns of that region strong for Owein. But we seemed safe enough as I looked round; and, for all my Druidry, no hand of prescience caught at my cloak.

As we headed south again at a steady pace, I cast round constantly for any feel of danger threatening; finding none, I fell into that mode I had been 'customed to use of old, a kind of walking trance, learned long since, when Ailithir that was Merlynn Llwyd and the six-year-old that was myself had walked another long secret southward path.

Much had changed since that journey nearly fourteen years ago; pleased though I was with those changes, I found myself wishing that my father could have lived to share them with me, and that thought led me inexorably on to thoughts of my mother. I thrust a hand inside my tunic, to touch the small flat gold case that hung on its gold chain against my chest. Arthur had crafted both case and chain for me, for birthday-gift one year at Coldgates: The case held, and was wrought in likeness of, the hawk's feather my father had given me on our parting in Tair Rhamant, that my mother had given to him. Never since my fostern had hung it round my neck had I removed it, save for my initiation as Druid, when all metal must be removed from the person—it was the last thing I shed before the rite, and the first I put on again after.

I closed my fingers now round the case, feeling the delicate chasing of the gold, the rock crystal that covered the feather within, taking comfort from the three living presences I sensed in it: Gwyddno, Medeni, Arthur. The strength that came to me from them made the road easier, so that I followed unwearied the tall figure of Elphin striding ahead, and steadily the shadow that was Corva Wood drew ever nearer.

We reached the eaves of the forest before nightfall, as Elphin had predicted. By this time I was very weary indeed, for over the last miles my companion had pressed the pace rather harder; but we had still some way to go into the wood itself.

"I know you are tired, Talyn," said Elphin over his shoulder, "but we will sleep safer and softer at Tinnavardan than on a bed of leaves and tree-roots. If you can go on, let us do so for any sake."

I said no word, wishing to conserve the few rags of energy I yet possessed, but he must have sensed my agreement, for we went on in deeper among the trees for another hour or two.

Though I had heard much of Corva Wood, I had never before been in it or even near it. A hundred miles from east to west, and near half that north to south, it was one of the oldest forests on all Gwynedd, most of it still virgin first-growth, the trees huge-trunked and towering, the forest floor thick with the detritus of centuries of leaf-fall. It came to me as we threaded through the giant trees, on a path Elphin seemed to know well though I could see no path at all, that there were few of the night-noises of beast and bird that so ancient a wood must surely be filled with. I thought that perhaps in my weariness I simply had not been paying much heed, but Elphin told me later that I had heard—or rather *not* heard—aright. Few animals, and no birds, dwelt in the deeps of Corva Wood; on the fringes of the forest there was creature life in plenty, but the farther in one went, the fewer the beasts became, until at last at the wood's heart there were none at all.

But we did not go in so far as that: Perhaps ten miles from the northern edge, I by then all but dropping where I stood, Elphin halted before a rockface that rose up among the clustering iron-oaks and redpines. Moss-grown and water-carven, the black stone of the ridge-spine stood a good forty feet high, and still the trees towered above it and upon it.

"Druimdhu," said Elphin with a sigh of satisfaction. "The Black Ridge—" He reached round and extracted a slim silver pipe from the worn leather case that hung by his side. Putting the pipe to his lips, he blew an intricate trill, then paused; and in that pause the silence of the surrounding wood became heavier than ever. But different: Now it was as if the forest itself hearkened to us, that great listening blackness holding its breath to hear what sound we might make next.

In the closeness of the silence, I shifted nervously from one foot to the other. Elphin gesturing me to stillness blew another, different, trill upon the silver pipe. Silence flowed back again; then came the sound of stone grating upon stone, splitting the shocked dark forest, and the sound came from the ridge before us. I gaped, weariness forgotten, as a crack of light appeared, running down through the rock, outlining a doorway in the ridge itself. Then the door opened, and light flooded out upon us, almost blinding eyes so long used to the forest dark.

There were figures moving now in the brightness, though my sight had still not adjusted enough for me to discern more than shapes. But they came out then into the night, and took each of us by an arm; and speaking words of welcome they led us out of the wood and under the hill, into Tinnavardan, the House of Bards that lay beneath the sheltering rock of Druimdhu.

Chapter 18

*A*pt as I had been to the study of magic, and content as I had been at Bargodion, all the same my schooling as Druid had seemed at times—to me at least—to lag and drag a little too much for my own liking.

This was not to prove a problem with my schooling as a bard: Indeed, if there was a problem at all, it was that there *were* no problems, that all went far too smoothly for one who had ever believed that for a thing to be well mastered and well won, it must be hard won.

That is doubtless true enough for most of us—and most often it was true for me as well; but that does not alter the plain fact that my years spent in bardic studies—there were to be fifteen of them in all—seemed no work worthy of the name.

I say this not to vaunt my prowess, nor do I mean that I did *not* work: Elphin and his fellow ollaves drove us hard, the thirty or so of us who had been sponsored to Tinnavardan by masters such as mine; nor was Tinnavardan the only secret school. For as long as Edeyrn continued to produce his false bards—even sullying the sacred precincts of Seren Beirdd itself with his half-trained, wholly bent mouthpieces—we in the hidden halls of true bardship must harden ourselves to counter him, and them.

It had not always been so, that bards must skulk and hide: In the early days of Keltia, and on Terra before, bards were among the most honored Kelts of all. Our art placed us next to royalty at royalty's own table, and the Chief Bard might wear as many colors in his cloak as the consort of the monarch. On a less lofty level, bards were much in demand as house poets and clan genealogists and teachers of the offspring of nobles and commons alike.

A fine thing, you say, to enjoy such standing; and so it is. But to claim that standing it is necessary to labor fifteen years together; and, should one then seek the golden starburst that betokens an ollave, a master-bard, to pass the most torturous of all tests of knowledge that any craft can demand.

Thanks to Elphin's instruction at Coldgates and at Daars, eight or so of those years were already to my credit, notched as it were into the flange of my harp. So did I enter Tinnavardan as a journeyman, or cliath as it is known, and began at once upon my term as institutional bard—to end, it was hoped, in ollaveship, to wear the gold star of master-bard upon my cloak as Elphin did now.

But though my teacher bore proudly that star of his rank, he bore it as did all his fellows on the inside of his cloak, beneath the lining where none might see, and that too was not as it had once been. It seemed to me cause for bitterness and anger, that one's great glory and rightful pride might be one's worst betrayer should the wrong folk come to learn of it; but when I spoke of it to Elphin he smiled in understanding.

"If pride were all it meant to me, Talyn, I had renounced it myself long since. Nay, it matters no whit how I may be seen and judged from without—look how long *you* thought me to be a mere rhymester and no bard at all, let alone an ollave, and it troubled me not."

Well, it troubled *me* to recall it, and my cheeks burned as I did so, but I persisted all the same.

"Yet even that was your skill at work, athro, to make me think it."

Elphin laughed outright. "I am well chided! But, Talyn, it is never the glory—as I know very well you know—but the love of the learning for its own sake. And had I not seen this love in you back in those first days at Daars, I had never even begun your training—nay, not had you shown flair and talent to equal Adoran's own.''

Adoran Tudur was a famed bard of old, called Aurllaw—Goldenhand—for his great skill and gift; traha of the highest order, for me to think myself capable of tuning my harp to the same pitch . . .

"Now it is I who am well chided," I said. "Yet it seems to me, athro, that I should not pride myself on that which comes so easy to my mind and hand. Druidry, as Merlynn will tell you, I had of force to work at; I loved it well, and had a certain modest talent for certain aspects, but it was pure slog and no mistake. Now this''—I spread my hands, to encompass the teaching hall in which we now sat, and by extension the entire warren beneath Druimdhu that was the bardic school—"this seems too readily won for me to be commended for its mastery, and I deserve no praise for it.''

I had never spoken to him of this before, though it had been troubling me some time now, and once I had got the words out I felt only a great relief, and glanced sidewise at Elphin to learn what he might think.

He had been listening to my words, and to that which had prompted them, with careful attention, that I could see straightway; and with that inner ear of his, the one that seemed able to discern truth from falsehood as surely and swiftly as any Druid truthsenser. Yet he had little magic save that which every bard learns as part of the discipline: Elphin's fíor-eolas was with him a thing inborn, as instinctive with him as breathing, as real a gift as his bardship.

I had watched him from under my lashes as I spoke, seeing his expression shift from the everyday into an attitude of attentive judgment as he weighed the undershades and over-shadows of that which I had said, and at the end of my speech he stretched his hands and flexed his shoulders and smiled at me again.

"Well. Doubtless the Chief Bard will use my guts for harpstrings when she hears that I have told you this, but time it is you heard it, and so I shall allow myself the pleasure of being the one to tell you first. And this is what you must hear: As Arthur will one day stand above all other rulers, so you will one day stand above all other bards. You are my master already, Taliesin, though you do not know it, and would not believe it did I tell you ten times over. But it is so all the same: You will be not only ollave in the end, but Chief Bard; not only Chief Bard, but for you shall be revived the ancient title of Plenyth ap Alun himself, and you shall be called Pen-bardd, and your name and Arthur's shall go together down the ages.''

Ah gods, yet *another* fripping prophecy, was there no *end* to the things . . .

"I do not want to hear about it," I said firmly.

Unexpectedly Elphin grinned. "You will, Taliesin," he said, still smiling. "And you shall."

Though my studies were to last almost six years more, I stayed this time in Corva Wood barely a sixmonth. For the safety of Tinnavardan lay in its flitting: It moved like the Solas Sidhe from wood to mountain to sea-lands to remote rocky isle, never the same place in twice ten years, sometimes the same place never again. There was no shortage of places in which to hide: Gwynedd had never been one of the heavily settled planets—indeed, no Keltic planet had ever been heavily settled, not by the standards of genuinely crowded worlds. In the years of the Theocracy, even such population as Gwynedd could boast had more than once been literally decimated, the survivors tending to cluster together for protection and reassurance, in small settlements such as Daars had been. In most cases the strategy worked rather better than had been the case with both my former homes . . .

But such clustering left vast expanses of the planet totally unpeopled; and to be safer still, folk whose very lives depended on remaining hidden—Druids, Ban-draoi, bards, Fianna, loyalists such as dwelt at Coldgates and elsewhere—had chosen the most remote and inhospitable regions for their refuges, places where Edeyrn's Ravens seldom if ever came.

The polar lands; the harsh cold arid steppes that lay below them; the bare islands in the Eastern Sea, where the winds were so strong and steady they had blown the very soil away; the thick forest lands of which Corva, though the oldest, was only one, and not the largest either; the burnt lands like the Long Valley—all these were cradles for Keltia's future, and if not easily dwelled in, they were gladly dwelled in, so that that future be assured.

The abrupt changes of habitat affected me less than some of my classmates: Accustomed as I once had been to living as did other folk in builded structures—castles or housen or whatever—I had learned at Coldgates and Bargodion to dwell quite happily in what were, after all, mere caves; and so I did not share the difficulty of some of the others in adjusting to life beneath the Black Ridge's sheltering stone, or in the tiny clochans of the isles, or even in the earth-houses of the southern steppes, dug like snuggeries into the permafrost.

Not that I would have much minded *where* I dwelt: My studies absorbed all my energies and inclinations. They may not have been any great struggle to master, and that was as I have already declared no especial credit to me; but they exerted on me a mastery of their own, a demand on time and mind and body, so that during my years with Tinnavardan I made no real friends. Acquaintances, aye, and good ones; comrades too—but no true friends, I was too taken up with my inner life in my art to have any attention to spare for outside matters. Even when it came time for my Teltown— that age-old ritual by which young folk are introduced, under the auspices of the goddess Tailltiu and the discreet guidance of their elders, to the pleasures of lovemaking—even then I begrudged at first the time and energy that compliance required; though once the revelry had begun, and I and a tall flashing Erinnachín had chosen each other out from the rest, I daresay I enjoyed myself as well as any.

Indeed, over the years there were many times I forgot altogether that past which had heretofore been ever with me—Daars, and Gwaelod before that—forgot even that Arthur my fostern and friend and the one I loved best in all the worlds was himself only two hundred miles to the west, or five thousand miles to the north, or whatever. But two hundred miles in those days was more daunting a journey than two hundred lightyears are now. We were in those times as confined to our homes and the townlands roundabout as were Kelts of old on Earth; for of course it was very much to Edeyrn's purpose that we should be so. Travel was for most of us a thing we dared not dream of, reserved as it was almost solely for Ravens and false bards and others in the Theocracy's good graces. Had I not been bard, I should doubtless have lived and died and never been more than a day's journey from my homeplace, as was the lot of most of my countrymen. As with so much else, Edeyrn had stolen the freedom of our own homeworlds from us all.

It was more than halfway through my term as institutional bard, and at one of our remoter refuges—far in the isles of the east—that I came to make that innovation for which, rightly or wrongly, I have been more celebrated than for aught else I have ever done—at least among my fellow bards. Not by any intent of mine did it come about, but rather, as most such happy discoveries do, out of boredom and chance and sheer expediency—in short, it was all by way of making things easier for my own selfish self.

That day I was supposed to be committing to memory one of the interminable lists of synchronisms—timelines of events and personages stretching all the way back to Earth—but early on I had grown bored with the repetition, and as so often when bored my hand had found its way to my harp. Without conscious intent, then, I began to play along with the lists I was studying.

Now bards had not heretofore been known primarily for music; though they often accompanied themselves on various instruments, and acquitted themselves well, the chief study of any bard had ever been words. Indeed, the memory-work that went into the making of a bard was little short of phenomenal, though I say it as should not. In our first homes on Earth, almost all knowledge was in the unwritten tradition, the spoken word; and little if aught was ever put down on paper or scroll. In that time, a bard's memory was often all that could be trusted, the sole bulwark between truth and falsehood, justice and injustice: In matters of inheritance, or relationship, or history, or simple entertainment, the bard's word was the final word. And for that to be so, and for the trust of the folk not to be betrayed or misplaced, the memory of a bard must be trained to unvarying perfection.

Some of us had less trouble with this than others, but at one time or another all of us would have difficulty, and it was out of that difficulty that my feat came to the birth . . .

As I played idly and unthinkingly to help my memory along, at some point something moved inexorably into place, and I found myself no longer chanting the boresome lists but making them into a sort of musical mnemonic. So well did this work that, once my synchronisms were set in my mind, I began to do the same for other rote-work, and after a few hours of this I had the beginnings of a great and subtle system indeed.

As near as I can make it, trying to recall it from my present distance of years and intervening events, it was at that point that the revelation burst upon my thought, and all I could think of was not how clever I was, but what a dizzard I was not to have thought of it before.

I have said that bards—true bards, not Edeyrn's creatures—were spies for the Counterinsurgency; here had I to hand a way of communicating information that could be encoded in the music itself. I could combine bardic dichtal, the secret finger-language, with any of the ancient lays and chaunts, to produce patterns that only a bard trained could detect and decipher. Anyone listening, or even watching finger-work on harp or pipe or fidil, would notice nothing untoward, and the sound of the music, and burden of the chaunt, would remain unaltered. Information could thus be passed along directly in front of enemies, even: Many times in the course of their travels bards would sing in the maenors and brughs of those high in the Theocracy, for in such places much could be learned by a clever spy who listened with more than ears alone, and saw with more than eyes.

But to pass on such knowledge to another bard was done at the price of great peril, not only to the bards alone. Now *this* that had sprung of my boredom might be a means to help reduce that risk to nearly naught . . .

I bent again over my notations, excited and alight with possibilities. When my scribblings seemed to read to my satisfaction, I began to play out some of that which I had labored to set down. I played for who knows how long, and it was not until I put by my harp awhile to ease my aching shoulders and wrists and hands that I realized I had had an audience all this time.

"Whence came that, Talyn?" asked Elphin quietly; he had, it turned out, been listening for over an hour as I had played.

"It is but a thought I had," I answered, suddenly doubtful, and shy of my half-formed creation. Suppose it was after all not a tenth so wondrous, a hundredth part so, as I had thought . . . I went on, a little defensively, "Bards have by tradition used music as well as words, if not as often, but I was wondering if the means of playing, the fingerwork itself, could not be made to serve another purpose?"

I began to explain, in a hurried rush of words and harped accompaniment, and as I did so Elphin's face began to take on that look I had seen so often on Scathach's in time past, when Arthur was explaining to her some new tactic or sword-trick of his own devising.

"And not only the dichtal," said Elphin after I had finished my explanation. "But the different instruments used— the music may be the same for all playings, but a message encoded into the dichtal devised for fidil-music would carry a very different meaning from the same message encoded to a pipe or a borraun or a clarsa."

I nodded eagerly. "And no outsider could break the code, for only a bard taught and trained would know the dichtal and its variants. Common folk would see naught, and false bards know not the finger-speech."

Elphin leaned back, hands behind his head, a grin upon his face that made him look scarce older than I.

"Do you know what you have done?" he asked presently.

"Something useful, I have hoped, out of my own sloth—"

"Nay, much more than that, bach! I mind you bade me never speak of it again, but this is your first step on that road we spoke of—and I claim for myself the honor of being the first to call you so . . . Taliesin Pen-bardd."

"Ah, do *not*," I muttered, embarrassed. "It is but a little small trick, anyone might have worked it out . . ."

"Yet until now no one ever has, and surely all the elements have been there for the mixing: dichtal, music, boredom . . . You will have to defend this before the Chief Bard, you know—I say 'defend' but defense is scarce the word, she will embrace this like a sister. It will speed news, and spare error, and most of all it will save lives. *That*, Talyn, is no 'little small trick,' and did you do naught else as bard for all the rest of your days it would serve to put you into the ranks of immortals."

"Enough," I said, shaking off embarrassment renewed, as the excitement of creating claimed me again. "Let us get down to some *real* work: If this is to be presented before the Chief Bard, in hopes that she will sanction its use, it must be as perfect a piece of bardery as ever came from any hand. My own life I would trust to less, but never the lives of my fellows."

And so we worked.

Sometimes—and any maker will know well whereof I speak—a created thing will create itself, and all its creator need do is guide it, provide it with the means by which it may make itself manifest in the world: a tale that tells itself, and you but the voice that speaks it or the pen-hand that writes it out; a sword that forges itself, and you but the one who tends the fire of the smithy; a song that sings itself, and you but the scribe to set down the notes. The thing is not made by you at all, but found.

So it was with my invention (if I may call it so for

convenience's sake). But though I knew from the start that it was not mine, others thought differently, and much against my inclination it came at once to be known as the Hanes Taliesin—'hanes' in our Vallican dialect signifies 'secret' or 'tale' or 'reporting,' and as such seemed a name most fitting. As for the other—well, I daresay my inmost vanity was pleased that the new code should be called for me, but that was not why I had made it—or found it—and it took me long and long before I could call it even 'Hanes,' and not some such by-name as 'system' or 'cipher' or whatever. Part of my reluctance was simple and honest modesty, but most of it stemmed from my conviction that this achievement was not mine to claim; and since I have been neither slow nor shy to claim otherwise, before or since, where I have created, I must have had the right of it here. The Hanes was a gift, and I but the one to pass it on to all its owners.

Any road, when Elphin and I deemed it fit to be shown, we brought it to Maderil Gabric, she who was Chief Bard in that time; and, again as Elphin had predicted, she fell upon it as a gift from the sacred Awen—an assessment with which I heartily concurred.

So Maderil worked with me, and Elphin also, to perfect the discovery, so that by the time my term of study came to an end, and it remained only for me to submit to the test for the ollaveship to which all my labor had been so long directed, the Hanes was already well established among the true bards of Keltia, and already working better than even Elphin had foreseen. As for me, I won my golden star in the end, not because of it, but almost in its despite; and for reward Maderil sent me, with Elphin, home to Coldgates, until such time as my craft should find need for me, and summon me to take my place among those who fought the secret war.

Chapter 19

*H*ome! It had been seven years since I had seen Coldgates—though I had in those seven years seen just about all there was to see of the rest of the planet, and been made bard and ollave beside. But then one day as Elphin and I went north again, there was Sulven behind her sheltering pale, wearing her summer crown of high snows. It was some weeks yet to Lughnasa; even here in the End-lands the air was heavy and sleepy and warm, though behind the languor it already bore the bite of coming cold.

When they say you cannot come again home they do not know the half of it: Home has changed, and you have changed, and there's an end. Though Coldgates was still the place I thought of as my home—indeed I had no other—I found it strangely altered. Or perhaps it was only my perceptions of it that were altered, for in all tangible senses save the smallest it was in truth little changed: The shieling itself was still safe and secure; Ygrawn and Uthyr, looking no whit aged, greeted me with loving delight; my sister Tegau was now a Fian general, and my other sibs too had advanced in rank; all my friends were well; no one I loved had suffered mishap, or worse. Yet still there was change, and I saw it most clearly when I looked on the babes.

But the twin Pendreic princesses were babes no longer,

they were young misses rising eleven years old, no more alike in spirit than they were of countenance. Morgan was tall for her years and slim of build—all bones, her mother lamented, but that was not so—with dark-gold hair and her father's direct hazel gaze, possessing that charming formality only a child can command. (And for all I had been hearing of our shared dáns and lives to come, there was as yet no way I could look on her as aught but a younger cousin or friend, by no stretch of thought as my lifemate to be. Indeed, the idea was most unsettling, and almost before I had recalled the prophecy to mind I had banished it utterly.)

Marguessan her sister was shorter and rounder, her hair a lighter, brighter gold, her blue-gray eyes disturbingly ringed round the irises with fine black lines. No biddable child, either of them, and their parents must be having an unenviable time of it: Marguessan was by turns a cool arrogant trimmer—aye, even at ten years—and a little scrat-cat; while Morgan, for the most part grave and mannerly as a child could be, could also turn wild and ungovernable as a spireling, that flaring storm of wind and fury offworlders do call the húracán. That would be a thing she must learn to master, and soon: Ygrawn, full of maternal pride and magicianly satisfaction, had already told me of her younger daughter's demonstrated flair for sorcery. The matter had been settled some time now, and soon Morgan would be leaving the shieling to begin her Ban-draoi studies, as Gweniver and others had done before her.

But for all the happy reunions, the one I had wished most, and waited longest, to see was not yet again in Coldgates . . .

"He has been near as busy as you yourself," said Uthyr, and my ear caught the warm burnishing glow of pride that lay upon the words. *So*, I thought with relief, *that at least has not changed; or changed only for the better if it has—Amris's son is still his uncle's treasure.*

"In a rather more perilous occupation, Lord," I replied, for even in the few short days I had so far been home I had already heard more than I liked to know of how my fostern had been spending the past years. In seven years' time Arthur and I had seen each other but thrice only; for safety's sake even our messages had been few and brief. Now I waited impatiently for him to return, and wondered even as I waited who it was that I should see when he came: my much-loved and long-absented brother, or the beginnings of the legend.

Ten days later, I stood in the gallery of the ship-cave, watching from a safe distance as the craft that had brought him up from the far south settled to the landing-floor, trying in vain to compose myself, to bear myself in a way that would chime with my newly acquired bardic dignity. I was an ollave now, and must behave appropriately, I told myself with some severity. Small chance: I felt as a borraun must feel upon being strucken, there was a shivering in my chest that all but shook me to pieces. Then the ship's main hatchway opened, and without knowing how I came there I was out on the floor, and then he was there too . . .

We ran together, flinging our arms round each other's neck, thumping each other on the back, embracing again, our words incoherent with joy, or perhaps there *were* no words, I cannot in all truth recall. But at last we drew away a little to study the other's face.

I do not know what he saw in mine save a few more years added—we were near twenty-six now, had known one another two full decades—and perhaps some wisdom gained; but *his* countenance was greatly changed, and I stared at him in wonder. Not simple externals—the beard that edged his jaw, the faint line of a scar across his brow—but subtle differences in the set of his mouth, the deeps of his eyes. And in the end they were not subtle at all but came from the core of his being—yet for all that it was still *his* face, and he still there behind it.

"You look *well*!" said Arthur. He flicked the golden star of my ollaveship that I wore openly here in the shieling, and that I had put on today to honor us both. "I see you have *done* well also, at least for one who has been holed up like a wounded stoat these seven years past—" But his smile, and what lay behind it, belied his teasing words; it was as if the moment's emotion were too overpowering for aught save brotherly taunts.

Not for him alone, either: I, master-bard that I was, was just as impoverished for the proper words, and fell back likewise on jest . . .

"Oh aye, and *you* come back as Ulkessar, mighty in triumph," I said through happy tears—and Arthur's eyes too were bright. "Or is it Alasdair Mór you are, weeping for that there are no more worlds to win?"

He gave a small disdainful snort. "Goleor of worlds—I have not so far managed to win even this one we stand upon. But even in our fastnesses we have heard of some masterful new thing called I think the Hanes Taliesin . . ."

"And even in stoats' dens we have heard of the reivings of Arthur the young, and what slaughter he does work upon the Ravens, that they might be fatling partridges, and he a hawk of the rock. We have both been 'busy,' as the King your uncle puts it."

As I spoke, I had put my arm round his shoulders—or as near as I might make it, startled to find how much taller he had grown—and he set his round mine, and together we went off to our old rooms. At my last words, though, he laughed aloud.

"Doubtless we have! But bards have ever loved to 'broider upon the fabric of plain truth—though I will not say there may not have been some Ravens the fewer to go croaking round Gwynedd once my sword was done with them. And not my sword alone," he added quickly, lest I should call him on his boasting, "but Grehan's, and Kei's, and Tarian's, and—"

"Mighty warriors the lot of you," I said, unable for all my bard's tricks to keep from my voice a feeling I had long time had, and which did me no credit whatsoever. His ear having ever been a quick one, I was certain he had heard it, but did not dare look to learn for sure, only babbled on to cover the break. "Methryn has told me all about it," I said, my voice strained and strange to my own ears. "And the King, and Scathach, and Merlynn—oh aye, they are all here. I have myself been here more than a sevennight now, and between the King on the one side and the Queen on the other, my ears are twice their natural thickness with tales of Arthur and his Companions.''

At mention of the King and Queen, he had shot me a swift sidewise glance, which I felt rather than saw, and now I sensed the look shifting somewhat.

"So they are called my Companions, are they?'' His voice shifted as well. "And why do I hear such a note of heartscalding as even an ollave cannot manage to control? There is naught and none can ever take your place with me, Talynno, though we be not together from now until Rocabarra rises."

"I know *that*," I muttered, shamed and shyly proud all in one. "It is just that I have been wanting to be with you and the others doing slaughter amongst the Ravens, and instead I am trapped in Tinnavardan wound about with harpstrings."

In his voice now I heard his smile, and the loving pride he had never been slow to show. "You do more for our cause with those harpstrings than all the rest of us with our swords. We have had more knowledge, and more certain knowledge, and more crucial knowledge, come to our camps by means of your new codes than ever before—and lost fewer lives to buy that knowing." Now the smile was gone. "Ah braud, I know well you have wanted sorely to be with us: I have wanted you there just as much, and so too the others of our friends who are with me. They have pressed me hard to send for you to join us."

"And yet you did not so." All my hurt and unhappiness was back, and my voice came small and tight and sullen. "Tarian and Grehan and Kei and Betwyr, and gods know who else—*new* friends—all *they* might be with you, but *I* your brother might not be."

Arthur was about to reply to this most unjust accusation when he was interrupted—indeed, almost knocked off his footing—by a new arrival.

"Artos, Artos! You are here! You are here at last!"

Arthur caught her up, swinging her off the ground as she flung herself upon him, her blond braids flying.

"Here's a graceless mannerless lass! No respect for your

brother, I see, but greet Master-bard Taliesin now as a princess should.'' He kissed Morgan roundly on the cheek and set her down again, and she hung onto the sword-belt at his waist, so that he could not walk away.

"Oh, Talyn has been here for *days*, I have seen him often— ''

I drew myself up with mock hauteur, and she giggled. ''A little more reverence, *if* your Highness pleases,'' I said loftily, vainly trying to keep my own face straight and severe as hers lighted up with merriment. ''Your Highness being an educated woman will doubtless be aware that an ollave may slay rats with an aer, does he so choose; and blotch the face of the discourteous. Think then what he might not do to an uncivil princess—turn her into the *Queen* of the Rats, I should not wonder . . .''

I made a feint toward her, teasing, a comic pretense of threat, and shrieking with delight she tore away again. Her sister Marguessan, who had watched all this byplay with her customary cool little smile, now came forward to greet her brother—and as afterthought, me—with a dutiful kiss, and then vanished after her twin, though at a more seemly pace.

"They are a proper pair, are they not?'' Arthur looked after them with a wide happy grin, and I answered his smile. Gone were the days when Arthur fenced his heart against even the mention of his mother's daughters: Though I myself had not been so fortunate, Arthur had in the course of his duties been obliged to return often to Coldgates over the past seven years, and one of the things he had managed to do in those years had been to become besotted with his sisters; as any self-respecting elder brother ought, to be sure, and of the two girls Morgan was his especial pet—and well she knew it.

So, speaking of such small matters as dear friends will do who have been long parted—and my jealousy that I could not have been with him set for the moment aside—we continued on our way, first to his chambers that he might bathe and change, and greet our faithful old Luath who was by now too stiff to do more than stalk from hearth to cookplace, and then go to Uthyr and Ygrawn who so eagerly awaited him.

But in all his torrent of query—and *never* was there one like to Arthur for questions, even Morgan did not ask so many, nor skip wider from topic to topic than did he—there was one who went unasked after and unmentioned, and it was not until many hours later that her name at last did cross his lips.

"Gweniver?" I repeated artlessly. "Aye, she is here, right enough; and what is more, she is come back from Vannin a full Ban-draoi Domina. Even your mother, Arthur, is impressed with her; she carries herself well, not proud nor boastful, and neither power nor learning—both of which are by now considerable—has puffed her up."

Arthur's face showed every scrap of the skepticism he felt as to *that*, and across the room Merlynn shook his head.

"Well, scoff as you like, but you will see soon enough. Any road, the Princess may soon be more even than Domina, have you not heard?"

To judge by the hawk-look, it would seem he had not; but the others who were lounging with us in our old grianán— Tarian, Kei, Betwyr, Tryffin, Elen, Grehan, some new faces from among his Companions whom I had not yet come to know—looked either blandly blank or hotly guilty, as they tried in vain to dissemble knowledge they possessed and Arthur lacked; and their efforts were grimly noted.

"And if I have not, I must be the only one in Coldgates who is ignorant. . . Tell me, then, if you think I can endure the knowing."

Merlynn's eyebrows, already near to meeting his glib, went higher still at the snap his beloved pupil put into his words, but answered mildly enough.

"There has been some talk in the months past—talk only— among some of the King's counselors that perhaps it has come time for Uthyr to name Gweniver Tanista in formal ceremony."

"What do you mean?" I asked over the sudden chill that had frosted the chamber. "Surely she has been Tanista since Uthyr became High King?"

"And you call yourself master-bard! Well then, ollave, cast your mind back over those succession laws you and I once discussed not far from this chamber: No heir to the Copper Crown, apparent or presumptive, is lawfully Tanista—or Tanist—until so named by the reigning monarch."

I was about to speak, but Daronwy—one of the new Companions, daughter of Anwas, the lord of Endellion—spoke up instead, from her pile of pillows by the hearth.

"If that is so, then Arthur might still be named as is his right, to follow his father."

"The Prince Amris was never King," pointed out Grehan with some annoyance, and Daronwy flushed a little; but his annoyance covered concern for Arthur's feelings rather than scorn for her observation, and she took heart to speak again, addressing herself this time to Merlynn.

"Even so, Merlynn-athro, he was the eldest of the three brothers—might it not lie within Uthyr's choosing, who his heir shall be?"

"It might," said Merlynn presently. "But do not look for it to happen. What must be, may be."

Arthur laughed. "Leave it, Ronwyn," he said comfortingly to his discomfited friend. "I am very well pleased to be Prince of the Name, since never did I dream even to be of that Name at all."

Some duergar seemed to have perched on my shoulder and was now whispering in my ear.

"But if it were possible to be more?"

Lucky for me I was his fostern, so that I got but a very straight look where any other would have gotten a clout . . .

"As Merlynn says, if it is to be, then it will be; if not, then not. Any road, if memory serves, no heir may formally be named to the Tanistry of Keltia before final majority is reached, and Gweniver—as do I—lacks two years of it. As for me, I have quite enough else on my hands just now—Llwynarth, and Owein, and about fifty thousand Ravens on Gwynedd alone—to fret over aught else."

Not for nothing was I bard: I knew a cue when I heard one,

and I sat up full ready to put forth another claim on what I had come to believe was my gods-given right . . .

He saw it and sighed, and got in first. "And before you try once more to plead your case, Talyn, the answer is nay and nay again. So do you not even think to ask."

I closed my mouth that had been open with what I was sure would be unanswerable dazzlements of logic, certain to win me my cause and place with him, and instead sat back, crushed. Why could I *not* be with him? Here were some of his daily comrades—most of whom were old friends of mine as well—and yet I could not be among them.

Over the past seven years—three if his learning years with the Fianna were taken from the sum—Arthur had formed friends and fellow students and strangers alike into a kind of train-band, a swift and silent striking force of a kind—and effectiveness—that had not been seen in Keltia since the days of Athyn Cahanagh. As she had done on Erinna, he too had established a secret camp—Llwynarth, they had called it, naming it after him: the Bear's Grove, deep in the Arvon mountains; as she too had done, he called those who joined him there his Companions.

And I was not to be one of them. . . Arthur saw the black scowl on my face, relented enough to explain a little more his reasons for refusing my martial services.

"Talynno, you are my brother, and I love you well; all here know you *and* your worth to our cause"—instant warm agreement from the rest, even those such as Daronwy who knew me only through him—"Also you are the inventor of the Hanes, and as I have said once today, *that* may prove to be of greater weight in the end than aught I or any other shall achieve by the sword. I honor you for it, and stand deep in your debt and reverence of it, and tell you plain that you would never have come to it had you been skulking in the hills with me."

"I might," I said sulkily, and caught his amused exasperation at my evil little mood.

"Well enough then, you might have! Not likely, let us say, but possible? Listen now: You are not the lad for what we do.

It is as I have said, simple butchery, mere Raven-slaughter. I do not much like it, but I will keep it up until by it I have attracted Owein Rheged's grudging attention. And then we shall meet in battle for Gwynedd, Owein and I, and it will not be I to come off that field the loser.''

He spoke simply and confidently, and looking round I could see that confidence reflected on the faces of his Companions.

"Besides," continued Arthur, in that tone of fine-reasoned persuasiveness I knew well from of old, "you are of ten thousand times more use to me as bard. As anruth, able to move openly through Gwynedd as none of *us* is able"—his arm indicated the room's occupants—"and after that, when you take up your petty place, it is to be hoped in the household of one close to Owein—you will be ten thousand times more use even than that. When I need your sword, be very sure I shall ask for it! Until then—"

"—until then just slinge round Gwynedd like a common tramp," I said, knowing full well that I was being sweet-talked and knowing just as well that he was right. "You make it very hard, Artos."

But I saw it as clearly as he had ever seen it: At Llwynarth I could do little save hang at his cloak-tail and make songs of his deeds. As a functioning bard, either travelling the planet collecting intelligence or sitting like a spider in some Theocracy vassal's court, where such information would fall into my webs, I could serve Arthur as few others could.

He saw that I had capitulated, with however bad a grace, and he smiled; and much against my inclination I smiled back.

"Do you always get your own way, Arthur Penarvon, or is it just that I am always around to see whenever you chance to get it? —Nay, do not trouble to answer; you have won yet again, far from *me* to cheapen your triumph."

"One thing that might make you more kindly disposed, Talyn, to your banning for the time being from Llwynarth."

The cool, amused voice was Tarian Douglas's, and I turned to her in surprise: In my self-pitying sulk I had clean forgot there were others present in the chamber who had been witness to my petulance. But, I consoled myself, we were all friends here, and had seen far worse pass between us, and would not mind. And for those new to our friendship, well, better they learned swiftly how we did amongst ourselves; and it was still well.

"Perhaps a summer spent training as a Fian would not come amiss," continued Tarian thoughtfully, glancing sidewise at Arthur and Merlynn as if for approval. "If you are to go round the planet doing spycraft it would be well to be as tuned to perils as your harp will be to music—and for you to be as fit to meet it."

"I am no warrior, Tari," I said honestly, though with real—and surprising—reluctance, for the idea mightily appealed to me. "Scathach and Berain will speak for that, from our days at Daars."

"As to that," said Arthur, and I heard for the first time the authority in his voice, saw for the first time how they took his least word as ironbound command, "let those whose business is war be judges. You and Fianship did not suit each other, that is true enough; but you are quick-handed and swift-footed, and any road, a summer with the sword can never be ill spent."

Chapter 20

So all my jealousies vanished like Samhain taish, fith-faths born of my own insecurities, and I spent a surprisingly pleasant summer being instructed in combat by Fian masters. My chief tutors were Daronwy and a new Companion I had not previously met, Ferdia mac Kenver, a cheerful sandy-bearded Erinnach. In the process of my re-education, the three of us became—in addition to respectful admirers of each other's particular craft—good and close friends; which, knowing my fostern's way, was doubtless exactly what he had had in mind from the first.

But improving my martial skills was also a goal of his, and he came by whenever he might, to put in his crossic's worth; we even fought a few touches ourselves, as we had done of old in Daars. But if Arthur had been my better then, he was now so far beyond me as to seem Fionn himself, or Malen Sword-queen, and our bouts were prolonged beyond three-stroke exchanges solely by his indulgence.

Even so, by grace of his holding back I learned much, and learned more from Ferdia and Daronwy and the other Companions who were pleased to add a hand now and again to my training. By Fionnasa, when the weather changed in earnest, the winds backing round to north and west, blowing gales of red and yellow leaves down through the passes onto the plain, I saluted my instructors for the final time, all of us most satisfied with the summer's result. I would never make a Fian, and I would ever be first to admit it, but I knew too that at least I might now hold my own against most Ravens that might cross my path; and that had been Arthur's objective.

At least with regard to me; he had other, and far graver, objectives that year, and it was those that took up his time and thought and energy. Uthyr had been ill during the spring past—desperately ill, as it happened, though I had not known it until my return to Coldgates. The news had not been kept from me a-purpose; it was only that Tinnavardan had been on the move, as usual, and since none had known just where a message might safely find me, it had been thought wiser not to send one.

Though the King was by now recovered, he was still worn and gaunt and tired, and Ygrawn, solicitous as a mother wolf caring for the litter weakling, was herself near as wearied as he. The strain told on her most of all, and there seemed little any could do to ease it: It was as if she had now three children to tend to, not the twins only.

But when I wondered, with a certain sharpness, why did not the Tanista Gweniver—the Domina Gweniver, returned this past year from her prenticeship in a hidden convent of her order—turn a hand, and more than a hand, to her uncle's healing, Ygrawn more sharply still bade me hold my tongue and my peace alike, and you may well believe I did so.

That did not stop me wondering, all the same, and I went to seek an end to wondering in the place I had sought such for years . . .

"There has been some—let us call it discomfortableness," said Merlynn, "between the Princess and your foster-mother the Queen. It is all to do with Uthyr, who knows naught of it, by the way, so see that you let nothing slip while you are with him. I know you go every afternoon to play to him."

"It is all I can do," I said defensively. "I am a bard, not a healer."

"And you do perhaps more for him thereby than any healer

has so far managed," said Merlynn soothingly. "I meant no criticism."

"Well," I continued, slightly mollified, "why then is there constraint between Gweniver and my methryn?" If I sounded puzzled it was because I was: Uthyr and Ygrawn had been wed near twelve years now, time was long past when Uthyr's wife and Uthyr's heir should not be friends.

"They *are* friends," Merlynn assured me, having divined my thought. "At least for the most part; and since Gweniver became Domina they have been better friends than ever."

"What then?"

"Time comes soon when Uthyr must name his Tanista—or Tanist—in formal ceremony." He tapped his fingertips together in the old gesture. "And there still remains that tiny detail of who shall indeed be named."

"That again," I said, annoyed that it should still be a cause of dissension and ill feeling.

"That again, and no nearer a solution than before."

"But why should it cause disharmony between Gweniver and Ygrawn?"

"And just who is the Queen's son by her first lord? A lord who I need not remind you had precedence over his younger brother?"

I was silent for a while. "What does Arthur say?"

Merlynn gave a small shrug, more in his face than in his shoulders. "What can he say? He attends to those matters Uthyr asks him to attend to, as does Gweniver. Otherwise he is too busy with the Companions and the beginning of the campaign against Owein to let it fret him, and too well-trained to let it be known openly how he might feel in truth. And all the more so, now he has begun to win ground in his fight."

I sat up a little straighter. "You mean folk might take his success in the field as a *threat*? To think *he* might think to lift sword against the King and take the crown by force?"

"It is not unknown, for power to be seized so."

"Well, never in ten thousand lifetimes will it be seized so by him!" I was momentarily blind with fury. *Gods* but folk could be stupid . . . I added presently, "Even did he not love Uthyr as his own—"

I stopped short, caught by the terrible irony: I had been of course going to say 'as his own father,' but Arthur had never known his own father to love him, though it was only through Amris that Arthur was a prince at all. And the man he *had* loved as a father had been, in the end, kin only through Arthur's love . . .

"That is plain to all," said Merlynn, and again his voice was pitched to soothe me. "And I promise you, Talyn, no one here thinks Uthyr in the least smallest peril from Arthur's hand . . . It is only that the matter daily grows more urgent and the King gives no clue. In little more than one year's time, both Arthur and Gweniver will be of age to be named heir in full law—though not just yet to rule—and Uthyr has been of late not always in health."

"Just how unwell is he?" I found the thought of Uthyr's death sharply affecting, sought the answer within and knew it almost at once: Uthyr gone would be my third father lost . . .

Merlynn shook his head. "No fear, he will be with us a good few years yet. Look how he was never as strong as either of his brothers—well, not in strength of the body—and here has he outlived them both. None of which diminishes, however, the need for him to declare his heir—or heirs."

I sighed. "It must be so, then, as you have said: that they rule together, joint sovereigns over Keltia."

"It must be," agreed Merlynn with a grave nod. "And that, I think, is a solution not they nor the King nor the people are ready to hear, at least not yet awhile."

"Impasse, then."

"It would seem so."

But I could tell by the look in his eyes and the sound in his voice that he did not *think* so; and, what was more, no more did I.

I had not seen the Princess Gweniver for near ten years. While I had been studying at Bargodion, she had been at Glassary on the planet Vannin training for a Ban-draoi; and when I had been off at Tinnavardan, she had been sent to still another hidden school of the Sisterhood, to become Domina, a high priestess of her order, and to serve thereafter her first prenticeship. Therefore our paths had crossed not at all in all that time, and only in the past sevennight here in the shieling had I met Gweniver again.

Had I not been Druid, trained to look past the mask of aspect, I might not have recognized her straightway. She had not altered so much in outward appearances, but rather in those inner sources from which all outer form does spring: the seeming taking its shape from the substance.

While Morgan and Marguessan had been changing from children to young lasses, and Arthur from stripling to warrior, and I from dreamer to bard, Gweniver had been changing more than all. Ten years ago, she had been still a creature of contentions, like any adolescent, lass or lad; half woman, half child, yet she had managed to be wholly royal. Now, royaler still, she was a sorceress as well, calm with power, confident, forceful, very much in control; and though she had not yet achieved to Ygrawn's wise and humorous detachment, she was well on her road to it.

For myself, I had neither qualm nor shyness in seeking her out: We had not begun well together, she and I, but since that long-ago afternoon up in the old watchpost, when she had wept and spoken from her sorrow, and I had watched and listened from my own, we had put away between us all our disliking and distrust. We were not perhaps the best and closest of friends, but we *were* friends, so that when I sought her in her rooms she greeted me with a smile, and bade me come in.

"For not every day," she explained, setting a chair for me by the quartz-hearth, "does a ríogh-bardan come to call."

I laughed and took the cup of ale she offered. "Ríogh-bardan only by default—the King your uncle will have no other bard near him, and any road there are in Coldgates but few to choose from. Thus do I owe my appointment as royal bard to proximity more than skill."

Unexpectedly she colored a little. "That is not how the Ard-rígh does tell it . . ."

I watched her as she set another keeve of ale to warm at the hearth. She had grown fairer as well as surer: Her beauty, like her power, had root in that deep, shining totality that grows from inner life—strength and skill, intelligence and integrity, all manifested in beauty of face and form. And the longer I looked, the plainer it grew; it, not she. . . The black hair and lynx-gray eyes and spear-straight posture were much as they had ever been, though now the hair was longer, the eyes clearer-sighted, the figure more rounded of breast and hip, with an assurance over all that had not been there before. It spoke of sensuality, and acquaintance with desiring and being desired; something that could be used as both weapon and defense.

And it troubled me, for this was something I had not foreseen: that I should look on Gweniver as any man might look on any woman, to find her fair, or that she looking back on me should return that finding—as I now saw she plainly did. And for an instant I panicked and despaired, for it would be a complication too complex to be borne—

Then I saw her smile, and I smiled too.

"Well, Talyn." It was all she said, and all she needed to say: Words and smile together carried amusement, and vivid regret, and a fine frank honesty. She would not deny her feeling, and she expected the same from me; but all else was denied, and that too she expected.

"Well, Gwennach." And then the moment was over, never to be repeated. We spoke for the next two hours as any friends might who had not seen each other for some time, constraint set by, to tell one another what has been seen and learned and known in that time of absence; we spoke as Druid and Domina, Ban-draoi and bard. Uthyr we spoke of, and Ygrawn, and Merlynn; of her teacher, the Mathr'achtaran Ildana; of Morgan and Marguessan; of Keils Rathen, Uthyr's war-leader, who had been her tutor in martial matters—and, somewhat to my surprise, in heart-matters as well; of

Elphin who had been my master in the harp and later my helper with the Hanes.

But all that time, as if by common consent, never once a word of Arthur. I would have thought, if I thought at all, that by now surely he might be mentioned, but it seemed it was not so. Yet I do not think, and did not think then, that we spoke naught of him: Arthur's name may not have been between us, but he was there all the same.

One night perhaps a fortnight before I was to leave Coldgates, to begin my professional career as anruth, or travelling bard, Ygrawn came to my chambers. Since she had wed Uthyr and mothered the twins, we had had few chances to be private as of old, when the Lady of Daars and her foster-son could share an indulgent lazy chat before retiring. Now it was Queen Ygrawn and Taliesin ap Gwyddno the King's bard who found time scarce for talk, but we were still ourselves.

She sank into the chair closest to the quartz-fire just as she had always used to, stretching out her hands to the warmth. Twelve years as Queen had changed her little; she was still slender and quiet and gracefully intense, but now there was a peace about her as well, a thing that had come to her in part from Uthyr and in part out of her queenship: that easiness of spirit one is free to show when one has achieved what one has long unknowingly sought.

I waited in our old companionable silence—so companionable a silence that neither of us thought of it as waiting—for her to say what she had come to say, and after a while she began to speak.

"I have a thing to ask of you, Talynno." She did not look at me but into the hypnotic shimmerings of the quartz. "It is a thing you may refuse as you do please, but also it is a thing I would ask of you and Arthur only. He has already consented, and I come now to ask you."

"No need to ask," I said at once. "What is it you would have me to do, mathra-chairda?"

Ygrawn threw me a brilliant smile at the name I had given

her: 'heart-mother,' of all our names for fosterer the tenderest and most loving of all.

"I expected you to offer so, amhic," she said, her voice deeper than her wont with her sudden emotion. "But listen first, and then say aye or nay as you will . . . You know that Morgan is to be trained as a Ban-draoi."

"I do so," I said, surprised at the turn of the talk. "I have seen her skills at work already; and felt them too, my sorrow to say! I had not been ten minutes back in the shieling before she had earthfasted me most firm and proper. She will be a most—exceptional sorceress."

Ygrawn laughed, a little sadly as it seemed to me. "Ah, the tactful tongue of an ollave. . . She will be far more than that, Talyn, as I know full well you have Seen, and as Merlynn warns me."

'Warns'? "Surely—"

"She will be no ordinary Ban-draoi." Now the amethyst eyes, clear as ever, were fixed on mine. "It seems to be my dán to give to Keltia children unlike any other's children: Arthur to be King and the doom of Edeyrn; and Morgan to be the mightiest magician since Brendan himself."

My whole being shivered and stilled. "I have felt it," I whispered. "And it *has* been Seen . . . But what have I just now to do with it?"

"She must go to learn, as I have said, but not to any common school. There is a place Merlynn has spoken of—"

"—and only there can she learn what she must learn."

Merlynn's voice came from the door behind me; I was not surprised to hear him, for I had known of his presence for some minutes, but what he had next to say astonished me indeed.

"She must go to the Lady of the Loch," he said, coming in and taking a seat between us. "No other teacher will suffice. And you, Talyn, and Arthur must bring her there yourselves. No other escort will serve."

"You have spoken once before of this Lady," I said presently. "You said that Arthur must take some sword from her hand—"

"In good time. But not yet."

"Well, who then is she?"

Merlynn and Ygrawn exchanged a swift, many-meaninged glance, and, for all my skill at interpreting, I could catch not so much as a splinter of its freight. Then Merlynn looked straight at me, and straighter spoke.

"Her name is Birogue of the Mountain. She is a lady of the Sidhe."

"Of the Shining Folk! And she is willing to be teacher to Morgan?"

"Indeed so."

"I have never heard of one of—*them* willingly to have to do with us," I said doubtfully. "Save for what you have told us of Edeyrn—" I stopped, cast a quick look at Ygrawn, for perhaps the Marbh-draoi's parentage was not known to her. But I saw from her tiny nod that it was, and went on. "But this is a different thing altogether. How can you know?"

"I should know," said Merlynn quietly. "She and I have been together these sevenscore years and more. And in the end, I shall join her under the hollow hill."

The chamber's silence went unbroken for many minutes. "And Marguessan?" I asked, when I spoke again. "What of her?"

Merlynn made as if to speak, but Ygrawn was there before him. "The learning is not for her."

All at once I had heard enough; more than I wanted to know of too many things, and I seized gratefully on the practical as a detail to save me.

"Where shall we go then, Arthur and Morgan and I, to find Birogue?"

Merlynn's gaze went past me, through the rock of Sulven that was all round us, and across many miles of dark air; he was seeing some far place, and a greater purpose even than this.

"To Collimare," he said then. "The Forest in the Sea."

Chapter 21

*I*n the dawnlight of a cold October morning, some weeks after Ygrawn's request and Merlynn's revelation, Arthur and I stood with Morgan on the shores of the Sea of Glora. The little waves lapped on the rocky shingle a few feet away, and thirty yards out a white woolly wall of mist came down to meet the surface of the water. It was very still, and none of us spoke.

We had travelled here from Coldgates, just the three of us alone, no guide or guard else. At first I had protested the plan, thinking such a journey too taxing for a ten-year-old child; but then I had remembered a worse journey far, made by a child younger still, and I had said no more.

For her part Morgan had seemed to enjoy it immensely: the riding, often by night; the secret ways through the hills; the grand, majestic country through which we passed. For myself, I enjoyed the faring near as much: I had not been so long with Arthur since our boyhood days at the shieling, and had never been so long in Morgan's company before; I was learning something new of her every hour. As the youngest of even so large a family as my own, I had not known many children well, so that Morgan's smallest quirks were revelations. She was very definitely a person of her own, cheerful and charming, self-aware though utterly unselfconscious, with

229

an unflagging interest in everything we encountered and anything Arthur or I happened to say.

Not that Arthur chanced to say much: He seemed pleased
and proud enough to play the role of protective older brother,
but ever since we had set out a kind of heaviness had clung
round him like a rain-soaked cloak; I could not pierce it even
with all my bard's subtlety, nor Morgan with her sunny
prattle, though even she sensed his mood—indeed, he scarce
strove to hide it, and that too was not like him.

So we stood now on the shores of the great inland sea,
waiting as Merlynn had instructed us, for the coming of
Birogue. And, waiting, I wondered yet again at my old
teacher: It seemed a thing reckless in the extreme, for mortals
to seek lovers from among the Shining Ones, and yet just
such a thing as he would do. I wondered too about the Sidhe
lady we now waited upon, and how her choice of mate had
been received among her own folk . . . But then my speculations died away, for the mist upon the water had shivered
itself and parted, and through the white rags now came the
prow of a boat.

Such a boat as none of us, and perhaps few Kelts ever, had
seen: Its prow was the carved head of a piast, with clear
rock-crystals for its eyes; its hull was gray and clinker-built,
and no sail did cling to its slim silver mast. Silently it moved
across the waves—*against* the current, I noted with interest—
and swung gently inshore, beaching itself at our feet.

I glanced quickly at Arthur, but he made no move either to
stir or speak; then down at Morgan, whose small face was
alight. Then a flash caught my eye, and my head snapped up
to look upon the figure that had been standing so quietly in
the stern of the boat as to seem another, smaller mast.

The flash had been one white arm throwing back the hood
of the gray cloak that she wore; for that it was a woman there
was now no mistake. Never had I seen such a face: young and
fair, and yet the eyes were older than time, deep wells of
starry knowledge; and as Morgan at my side disengaged her
hand from mine and stepped eagerly forward, I moved invol-
untarily back.

A smile lighted the lovely face. "I am Birogue," the woman said then, in a voice not unlike Ygrawn's, low and vibrant, subtly amused. She looked from Morgan to Arthur, whose head came up like a hound's under her stare, then to me—it was like drowning in silver light—and then back to Morgan. "Come, Morguenna Pendreic."

Morgan surged forward in her eagerness like the wave we call the sea-bear; then suddenly she seemed to remember the two who had come with her to this place. Turning swiftly, she embraced first me, then Arthur, thin little arms hugging us fiercely, and then stepped into the gray boat.

I looked up to meet Birogue's glance like a glowing flame, and I who had once thought Merlynn's gaze hard to bear now learned an entirely new level of difficulty. But I was not unschooled, and I held my mind and my gaze steady before hers, with all that I had learned and all that I had possessed to begin with plain in my eyes, and again she smiled.

"Well stood, Medeni's son," she said, and my mother's name was like the slap of a breaking wave in my face.

"Lady, how come you to speak of my mother?"

The silver light took on a glint of steel. "Another time for that," said Birogue. "But for now, know that she was my friend, and if by taking her under the hill I could have saved her, know too that I would have done so, even in despite of my king's command."

Looking into those eyes, I knew that I should hear no more just then than I had just heard; and perhaps could have borne to hear no more: The utter unexpectedness of it—that a Sidhe lady should claim friendship with my long-dead mother—had all but staggered me right there where I stood.

But now the little craft began to quiver, as a horse will shift leg if kept too long standing under saddle, and I knew that it—or perhaps its mistress—wished to be gone. It seemed that young Morgan knew also, for suddenly she reached out a hand to each of us, leaning perilously out over the boat's low side.

Stirring from his motionless stance, Arthur took the cold little fingers, kissing them as he would have kissed a queen's.

Then the child turned to me, and with speed and shyness tied a knot into the gold tassels of my cloak-fringe.

"A knot of remembrance," she said, cheeks flaming with her own boldness. "Do not forget me, Talyn, while I am gone!"

I kissed her hand as Arthur had done. "It needs no knot," I said in answer. "But, Guenna, do not *you* forget *me* . . ."

Then Birogue drew her gently again to her side, and as gently did the gray boat draw back into the morning mists, leaving Arthur and me to shiver on the strand.

He did not ask me as we stood there, nor when we turned to ride slowly away; nor all that long day of travel, nor yet at the fireside that night, when we broke the day's fast with a hot meal. That was ever one of Arthur's graces, that he knew always when you had rather say naught of some deep matter and when you longed dearly to speak of it. He assumed you had your own very good reasons for either course, and honored them—however he himself might have felt about it.

And however you yourself might have felt about it, soon or late, surer than any tugging or taunt, his restraint would coax speech from you; and you would never even know you had been coaxed . . .

"I have never met any who knew my mother," I said presently. "Well, not *truly* knew her—save for *your* mother, and Gorlas and Uthyr and Merlynn."

Arthur all at once found something of great concern in the precise arrangement of our broiling meat.

"Surely folk must have spoken of her to you?" he asked after a moment, voice carefully uninflected.

I laughed, not unkindly, at his carefulness. "Oh aye; about as much as folk have spoken to you, I think, of your father—your true father."

Arthur grinned, a little wryly; but the days were long gone when any mention of Amris Pendreic caused him to pull into himself, like a snail prodded with a stick.

"Aye to that—even my mother has not been exactly forthcoming . . . Is it that they think we cannot bear the knowing, or what is it?'' He did not pause for answer. ''But it seems hardly the same, Talyn, for all that: I did not know that Amris was my father, while there has never been doubt as to who was your mother. Unless you are after all a changeling from under the hill, and no human child at all? That would explain much I have often wondered at—''

I flung a bit of moss at his head. ''You need not look so pleased at the possibility.'' Not for worlds would I admit even to him that I had been thinking along those same lines myself, questing out on the inner planes—a quick silent sensing. But what I got back was only the answer I had known was truth before even I had asked: Gwyddno and Medeni were my true and only parents, this life round; I, and they, indisputably human.

''Well,'' said Arthur, sharing out between us the savory charred meat and crisp hot bread that made our meal, ''if you are yourself no child of the Sidhe—though I still say I could easier believe it of you than of Edeyrn—then it must be as Birogue did say, and the Lady Medeni was one of those Kelts who dare to seek the dwellers in the hollow hills.'' He puffed in air to cool a too-hot mouthful of supper. ''She sounds the sort of mother you *would* have been born of—though I am still sure there is more to it, and to her, than that.''

''I know there is, and some time or other I shall learn it.'' I reached for the flask of shakla that had been heating on the hearth. ''But what *I* was struck with—''

''—was Birogue,'' he finished for me. ''I too; to think that Merlynn all this time has had for beloved a lady of the Shining Folk, and we knew naught of it.''

I nodded thoughtfully, drinking my shakla. ''I wonder what else there may be about him we know naught of . . . or about this whole coil.''

''Well, for one, where Birogue did take my sister. I tell you, Talyn, that was no easy thing, to watch her sail off into the fog like that, and I not even knowing what was on that fog's other side.''

''I can tell you that,'' I said at once, apologetic and annoyed with myself that I had not thought to do so sooner;

surprised too, that he had so long restrained himself not to inquire. "They go to Collimare, the Forest in the Sea. It is an island in the middle of a finger-loch, a long curving arm of the Sea of Glora."

"Why then is it called 'forest' if it is in truth an island?"

"For that the trees upon it do grow right down to the water's edge; to one looking on it from the shore, it seems that the forest stands rooted in the very waves."

He considered that awhile. "I should have asked sooner, I know; it was just that— She will be safe there, do you think, with only this ban-sidhe to ward her?"

"Oh, I have an idea the isle is well fenced against any who might try to land unbidden; Guenna will be safer there, I think, even than she was at Coldgates. Merlynn would not allow it else; and his lady will be no careless guardian. As to alone—who can say?"

Not I, for one: Who knew what helpers of her own race Birogue might not have to dwell with her in Collimare? And if not folk of the faerie race, then surely faerie creatures to bear her company—cait-sith, those huge sand-colored panthers; or the red-eared, white-coated hounds bred by Nudd himself . . . No, Morgan would not lack for company there on the magic isle.

But as we curled up beside the quartz-hearth for a few hours of sleep before setting out again back to Coldgates, I found myself thinking once more of my mother; and just before slccp took me I put my hand inside my shirt, to close round the gold case that held her legacy and message to me, the hawk's gray feather.

On our return to Coldgates, Arthur and I made due report of our journey and its successful conclusion to the parents of the one that journey had most closely concerned. Ygrawn seemed well content with our account of Birogue, and Morgan's conveyance into her protection; but Uthyr was seized anew with paternal fretfulness, which I did my best to allay.

"Had you been there yourself to see her go, Lord," I said at last, "you might be better assured, but she would be no safer, I promise you and the Queen both." I ran a hand through my hair, for by all gods it is no light task to soothe a worried monarch. "The Princess was most happy and confident, and the Lady Birogue—"

I fell silent as I saw Ygrawn cover her husband's hand with her own, sensed the calm that radiated outward from her to him. Uthyr, it seemed, sensed it too . . .

"And do you not, lady, think to try your tricks on me," he said, not looking at her; but he said it with a smile, and the tender and grateful squeeze he gave her hand gave his words the lie.

We were all ensconced most comfortably in the Queen's grianán—a cozy, warm, pillow-strewn chamber. Merlynn and Arthur had both been with us, but after Arthur's initial account they had left on some business of their own. I was far too comfortable to stir myself to follow, and besides I sensed that there was more afoot than had so far been revealed . . .

"The Queen is right not to fear for Guenna," said a voice from the other corner of the chamber: Gweniver, who had been sitting on a low couch letting her uncle's new puppy gnaw happily on her hand—great-grandson of our own Luath, who had a few weeks since been called at last to a new Hunt. With a final teasing tap on the indignant puppy's nose, she sat up and fixed her uncle with a stern gray glance.

"Your worries are causeless, uncle," she said then. "I love my young cousin dearly, but time it is she begins to learn her craft. And as a protector and teacher there is none better than Birogue of the Mountain. As Merlynn would have told you had he still been here, I have learned from her myself."

This was news to me—though not, I could see, to Ygrawn— and I leaned forward with interest, to hear more of it. But having imparted to Uthyr her best assurance, Gweniver withdrew into herself again, and I received an impression of some trouble; sensed too that it was a trouble of long standing.

"What is it, Gwennach?" Ygrawn's voice, low and achingly kind, could have lured souls from Gwynfyd; so subtle were the evokers she employed that none, seemingly, could have failed to respond.

But it seemed even so that one could . . . "Naught to speak of, Lady," said Gweniver, which meant only that it was naught she *would* speak of.

Whatever it was—and I had a feeling it was the same strain that had been between Ygrawn and Gweniver for some months now, and all to do with Arthur—Uthyr seemed well aware of it. Giving his niece a very sharp glance, he rose from his place beside Ygrawn and crossed the chamber, to one of the great chests that stood against the wall. Opening the lid, he took from its depths a battered brown leather casket, and setting it on the floor before Gweniver's feet, he opened it with the small silver key that had stood in the lock.

The light of the sconces fell fierce and brilliant on the jewels tangled anyhow on mushroom-pale velvet: crown jewels of Keltia, brought perhaps from Earth, or before that, maybe even, from farther still. Heavy chains of bright gold thick with emeralds, glowering garnets, water-clear diamonds like silvered ice, carved beads of fat white jade, sunset-hued rubies and summer-sea turquoises, black pearls and blue pearls, pearls the rose-gold of an April dawn and pearls the color of cream on snow, amethysts framed in findruinna and sapphires set in silver—

I gasped aloud, for never had I seen anything like to it, and even Ygrawn looked impressed. But Gweniver merely scowled.

"What have trinkets to do with me? I am not the kitchen-wench, that you offer gauds to as a sop."

"No sop," said Uthyr. "Your father left these and more in my keeping. Some were private jewels passed on to us from our mother, and these I have passed on in turn: to my Queen, to my daughters, to you; or will pass on, to Arthur and to Talyn, when they wed"—he smiled at my start of surprise—"who are as my sons. But these are kept in trust for one only: the next Ard-rían of Keltia."

That, I saw, went home: Gweniver's thin straight shoulders went straighter still. But not yet would she give over.

"Why show them then to me? You have two heirs now by your own wife, Lord, either of whom could be named by you Tanista, to be Ard-rían after you."

Uthyr's face darkened with rare anger. "Do you then think, Gweniver ferch Seren, that I would flout both law and love, to set you aside? Listen now and listen well: You are my right heir, by true descent from your father Leowyn King of Kelts, and none other but you shall be High Queen after me. Though I pity your uncertainties, Gwennach, they have no cause but within yourself, and I do not wish to have to tell you this ever again."

That was no uncle chiding his niece but an Ard-rígh rebuking his heir; Gweniver flushed and dropped her eyes, and said no word. But Ygrawn and I exchanged a look in which there were many words, though all unspoken: Uthyr had said truth, but not all the truth, for as yet he himself did not fully know it—Gweniver might be High Queen as he had said, and had ever intended, but Arthur ap Amris would be High King to sit beside her.

Though Uthyr's chief concern at that time was for his younger daughter, he soon found that his elder daughter was giving him cause for equal worry, though for vastly different reasons. And before I left Coldgates, I was to see for myself what root his fears did have in solid fact . . .

Marguessan Pendreic, firstborn of Uthyr and Ygrawn, was in all ways as unlike to her sister as could ever have been thought of; had I not known them for sisters, and born of the same birth, even, I would have believed them not related in the least degree, so different were they from each other, and in themselves. Where Morgan was quietly dignified, possessed of a grave air that spoke of inner reserves and compassion startling in so young a child, Marguessan was uncaring and selfish, even cruel at times, and desperate above all things else to prove herself her sister's equal.

But in one thing at least had she not been thought so, and by those equipped uniquely to judge: Despite her terrible longing for the chance to do so, Marguessan was not to become a Ban-draoi.

It had surprised many, indeed, that she should not be allowed even to try; but Ygrawn, with a rather frightening inflexibility, had herself decreed that magic should be denied to her elder daughter, though when I wondered at it she was as candid with me as she had ever been.

"She is not fit for it, Talyn, and that is a hard thing for any mother to say. But there it is." Ygrawn's lovely face was taut with the cost of those words, and of the decision that lay behind them. "Morgan is gifted in magic, but also she is gifted in those things without which the greatest gift for magic that ever was would be but vain and empty pretense. It is just these that Marguessan lacks, and I fear she ever will."

No need to say further: Being Druid, I knew well what she meant. For the flair for sorcery, the simple talent, is never enough: The aspiring sorcerer must possess also a proper character upon which that talent may anchor—such fixed bedrock as honesty, and loyalty, and strength of character, and empathy; self-mastery and compassion; above all else, the need to seek and the will to serve.

"Yet Marguessan is by no means untalented," I said aloud, and Ygrawn's head came sharply round to me.

"And that is part of the problem," she said. "She has enough raw skill to make more than a little trouble does she so choose, and no great wish to use even that skill to benefit anyone save herself only. That might have been just acceptable in another time—for the talent's sake alone—but not now. Now we need only our best, and if they are few, well enough; we cannot afford the risk these days of confirming power in those who are but half-Called."

I hesitated to voice my present thought; but Ygrawn was not only my foster-mother—indeed, the only mother I had ever known—but also my Queen, and I owed her in both roles my perception and my doubt alike.

"At Bargodion," I began carefully, "we were taught that a person who has the gift for sorcery but not the conscience for its proper use might be—controlled."

The grave lucid eyes met mine straight on. "Think not that I have not considered it, Talyn . . . And I will not say that even yet have I ruled it out entirely. But to set such controls on a person—on one's own daughter—is a decision not lightly takcn nor maintained. But the Mother may grant it may not come to that: We must trust Marguessan to grow into herself, and to govern herself; and, perhaps, later—'' Her voice trailed off into uncertain silence as she looked into the still more uncertain future.

I too was silent, but for a rather different reason: Prescience had unexpectedly touched me, and I was suddenly sure that not only *would* it come to the desperate straits Ygrawn dreaded, but that, no matter all our Sight, we would be too late to avert the disaster that would come of it. And that disaster—

But as swiftly as it had claimed me the Seeing was gone again—if Seeing it had been, even, and not merely hareheartedness. I agreed with Ygrawn that to control someone so—the Druids call that particular rann 'Buarach,' the Stallrope; I do not know what name the Ban-draoi give it—was a fearful thing. Yet a necessary thing, as it befell; and though it was not often done, never was it done save where the wellbeing of the many must outweigh the restricting of the one. We have never been ones for restrictions, Kelts; freedom is more than life to us, but sometimes even freedom is not the clear and highest good.

There it was we left things for the moment; but I felt as if I had come home to Coldgates only to step into a scalding, one of those bubbling hell-pits like the ones below Bargodion. Only this one was full not of molten stone but of the scions of the House of Dôn, Arthur and Gweniver and Marguessan and Morgan, all bubbling round and round, exploding and subsiding and steaming up to explode again, never at rest, ever ready to drag unwary watchers down into the vortex.

But only a few days later, I was to have my first evidence that perhaps Ygrawn might need to rein in her daughter after all, and sooner than she had thought.

On my way to the ship-cave on some errand for Uthyr's warlord, Keils Rathen, I was crossing the watch-room, the great cavern where were installed the many viewscreens that overlooked all approaches to Coldgates, and gave warning of impending visitors friendly or other. Some of the screens showed places even more distant: the pass that led down to the Sea of Glora, for instance, on which screen Arthur and Morgan and I had been watched over during our journey, or stretches of sea-coast miles away to the west.

As I passed by a bank of screens off to one corner of the cavern, my attention was caught by a sudden gleam of movement, and I halted to see what it was that went on.

Marguessan was standing there, hidden away in a little nook formed by the screens. Her attention was not on me, nor indeed on aught else in the chamber, but rather fixed on the screen before her, which showed the coast at the feet of the Spindles, fifty miles away. In her hands was a small silver bowl—it was this had gleamed and caught my eye—filled halfway to the rim with water. For no reason I could name I was seized with vague dread, and I spoke quietly, so as not to alarm.

"What do you do, Marguessan?"

The dark-ringed blue eyes, disturbing as always, flicked up to my face, then away again. "I can make the birlinn come in upon the rocks. See, Talyn, how I do it."

Now it was I who was alarmed, and alerted; every sense in my body and mind seemed to come at once to full stretch. I took a closer look at the screen. There was a small birlinn sailing in the bay, a fishing-vessel most like, out of one of the few villages that stood along that hard cold coast.

Marguessan stirred vigorously the water in the silver bowl, stirred it widdershins, against the sun; and on the screen, far westaways in the bay, the little birlinn twisted suddenly and violently onto a shore tack, almost against its own will and counter to its helm, as if some hand had reached down from the sky and wrenched it over.

Which in fact one had . . . I put on calmness as I had been taught at Bargodion, thrusting from my mind the picture of the boat-folk in terror aboard their doomed craft, fully prepared to act as Druid from my own power if I could not convince her to pull her magic back.

"A most impressive trick, Highness; but as you see the

coast just there is all rock, and the boat will break to pieces and the folk be drowned. Can you push it off again out to sea, just so easy?''

She was watching the boat heading to certain destruction on the fanged and streaming rocks, a small glassy satisfied smile playing over her lips, the strange eyes abloom with dreamy light.

"I *could*—if I would."

I continued to feign unconcern, though by now my guts were churning, and my power as it sensed the growing need was swiftly building behind shields.

"Ah well, perhaps you cannot after all, no matter your vaunting."

That was how to do it: Marguessan glared at me, her vanity mightily stung, and stirred the water sunwise. As if released from some eccentric current, the small boat popped quite suddenly back on a seaward course, and after a quick remote thought-touch to soothe the fisher-folk's panicked souls, I allowed myself a deep silent sigh. *A near thing—and it must not happen again. I will speak to Ygrawn. But first—*

Reaching out, I knocked the bowl from her hands—the water hissed on the stone floor, steam rising where it ran— and Marguessan turned on me like a striking nathair.

"Clumsy fool! See what you have done—"

"Call no Druid fool, young madam, at least not to his face." My voice was freezing iron, and her cheeks stained a slow dull ugly red. "Behind his back, as you please and your insufficiencies may require. To his face, and be prepared to bide the issue."

By now Marguessan had regained her self-possession—never far lost—and she bent to pick up the silver bowl, careful to keep her eyes averted. But as she had brushed past me I had caught a quick glimpse, and was almost staggered at the cold depths of fury and hatred I saw in them, so that I had deliberately to remind myself that this was Morgan's sister, and Arthur's also.

"Oh, that is nothing," she said in an even voice. "But I shall remember what you have shown me here today, Taliesin. By all gods I shall."

Book IV:
Galtraí

Chapter 22

*T*hat was the year we both began in earnest that battle for which we had been all our lives preparing, Arthur and I, that autumn out of Coldgates. The sword for him, for me the harp; but the same fight for both of us.

Which fight would begin for me at least with yet another test, though of all tests I ever faced this was the only one in which I was assured of victory before even I had faced my questioner.

After a youth or maid has reached the rank of journeyman bard—or so at least it was in the old days—he or she may then leave the Colleges to serve at that level of training. Many positions are indeed open to such a one, for trained bards are much in demand, even the half-schooled impostors that Edeyrn would alone permit to call themselves bards. And that was irony beyond irony, that true-trained bards such as Elphin and myself and all the others like us must now study to impersonate these ones who were themselves impersonators.

I think it was just this that rankled the deepest: that art should be so betrayed, that these counterfeits should take no shame at their own actions, that the noble and wealthy families who were the bard's traditional employers should care so little for that tradition that they would pay any fee to secure a bard of their own, no matter his skill or how his training was come by.

It may not have mattered much to the false bards and their masters, but it mattered more than anything else to me and to my true fellows, and to other artists as well. For each art partakes in the end of each other art, and each artist shares in the crafts of his coequals. The bard must be musician and lymner, not merely a storyteller: The words must be painted, they must be portrait and landscape and sculpture all together. There must be music in it too, the words must sing; and dance, they must move to a palpable rhythm. Likewise the lymner or carver, for their part, must tell a story in their works, make statue or painting move, put frozen music in pictures. And the musician must be poet and painter together, his chaunts must be a thing one can put hands upon, as upon another person in a dance, or move through as tangible as a landscape, or read as clear and plain as an ancient text.

But now it became my duty, just as clear and plain, to put all this aside for a while, so that I might serve it in secret; and, perhaps, to serve it so better than I had ever done before . . .

One of the controls Edeyrn had over bards at that time—which was to say, since bards did nearly all the general teaching in Keltia, over the minds of Kelts as well—was the requirement that they be tested, and granted leave to practice only by means of such licensing. Some of us, it was true, had actually passed through his bastard bard-schools, and so qualified. Yet this ploy presented the rest of us somewhat of a problem: Though there were not all so many of us around, still there were enough of us to give the dimmest enumerator pause, should it ever come to counting of our numbers. After even the most cursory census, it would be plain to all that there were far more bards about than the false schools could have possibly produced, and the whole secret structure, so laboriously constructed upon a foundation of so many lives and deaths, would be laid bare before the Marbh-draoi's wrathful eye.

So to forestall such disaster, we had contrived over the years to get some of our own into places of influence within the Theocracy edifice, so that they would be among the ones doing the testing and granting the licenses to practice, or altering the records to allow for an extra few bards each year out of each of the approved schools.

Therefore was I so confident of my triumph, when I went for my testing before a panel of a Druid, a senior Raven, and the bard who had tested Elphin before me—the bard who had granted impeccable credentials to many others like us, sworn to destroy the system that required such deceptions of its folk.

The test itself was almost anticlimactical: first a bored Druid of Edeyrn's faction, dull and untalented; then an equally bored Raven with an ear of lead. Then came my final inquisitioner, a merry-faced woman of an age to be my grandmother, with the hearing of a lynx and the tongue of a serpent. We went through the thing under the noses of the other two as if it were some dance to which we knew secret steps; she granted me my license as if it were an afterthought, a foregone thing—which in truth it was—and the other examiners left, clearly relieved to be done with a tedious duty. Upon which we spent the rest of the afternoon chatting about Tinnavardan, in dichtal of course; for my part I had to explain the Hanes, of which she had heard much but in which she had not been instructed—the which I was pleased to remedy.

It was done, then; I had not expected to have such a feeling of exhilaration, but there it was. Tracing the feeling to its source, as I went to rejoin Elphin, I realized that I had achieved more than mere ratification here today: I had achieved empowerment. Now I could begin in earnest, as Arthur already had, to put my gifts to work for my country—or what would once again be my country, after all our gifts and arts and swords had worked together to make it so.

To that end, then, with the blessing of Uthyr and Ygrawn and Merlynn and Elphin, I left Coldgates to set out on my journeying years. I was an anruth, and so did I begin as bard.

And continued so for seven years together, wandering round Gwynedd from hall to hall, sleeping rough, sleeping fine—

not unlike the journeys I had made with Elphin years before.
Little of note befell me; it was for me a time of learning, of
looking with all senses open, not just eyes alone.

I have mentioned now and again in these pages how Keltia
was a sad, poor kingdom just at that time: Held down by
Edeyrn and the rule of Ravens, we had no technology or trade
to speak of, nothing to offer in commerce beyond our borders; we had all but forgotten that we were born a starfaring
people—few folk these days save those favored of the Theocracy had ever seen their own homeworld from space.

And the more I went round Gwynedd the more I saw: folk
worn down before their time, poor souls; folk embittered by
lost opportunity and soured by thwarted dreams; folk clever
enough to know they had been cheated of their birthright, but
too angry to be able to do aught about it save only to
rant impotently. Sad and sorry did it make me; more than
that, it all but broke my heart, and sore did it tax my vow of
secrecy. It was all that I could do to keep from crying out to
them, 'Do not despair so! Do not grieve! Do not lose that
angry edge!,' to keep from telling them that all would be
restored to them, and more, and sooner than they might well
believe.

So I sang them what comfort I could; and, seeing it,
singing it, I began to believe it myself. I had been privileged,
as few others had, to see the process of our salvation beginning, and yet I had not been able truly to believe in it even
so. I had seen in my own foster-brother the shining heart of
the power that was beginning to rise, as power will clothe the
one who works the magic in the circle's center, though that
power is raised not by him but by the others who spiral round
to raise it.

But still I had not been able to accept it, not completely,
not until now, now that I saw the ragged minds and poor bare
souls and scarred hopes that two hundred years of Edeyrn's
rule had left to call Keltia. And all the time as I travelled, I
heard rumor of some upstart rebel in the western mountains,
who, striking swift and hard and seemingly out of nowhere,

had begun in the past few years to make the lives of the Raven garrisons true and warranted hell.

None of those who reported of him knew his name or parentage—it was said he had come out of the far north, but there were as many tales that held him for a southerner, or for a man of the remote eastern isles, or even that he had come down from Arianwen, Gwynedd's small white moon, where wild savage folk were rumored yet to dwell.

No need to tell you how much this talk interested me: Not only did I most shamelessly use every trick I knew, bard's trick and Druid's trick alike, to coax every word known of this mysterious ravager from the lips of my informants; but I then passed on the tales, suitably enhanced and enforced, to the next little gathering for which I chaunted, in the next little townland.

I was not entirely alone on these rounds: Elphin and I encountered each other often, and exchanged, besides those embraces of greeting of friends unsure if each might be the last, all such news as had come our ways since our latest encounter. And from time to time I travelled with a companion —another bard, perhaps, on an errand like to mine, or a Fian spying out the land and the forces upon it, but always one of our own; and if from time to time these companions should chance to be lasses, and companionship took on a warmer hue, that too was as it should be. Neither I nor they could risk romance with any who did not share our cause and secrets; one more reason for us to share as we could.

And sometimes even there were friends: Daronwy, met one summer afternoon at a market square in a town called Talgarth; Betwyr and Tryffin, most convincing-looking lay-abouts, feigning drunk in a roadside bruidean near Caer Dathyl; one time even Tarian—her tall blond elegance impossible to alter, she had not troubled to try, and was putting on a very creditable performance as a high-ranking, arrogant Theocracy lady.

And once even Arthur himself, though it was folly beyond belief that he should dare to show his face in public without a sword in his hand and his Companions at his back.

"Good enough reason for it, Talyn," he said, setting down his ale-mether. "Though perhaps like all the others you may not think so—"

"That shall be when I have heard," I said, unable to suppress a stab of alarm. We had met, by arrangement, at a horse-fair in a country town in the far southwest of Arvon, and after the ritual examination of some very fine beasts offered for purchase, had repaired to the tap-room of the local inn, ostensibly to discuss business. Yet even in so remote a place we could not avoid the occasional Raven, and two already had taken cursory note of our presence—though with the town full of strangers for the fair we were most likely safe enough.

But for once Arthur, as a rule the most straightforward and plainspoken of individuals, seemed to find it hard to come to his point, and after an unbearable minute or two of watching him struggle for words, I sought to find some for him.

"Is it to do with your uncle?" I asked—the first rule of the Counterinsurgency's operatives was that the name of Uthyr Pendreic, and the names of his kin, should never be spoken outside the shielings save in a known safe place, which, gods knew, a tap-room in a back-country village was not like to be.

He shook his head. "Nay, nor with my mother or sisters or cousin—I fear this time it is I who cause the problem."

"What have you done this time?"

Arthur looked up at me at last with a strange smile upon his face. "I have fallen in love, braud. I am on my way to wed, and to take her home with me to Llwynarth."

Out of all the thoughts that crowded my mind, out of all the words I might have said, thought and word came out the same. *"Whyfor?"*

"Oh, for a few, any road, of the customary reasons . . . Her name is Gwenwynbar; she is the daughter of the lord of Plymon. And before you ask, aye, my uncle and my mother have been told."

"And they approve?"

"They think it—ill-timed."

And they are not alone to think it so . . . "Then if I may ask again, whyfor? Do you love her so greatly?"

"Whatever 'love' means," he said with an impatient flick of his fingers. "At least I am not at war with her as I have been with— Well, there is peacefulness between us, and I have been fighting alone these many years now; have I not earned the chance of a little happiness for myself?"

I nodded, but my eyes were on the table in front of me, for I knew the lady somewhat from my travels. Her father, Gerwin, was one of Uthyr's staunchest supporters, who had more than once saved the lives of Counterinsurgency spies fleeing Ravens, and who was regarded by Keils Rathcn, Uthyr's warlord, and the Taoiseach Marigh Aberdaron as one of the surest and safest sources of information we had on all the planet.

But the daughter—whom I had met once, briefly, in her father's hall while I was there on bard's business—was cut from inferior cloth; or so at least I had thought. She had seemed pretty enough, but brainless, a sly-eyed baggage, where what Arthur wanted was a mate of character and courage. He wanted Gweniver, though he did not yet know it, and no more did she know she wanted him; they would, I knew, but it appeared that in the meantime we were doomed to suffer Gwenwynbar queening it over us all. Not a happy thought—but Arthur was speaking again.

"—when you meet her, Talyn. Come with me now to Rhosyran, to stand with me before the brehon, and then come back with us to Llwynarth."

Sunk in gloom as I was by then, I caught the only word he had said that seemed to cheer.

" 'Brehon'! It is a brehon union, then?"

Arthur looked surprised. "Did I not say so? Aye, for the space of a year of Beli; my uncle thought it best."

I did not say how very fervently I agreed with the wisdom of Uthyr the King; at least, not then. But that night, lying awake next the quartz-fire, Arthur a shadowy sleeping shape just beyond the circle of light, I stared unseeing at the summer stars, full of a dread I could neither shake nor share, nor even clearly define.

That day for the first time I had looked on my fostern as another might, to see him as another—as a woman—might see him. Tall by now as a young rowan—and even in Keltia his height did mark him out, yet another reason why he should not be showing himself—hair red-brown like dark copper in sunlight, skin ale-brown where that sun had touched it, pale as a true Kelt's where clothes covered: Arthur was thirty-three this Wolf-moon past, still not grown to full strength and wisdom, but full of youth and fire and grace. Most attractive to any maid, and I assumed that in spite of his growing burdens of war there had been a few he had found attractive in his turn. Still, I saw no need for him to wed one of them . . .

I should not have been as surprised as I was, indeed, surprised to find myself: Though it seemed to me a thing irresponsible in the extreme, to choose this time—and this woman—to wed, a brehon union was by far not the worst fate that might have befallen, and perhaps all would yet be well. And too, as he himself had said, surely he deserved some joy, and if he had found the possibility with this daughter of an old and loyal house, may he be welcome to it.

Yet as I lay there, one word echoed and re-echoed in my mind, until it seemed that not my soul alone but all the sleeping darkness round must ring with it: Gwenwynbar. A pretty name, as Arthur thought it. But to me it had another aspect altogether: In the bardic usage, the ancient meaning of that name was 'Poisoned Spear.'

Travelling openly, it took us only three days to come to Rhosyran, a fortified manor on the sea-coast below Caerllyon. There we were received by Gerwin and Tamise, his lady, and entertained most royally by the household. How royally was made apparent when on the morrow of our arrival, Ygrawn herself arrived.

"Did you think I should stay away?" she asked with some heat, when, alone with her in her chamber, I asked cautiously as to whether she should have dared to come. "Tell me, Talyn, what do you think of this one who is to be my daughter?"

"Have you not met her yet, methryn?" I asked, surprised.

Ygrawn shook her head. "I have not, and little am I looking forward to it . . . But I asked what you did think."

"She is no Gweniver," I said flatly, and was grimly pleased to see Ygrawn smile.

"Nor, for all her patent hopes, will she rule at my son's side."

In spite of myself, I laughed. "That, I think, she has already learned: that queenship is reserved to another—now, and in time to come."

"Has she indeed?" said Ygrawn, still smiling. "Then perhaps she will be as quick to learn the rest of it."

That night in hall was the first time I had seen Arthur's lady at close hand; indeed, I had seen her only twice before, that one time many years ago, and briefly when she had welcomed us on our arrival. I watched her now, trying to see her as Arthur saw her. She was very fair, even beautiful in a showy way: thick curling hair of red-bronze-gold, huge brown eyes, a tall and slender form. She was magnificently clad but much overpainted, and wore too many jewels at neck and ears and wrists and fingers. Lovely indeed; and yet there was something not lovely at all behind her fairness, something as subtle and deathly as blight on a rose—the faintest taint of unwholesomeness, as something that has been permitted to ripen past perfection, into rot.

Gwenwynbar came forward with the guest-mether, to offer to Ygrawn as we sat at table, a fine show of deference on her that I knew Ygrawn saw through as easily as I did. The great mystery for both of us was why Arthur did not . . .

"And this is—?" Ygrawn knew perfectly well the girl's name and her descent for the past two thousand years; this hesitation was calculated and two-edged: to disconcert the young woman, and to hear her speak for herself.

"Gwenwynbar, Lady," she said in a soft, childlike voice. "But I am called Gwenar, if it please you."

I could tell without looking exactly how much it pleased Ygrawn—not one smallest bit—but she was Queen, and she was Arthur's mother, and she owed Gwenwynbar at least the outward seeming of civility and welcome. So she took the guest-cup, and drank, and pledged the household her friendship and Uthyr's together, and bade the ceremony begin.

Next day Ygrawn prepared to return to Coldgates—she had come herself as much to spare Uthyr the journey as to see what manner of woman would now call her mathra-chéile, and she had seen. As for myself, I would be accompanying Arthur and Gwenwynbar—I alone refused to call her as she preferred, and gave her her full and fateful name on all occasions; which did little to endear me to her, and which of course was not meant to.

It was a strange and strained journey, to say the least. Though I was scrupulous in giving them all the privacy they could have wished, still it seemed that to Gwenwynbar my mere presence on the same planet with her new lord was threat and annoyance aimed at her personally. Well, good luck to her: I had been with Arthur rather longer than she, and gods willing, I would be with him still long after she had gone. This too she knew, and much did it chafe her.

But though I detested Gwenwynbar every bit as much as she loathed me, even so I found cause for delight in this seemingly interminable slog: We were going to Llwynarth, and it would be the first time I had ever been permitted to come there. Though the circumstances of my coming were not perhaps as I would have had them had I been master of the arranging, still at the end of this march I would be at the Bear's Grove at last, and I would have endured far more, and far worse, than Gwenwynbar's cross, jealous presence to get there.

Chapter 23

*T*he news of Arthur's marriage had travelled before us to Llwynarth, so that by the time we arrived there the first astonished speculation had long since died down, and those who dwelled in that sanctuary were able to greet their leader's lady with what passed, at least, for civil welcome.

In truth it spoke more strongly for their powers of control than for their obedience to hospitality's laws: Tarian and Grehan met us, as commanders in Arthur's absence, with most of the Companions ranked at attention behind them. Now these two were after all members of princely families, kindreds that had been royal since Keltia's first beginnings; there was little they did not know about putting on a mask for public occasions, and the masks they had that day donned would not have cracked under blastfire. Oh, there was naught outward any might have called them on—stiff expressions of welcome, smiles of seeming warmth that all the same did not reach the eyes—in short, the sort of polite condescension for which the perpetrator cannot be accused without insult and under which the recipient can do naught but writhe in impotence.

Standing a little to one side of Arthur and Gwenwynbar, I confess I was myself surprised at Grehan and Tari; usually their manners were far better than that, and whatever their inner feelings might have been, they would sooner have perished on their own swords than allowed those feelings to show on their faces. But as I casually scanned the faces of the Companions behind them, I could see that the same control and the same appallment prevailed, and by no means the same skill exercised to hide any of it: Kei, furious and uncaring who knew it; Tryffin, Arthur's own cousin, who came forward to give Gwenwynbar a kinsman's greeting and his relation a troubled glance; Betwyr, coolly correct; Daronwy, hot-faced and hostile; Ferdia, puzzled but resigned to courtesy; Elen, smiling slightly, as if she had weighed Gwenwynbar in some arcane balance of her own and found her distinctly wanting. The faces of the others read anything from annoyance to disgust, variously—or indifferently—concealed.

Arthur, of course, was unaware of none of this: As he had presented his wife to his Companions he had run that swift raking glance of his down over the ranks of mutinous faces, and only his raised brows betokened that he had taken note. But he made no comment, then or later, and if anything his air of chivalrous protectiveness toward Gwenwynbar grew only more pronounced.

Yet, even against my strong inclinations otherwise—and too, you will recall, after suffering her company on the long, *long* road here—I must commend Gwenwynbar for how she carried herself, for the most part, that day.

It can hardly have been easy for her, being flung will she or nill she into a throng of sullen strangers and an ember-bed of rebellion. Presumably she shared her husband's views and dreams on that last—certainly her parents were among the most loyal of loyalists—but still it must have been difficult suddenly to find herself as much a fugitive and outlaw as all the rest of us. Yet she had stepped forward bravely as Arthur presented her, head high, her whole posture daring us to fault her, challenging all or any to deny her place.

But if the displeasure of the Companions was easily seen, so too, behind the defiant courage, was Gwenwynbar's jealousy: that all of us had more share in and claim on Arthur than ever she would have, no matter his love—and even I must grudgingly admit that it *was* love—that the Companions and what they stood for would ever take place before her in Arthur's heart, and she the outsider forever.

It need not have been so, truly: We were not set against her from the start, and gave her a fairer chance—and more than one chance—than she gave us. If she had worked to make any kind of place and position for herself among us save only that of 'Arthur's wife'— But she did not see it so, or did not think it needful, or held it beneath her new, supposed, royal dignity; and by then not even Arthur's direct command could have won her what she had scorned to earn for herself.

Still, it is their *problem now,* I found myself thinking, with a strange mixture of sorrow and relief, watching them move off through the ranks, accepting the subdued felicitations offered them, to Arthur's hastily refurbished rooms deep within. Rooms that, refurbished or not, Gwenwynbar would doubtless find too small, too bare, too poor and shabby for a prince of the blood—and that prince's wife.

Yet furnishings would be but first and least of the things at Llwynarth with which Gwenwynbar would come to find fault.

Much-loved though I knew I was by my foster-brother, I knew also that just now I was not his chiefest priority. I would have felt less put-upon had I known that concern of his to be someone of greater merit, but that too was his problem and not mine. I was only happy and grateful to be, for whatever cause and for the first time in many years, in the same place as Arthur; and Llwynarth, the Bear's Grove, was as fascinating a place as I had always imagined it.

Like Coldgates, like Tinnavardan, like so many other of the strong places of the Counterinsurgency, Llwynarth was built of the bones of Gwynedd: and yet not so much built as formed, for it was in origin a series of natural caverns, vast and interconnected, lying deep beneath the Arvon hills. They were scarcely plain holes in the rock, but rather places of unbelievable natural beauty: stone columns and curtains, dripstone veils and flowstone screens, all gloriously colored; massively intricate calcite pillars, ice-white and ice-cold; cascades of stone layering like melted candlewax—of all the caves it has been my lot to dwell in, quite the grandest.

However lovely the caverns were, though, our need had been paramount, working upon them to enlarge and fortify them, to extend them and shield them, until at last Llwynarth, at capacity, could shelter comfortably and safely upwards of a thousand inhabitants. All those were never there at the same time, or very rarely; always some were out on reivings, or scouting expeditions, or spying, or on circuit to Coldgates and the other shielings, training up new Companions against the day of their need—for needed they would surely be.

And as I had at Daars, as I had at Coldgates, I felt at once very much at home at Llwynarth. I was given two small chambers not far from Arthur's, most pleasant, with Tarian's rooms to one side of mine and Betwyr's to the other; given place at the high table beside my foster-brother, as not even Gwenwynbar could deny was my right by law; admitted to Arthur's councils as a valued and trusted advisor.

As the weeks wore by, I went out with Kei and Elen on reivings, putting to good use at last some of my hard-won swordcraft, learned so long since, and at such pains, from Daronwy and Ferdia; and once my confidence grew in my mastery of lands and townships roundabouts, I even ventured alone, or with at most one companion—usually Daronwy, who loved this sort of thing as much as I was swiftly growing to enjoy it, and whose company enabled us to pass for a travelling couple, and so be less suspect than either would have been alone—into the towns themselves.

There I would meet with other bards, to pass along by means of my own Hanes information that might mean life or death to many, or to receive news of Uthyr or Edeyrn or Owein, or to glean for myself, as I strummed upon Frame of Harmony and Daronwy sang in that bell-voice of hers, knowledge that those who imparted it—seduced by ale or by Ronwyn's singing—never even knew they gave.

So did weeks become months, and at the end of that first year Llwynarth received a royal visitor; and though most others in our campment were surprised indeed to see her, my only surprise was that she had so long managed to restrain herself, and stay away.

The reason outwardly given for Gweniver's journeying to Llwynarth was predictably commonplace: some message or other to Arthur from the King, that could not be entrusted to a lesser messenger; but I was not alone in suspecting Ygrawn's hand—as well as her own curiosity—in the Princess's coming.

So I was there to witness the first meeting of Gweniver Arthur's cousin and Gwenwynbar Arthur's wife. It was on the evening of the Princess's arrival: Gweniver had pleaded travel-weariness, and had met with only Arthur and Tarian and myself before withdrawing to the guest-rooms prepared for her, the grandest we could offer, to rest and ready herself for the nightmeal.

Not that we kept much state in Llwynarth, but one of the traditions we made a real effort to maintain was that of the nightly gathering in hall—or what passed for hall here at the Bear's Grove—for the evening meal and mild revelry after.

We Kymry have a strange and bardic bent for triads, the grouping of things in threes for poetic purpose: the Three Sacred this, or the Three Miraculous that, or the Three Astonishing whatevers. Were I to make a triad of the Three Fateful Suppers of my life, that night's meal would stand among them, along with a banquet I have yet to speak of, and that feast which followed Arthur's naming as Prince of the House of Dôn.

This unpleasant and most strainful supper began with Gwenwynbar's fury as Arthur led in Gweniver instead of her—as lord of the camp and Prince of the Name both, he scarce could have avoided the duty—and her mood did not improve when, on being presented, Gwenwynbar realized she must curtsy to the Princess as her superior in rank. She did so, if one can call a flick of skirt and a barely bent knee due and proper reverence to the next High Queen of Keltia; but Gweniver for her part displayed a lack of courtesy fully the match of it, looking on Gwenwynbar with a face of stone and thunder—a face that would take no prisoners—and muttering a few words that barely passed for civil greeting to a kins-woman by marriage.

Had it been any other folk than these three, I would have been shrieking with inward laughter at the utter absurdity of the thing; but far too much depended on smooth dealings and lack of discord among them for me, or anyone else, to be amused. So as I took my place beside Gweniver—as Arthur's foster-brother I shared his duties of host on such occasions—I summoned up all my bard's tricks to help ease the moment along.

Gweniver seemed strangely grateful for my attentions, bab-bling on most uncharacteristically of Uthyr and Ygrawn, and of Marguessan who was still at home—though already marriage-talk was in the wind of a union between Uthyr's elder daugh-ter and the dashing heir of a staunch loyalist family, one Irian by name; of Morgan there was little news save that she was well and happy, and still at Collimare. But though the Princess discharged her guest-duty of tabletalk to me and to Grehan and all the rest at that end of the board, her customary courtesy seemed not to run to her hostess, and not once did Gweniver address herself to Gwenwynbar who sat palpably seething at Arthur's left.

In my distraction I did not see it straightway, but bit by bit it dawned on me that Gweniver was behaving so out of jealousy, and Gwenwynbar likewise, though her conduct was sadly more obvious. Ignored by the Princess, Gwenwynbar was determined not to be treated so by the Prince her hus-band, and by now she was all but seducing him in front of the hall, kissing him, fussing with his food and drink, thrusting herself against him—most trying and tiresome, and, as any could see, utterly in vain. Arthur sat there cold and unmov-ing, his face as remote as the moon—his usual demeanor when he was angry and embarrassed and wished not to show it—and was as attentive to his guest as he was dismissive of his wife.

Which only made her the more desperately demanding; and at last even Arthur could no longer ignore her, and turned to her—though perhaps 'rounded on her' would be more correct a description of his attitude—and in a quietly furious tone delivered a tongue-lashing that swiftly sobered her, if it did little to correct her mood. But at least she ceased her frantic bid for Arthur's attention, and I took the moment to address myself to Gweniver.

To my astonishment, I surprised upon her face an expression of bleakness such as I had never before seen her wear—or perhaps once only, that time in Coldgates, when I had found her weeping in the watchpost—and my heart went out to her.

"Why do you look so?" I murmured, under cover of refilling her winecup. "She is not worth a thousandth part of you."

Gweniver's mobile face quivered and shifted into laughter, and she drank off in one draught the cup I had just filled.

"Say you so? My thanks to Lord Taliesin ap Gwyddno—or is it rather the master-bard whom I must thank? Well, it might be, what you say, and again it might not . . . She is very beautiful," she added, toying with the empty cup.

I made the usual courteous protestations, as to how her own beauty was such as to eclipse Gwenwynbar's—to which Gweniver listened with a faint smile and a raised brow—but as I looked at Gweniver's face glowing scarce three feet from my own, my words that had been honestly spoken took on new meaning.

Gweniver was one of those women who grow lovelier with their years, like late-blooming autumn flowers: Weedlike through summer days when all round them riot in splendor, when the showy summer blooms are blown they burst into a strong shining beauty that outlasts the snows. Tonight she seemed on the edge of that blooming: hair like a soft dark mist, gray eyes silvery in the sconcelight, creamy skin set off by a collar of rubies and a ruby-colored gúna.

And it must have been the wine—I am sure it was the wine—but it seemed that the same thought and need were set alight in both our minds, for when, in the deep quiet owl-hours past middlenight, a faint tiny tapping came at my chamber door, I did not find it surprising nor yet unwelcome;

and, by emberlight alone, and no word spoken, drew Gweniver in, and so we stayed till morning.

When that morning came a new ease came with it: If wine and jealousy and hurt and loneliness and long curiosity had all conspired to put Gweniver and me into each other's arms that night just past, that same night's intimacies had seemingly contrived a conspiracy of their own, bringing about not only the ending of all those reasons and rationalizations but the beginnings of a strange and splendid freedom.

We had been friends, Gweniver and I, and we had been lovers for a night, and now we were friends again in this morning, but we awakened as altogether a different sort of friend: It was as if the act of physical love, delightful as it had undoubtedly been for us both, was also for both of us a seal we had placed on something of much greater permanence and worth; that the sharing of our bodies was all the same incidental to what we truly shared between us, and would ever share. Though this night was not to be repeated, and never to be regretted, it was something we had needed to do, and now we had done so.

Indeed, its most immediate effect was felt as soon as we opened our eyes: We turned to look at each other, and our smiles of morning greeting, that had been frank and open and carried neither shyness nor shame, suddenly flared into laughter.

"Ah me," said Gweniver, when she was able to speak again, leaning her forehead against my shoulder as if in helpless apology. "No offense, Talyn—it was a *most* pleasant night—but I think now we know this is not for us, not with each other. I had thought once that it might be, do you know."

"And I had thought the same," I answered, still smiling, and taking her hand kissed the cool fingers. "And therefore no offense taken—pleasant indeed though it was, and something that we needed to learn." I sat up, pulling her with me. "And before all Llwynarth learns alike—"

She looked amused and mock-alarmed. "Oh aye." Slipping from the warm huddle of furs, Gweniver padded across the floor to scoop up her scattered garments, then turned round to face me clad only in her ruby collar and her streaming hair, a smile that seemed perfectly to express our new openness and understanding lighting her face.

I paused in my own dressing to look at her—a sight that it must be said well repaid the looking—and felt my smile answering hers. My smile only, however; not any other part of me, though she was no less desirable that moment than she had been at the banquet-board beside me all last evening, or in the bed beside me all last night. She had had the right of it, of course: This formed no part of the bond that was between us; was in fact rather a distraction from the reality of our friendship, and it was good it should be put by early on.

Yet though neither of us felt shame or secrecy for what had been last night—and there was no reason in all the worlds why we should have felt either—the same thought stood now in both our awarenesses, though we did not speak it aloud: What we had shared was our concern alone, and not even Arthur would hear of it from either Gweniver or myself.

But though he did not hear, Gwenwynbar did; how, precisely, she contrived to do so forever remains a mystery. Perhaps it was simply the same sort of uncomplicated kenning that had told Gweniver and me that we needed each other just that once; or perhaps it might have been that mean probing certainty that can come into play when jealousy is afoot—man or woman, it makes no differ; that hot green emotion is all one, and indifferent to gender.

Whatever, clearly Gwenwynbar had learned by some means of our night together, for the glance she shot at Gweniver and me when we came in to the morning meal—together, I admit, but we had scorned to dissemble, or stage some charade of mock encounter—spoke volumes. Why it should so enrage her that we had shared ourselves I had not the smallest idea, and Gweniver seemed equally bewildered; unless it was simply that Gwenwynbar hated me and hated Gweniver and detested the thought that we should have turned

to each other for brief loving comfort. And why, knowing
this, Gwenwynbar did not tell Arthur, baffles me still.

Not that Arthur would have minded; for he minded not at
all, when in time he came to learn of it—but Gwenwynbar
perhaps thought he might mind very much indeed, and so
chose to save it, to keep the knowledge as a weapon in time
of need, to use against Arthur what time she should have
naught else to hurl against him. Yet when it came to that
moment, years later, she proved only how little she did know
her own lord . . .

But as I say, that was years away, though after that time
those years did seem to take wing alarmingly, in that speeding way they will do the older one grows. In childhood it
seems time moves at less than footpace: A week passes like a
month, a summer like a year, a year is a century; while in
youth and mid-age the pace picks up, until at life's end the
years hurtle by like weeks—turn, and it is Beltain; turn
again, Samhain two years hence . . . No wonder old folk
sometimes forget where they are, and when; hard it is to
mount time galloping.

Yet time went all the same: I stayed at Llwynarth, and the
Companions grew closer, and there were a few more of them;
while far away in Coldgates Uthyr and Ygrawn stayed safe
and well, and farther still in Collimare Morgan grew and
learned. It was a quiet time of consolidation and growth in
turns: We kept up the raids and reivings that had become such
a thorn to Owein—still a small thorn, by compare to what
would come later, but sharp enough for all that. And most
astonishing of all, Arthur and Gwenwynbar stayed wedded,
for near full seven years, renewing their brehon promises
every Midsummer, dashing the hopes of Llwynarth.

For by now Arthur's wife was openly detested by most of
the campment; at first it had been simply a general disliking,
on her part as much as on ours. But as time went on, and not
only did she make no effort to be *of* Llwynarth rather than
merely *in* Llwynarth, but began actively to throw caltraps in
our path and speak ill of us to her husband whatever chance
she could, our disliking flamed into hatred, and hers blazed

backfire against us, and only our obedience to—and love for—Arthur himself kept our hands from violence.

Even that not always: Daronwy and Betwyr and Elen and Kei, each on separate occasion, had literally to be restrained from seeking Gwenwynbar's blood, in lawful combat or not as each's rage did require. It was Arthur, of course, did soothe and smooth the quarrels over; but in the end even he seemed to lose the will and the heart to do so.

At the last the marriage seemed more habit and custom than aught else, at least on Arthur's side; on Gwenwynbar's, perhaps only reluctance to give up something in which she had invested so much over so many years. Whatever may have been the truth of it, it was clear to be seen that Arthur and his lady were not so much drifting apart as being sundered by a rising tiderip; whether it would engulf either, or both, was yet to be shown.

The end came with merciful suddenness, cleanly, like a sword's fall; and though it was not a peaceful end, at the least it was a swift one, and its cause—as so often is the case in such matters—was an old and a small matter indeed.

In all the seven years of her marriage, Gwenwynbar had not once been permitted to visit Coldgates. It was one of our most adamantine of rules among the Companions, that none should go there who had never been there, and even then as few of those as possible. It was purely for safety's sake: Many of our own sworn Companions, even, those who had joined us through the years at Llwynarth and had not been born or sheltered at Coldgates as had we others, had never come there and did not even know its location. And so Gwenwynbar, wife though she was to the Queen's son, continued to be denied both the going and the knowing.

At first this had not seemed to trouble her—at least she had so said—but of late she had chafed more and more at the restriction, and at last had come to take Arthur's steadfast refusal as personal insult; and this it was that brought about the end.

Their final quarrel was brief but ferocious, or at least Gwenwynbar's side of it was so: Though she could be heard shrieking over half Llwynarth, Arthur as usual had refused either to lose his own temper or to give in to his wife's demands, and his calm only fueled her fury. So that she brought up other matters long festering in silence: how she had never been granted the respect her rank deserved, how all the Companions secretly detested her, how Arthur himself did not pay her proper attention but would desert her any hour for a council or a raid.

He did not trouble himself to make answer to her charges; for what reply could he have made save the truth, and that she knew already. We of the Companions *did* detest her, and not so secretly either; Arthur *did* neglect her, but his first loyalty had ever been to duty, even a wife could not alter that; *never* would Gwenwynbar be given the queen's honors she coveted, and thought herself entitled to—the only women rightly to queen it in Keltia were the Queen and the one who would become Queen, and both Ygrawn and Gweniver had far too much wit and sense and humor even to wish to try.

Which was where they differed from their angry kins-woman: Gwenwynbar would never cease hungering for homage—those who did not deserve it seldom did—and that cold calculation that I shall always believe led her to wed Arthur in the first place led her to leave him in the end. If he would not give her what she wished, she would obtain it elsewhere; or so she must have thought, for the morning after the quarrel, Llwynarth woke up to find her gone.

Informed of her going, Arthur declined to pursue her.

"She ended the marriage by declaration"—he indicated a letter lying on the table between us, as I sat trying to console him, though he seemed not to need consolation—"and that is all the law requires. We were not wed at the stones, so a formal divorce is not needed; only either party's written or publicly spoken repudiation of the bond."

"Well, Artos; but what about what *you* may require?" Though it chafed me to plead Gwenwynbar's possible return, it chafed me still more to see him so diminished; he seemed smaller, somehow, this morning, downcast and quiet, his usual vibrant fire banked low. And so strangely, sadly calm . . . "Did you not know when she went?"

Arthur shook his head. "She slept apart from me last night. When she did not come to bed, I thought she must still be angered, and that it was best we spent the night away from each other. I fell straight to sleep, but plainly she did not sleep at all; only packed her gear and left. None saw her go; she used one of the unsentried gates, she knows—knew—the codes to raise the barriers."

"Are you sorry, then, braud?" I asked after a little silence.

"Sorry? Sorry that it did not prove to be my best, though it lasted longer than all you here might have thought—or hoped—at the start. Not sorry at all for that she is not now able to betray Coldgates, and the King, as well as Llwynarth."

I gaped, for this most obvious of vengeances had not occurred to me. "Llwynarth! Would she do so?"

"Nothing likelier." Arthur stretched, a bone-cracking, sinuous movement. "She will be feeling hurt and humbled; how better to take revenge on the one who has caused her such pain than to betray him, and his, to Owein? Any road, she promises as much—in this."

He tossed me her letter, and after a moment's hesitation I began to read.

"I was mistaken from the first, Talyn," he said presently. "I saw in her something that was never there save that I wanted it to be. But though she lacked that, still she was loving and cheerful and fair—" News to me, for though I might just allow 'fair,' never had I or any in Llwynarth save only, apparently, its master seen in Gwenwynbar the least trace of the other virtues he claimed for her. But perhaps as her husband he had seen more, and deeper, than the rest.

"She says here she will have vengeance on you and all of us," I remarked, putting down the sheet—my othersenses were reeling, so imprinted was the paper with her hate.

"It is no more than I am sure you heard her shouting last night." Arthur stretched again, and I was more than ever suspicious: He was taking this far too calmly even for him, or so it seemed to me. After all, the woman had been his wife for seven years . . . But before I could ask, he spoke again, and now he sounded almost his own old self. "The first thing we must do now is move Llwynarth."

"Move it! But how? Where to?"

"As to how, the same way we did build it. Where—almost anywhere; there is no lack of such cave systems in this part of Arvon. Time it was we moved on, any road; we have been here too long for strict safety." He smiled suddenly, and it was a real smile. "What say you, Talyn—it may be that Gwenar has done us a service after all."

"Are you out of your wits entirely, or mad but for the moment?"

The words—I had meant them as rhetorical, for surely no sane individual could have in seriousness put forth the pro-posal that Arthur had just put forth—hung in the air between us, until Arthur looked up at last to answer me.

We were in our new refuge, the new Llwynarth; had been here barely two months, following our hasty and enforced removal from the first. The finding and fitting out of the second shelter had gone better than we could have dreamed, though there was still much to be done to add to our comfort; at the least—though scarcely least—nothing remained to be done to assure our safety there, and we had removed our-selves from our former home well within the deadline that Arthur had imposed.

Though during the relocation we had dreaded every instant Owein Rheged, sent by a vengeful Gwenwynbar, falling upon us, had looked over our shoulders imagining fleets of Ravens raining fire and death, nothing of the like had happened. We had moved into the new refuge—as lovely as its predecessor, lovelier even, with a subterranean stream foaming and falling over the rocks—and destroyed the old one, without hindrance from our enemies and with no error of our own making.

No error, until now—

"Well, I had not thought myself either," said Arthur evenly.

"But it seems you think I am mistaken. Say then the ground of your convincing."

I threw back my head in boggled despair. "Oh, well, then, it must be that *I* am the madman here, to think I just now thought I heard you say you mean to go to Caer Dathyl, to have a look at Edeyrn when he comes on progress to visit Owein. But since you cannot possibly be so great a lunatic as to suggest so stupid a plan, then obviously I did not hear it, and so I must be mad."

He laughed. "Come, Talyn, hold not back; tell me how you *truly* feel— Well, perhaps it *is* the thought of a madman, but I am going nonetheless."

"In the Mother's name, whyfor?" gasped Grehan, as appalled as I at our friend's intention.

"I have never seen Edeyrn," said Arthur after a little pause. "Nor Owein neither; and in the Fianna, did they not teach us to know our enemy?"

"But you know perfectly well who your enemy is, both of them!" I shouted, cross with terror; for I knew that no matter all our protests, he was going and that was that.

"I would see them all the same. But *you* need not come, Talyn," added Arthur kindly, "since you think it so ill-found a plan."

"Oh, I know I *need* not, right enough," I said, in a voice that carried all the sarcasm and sting I could put into it. "But—with your leave—I think I am coming even so."

Chapter 24

*I*n the end there were four of us did ride to Caer Dathyl: three too many to Arthur's way of thinking, and he was still vexed that he had not been taken at his word and allowed to go alone.

Not likely!, I thought more times than a few, as we made our way cautiously eastward to Owein Rheged's stronghold. I kept from my fostern as best I might my real suspicion—more than suspicion, truly—my certain knowledge; then, that this insane venturing, and the months of near-as-reckless raiding and risking that had gone before it, signified more than military motive. To my mind, it was Arthur's way of dealing with the going of Gwenwynbar.

In truth, I was not the only one who had looked on all this and wondered whether Arthur were trying to kill himself on another's sword: Grehan, and Kei, and Betwyr, and Tarian, and all the others closest to Arthur, had seen what I had seen, and, one by one, had come to me privately to voice the shared fear. And, one by one, we had each arrived at the same unwelcome conclusion: In his pain he was doing this, and despite our love for him, there was naught we might do either to halt him or even restrain him somewhat. All we could do was watch, and pray.

Which was why Ferdia, Daronwy and I were now riding

with him on this very maddest of exploits: In the end, only the fact that the three of us would be with him had won over the rest of the Companions to give grudging consent, and even then Grehan and Tarian had been slow to agree. It had been unanimously undertaken, almost without the words even needing to be spoken, that no smallest whisper of this venturing should reach the distant ears of Uthyr or Ygrawn.

We went in the guise of travelling bards—it seemed the safest choice, as everyone in the party could handle a harp sufficiently well not to explode the fiction; though we were also agreed that if by bad luck it should ever come to actual bardery, I alone should be the one to save our honor—possibly also our necks—and play. Which led Ferdia, the only non-sorcerer among the four of us, to wonder why we did not simply cast a fith-fath upon ourselves and go so masked among our foes.

"For you are both Druids, and Ronwyn is Ban-draoi," he had argued, "and therefore powerful enough in magic to manage a little glamourie for good cause."

"And therefore too powerful in magic to dare wear it into Edeyrn's presence," countered Arthur. "Trust my saying, Feradach, he would pick us out in an eyeblink—we should do better, and last longer, did we wear signs proclaiming our names in foot-high script."

At last Ferdia had given in, muttering what use was it to train and torture oneself into a magician if one could not use it when one needed. He was right, so far as he knew; but had we worn fith-faths, the Marbh-draoi would scarce need to be told our names—we would blaze like torches to his inner sight. So we wore openness instead, the best disguise there is; and he knew us soon enough as it was.

Caer Dathyl, seat of the princes of Gwynedd since Gwynedd first was born, rises up like a gray ghost on the southeastern edge of the northern continent. It is the first settlement of all the Kymric worlds, and the castle at its heart is one of Keltia's great fortresses: Save for Ardturach on Erinna, and the royal palace of Turusachan on Tara, Caer Dathyl is the largest stronghold in the kingdom; and perhaps only Turusachan itself is more formidable, to approach or to escape. The Marbh-draoi himself would be there, in the ancient palace of the Princes of Dôn, and Owein who was now Gwynedd's master, and doubtless dozens of their creatures—Ravens and courtiers and lackeys all together; and here came too the four of us to invade it, armed only with our harps, and our hatred, and Arthur's wits.

We were received with all courtesy at the great gates, as bards should be—and mostly were, even in these degenerate days; and from there we were passed up through the streets that climbed to the palace. Always our bardic garb gave us admittance, though I think we were all more than a little surprised that not once were we challenged to prove ourselves, by showing passes or tokens that we were indeed what we claimed to be. But apparently Owein in his traha deemed none dared approach the city, far less enter the palace, who had not been summoned or had no lawful business there; and never dreamed that his chiefest foe would dare far more.

Any road, we arrived at last in the palace's main hall, just in time for the nightmeal, at which Edeyrn and Owein would surely preside. A harried-looking rechtair gave us place on the lower benches, among others of our assumed humble station who were already beginning to fill the long tables.

Although I had been schooling myself against it, in the end I could not help it: My gaze flew at once to the high table at the far end of the room. Some of the mighty who were soon to sup there were already in their chairs, or standing in small groupings behind the goldware-bedecked, silk-clothed board, conversing idly amongst themselves. I dared not stare overlong, lest my scrutiny should itself be scrutinized, but I did not see anyonc I could recognize as Owein, and I assumed he would enter later, in full pomp, escorting his exalted guest.

At my right elbow I could follow Arthur taking mental note of everything he saw and sensed, as he had been doing on all our long ride here: Everything from the state of repair of the roads and the mood of the tavernkeepers to Caer Dathyl's

defenses to the names and faces of the folk in the seats of
honor was being sorted and salted away in that prodigious
memory.

I could put names to a few of the faces myself, mostly
lords and ladies of opportunistic houses, lesser lines, seeking
increase in their own fortunes by having allied with the power
that now ruled. And also there were those whom the Marbh-
draoi himself had created—his creatures in the true sense of
the word—men and women jumped-up by treason and boot-
kissing to ranks they could never have hoped otherwise to
attain. Some were trimmers, thinking to run with the hounds
and yet still scratch among the other hares; but many had
dedicated their hearts and souls and bodies to the Marbh-
draoi's cause, and these it was that Arthur feared the most.

"It will be easy enough to buy the others back," he had
said on the journey here. "What was once bought can be
repurchased anew for the proper coin . . . I shall not be
buying the best goods, truly, but at least I shall be buying us
some peace and easy roads. But the ones who have gone in
loyalty to Edeyrn—they will not be bought and cannot be
turned; and therefore they must be destroyed."

For the moment, though, it seemed that we might be
ourselves destroyed before ever that time should come; before
even our meal came, perhaps. Notice had been taken of us by
some of our neighbors at table, and though I prayed with all
the fervor of my being it was but casual suppertime interest in
unexpected strangers, I had the most terrible feeling that it
was more, and worse.

"This is insanity," I whispered savagely to Arthur in a lull
in the converse around us, then switched to thought-speech,
hoping beyond all hope that Edeyrn, or indeed others, would
not sense it.

We must risk it, came my fostern's reply in the familiar
mind-voice. *I must know my enemy.*

Then do you see to it that he does not likewise know you! I
snapped, and felt the flashing warmth of his mental grin. But
I sensed too that he would obey: Edeyrn would not know

Arthur by anything Arthur might do. It was what Edeyrn
might do that had me worried.

I felt his presence before he came into the hall; indeed, had
been feeling it from the moment we passed within Caer
Dathyl's walls. And I saw him now with othersight before I
viewed him with the eyes of the body: Edeyrn, son of Seli and
Rhûn. He was clad in some dark plain stuff, wore no jewel or
sign of rank—a relief to Ferdia, who had, I think, expected
him to enter wearing the Copper Crown itself—and, save for one
who could be none but the mighty Owein, was unattended.

I found that I could not take my eyes from him. It was his
aspect that astonished: Edeyrn looked to have fewer years on
him than Merlynn, though I knew very well that he had seen
twice my teacher's span, and maybe longer still. His eyes
were dark and deep-set in a face the color of ivory; the thick
hair brushed back from the high brow was a rich charcoal
hue, neither black nor gray, and fell to his shoulders. And he
was tall and straight, where I had been resolutely picturing
him as small and hunched, misformed and ill-shapen as a
duergar, ugsome, shadowed with the dark wing of his own
evil. I had not thought to see him so—a controlled majestic
presence, confident with power.

He swept his glance just then over the hall—all of us had
risen for his entrance, and now we bowed deeply as he
acknowledged us, much though it grated the four of us to do
so—and as that distant glance passed over me palpable as a
cold wind I felt it check an instant, as if it were caught by us,
as the wind may be caught in a tree's branches. Though his
gaze can have rested upon us for mere seconds, no more than
five altogether, in those few seconds I felt Arthur kindling to
wrath beside me, and Ferdia to cold panic.

This was no time for either, not if we hoped ever to leave
that hall alive: So, thanking the Mother that Daronwy seemed
unaffected, I seized her mind to join with mine, and together
we bade Ferdia cast out his fear, and counseled Arthur to
calmness, and bent all our strength to raise a defense against
Edeyrn's scrutiny. But a solid wall would only confirm his

suspicions, and doom us all out of hand: Our rampart had to be light as air and thin as light, a shield of vanishment, that he or any could probe and find naught there to resist the probing. After a moment, it was with deepest thankfulness that I sensed the others join the effort; and—I know not how else to say it—we became transparent, we four; we were invisible, we were absent, we were *gone*.

And I saw Edeyrn shake off his hesitating attention as a horse will shrug off a bothersome cleggan, and I gave a huge inward sigh of relief to see it, though still I did not allow the magic—if magic it was—to slip away just yet, in case . . . well, in case. But if I had thought *that* the worst we should have to face this night, I was about to be shown yet once more just how mistaken I could be.

In the tail accompanying Owein and Edeyrn were several women who swept to their places at the high table with an air of what they plainly thought, or hoped, was queenly arrogance. I, who knew a true queen in whom arrogance had no part, cast a quick scornful glance their way: fair enough, some of them very fair, but all of them most overjewelled and overdressed and overpainted for the occasion; and I began to turn away.

Then, as Owein, having seated Edeyrn in the place of honor, stepped aside with great show of courtesy to hold a chair for one of the women, I saw her face against the rich figured silk of his tunic, and the seeing near stopped my heart. The woman was Gwenwynbar, and, to judge from the fall of her velvet gúna, she was heavily pregnant.

Give me this at least: I am not slow to recognize dán at work, though I may not always see it coming, and I recognized this at once as the most fateful of that triad of Fateful Suppers of my life. Most fateful—perhaps most fatal—and most endless also: I thought that meal should go on until time itself had died, and certainly until we ourselves had perished. And indeed I was beginning to think that that last was nearer than any of us might like: Though Ferdia and Daronwy had by skill of banter turned the suspicions of our tablemates, and

the four of us together fended off Edeyrn's eye, I despaired
anew when I thought of our chances of escaping Gwenwynbar.

I had not dared glance at Arthur, but judging by the
clenched fist that lay in his lap, and how his whole arm shook
against mine with the violence of the clenching, I knew he
too had seen and recognized his disespoused wife. But, save
for a sympathetic touch of mind and hand, I could do naught
just now to help him, and presently I felt the terrible trembling
ease. His face, when I dared glance at him, was serene and
unclouded, and with a shiver of my own I knew he had shut
down upon his feelings that control of his that was like a
findruinna gate: to close Gwenwynbar out, and close himself
in.

But the meal had begun, and for the next three hours we
endured perhaps the greatest trial of our lives so far. Certainly
it was *for* our lives that we endured—had we attempted to
exit the chamber or the castle we should have been summarily
seized, and our lives past that point both brief and painful. As
it was, every moment, every mouthful, every breath and
every word, we thought to be our last.

In one small thing, or perhaps not so small, we seemed
blessed: So far as we could tell, Edeyrn made no further
attempt to seek out either us or any other suspected renegades
who might be in hall that night. Indeed, from all appearances,
he was enjoying a very pleasant nightmeal, on this the next-to-
final evening of his stay on Gwynedd. Though he seemed
sociable enough, as I watched him with Owein and the others
who sat at the high board, his power and his—his *otherness*
were as plainly to be perceived as his very face. No one
looking upon Edeyrn could fail to be aware that here was one
who was master over men and magic both, and though I
detested it, and myself for feeling so, I knew that I felt an
awe near as strong as my long hatred, for my father's mur-
derer, and Gorlas's, for the destroyer of Gwaelod and of
Daars.

"Aye, that's as may be"—I heard then to my horror from
two places away—"but what *I* want to know is, what might
his *mother* think of him?"

Unable to believe my own ears, I craned past Arthur's suddenly rigid form to glare at the speaker: Ferdia, with blithe cheerful heedlessness, had succeeded in killing his earlier fears with the help of ale. Not as a rule one for the mether, he seemed to have done a good job this night, to judge from the flushed face and tousled hair; and now he was deep in sozzled discussion with one of our tablemates, a thin, overeager, furtive-faced man who had boasted earlier to the table of his exalted status: kern-equerry to one Pyrs Vechan, a vassal of Owein's who held a dúchas in the Deer Hills behind the city.

Ferdia's ale-born question seemed to have turned to stone all those near enough to have heard it: I gathered by their uneasy reaction that speculation on the Marbh-draoi's maternal parent was not a thing much done, here or elsewhere—though doubtless none knew the truth of it as did Arthur and I; even Daronwy was ignorant of it, and certainly Ferdia had no idea—and for a drunken stranger to do so was little short of declared disloyalty, a true guest-sin. I opened my mouth to say something, anything, but Arthur was quicker.

If any one of us had had lawful cause to sink a drench too many this night, surely it had been my fostern. I had scarce dared look at him for near the entire duration of the nightmeal, for fear of what I should, or should not, see upon his face. To have looked for the first time upon the dark lord of Keltia, who by his arm and his dán would be brought down, was surely enough to unnerve even the boldest; to have seen his former wife not only sharing plate and cup but seemingly her bed as well with the man he would one day face in battle for Gwynedd . . . I do not know how he did it, Arthur, to keep himself calm and clear-headed in the face of all that and the continuing peril of our lives as well; and I wondered, by no means for the first time nor the last neither, whether he himself was entirely mortal and human.

But then, seeing the pain in his eyes when at last I turned to look at him, I saw that he was both; and when he skillfully interposed his own slyly humorous comment between Ferdia's blunder and the suddenly bristling suspicions of our unpleas-

ant tablemate, to turn the danger of the moment, I saw too
that he was, for all that, more besides.

Still, even such prolonged torture as this must come at last
to an end, though—dán's final twist of the pirn—there was to
be one trial yet to live through.

Owein had stood up in his place, cup in hand, to offer the
traditional health to the ruler of Keltia that had once been
reserved as rightful tribute to Keltia's rightful monarchs.
Now, as I watched it offered to the Marbh-draoi, and saw his
complacent acceptance of it, as if indeed he merited it by
right, I thought of Uthyr, so kind, so patient, so worthy, so
far away in Coldgates and so far away from ever being
offered even this tiny thing that should, with so much else,
have been his, and my anger rose up bitter to choke me.

Yet it did not need Daronwy's warning hand on mine to bid
me compose myself: Owein was leaving the high table, and,
with Ederyn at his side, was beginning an apparently customary progress down the hall's main aisle. An unnerving prospect, particularly since that stroll would bring them within
five feet of us as we sat there. Our table was the outermost of
those ranked on that side of the hall, and the bench upon
which we four sat was the outer bench of that table, so that
we had been sitting all evening with our backs to the wide
center aisle down which Edeyrn and the rest would be passing.

Not only that, but we would of course be obliged to rise and
turn to face them as they did so, and there would be no one
for us to hide behind: Edeyrn, Owein—and Gwenwynbar—
would be near enough for us to touch.

I resigned myself to the inevitable: This was without doubt
the end of us. Though Owein might not know us by sight,
surely the Marbh-draoi could not fail to see at five feet's
distance what he had been able to sense at five hundred's. But
if by some miracle he should miss us, there was no way in all
the worlds that Gwenwynbar would do so. She would see us
as she went by—Arthur, Ferdia, Daronwy, myself—would
see and know us, and would cry a seizing down upon us,
and that would be that, an end neither painless nor swift.

That was what my brain told me, as I watched Edeyrn and Owein, with Gwenwynbar three steps behind, come stately down the hall between the bowing rows of courtiers and servitors alike. But what my othersight told me was very different, and I could only assume that my very natural wish to survive was coloring my senses . . .

They were twenty feet away now, then ten, then five, and now they were passing us. I bowed as deep and respectful as any Theocracy lackey in that hall, and to my right Arthur and Ferdia did the same; on my other side Daronwy dipped in a court curtsy—even in that unbearably crammed instant I could sense her fury at having to do so to Gwenwynbar of all women.

As Edeyrn's glance touched upon us, brushing over our faces like a black feather, I summoned all my strength to keep body and soul and mind most still and silent, as a baby rabbit will freeze to immobility when a hunting owl flies by overhead. The only part of me that moved, besides my pounding heart, was my hand, that as ever in times of need and stress had closed upon the gold case that held my hawk's feather.

Arthur too seemed to have closed his hand upon something, though I could not see what it might be. But even as he did so, Edeyrn's eyes that had been keen and bright upon him suddenly blinked and unfocused, and he moved on. Owein's own gaze ran incuriously over us, and he nodded—perhaps a little more respectfully than he might have done had he not noticed our bard's insignia.

Then Gwenwynbar was before us, and I prepared myself anew for the outcry and battle that seemed certain to follow, resolved that none should come to Arthur save over my slain form and at great cost to themselves.

She looked each of us straight on, her dark eyes going first to Arthur, then to me, then flicking briefly over Ferdia and Daronwy and back again to Arthur, and I held my breath.

Arthur bowed as he had bowed to Edeyrn, but now he bowed to her alone, his face showing nothing I could read. But plainly his onetime wife had seen rather more, for she hesitated, just the barest check of stride and speed, and something passed over her countenance to which I could put no name. Then she inclined her head to Arthur, and followed Owein out of the hall.

Though we waited every second for guards to fall upon us, and when at last we ourselves left the hall our backs crawled every step of the way, we passed unhindered, and departed Caer Dathyl unpursued by guard or thought.

"Why did she not *tell* him!"

It was perhaps the twentieth time Daronwy had asked the question, and she no more thought to get an answer now than she had done when first she asked it.

We were at the moment as safe as we could be short of Llwynarth: Having put as many miles between us and Caer Dathyl as our horses could give us, we lay now hidden up in the summer shieling of a family secretly loyal to the Counterinsurgency, some thirty lai into the Deer Hills.

And as we had done twenty times already as response to Daronwy's question, we shook our heads in baffled unison. For indeed none of us had an answer: as to why Gwenwynbar, who had last been heard of swearing vengeance on her husband and all his kin and friends and cause, had saved us there in the hall from the swords of Owein's Ravens. By now—and none of us had any illusions on that account—we all of us would have been either slain or praying for it as release from torture. No question but that Gwenwynbar had saved our lives; but still the question remained.

If Arthur had any answer—and he was the only one among us who might—he was keeping it to himself for now, and perhaps for always. On our carefully circumspect trot out of Caer Dathyl, and subsequent wild drumming bansha-ride into this present doubtful safety, he had said not one word, and he said none now.

"Well," said Ferdia heavily, "she may have saved us and it is not that I am not grateful—but to be beholden to *her* . . . Clearly she is Owein's bedmate now, ban-charach or lennaun or lightskirt or whatever."

I lowered my eyes and carefully shut my mind as he and

Daronwy idly disputed Gwenwynbar's status in Owein's household, but the thought blazed in my mind until I could not believe they did not see it plain upon my face: the thought that the child Gwenwynbar was great with was no child of Owein Rhcged's, as all seemed to assume, but a child of Arthur's.

That he was thinking the same, and had been all night, I knew well; and later we spoke of it privately, away from the others.

"You have only to count the months, Talyn. It could well be mine."

"And if it is?"

Arthur ran a hand over his face. "If it is—then it shares heirship with Gweniver and Marguessan and Morgan and myself, for it is blood of the House of Dôn."

"And if it is," I heard myself saying calmly, "then you must destroy it before it can destroy you." I pretended not to see the shocked, guilty face that turned toward me—shock to hear the unspeakable spoken, guilt for having thought the same long since—and resolutely continued, "This you know already. But, Artos, *I* know that it is not. It cannot be. Why else do you think Gwenwynbar saved us?"

Now Arthur looked only surprised. "I had thought, that must be the one sure proof that the child *is* mine; for her to so spare me and the rest of you." A harsh, desperate laugh. "Which do you think Owein might prefer it, his or mine? Or Edeyrn? More to the point, whose would Gwenwynbar wish it?"

Even more to the point, I thought, though I did not say it, neither then nor later, *whose will Gwenwynbar claim it?*

Chapter 25

Safe again at Llwynarth, by the next day after our return I was feeling confident enough to tackle Arthur on several matters; and after breaking that morning's fast with a much chastened Ferdia, I headed for my fostern's quarters to do just that.

This new Llwynarth was still new even to us who sheltered there, and although it was larger, more comfortable, better planned and better hidden than its predecessor, still I found myself resenting the reason, and the author of that reason, for our enforced relocation.

"Are you going to blame Gwenar for everything then, Talyn, from now to Nevermas, or just for such things as suit you?"

To judge by the look in his eyes, Arthur had been up most of the night; to judge by the unprecedented tidiness of his chamber and the bareness of his workdesk, he had defended himself well against the night's hauntings. And seeing the weariness and sorrow that were on him, I was instantly remorseful that I had just carped as I had against the admittedly far-from-blameless Gwenwynbar.

But not remorseful enough to repent of it . . . "Nay," I snapped back, "only for such things as she can be rightly credited! She could not betray Coldgates, for instance, so most like I would not hold her to account did the shieling come to be laid bare—though perhaps I might even so, now I think on it. And do you not go telling me yet again how she did save us from Edeyrn and Owein; even you cannot absolve her from obliging us to find a new Llwynarth.''

"I had not thought to try." He stood up, flexing his neck and shoulders as if to rid himself of some invisible burden. "And as I have also told you before, we should have had to find a new lair sometime; now or a year now makes little differ. As for Gwenar, leave it. She has chosen her own road and her own dán will chivy her down it.''

"But the—''

"I said *leave* it, Glyndour.'' The dark eyes flashed warning to match the sudden steel in the voice—it was ever a bad sign when Arthur addressed one of us by surname—and I subsided. "All the same," he continued after an uncomfortable little pause, "I am still glad we went to Caer Dathyl as we did, for now I have seen as I have wished to see who we have so long been fighting; whom in the end we shall destroy.''

"And he has seen you, maybe," I muttered.

"Now do not start that up again— Any road, I think not.''

"Artos, he looked straight at you! At all of us, come to it.''

"Even so, I do not think he saw us—any of us—by grace of this.'' He had been fidgeting with something in the pocket of his tunic—as he had been when Edeyrn passed us by in Owein's hall—and now he brought it out upon his open palm. "Morgan my sister sent it to me before we left for Caer Dathyl. She and Birogue constructed it at Collimare. There is mighty magic in it, and on it.''

"I can see that; or rather do not need to see, for it is plain to any sense. She grows skilled . . .''

Glancing up at him for permission, I carefully took the talisman from his hand. It was a water-white sphere of purest rock crystal, smooth and polished, ice-cold even though it had been in Arthur's hand, and in his inner pocket before that. Bound round by two intersecting bands of incised silver—runes, but I could not make any sense of them—it was of the bigness of a grape or cherry, and it prismed the light like a cabochon diamond.

"This is what saved us from Edeyrn, Tal, not I or you or Ronwyn or anything we thought in our conceit to do." He watched me as I turned the thing in my fingers, marvelling at its beauty and the supreme skill that had made a thing of power from a piece of rock. "And, like it how little you might, it was Gwenar saved us from Owein. As simple as that."

"Naught is ever that simple." I returned the crystal to him and sat back, putting my hands behind my head. "But, just for now, let us say that it is so . . ." I turned the topic. "I had not thought young Morgan to be so far along in her studies. Birogue must be a queen among teachers, though of course she has good stuff on which to work. That is no magic of Druid or Ban-draoi, that talisman, but some practice of the Shining Folk. Never did we learn such ranns at Bargodion, nor I think your mother and Gweniver, at their own schools."

Arthur's face, that had been clouded, cleared like sudden sun. "Guenna does do well, though I seldom hear from her save through our mother. This was the first direct communication I have had from her for three years, as if—"

"—as if she knew her brother had need of her craft," I finished for him. "And doubtless she did; no great surprise there."

He shook his head. "Nay, that is not it; I was thinking that she has been now fourteen years on that isle with one of the mighty among the Sidhe. If this is the measure of her now—to craft a talisman to thwart the magic of the Marbh-draoi himself—what must she be like when she comes into the fullness of her power?"

"Well, whatever she may be like, she will still be our Guenna." But I was caught by the thought as he had been: Fourteen years learning the teachings of the Sidhe! What Morgan must know by now, what she must be by now capable of doing . . . And yet it was the 'fourteen years' part of it that held me most in wonder: It seemed hardly possible that it had been so long; and yet, as I ran back over those thousands of days—these the years of wandering, these the years at the first Llwynarth, these the months of our abiding here—I knew that it was so, and sighed for time passing. Morgan was now a young woman of twenty-four springs, I might not even recognize her when next I did see her— whenever that might be; Arthur and I had ourselves passed our fortieth year this last Wolf-moon and Badger-moon.

And yet to Morgan's companion in Collimare those four- teen years would be no more than a week's-end at the most, for who knew to what strange slow clock or calendar the mortal forms of the Sidhe did make temporal answer? For a moment I let my mind run: The Hail, that tall fierce feathered eagle-race who dwell on Galathay, live to see their own millennium and more, and they are the longest-lived folk that so far is known. But in Keltia it has ever been believed, though of course none can say for certain—or at least none *has* ever said, which is not quite the same thing—that the lifespans of the Shining Folk may surpass those of the Hail ten times over, maybe longer still; indeed there are those who hold that the Sidhe do never die.

And, thinking on all this timelessness, I knew suddenly that time had come for me to move on . . .

"I shall not be here past the summer Sunstanding," I said abruptly, and Arthur's glance shot at once to meet mine.

But he seemed to have known already, and to understand my reasons, for instead of the protest I had expected to hear, all he said was, "And after all that great lamenting and cajolery you sent up to come here with me?"

"Say rather, after the seven years I have spent with you and the rest! But you know as well as I that I must be gone, I can tell it. Time it is I took up my petty place, and if they were here to say so, Elphin and Merlynn and Uthyr and Ygrawn would all agree. Any road, have we not ever planned it so? You yourself, if I recall correctly, once did say that I can serve you best from a place in some well-connected household."

"I did," said Arthur ruefully. "Though now I repent me of

it, since it means I shall not have you by me when I need your company the sorest . . ."

"Well, we cannot have it all ways. I cannot take a petty place to spy for you and yet remain in Llwynarth. Perhaps I should try to enter Owein's service," I added, only half in jest. "There is naught like robbing an orchard when you have need of apples—"

"Do not even think it! Well, though I am loath to lose you, braud, you are in the right as to the rest of it; and to have you in your petty place will be of more help to me than five Fian battalions. But, gods, Talynno, how I shall miss you."

I felt tears sting my eyes, and looked hastily away. Yet though I knew already how very much I myself should miss him, I knew too that my feeling was by no means the same as his: For the loneliness that was to wrap Arthur round for the rest of his life, even in the midst of Companions and campaigns and the crown that would come, had settled down already upon him. Partly it was that terrible solitude that distances princes from the day of their birth; yet Arthur had not been born a prince, but only come to it later and unlooked-for, and still this remove had been part of him for as long as I had known him, and most like even before.

It was never coldness nor aloofness, never once that: He had a warm feeling for folk, whether in the general or each by each, and this reserve of his did not seem to hinder him reaching past it to touch folk's minds and souls and hearts. Never was *that* gift to fail him: He was ever able to touch others, but only rarely was he able to let them touch him, much though he did wish it. Instead, that remove kept him from entering fully into such small everyday joys as most folk take for given; perhaps this was what he had sought to escape by wedding Gwenwynbar—perhaps he may even have found it, a little, for a time. . . But, though it is a hard saying, and a harder knowing for us who loved him, and for him hardest of all in the doing and enduring, Arthur was not made for private happinesses; and though he knew it as well as any, every now and again the very human longing to be as others

were, and have what others had, would break through both
resolve and reserve; as it did now.

"Oh, you shall soon be far too busy even to think of me
save as another intelligencer." I had shaded my voice to
unconcern with all the skill of my craft, but I was as moved
as he at the thought of our parting yet again. For most of our
lives we had been closer to each other as fosterns than either
had been to his own blood relations, how should we not
sorrow now to be once more apart? But I sought to do as he
had already succeeded in doing, and moved past it.

"I shall go to Bargodion first, I think," I said then, "for a
month or two of retreat—and to get in some practice time, the
which I have been sadly neglectful of here amongst the
heroes! Merlynn will be there, I have heard, and I have not
seen our old badger for too long a time."

"You will find him the same as ever," said Arthur with a
laugh. "Sometimes I wonder if he has not after all learned
from his lady the unchangeful long-living of the Sidhe."

But for all my sudden decision, it was near another sixmonth
before I managed to extricate myself from Llwynarth and set
out as I had planned. No sooner had I fixed on a day for
departing when some difficulty arose with the Hanes that only
I could deal with, or then it was one of the Companions
needing my help as master mapper to plot a new raiding
route, or if not that there was ever and again some task that
needed taking from Arthur's shoulders; and none of these
chores could be refused, even had I wished to, and I did not.

If naught else, though, at the least the delay meant that I
should leave Llwynarth's master with an easier heart than
might have otherwise been the case: He had been sunk in
gloom for some weeks following our venture to Caer Dathyl,
and not unnaturally, for it was all to do with Gwenwynbar.
He never said so to me, and so I presumed never to anyone
else either, but I knew well enough how he had felt to see her
there with Owein, and with child. And when word came
about two months later that she had borne a son—a strapping lad by all accounts, tall and well-made, with chestnut-red

hair—Arthur's silence was more thunderously eloquent than ever.

We had of course discussed the matter amongst ourselves, most privily—we the Companions—and most of us held with Kei's philosophical judgment: "If it is Owein's," he had said, "no great matter. If it is Arthur's, we will all know soon enough." I had my own ideas on the subject, but took care to remind myself that Gwenwynbar had red hair, and Owein's was not far off that same hue, and both of them were tall above the average; and therefore naught was to be proved by *that* road.

Arthur himself recovered from his dubhachas—the word is untranslatable, it means a savage evil humor of blackest despair, impossible to counter and almost as hard to conquer—defeating it by some strength he found within himself; though it would not have surprised me greatly to learn that Morgan's crystal, that had confounded Edeyrn, had made shift here to comfort Arthur, or at least to clear his mind and mood of the dark and dazeful mists.

However he had done it, long before I left Llwynarth he was back again his old self, and saw me off with unfeigned good cheer and unconcealed envy and many messages for Merlynn and our other Druid preceptors; and for my part, though still reluctant to leave him, I was also glad that I could do so with so relieved a conscience.

My intent in going to Bargodion was not only as I had told Arthur and the others—to rest, to contemplate, to retune my fingers to the harp, to see Merlynn—but to meet another need I had had for some time now. I had never forgotten that Birogue of the Sidhe had spoken my mother's name as a friend, and though she had refused at that time to enlighten me, perhaps at Bargodion I might find answers from another source. But when I spoke of it to Merlynn, for once the sorcerer seemed loath to answer.

"I understand your need, Talyn," he said at last. "To know of Birogue, and how she came to be your mother's friend and how Medeni died. But if Birogue did not tell you, then I may not. At least, not yet; it may be the right time has not yet come for that telling. But you will know, one day, that I promise. Your mother would not have wished you to remain in ignorance of the truth—and I promise too that there is nothing about it that would be better left unknown—and your mother's friend will honor that wish. The Sidhe do keep their promises—though sometimes it may take longer for them to do so than other folk are willing to wait, still they have excellent reasons for delaying, and we can be sure of that, at least.''

But I was sure of nothing just then, and of that least of all. It seemed the height of vain hoping, that I should have thought Merlynn would tell me what even my sister Tegau could not tell me, nor any other of my sibs. But then I recalled that never in my life had Merlynn spoken aught but the truth to me—whether he spoke as Merlynn or as Ailithir—never but the truth, be it howsoever hard to bear, and I was a little comforted.

Though I failed in my endeavor to learn what I would know, much else at Bargodion was more to my liking that time. The actual school had moved elsewhere long since—like Tinnavardan, moving for safety's sake—but the old location was still maintained as a kind of supercollege for the Pheryllt, those Druids above Druids. Renamed Dinas Affaraon—a name it still bears, and perhaps ever will—it housed fewer than fifty just then, which suited me very well indeed.

There was time for the harp there, time for refinements of the Hanes, time to debate magical theory with the lords of magic and time merely to sit and stare, and sometimes it was that which was most productive of all.

But however much I had been enjoying my stay, and however much more I had needed the respite—between Gwenwynbar, Gweniver, Arthur and the omnipresent though ever-absent Owein, I had felt pulled to pieces of late, like a strawcross when the harvest festival is past—I knew better than any other that I had been long enough in preparation and in indiligence both together; and that it was time indeed to move on, to that place which Arthur and I had so long since foreseen for me.

Chapter 26

So I set out from Bargodion much as I had left there for the first time, so many years ago now; but this time I went alone.

Travelling slowly and in easy stages, I went down along the edges of the black glass plains that lie to the south of Bargodion's knifeback ridge, and came after some days to the border of the ancient volcanic desolation. Even now, centuries after those times of fire, if you stand there you will see for yourself that strange boundary, where the devastation of the exploding chain of craters finally ceased and the living lands survived. Though not unscathed, to be sure: There are rifts still in these marcher-lands so deep and narrow that snow falling to the bottom in winter oft will remain unmelted until the height of summer following, so deep are the rifts cut by the great earth faults and so high uplifted are the lands.

It was a country of great harshness and greater beauty: I would look up as I slogged southward to see towering, sharp-edged cliffs, carved out long ago by vanished glaciers grinding by, hanging above me like knives in the clouds. I was leaving the burnt lands behind, with their sleeping fires and mutterings below, moving now into a country of honey-colored sandstone hills and wide-mouthed valleys.

Summer was over—I had tarried longer than I intended at Bargodion, and once again I was on the road in autumn—and

I could watch the white cranes heading south with me, long curving strings across the sky, their flight mirrored in the shallow salt lakes that lie all through that region; but as I passed nearer I saw that the rippling lines upon the water were no reflections but strands of salt froth, blown into arcs by the freshening wind.

I was headed into the heartland of the enemy: Against all counsels of those whose counsels ordinarily mattered most to me, I was going down to Caer Dathyl itself, where Owein Rheged held sway for the Marbh-draoi over all the world of Gwynedd, and where once before I had rashly ventured. I did not know why or indeed by what—or by whom—my steps were so directed; but every sense I possessed, as Druid or bard or believer in dán, had united to lead me this way, and far from me to think to turn to another road. I had gone once to Caer Dathyl, and come safe away again, and those senses urging me there now told me in no faint voice that I should do no less this time.

So it was that on a snowy afternoon between Samhain and the feast of Midwinter I came to the maenor of Pyrs Vechan, lord of the district of Ruabon in the Deer Hills, and one of Owein's chiefest lackeys. Perhaps the half-forgotten memory of that ferret-faced equerry we had had for tablemate, that never-to-be-forgotten night at Caer Dathyl, had prompted me to turn my steps toward Ruabon, or perhaps there was some other reason; but there it was I went, and there sought shelter.

I could not fault my welcome: They must have hungered greatly for bards in this backhill district, if even such a patchcloak wanderer as myself was greeted with courtesies more suited to a visiting prince. In one respect only was my treatment somewhat lacking: I was given to sit at the top of the cross-table below the high dais where the ranking lords and ladies would sup. This was not in accord with strictly correct practice, which should have given me place at the high board itself, and indeed may well have been honest ignorance; but I was in truth better pleased that I should be seated so, for my placing allowed me a clear view of the hall and those who sat within, both above and below the horn. Our former fellow-diner, the kern-equerry, was nowhere to be seen, and I allowed myself to relax a little; not that I had been qualmful to begin with, and that too was strange.

I was hungry, and it was some little time before I managed to lift my face from plate and mether and look round at the company. First of all my gaze went to the dais, where sat the lord of Ruabon among his honored guests.

Pyrs Vechan was a minor chieftain, of the same rank as my father, and Gorlas, and many others; influential for no great merit of his own, but for that he ruled a strategic dúchas—Ruabon, remote as it was, protected the passes through the Deer Hills, guarding Caer Dathyl to the north. And there lay the difference: Unlike my father and Gorlas and those others, Pyrs had taken Owein's coin, he was a bought dog of Edeyrn; the like of which many had perished rather than themselves become.

The guest-seat beside the pig-faced Pyrs was empty, and I assumed that there was no visitor of rank this most inclement evening. I never learn: No sooner had I assumed so, and begun to relax in earnest, and devote myself to my mether, than the doors of the hall swung open and a party of latecomers strode arrogantly in. They separated as they did so, a few going to the high table where Pyrs was gabbling and gesturing in abject hospitality, the rest to the lower benches with us commoners.

And I hid my choke of surprised dismay behind the wide wooden shield of my mether, for the late-come guest in the snow-damp cloak, now taking the seat of honor as if by right born, was none other than Owein Rheged himself.

It was plainly a surprise flying visit, for all round me I heard only muttered astonishment mingled with consternation and indeed speculative comment, that the lord of the planet should turn up for the nightmeal unheralded and unannounced in the hall of a minor vassal; and I confess the thought went through me like an arrow that somehow Owein knew I was here, knew who I was and had come a-purpose to trap me.

Quick as that thought died, though, killed by cold reason, another had formed, born of the calm inevitability of dán itself, and I suddenly knew what I was going to do, what I had been led here to accomplish. Arthur would either kiss me or kill me when he learned of it, but I was going to do it all the same.

So I waited in patience until the meal was done with— Owein's late arrival scarce delaying it, for he ate almost as an afterthought, swiftly and sparingly, with a minimum of talk to his tablemates or indeed to his host—and then, in that relaxed, easy pause that comes when the meal is ended and the board cleared, when folk sit back to finish methers at leisure and talk in comfort, I rose in my place and caught Pyrs's eye. Standing forth before the high table, I touched my harp-satchel, in the ancient gesture of a travelling bard craving leave of the lord of the hall to chaunt. Before Pyrs could order it, the entire room had quieted in delight; and I thought as I had thought before how hungry the folk here seemed for what a bard could bring them.

Owein, who had been talking quietly to Pyrs and a sol-dierly-looking sort who I guessed must be his lieutenant, now glanced down to where I stood. For the first time since that night in Caer Dathyl I felt his eyes on me, and under that curiously light-filled glance my skin began to chill, though it did not seem that he recognized or remembered me.

He was perhaps seventy years old at that time, still a young man as my people reckon such things—when one's lifespan can reach the double-century, one's youth lasts rather longer as well. A handsome man too, in appearance more Scotan than Kymro, with reddish hair and blue eyes, and a terrifying air of latent power that hung round him like a cloak or a cloud. With eyes that Merlynn had trained, though, I perceived at once that the power was by no means his own, but only borrowed as the cloak may be borrowed—lent him by Edeyrn, and, presumably, subject to its proper owner once again reclaiming it.

Well, I thought, *this time Edeyrn is not here, and I am,*

and so we shall see what we may see . . . I bowed deeply in
answer to his nod of acknowledgment and permission, un-
slinging my harp from my shoulder and taking it from the
worn leather satchel. All round me the hall settled down into
anticipatory silence, eager and ready to hear. I fitted Frame of
Harmony—its betraying name-runes and Glyndour armorials
long since covered over—in my lap and gave them of my best.

It must have been good indeed—I could not recall afterwards what I had played, or how well—for all at once I
seemed to awaken to a storm of approval and applause, and
looking up I saw Owein himself smiling at me: under the
circumstances, perhaps not the most reassuring of sights. But
he was clapping heartily with the rest, and tossed me a gold
ring as guerdon, and again I bowed, though less deeply than
before.

Pyrs seemed to feel the need to assert himself; and any
road, he, not Owein, was master in this hall.

"Such artistry should receive greater reward than a gaud,"
he said, in a surprisingly high, light voice. "What would you
ask, master?"

I had my answer ready. "Lord," I said, "a place at your
table."

That woke them all up again: I could hear the gasps run
round the room, and they sat up as if jerked by a single
string. Pyrs looked discomfited—doubtless he was wishing he
had given me another gold gaud after all—but Owein merely
smiled a sleepy smile, and spoke lazily; but he was heard.

"The Lord Pyrs already has a bard in his service. And is it
not said that two harps in the same hall will never play in
tunefulness together?"

Once more I bowed before I replied. "It *is* so said, Lord
Owein; therefore do I challenge the bard of the house for his
place, according to ancient custom."

The instant the words left my lips I was sorry: The custom
I had just invoked was indeed a true and an ancient one, but I
did not know if any save a true bard would be aware of it in
these degenerate days, and I was in terror lest I had in my

traha revealed myself. This had *not* been part of my original plan . . . But it seemed that I had not, or at least I had not yet.

"We know of course of this old and worthy custom—" Owein was watching me now with genuine interest in his eyes, though I could detect not the smallest suspicion that he thought me anything but the wandering bard I posed as, just another threadbare anruth hoping to win a place. But Owein was still speaking.

"It is written that any bard seeking his petty place may challenge any incumbent placeholder. Let us settle the matter then—with a bardic duel."

Owein waved his hand, and the space between the tables was magically cleared. Another stool was brought and set five paces from my own, and then the house bard, one Anlaudd by name, came down from the seat in a corner of the dais where he had been listening to me play. His harp was already in his hands—a nice little instrument, but not fit to share the same shelf with Frame of Harmony—and he wore an air of mingled annoyance, apprehension and superiority. I could tell by his bearing that he was but one of the half-bards; still, who knew but that he might not prove my master all the same. As he came to the little carved seat placed over against my own, I rose, and as one we bowed to Owein and to Pyrs, and to the rapt onlookers, and to each other. We seated ourselves in a ringing silence, and began.

As challenger I had the right to sing first: Frame of Harmony leaped under my fingers, and I sang a song of the Arvon mountains; intricate and pretty, but by no means a major music. It was well received, but I could hear in the quality of the applause the faintest tinge of disappointment, that under the circumstances they had hoped for something altogether more spectacularly fine—and that was just as I had planned it.

Then Anlaudd took his turn—a Vanx melody, I think—and then I played again, and so it would go on, until one of us conceded defeat or until Owein—Pyrs having been overruled, seemingly, in his own hall—declared one of us the victor.

*   *   *

After a while I had suddenly had enough: I had been chaunting most inspired for over an hour, but so, surprisingly, had Anlaudd, his skill rising to the need of the moment as art so often did—commendable for one who was after all no real bard. But I had need to win this contest, for motives far beyond my own personal glory, or even the wish for a place that I had claimed as the contest's cause. I had thought I was playing the best I knew; but clearly more was needed, so in the uncertain silence that followed Anlaudd's last effort—and even I must admit that he harped superbly—I closed my eyes and opened myself to whatever power there was, to the power Elphin had long ago said was my own. After a moment I felt something stirring, somewhere far away, as if it had just then been awakened from stasis or sleep, and then as I called again it came in like a rush of waters.

Oh, I had felt the bardic force stir in me before, as it had been moving just now in Anlaudd; but this that now possessed me was a thing altogether different. The Holy Awen came down upon me like a singing flame: Suddenly I was vast, I towered above the castle, above all Gwynedd; if I lifted a finger, oceans boiled; if I shook my hair, storms arose; I touched the strings of my harp, and mountains walked . . .

I do not remember singing, but I shall never forget what it was I sang:

"Owein, learn thou what may be
That mightiest creature from before the flood.
Without flesh, without foot, without bone, without blood,
Neither older nor younger than it was at the first.
When the Three Shouts were given,
It was on the hill, it was in the wood,
It was upon the fields, it was above the waters.
A cry in the dawning, a whisper in the darkness,
It was not born, neither was it made.
Consternation does it cause, and lamentation,
Wherever the Highest shall will it.
It is the blast that blows against Owein Rheged,
And the name of that wind is The Bear."

When the Awen left me—and it left between one heartbeat and the next, going like a thunderclap, with the unheard boom of mighty wings—the hall came roaring back around my ears. I stood sweating and shaking, cold and hot at once, blinking in the sudden noise and light, noticing particularly Owein's guards as they fingered their weapons, prepared at their master's lightest nod to drag me out and give my insolence the reward they clearly thought it merited. But for his part Owein only looked at me, his fingers to his chin, and under that measuring, weighing stare I grew cold and quiet.

"Death to lay hands upon a bard," said Pyrs doubtfully. "Even so brazen a one as this—let him go as he has come, and no more."

"Nay," said Owein, rising from his seat. "Let his insolence have more fitting reward: I shall take him as bard in my own hall. Many other bards do I maintain at Caer Dathyl, but in thirty years this is the first who has sung me aught but flattery to win a place." To me then: "What is your name, master?"

I looked him straight in the eyes. "Lord, in my craft I am called Mabon Dialedd."

'Son of Vengeance' . . . overdramatic perhaps, and dangerously near the truth; but a name to hide my own that I had vowed to use long ago, should this moment ever come; as now it had. Just for an instant I saw Owein's pale eyes flicker; then the mask was back in place.

"Well," he said lightly enough, "it seems I have acquired more here tonight than a bard only. But however you may be called, you will ride with my company in the morning for Caer Dathyl. One of my men will come for you, so be ready betimes."

As he left the hall with Pyrs and the others of his tail, I sank back upon my little stool, quietly shaking, oblivious to the tendered—and clearly heartfelt—congratulations of Anlaudd. Dazed and delighted and daunted all together I may have been; but I had won my petty place, won it in the afanc's lair itself, even as I had jested to Arthur that I might; and still I could not decide if Arthur would be pleased or wrathful.

But one thing I did know, and reflected on most soberly:
Once again the gods, or whoever it might be that manages
such matters, had ordained that a casual word, spoken in what
amounted to rashness and jest, should become cold reality.
And if that does not instruct us yet again that we must be ever
vigilant as to what we wish for in our heedlessness, I do not
know what might.

Chapter 27

I was five years in Owein's court and service; five years in
Caer Dathyl, that place of strength and stone. By and large it
was a pleasant enough servitude, once I had accustomed
myself to the terrifying reality that, through dán or traha, I
was in the employ of the Marbh-draoi's sword-arm, the master of Gwynedd, my enemy and my brother's enemy. Certainly my tasks were not what I should call burdensome: As
Owein had said, he maintained a goodly number of other
bards to suit his state, and I, however hand-chosen, was the
most junior of the lot.

So it fell to me to harp for guests and visitors, mostly—
though never, thank gods, Edeyrn; he came not again to Caer
Dathyl—and, perhaps once or twice a fortnight, to entertain
in hall after the nightmeal. Now and again Owein himself
would call for me to soothe with my harp a troubled mood or
sleepless night, and on those occasions I took advantage to
learn of him what might be learned—though, as ever, I took
care to keep the quality of my harping to a level that any
half-bard might with art and diligence achieve.

My master was a complex man, which I had not thought to
find him; I had ever imagined him as merely the Marbh-
draoi's creature, a hired sword and a hired soul as well. But I
soon came to learn that he was vastly more than Edeyrn's

obedient servant: He was quick of mind and quick to act; yet
he never acted save from strength and from reasons that were,
to him if to none else, good and sound ones. And by no
means was he the unstable despot common wisdom held him
to be: There was cold brutality, certainly, and amply displayed; but it was equally cold necessity that lay beneath it,
not simple savagery. Owein was not one to let reluctance
come between him and his duty; if after so many years of it
his resolve had grown to look like ruthlessness, so be it, and
perhaps in the end it was.

But it was not unremitting grimness either: He took a
perverse fondness for me from the first—perhaps as he had
said, for that he knew I was no glozer, no speaker of honeyed
words to princes, and he saw and relished the mockery beneath my chaunts as much as did I. We were never friends—
too much blood of too many I loved lay between us, though
he was not to know that until the end—but there was ease and
even laughter, and in a strange, wholly unexpected way, I
soon learned I could serve him without dishonor; even, sometimes, without dislike.

But never did I forget my chief purpose for being in
Owein's service, and almost from the hour of my arrival at
Caer Dathyl I contrived to send messages—by way of the
Hanes, now coming into the fullness of its usefulness—back
to Arthur and the Companions, and even to Uthyr in Coldgates.

Of the one I had dreaded above all others to see—Gwenwynbar—there was no sign. I had half-expected to find her
waiting for me at Caer Dathyl, poised to pounce, and what I
should have done in such case I have no idea even now—had
none then, save some vague, and no doubt vain, thought of
fith-fath.

But again luck—or dán—held: My cautious questions even-
tually elicited the information that upon the birth of her son a
year since—Malgan, she had called him; a name traditional to
Owein's family, and already the boy had been proclaimed
Owein's heir—Gwenwynbar had decided that Caer Dathyl
was not the healthiest place for an infant; and she had gone
with the child and a court, indeed, of her own to a seacoast

maenor of Owein's in the province of Sarre. Having established herself there in the queenly splendor she had long craved—and had never had with Arthur—she did not return to the capital but instead waited, by all accounts scarcely impatiently, for Owein to visit her.

This was interesting knowledge, and after I had passed it on in the usual manner—allowing for the swiftness of the Hanes, it should reach Arthur in a sevennight or so—I gave thanks for Gwenwynbar's absence, and wondered a little on it myself.

Though I doubted Gwenwynbar had ever informed her new lord of her past status as wife to his chief adversary—and, grudgingly, still bore thankfulness to her for our deliverance that time under Edeyrn's very nose—I had long given up speculating as to whether her child had been sired by Arthur or by Owein. Only Gwenwynbar herself knew that, and it appeared that for the moment, at least, and the foreseeable future, she had chosen that Owein should be credited with Malgan's paternity. Since Owein had until now not troubled himself to get any heir at all, I wondered also if perhaps he had not found it as much to his purpose as Gwenwynbar had to hers, that the boy should be acknowledged as his.

What that purpose might be was made abundantly clear some three years later, when it was proclaimed across Keltia that Edeyrn had adopted Owein to be his own heir; the unspoken intent clearly being that as Owein should succeed Edeyrn when at last the unthinkable should occur and the Marbh-draoi no longer walked among us, so then should Malgan come to succeed Owein. Just as clearly, this had been a thing long determined, and the timing of the announcement contingent upon the birth of a suitable heir of Owein's body: Presumably, now the child was four years of age, he might safely be expected to live and thrive; and so did Edeyrn at last declare his grand design.

Though there had been some curiosity in Keltia as to what, indeed, should befall when Edeyrn was no more, so long had the Marbh-draoi ruled that I think folk thought in their despair that he should rule forever. I, who knew the truth of his long-living, found my own speculation running on a different track: Edeyrn was by Merlynn's own accounting at *least* four hundred years of age—twice a Kelt's natural outside lifespan. Granted that he came by this thoroughly unnatural span for that his mother had been of the Shining Folk—could it mean, even so, that his years ran short at last; hence this new concern for the usurper-succession? And if he who was half-Sidhe could live undiminished to twice the double-century, what did that say of the spans of those who were full-blooded of that mystic race?

Intriguing questions: But though I dutifully passed on my reflections to Arthur, I received none back again; and as for the common folk of Keltia, once the first stir of Owein's adopting was past, they sank back into the same seething of apathy and unrest in which they had been caught for the past two hundred years, and little changed.

Even Arthur's activities seemed shaded down into half-strength: Though he kept up the same raids and reivings he had been making for years, he had grown more wary of late, pulling back into his beloved Arvon fastnesses, emerging from time to time only to remind folk, forcefully enough when he did so, that Owein did not have all things his own way.

Gwenwynbar I never saw, save at a safe anonymous distance on a few occasions of state when she deigned to return to Caer Dathyl. Though it seemed that Owein was as besotted with her as he had ever been, she herself seemed to have cooled somewhat in her passion; if passion there had ever been on her part, and knowing her as I did I rather doubted it. No, she had set out to snare Owein as coolly and calculatedly as earlier she had set herself to trap Arthur.

Yet by all accounts she was devoted to her son: Malgan ap Owein was a well-grown five-year-old now, old enough to come to court on his own—attended of course like the princeling he was. He was a careful child, well-behaved, tall and lithe like his mother, already receiving instruction in sword-play from his father's lieutenants, and a more accomplished rider than I had been at his age, or was even now. Though I made it my custom to go to ground outside the city whenever Malgan came to visit his father—in fear that some word or thought of me should through him reach Gwenwynbar, and my masquerade and mission be exploded—I contrived to observe him from afar, to see what might be seen.

From such limited scrutinizings it was hardly possible, of course, for me to deduce the child's paternity: I saw traits in him that I had known in Arthur these forty years past, and traits that I had discerned in Owein over the past five, so clearly there was no answer for me there.

But then one day, full five years after Owein had beckoned me from the hall at Ruabon, I had an answer to a question I had long forgotten I had ever framed in words, and all my Sight gave me no warning.

It was a nightmeal during one of the days of the Midsummer festivities. Owein had gone as was his custom to spend the feast days with Gwenwynbar and Malgan at his castle of Saltcoats, south of Caer Dathyl on the shores of a great shallow bay, where Gwenwynbar had made her abode since the birth of her son. Again as was his custom, the lord of Gwynedd had taken a sizable tail with him, as well as off-world guests, and so the benches of Caer Dathyl's Great Hall were less full than usual for the evening meals.

As I have said, I was not Owein's only bard or even his chief bard, and so had managed to avoid being included in the party for Saltcoats—which of course suited me very well. If my presence *had* been commanded, I should have feigned illness or found some other excuse, but I had never been asked on such jauntings and was fervently glad of it.

But the thinness of the bard-roster for the feast days meant my playing in hall rather more often than was my usual duty, and this was the third straight night I had been chief chaunter. Ordinarily such prolonged bard's service would have been a strain—and indeed my voice this third night was more ragged than it should have been—but my audiences were undemanding, and the mood with Owein away was one of relaxment,

and the summerwine for the festival was an excellent pressing
this year. Altogether an easy and pleasant time . . .

So I invite you to imagine my utter staggerment when,
looking out idly over the hall as was my habit when I played,
I saw Arthur Penarvon on the lower benches, among the
rough-clad servitors and galloglasses and grooms.

He stood out among them like a Beltain fire on a rocky tor
at middlenight, so that I marvelled that I had not noticed him
before that instant. But when my heart had stopped pounding
I realized that his invisibility had been his own doing; he had
blended in perfectly with that rough company, and only my
stupidity could now betray him. He made no sign of recognition, of course, as I made none, only watched me and listened
with the same polite and appreciative attention that the others
gave me. But even so I could sense by his bearing—the
alertness that was impossible to disguise—and the total shielding of his mind from the one swift probe I ventured that he
had come for no small purpose or senseless exploit, and that
he had been waiting for this moment for some time.

I played on—at least I think I must have, for none, not
even Owein's lieutenant Daigh, who was master in our master's absence, reproached me with fumbled harping, though I
have not the slightest recollection of how I played or what or
until when. I was conscious only of the overriding need to
keep my gaze from Arthur's face—both of our lives, and
more beside, without question depended on it—yet all I could
see *was* that face, shining in the corner of my sidesight.

"*WHY?*" was all I said. The ordeal was over at last, and
Arthur and I had met as if by merest chance outside the hall,
he pausing to commend me on my playing; and now we were
alone.

But Arthur shook his head in warning, and drew me farther
down the passage. "Not yet; gather your gear, you are done
with your service to Owein, and to all others like him. You
are with me, Talyn, from now until—well, until. Did I not
tell you once that when I had need of your sword at last, I

should ask for it? Well, I ask now. If you will wish to come?'' he added anxiously.

I laughed. ''I think I might be persuaded! Any road, I have little else but what I stand up in. Only let me get my cloak and harp, and a few small bits of gear and garb, and we can be away. You had best await me by the stables, it is less public and we can be the swifter gone.'' As I turned to go to my chamber: ''Just where is it that we shall be gone to?''

''Does it matter?''

''Not in the least,'' I answered with a grin, ''but I should like to know all the same.''

''And so you shall,'' said Arthur, matching my grin with his own. ''But not here, and not now. Owein, though he be not to home, has long ears, and many long tongues to wag at them.''

''I am come to take you with me north,'' he said, as we rode more slowly now, slow enough for speech; our first wild gallop out of Caer Dathyl, reminiscent of that flight six years since, had put some real distance between us and possible pursuit. Though I by no means expected any: I was well known in the city by this time, and the incurious guard had waved us by without even a casual challenge. Which possibly he would soon come to regret; as for Owein, by the time he returned from Saltcoats I would be far beyond his reach, and if he puzzled out the truth it no longer mattered. But:

''North!'' I echoed, my spirits soaring. ''To Coldgates then?''

Arthur shot me a swift glance that I felt even through the darkness; then he turned his eyes straight ahead, to the moon-blanched road that rolled before us, between the horses' forward-pricked ears.

''Do you remember,'' he said after a while, ''Merlynn once laid geis upon me—or perhaps he but foretold my dán, it makes little differ which and with him it is ever hard to tell—that I should one day go to Loch Bel Draccon—''

''—and take there the sword Llacharn from the hand of the Lady of the Loch,'' I finished eagerly. ''I remember well! Then—''

"Though I did not know it then," continued Arthur, with a strange deliberate air, "Loch Bel Draccon is the ancient name of that arm of the Sea of Glora in which lies Collimare."

I swung in my saddle to stare at him. "Then the Lady you must seek for the sword is Birogue? She knew all this time that you should come to claim it?"

Arthur shrugged under the swathings of his cloak. "She might be, and she may have known—I daresay she can keep counsel on such matters even better than Merlynn himself! We shall not know until we come there; and so until then let us speak of it no more." His face, that had been grave, grew animated. "But let me tell you how it has been with us, and I would hear as much from you—"

So I listened to him, and learned that all was well at Llwynarth with the Companions, and at Coldgates with Uthyr and Ygrawn and all the rest, though he spoke no word of Gweniver and I asked for none. One surprise there was: Marguessan had been wed this sixmonth past to Irian, son of the Lord of Lleyn, and had gone to live with him and his kindred, in that part of Gwynedd that we call the Old North.

And though with one ear I listened to Arthur maundering on about the wedding, and the utter loyalty of the bridegroom and his family to Uthyr and the Counterinsurgency, I was in truth back in a conversation of many years since, looking down into a pair of dark-rimmed, blue-irised eyes, watching on a viewscreen a hapless birlinn being driven by magic onto distant sharp-fanged rocks.

Marguessan. I had not thought of her, save in passing, for many years; now all that old uneasiness came flooding back, and I remembered how I had spoken to Uthyr and Ygrawn not ten minutes after that long-ago incident, telling them—evenly, dispassionately—of what their daughter had done; and mentioning, with diffidence, what steps might be taken to prevent any repetitions. Clearly she could not be watched forever, on the off chance that she might try the same malevolent trick again; but just as clearly she could not be permitted to go about wrecking ships for sport, or worse, by distant sending.

My deepest unease lay in the fact that although Marguessan,

by her mother's own foresighted decree, had not been given the training in magic that her sister and her cousin had received, she had all the same managed to master this evil, and by no means simple, trick; and doubtless more beside. So I pointed all this out to Ygrawn and Uthyr as forcefully as I might—however beloved I might be to them, I was still only foster-son and cliamhan, and they were, after all, the King and Queen—and suggested possible courses of action and precaution.

But for all my undisguised disquiet, the response of Marguessan's parents had been strangely subdued and non-committal, and in my dull-wittedness I went puzzled and even angry away. Now it came to me, as it had not then, that they had been every bit as shocked and horrorstruck as I at Marguessan's actions; and indeed I later learned that Ygrawn had secretly set upon her elder daughter that binding-rann we had once spoken of, so that such a thing did not reoccur. As so far it had not; but who knew what skills Marguessan had by now mastered . . . But now the truth was plain to me: She had been all they had left to them besides each other; and in their loneliness Uthyr and Ygrawn had not wished to set any wedge between their daughter and themselves. Arthur had gone, and I, and Gweniver, and Morgan; only Marguessan had remained with her parents, and they had been loath to distance themselves from her until there plainly was no other choice.

Yet my feeling of unease remained: Soon or late, Marguessan would show her true colors—as, indeed, she had promised me—and naught good should come of it.

And thinking of Marguessan, I found my thoughts naturally leading on to her sister. Marguessan wed, Morgan—what *would* Morgan be like by now? I had not seen her since that day two decades past when Arthur and I rode to Collimare, as we did now, to leave her with Birogue. Now we rode to claim her back, perhaps, and take her home; or perhaps we rode there to another purpose—Arthur's purpose. Or perhaps all purposes were now the same purpose: We should not know for certain until we came once again to the Forest in the Sea.

Chapter 28

*I*t was a mild, still morning of middle summer, the air sweet and heavy with that milky scent of grass and leaf, the ground under our boots drenched with dew. We stood on the shores of Glora, Arthur and I, as we had stood years since, and waited now as we had waited then.

"At least there is no mist today," I said, my voice unnaturally loud in the absolute hush; and indeed the sea stretched blue and calm and clear in all directions. "This time we shall see her boat before it is upon us."

Arthur raised his brows, then pointed, and I followed the sweep of his pointing arm. "Mist or no," he said, "that craft goes unseen as it does wish."

For indeed the gray-hulled boat was almost to shore by us as he spoke, and yet I swear now, as I did then, that the sparkling strait between us and the island of Collimare had been empty until that instant.

In the stern of the ghostly craft, as before, stood a gray-cloaked figure; but as the boat touched sand beside us, with a very real crunch of keel on gravel, I frowned, for something about this shrouded figure seemed both strangely familiar and utterly unknown . . .

From beneath the gray folds of the hood, a shadowed smile. "Do you not know me then, Talyn? Or is it that you have forgotten me after all?"

In my bemusement I found my fingers going to a tangled scrap of gold fringe on the edge of my cloak, and I spoke as a man will speak in dreams.

"Your knot of remembrance is tied still, Guenna, if tattered."

At that she laughed, and it was her old laugh, and swept the hood from her head. Morguenna Pendreic it was, and yet not so: The girl that I had known was both vanished and somehow present, and the woman who stood in her place, calm, confident, lovely, I did not know at all.

If I dithered, Arthur had no such difficulty: Striding ankle-deep into the wavelets that broke beneath the boat, he reached out and pulled his sister into his arms, bestowing upon her the same brotherly kiss he had given me, once we were gone from Caer Dathyl and it was safe to exchange warm greetings deferred.

"I had a thought, that it might be you," he was saying joyfully. "But where then is the Lady Birogue?"

Morgan gave him a smile brimming with secrets and straightforwardness in equal parts. "Oh, not far; she has other calls upon her now, and so I have come to be Lady at Collimare." She spoke to him, but her eyes had not left my face; before I could drown utterly in their deeps I heard Arthur's cheerful voice, and startled back to life.

"Talyn, have you no kiss for Guenna?"

It was what I had been longing to do, and fearing to do, and dreading lest I ventured and was rebuffed; and never would I have dared it on my own. But now at Arthur's prompting I stepped forward, and taking Morgan's hands in mine I kissed her given cheek, soft and cool beneath my lips.

Then, to my utter confoundment, she turned her face straight on to mine, and her mouth briefly brushed my own, with a touch like frost and fire. I looked down at her, amazed, yet not at all surprised: This was dán, then, come at last; how simple it was in the end. I saw by her eyes that she shared my thought, doubtless had known it before I had, even; and both of us saw too that from now until the end of our days we should know all things together.

Morgan stepped back then, and when she spoke her voice

was clear and grave, nothing of what we had just shared reflected in it.

"Come then, both of you. There is something must be done, and only we three may do it."

We stepped from the gray boat onto the island's shore; without a backward glance to see if we followed, Morgan plunged into the trackless wood that came down nearly to the water's edge. As we trailed obediently after her through the silent dripping thickets, I could not take my eyes from the graceful figure that moved so silently before us. Not only to avoid being lost in the many trees did I stare so hard upon her, but because I found it hard to accept that the colt-awkward, blond-braided tearaway that had been Morgan as I knew her was now this stately young sorceress in the long gray cloak. But the eyes, if farther-seeing, had been the same.

All at once the trees thinned and we were in a clearing at the forest's heart. Across the grassy ground stood a white stone llan, of the ancient shape and style, the kind that had been sheltering anchorites since first the Kelts did dwell on Earth. Such an air of dread and mystery lay upon the clearing that I hesitated to step from the trees' protecting shadow, and Arthur, a half-stride in front of me, likewise held back. I read in his reluctance the same cause as fueled my own: For all our Druid training, our Fian or bardic experience, there was in this place a power, and a Presence, that neither of us had encountered before.

Then Morgan turned and smiled and gestured us to follow, and without a heartbeat's pause we went, biddable as lambs under the nippings of a working hound.

The llan was bigger within than it had appeared from across the clearing's width: The rooms—a grianán, several sleeping chambers, a pool-room and cookplace and annat—were clean, bare, spacious, airy; the few furnishings of carved honey-colored oak were draped with jewel-bright fabrics and thick furs. Arthur disposed himself upon a broad pillowed divan, immediately at home, while I paced around like a cat in a new place, poking into things, unable to settle.

This was where Morgan and her Sidhe teacher—or teachers? —had dwelled and studied and practiced all these years; their activity, and perhaps that of others before them, had left an imprint that seemed to cling to the white walls as closely as did the coats of clean limewash that brightened them. Palpable magic, and not just here, either—

"Does your fur crackle then, Master Cat?" Morgan was watching me from an archway across the room, her face alight with mischief. She had shed the hood and swathing cloak, and stood there clad in the plain gray robe that the Ban-draoi wear indoors and out. Its plainness served only to highlight her beauty's richness: the tallness of her, the gold of the smooth hair, the hazel eyes like a pool deep in Collimare's own woods.

I laughed, a little shamefaced to be so caught out. "Oh, perhaps a few random sparks . . . There is more to this place, I think, than what we do see here."

She nodded gravely, mischief vanished. "Oh aye, there is more! Shall you see it now, or had you rather wait?"

It was one of the sacred caverns of the Ban-draoi: like to, though far smaller than, Broinn-na-draoichta at the great convent school of Scartanore. We had reached it through a hidden door in the annat's north wall—Morgan had not touched it, but it had opened for us all the same—and then a shallow set of steps and a tunnel into the island's heart had led us down into darkness. It was no place for men, a women's hallow pure and plain—and before you cry scorn on me for what may sound like prejudice of gender I would speedily say that neither are our Druid hallows places for women. Some mysteries are not for sharing.

But Morgan knew what we were feeling—the hairs on the back of my neck were standing up by now, and Arthur's eyes were wide and wary—and she laid one hand on my arm and the other hand upon her brother's; we both flinched at even that light touch.

"Be easy, careddau. It is naught, and it will pass. You are expected here, and you have been long awaited."

Now though she had meant those words to comfort, they had precisely the opposite effect, at least on me: I felt as if some very cold, very strong, very sudden tide had washed over me from neck to toes. I opened my mouth to speak, but Morgan was no longer with us.

Oh, she was still 'there,' in the body, but she had gone all the same: had in the Ban-draoi manner gone out by going inward, and was so caught up now in the demands of moment and magic as not to notice us at all.

She drew herself up to her full tallness, and though she made no gesture that either of us could see—as she had made none to open the hidden door—suddenly light began to bloom upon the cavern walls.

No light from sconces or crystals or torches, just cool blue luminance called from the stone itself; neither brilliant nor blinding, but more than sufficient for us to see one another, our faces pale and apprehensive in the glow, and to half-glimpse the carvings upon the walls, where the stone had been made flat and smooth. From these, after one quick look, I averted my eyes with great firmness of resolve, and Arthur did the same: Though we knew many of the incised symbols from our own tradition, many more belonged to the Sisterhood, or perhaps to a tradition older still, and were in any case not to be stared upon by even favored intruders.

I looked past Morgan to the center of the cave. A dolmen stood there, one of those ancient pillar-stones that point like fingers from earth to sky. As a rule, too, they stand beneath that sky, either alone, like the one I had passed so long ago on the road to Daars, or in conjunction with nemetons, the great stone circles that are our holiest hallows. Never had I seen or even heard of one in the deeps of the earth. It looked as if it had grown there, rising out of the rough-cut floor; it was hardly hewed, seeming shapen only by patient chipping, if even that. But there must have been some, once, who had set their hands to it, for as Morgan moved her own hand, and the light fell upon the dolmen's face in obedience to her wave, I caught my breath in awe: There upon each of the stone's four sides, faint though unmistakable, was the carved outline of a hilted sword.

Beside me Arthur too had seen, had caught his breath in the same shivering awe that had claimed me; unlike me, he stepped forward, hand outstretched, unthinking. But Morgan spoke to bar his way.

"Not yet," she said, and he stopped where he stood. "This is the weapon that has been prepared for you: the Sword from the Air and the Sword from the Water, the Sword from the Fire and the Sword from the Stone. And the way of the test is this: Face each of the four in its turn, without fear or failing, and at the end shall Llacharn be yours."

Morgan had not looked at us as she had spoken but upon the sword prisoned in the rock; now she turned to face us, and something of what she had learned all these years was in her eyes, some unimaginable sorcery of the Shining Folk, or holy Nia, or the blessed Brendan, or all those together, or none of those at all. Whatever it may have been, before it I felt once again the five-year-old boy I had been, awed by my tutor's magic, and all the years between, that had made me Druid and bard and ollave, were suddenly vanished away.

But Arthur and his sister looked into each other's eyes, deep and long and hard, and as I looked from her to him and back again I could see in them the mother they shared, and the royal brothers who had fathered them. *Sibs and cousins both . . .* Then I forgot my musings in the wonder of what came next.

There had been a wordless questioning, and an equally wordless assent: Then Morgan bowed her head, and as if it had been a signal, a wind arose in the cave, a wind in the depths of the earth that howled and boomed and ripped the very breath from my lungs. As abruptly as it had come, it was gone, and in its place was water. A strange water this, that poured past us and over us and around us, the blue light glowing eerily through it. Yet though it nearly knocked us off our feet with the force of its passing, as if we had been standing in a mountainstream when suddenly it rushed down in spate, we were dry-shod and dry-clothed, not a drop did touch us.

Then the water too was gone, and now the blue light that came from the cavern walls was all at once burning gold. All the cave seemed filled with fire, there was no air to breathe but only flame, the heat was as the inside of a star; yet we did not flash into cinders, our garments did not kindle and blaze, we were not even singed by the heat.

And then the cave was as it was, stone only, gray stone and green stone, stone the color of new wine and stone the color of old blood, stone like snow beneath the moon and stone blue to blackness. We felt the weight of it, everlasting, insupportable, heard the planet's slow groan as it shifted itself through space. Then the sword that was carved upon the dolmen, the sword that had been buffeted by wind and washed in water and bathed in flame, was there before us, more plainly to be seen than ever, almost visibly trembling to be free of the stone that held it firm.

"It was left here for you, what time you should come to take it up." Morgan's voice echoed in the cave's confines; but though I could not see her face, and dared not turn to look for her, I knew she had not spoken to me, nor had she spoken aloud. "Arthur. Take the hilt."

At that Arthur's head came up, and I felt him reach out to the sword with his senses as he must reach out with his hand. If indeed the weapon was such as could be taken up with hand alone . . . But it was a carving still; or was it?

Stepping forward, without hesitation Arthur set his right hand to the gray granite, where the sword-hilt was wrought in curving interlace. What happened next I could not see, for his back was to me, but I did see him flinch a little, drawing back his hand rather more swiftly than he had extended it, and when I saw his hand clear I gasped aloud. Blood dripped from his fingers, as if something had slashed across them; and when he turned his palm outward to us, the blood flying out in an arc, like a spray of red rain, we could plainly see the cuts across the skin, thin and fine, as if he had grasped a fistful of whipping wires.

My face reflected my pain at his pain, but Morgan's expression did not alter. "Again."

Arthur had never lacked for courage, and he was already reaching out again as his sister spoke, this time with his left hand. And this time he did not flinch, but went stiff as his palm seemed to freeze to the stone. After an instant he set his mouth and ripped his fingers free: Some of the skin had been torn from the palm, so fast had it frozen and so swiftly had he pulled his hand away; and the remaining skin was seared blue and mottled white, as if it had been touched to freezing iron.

He did not need to be bidden try yet a third time. With the look of someone who has suddenly out of blackest bafflement seen the answer to a riddle, Arthur stepped forward again, and this time—it is hard to explain, for though I Saw what happened next, I do not think I truly saw it—using both hands, he reached *into* the stone, and closed his fingers upon the carved hilt of the carved sword.

It seems impossible now as I recount it—indeed, it did then, when I was but observing it—but the dolmen had become almost transparent, and even as the stone was losing its density and very physicality, the sword could be seen taking it on, growing real, growing solid, so that now it blazed silver and gold in the cavelight, and the great square stone in its pommel flamed red. But the greatest wonder was yet to come: As Arthur took the hilt in both hands, the bleeding hand and the burned hand alike, the stone was gone in a flash of light, and only the sword remained; and his hands that had been slashed and skin-torn were full healed.

"Llacharn," said Morgan, and I heard in her voice an echo of Merlynn's. " 'The Flamebright' . . . not the Sword that will do the true task in the end, but it will serve for the work to come."

"It will serve," said Arthur in a drowned, wondering voice. He lifted the sword, and the blade flashed like silk in sunlight.

"Bring me the sword, Arthur Pendreic," said his sister, and such was the depth of the magic that he did not jib at the name she used in that moment—the royal surname they shared

through different fathers—but came and knelt before her, as a
man before a mighty queen, and gave the sword Llacharn into
her hands.

Morgan held up the blade balanced on her palms, and
blessed it, then kissed the hilt and gave the weapon back to
Arthur, and kissed him. As he rose from his knee, and turned
to look at me, I let out a deep breath that I did not realize I
had been holding, and met his eyes. Though we said no
word, we saluted the moment, for the dán of Keltia and the
doom of Edeyrn had been born here this night in this cave.
Born of Arthur, born of Morgan, born of me, born of Birogue,
born of whoever had wrought Llacharn for Arthur to bear—
this night had been long in the making, and though it must
soon pass if that making were to have meaning beyond this
night, these walls, we three stood a moment motionless,
honoring the moment, glimpsing what would be.

"Now," said Morgan then, relief and delight in her voice,
and it an everyday voice at last, "now let us go from here.
Time it is this place must rest, and so must we."

We did not leave directly, of course: Working for the first
time together as sorcerers, the three of us sealed the cave until
such a day as it might again be needed, with thanks and with
blessing. Morgan directed the magic herself, and when we
had finished, not I nor Arthur and perhaps not even she could
see where the entrance or the cave itself had been. It was as if
the hill had closed up behind us, as water will close after a
swimmer's arm has passed. Though the rock still held the
memory of the cavern, and the cavern would exist again at
the proper time or in the lawful need, the place where the cave
had been was solid now as if no cave had ever yawned there, as
filled with stone as it had been an hour since with darkness
and with light.

After that, we were tired and hungry indeed, and dizzily
elated with the winning of the weapon. So Morgan fed us;
and though she was no more skilled a cook than any other
great sorcerer I have known, we contrived all the same to be

full and warm and happy, and slept dreamlessly that night on beds of furs and rushes.

Yet all that night was not for sleeping . . .

I woke suddenly, my heart hammering as with some uncaused terror—an awakening such as I had not had for many years. Had there been a noise, had someone cried out, was there some intruder on the island, or in the room? I held myself to stillness until I had taken inventory of my chamber; once satisfied that no one was lurking in the shadows or behind a chair, I cast out in thought to Arthur's room and to Morgan's. But I could detect there only peaceful sleep—though Arthur slept with one hand on Llacharn's hilt—and two steady hearts; and farther too all was safe and calm.

Well, it seemed to be my trouble alone, then. But I had ridden ghostmares before now: I lay awake for a while, watching the moonlight on the floor, breathing in a mode to induce sleep, then sighed deeply and cast off the coverlets and began to dress. In my years as Owein's man I had known many such awakenings, and knew too from those experiences that my chances of attaining sleep again any time soon were few to none. So I did what I had used to do at Caer Dathyl: went out to breathe the night air and be at one for a while beneath the stars, hoping to trick myself into sleepiness thereby. If it worked at Caer Dathyl, I told myself, moving silently past Arthur's door—Morgan's chamber was on the llan's far side—it should work here; if not, a little clean night air never harmed anyone.

Once outside, and the others not awakened behind me, I stood for a while in the llan's sheltering angle, letting my eyes grow 'customed to the moonsplashed world before me, all my senses slapped to wakefulness by the light and cool air. Though Glora was called a sea, her waters were fresh rather than salt, and so the tang that breathed from the waves was not of the ocean but of high snows and glaciers and rivers and tarns and streams—all the waters that had flowed down to Glora, and there remained.

During the evening's long lazy converse, after the nightmeal and before retiring, Morgan had spoken of a small pinegrove on the edge of the rocks above the sea, where she liked to sit—in meditation or in idleness, it made little differ which, in that place they were much the same—and after a pause to get my bearings in the glamourie the moonlight cast upon Collimare, I turned my steps that way.

As I approached the grove—more a dell than a grove, sheltered and shadowed—I thought that someone else stood there, tall and straight and motionless, and stopped dead in my tracks. Stupid, I chided myself; for if it *had* been an enemy not only would I have betrayed my knowledge of his presence by my abrupt halt, but I would have provided a perfect target for his weapons. Yet I think I knew even in that surprised blinking instant that it was neither enemy nor stranger, and so when she spoke I was not surprised at all.

"You took long enough in the coming," said Morgan.

I could see her face now, white as the statue she had seemed at first to be; but as I came up to her I could only marvel at how she had come there before me when I had sensed her deep asleep as I left the llan.

Her eyes danced under the moon, for she knew well how puzzled I was, and after a moment she relented.

"And you call yourself Druid! Ah Talynno, what kind of sorceress would I be could I not make you think I slept though I waked and walked?"

"But you *were* asleep, you were *there*! I kenned you and Arthur both, so that I should not wake you as I went. I take oath you were both well under, for I even felt you breathing."

The smile widened. "Nay, I have been here this hour past—an hour spent, I might add, in calling to you. You take a deal of waking—or perhaps you were still wearied from your journey." That was a deliberate taunt, though a loving one: I to be wearied, who had spent much of the past twenty years on Gwynedd's roads!

I forced the words out past a sudden shyness, though I needed no answer from her. "And why is it, lady, that you did call me?"

Morgan did not trouble to answer, only took my face

between her cool hands and kissed me gravely, lightly upon the lips. And that was the last of our past and the beginning of our world, as the stars spun above us and the deep grass was soft below.

What we did was no more nor less than all others do, or than each of us had done before—Morgan too had known her Teltown, and other nights after, as had I—doubtless it was little different for you, or for any.

What we did was simple; what we did was fathomlessly complex. Sharing minds as well as bodies; all consciousness receding to that ancient place in the back of our brains that remembers things our forebrains never dreamed on: lights dimming in the regions of thought, all sensation exploding out from one white silent blazing center.

I have been caught up before and since in something bigger than my own small finite being, and it was both like and unlike to this—though there can be the same urgency and ecstasy in one's art as in one's body. Oh, it was a wonder, and no mistake; joy there was, even rapture, though not the soaring communion that was to come later—both of us were, I think, too frightened by the overwhelming inevitability of the thing. It is hard to get what one has long wanted.

And what we did set the seal on what had been done in the cave; for the first time the long battle waged and the distance yet to go seemed capable of achievement. That Morgan and I should come together then, at Collimare, was Sight long Seen, another corner of the pattern tying itself off, another square completed; in years to come it would be deeper and higher and wider, but never could it be more certain than it was that night.

And when Arthur and I left Collimare next morning—only one of us ever to return there—Morgan rode between us.

Chapter 29

*T*hus began the beginning of the end of the beginning: the last days of the secret war that Arthur had been waging and all those before him for all the years of the Marbh-draoi's rule. It ran quick enough now, but for all that, it was near five years more before it ended.

Five years we were in hard campaigning, such campaigning as we had not yet seen, as perhaps Gwynedd herself had not seen, not even in the earliest days of Keltia. We fought now for the planet, fought openly; the actions that had gone before were mere pinprick reivings, by compare to what Arthur now commanded.

No more now were we just a few loyal comrades, a handful of Fians hidden away in shielings, endlessly training for fights that never came. Now they were upon us, those fights, and we were a true army that met them gladly. For with purpose and method both deadly alike, Arthur had begun to claim Gwynedd back from Owein, lai by lai, foot by foot, inch by bloody inch. Some of those claimings are wreathed now in legend; many are lost, or remembered only by those who helped to make them, or who were themselves caught up in them—soldiers, townsfolk, Companions, landholders whose lands became the battleground whether they will or nill. There could be no bystanders anymore: The day had dawned

at last when Gwyneddans, and their fellow Kelts on the other
worlds soon to come to it as well, must declare for Edeyrn or
for Arthur, for the Marbh-draoi or for the Bear; and from
either choosing there could be no appeal, and no return.

I myself do not recall every skirmish we fought in those
earliest days, every stronghold we toppled, every town we took.
But some shall live in my memory until the day I no longer
can recall them or indeed anything else, and they are not
all of them the grand fights of glory that Keltia will never
forget.

Those epic battles are well enshrined otherwhere: Here I
am free to raise shrines of my own, to erect cairns of memory
that perhaps none other may think to build, and I have five
years and more of building-stones to choose from . . .

The high tops were whitening now with winter coming on,
the streams running down from the slopes braided brown with
leaves and twigs and laced with foam. All sensible creatures
were making ready for, if not actual sleep, then at least
protracted inactivity for the duration of the approaching cold
times, obedient to the inborn ancient commands: Beasts that
had been fattening were going now to lair, the gray geese had
long since flown south, the red deer were down on the flats
from their upland haunts, townfolk and hilldwellers alike had
prepared themselves to face the frosts.

All creatures indeed; all, that is, save Arthur, and those
who went with him in his madnesses . . .

It must be said that campaigning in Keltia in those days
was not as it had been formerly, or is now. It used to be that a
winter campaign was the mark of an inexperienced captain, or
a lunatic one, or one with no alternative; and now, of course,
we have such technologies as make winter battle not even an
inconvenience. There was that, if naught else, to be said for
Edeyrn's rule: By depriving us of enginery and other tools of
science he had given us a life of winter quiet and rest, like to
that of our long-ago kin on Earth.

Arthur changed all that, as he was changing most things
these days: Never one to waste the snow-months in sleepiness

like the bear whose name he bore, he roused the rest of us as well. Some of us liked it not at all, while others thrived: We went never hungry, though sometimes the board at Llwynarth was sparser set than we might have liked it; nor were we ever idle, though after bouts of prolonged inaction—due more often to fierce weather than to Arthur's strategies—the more restive souls among us began to suffer from what we called 'cavern fever.' But for the most part Arthur had us out and doing in all weathers until we dropped—he himself seemed never to tire, which can be most tiresome for those who do—and sometimes we cursed him as passionately as Owein's Ravens cursed us all.

Now we were often together, he and I, as we had not been since our shieling days; Morgan of course was with us—with me—and Ygrawn too, sometimes, though it was still judged too unsafe for Uthyr to venture from Coldgates. Keils Rathen, warlord paramount, joined Arthur that winter I speak of; and though Tarian and Grehan, who had long been counted chief commanders, were a little daunted by him at first, and fearful that Keils should usurp their place by virtue of greater experience or age or mastery, they soon learned that their fears were groundless. Keils was a professional warrior, to him victory was all; he cared no whit how it was gotten. Though his help was matchless, he confined himself to advising only, and he was the first to give the praise, where merited, to his two young counterparts.

As for the rest of us Companions, we were much the same as ever; Tarian and Grehan, of whom I spoke just now, and Betwyr, and Kei, and Daronwy, and Ferdia and the rest, that inner ring of Companions within the Company, and the outer circle as well. Indeed, so confident and forward had Arthur grown with his successes that we began about now to seek irregular levies: troops committed to Arthur and to our cause who were not permanent members of our kinship, who came and went with the seasons, recruited for specific objectives— the taking of a certain town, or the raiding of a particular stronghold—and then disbanded, never to come to Llwynarth. The strategy worked surpassingly well for these short-term goals, and left in place a framework of warriors all across Gwynedd, when Arthur should in time to come need every fighter he could call to him.

But that winter began the sword-dance across the Arvon hills for which he was so famed in after years. From the Rough Bounds in the east to the slopes of the Grain Valley Range far to the west, Arthur led Owein's forces thrice round and three times thrice more, in a teasing, slaughterous progress—feinting, drawing them on deep into the trackless hills he knew so well and they feared so greatly, then turning round to strike. There was blood on the snow that winter from Agned clear to the sad ruins of Daars, and we were pleased indeed that so little of it was our own.

All the same, there were times when even Arthur cut things a little too fine for anyone's liking—

Deep midwinter, past Sunstanding and the feast-time that followed. Snow had been falling for three or four days straight; then a thaw had set in, and then a freeze again. The ground was hard now and bare, the sky a brilliant blue.

We had been caught by the snows too far from Llwynarth to replenish our supplies, and now we had not enough food among us to make even a forced march there without perishing like fawns on the howling hills. We had new levies with us as well, to whom Llwynarth was no option; and worst of all, we had not enough power to recharge the new weapons sent us from the scientists at Coldgates—laser flains and balisters, glaives and even a few small field pieces—and should an attack come we would be hard pressed to stand it off. Our only comfort was that few Ravens would be willing to brave the harsh weather; but that was by no means a thing assured.

I came to Arthur's tent that afternoon to find him deep in converse with Tarian and Kei. To judge by the grave faces, we were in worse straits than even I in my usual pessimism had thought; but to judge by Arthur's face alone, we might have been in the midst of a summer revel.

"Well?" I dropped down into a field-chair. "Where away now? We cannot stay here much longer, unless you fancy eating snow."

Kei rolled up his eyes to heaven. "Tell that to your fostern," he said, clearly vexed. "*We* have been trying to get it into his head this half-hour past, and if Keils or Scathach were here they should have *pounded* it in."

"No need of pounding," replied Arthur sharply. "It has gone in long since, Kei, so you need not think you have lost your labor."

"To enter a walled town—" began Kei with some heat.

I cut him off. "A *walled town*? Artos, you cannot mean this? Nay, I see that you do—ah gods, surely we can come by some other plan."

"Oh aye? What then?" That was Tarian, sounding more snappish than I had ever heard her. Surely she had cause: I could see that she had begun by opposing Arthur, and had been swayed by his eloquence to come to hold reluctantly with him in his lunatic intent. No wonder she was cross . . . "We have not enough power for the weapons to hold off one—*one!*—determined attack by even half-competent Ravens, Talyn, nor have we enough food for ourselves past tomorrow's nightmeal. And though we of the Companions have learned to fight on shorter commons than most, the levies have not, no matter their own valiant efforts. So by tomorrow's morrow we shall be starved and stiff with cold, if not cut down first. Is there aught else you care to ask?"

I blew out an explosive sigh and ran my hands over the middle of my face. "I had not thought we were in quite so evil a case . . . What shall we do, then, for food and arms?"

"We shall go and take them," said Arthur.

The place Arthur had in mind to acquire what we needed was called Talgarth, a small walled city not unlike to Daars, perhaps forty miles away from our present camp. The town sat well down in a river plain, though there were hills not far off—as ever on Gwynedd—and for pure safety's sake we dared not venture out of sight of them.

But otherwise Talgarth was perfect for Arthur's purposes: It was no Counterinsurgency hotbed, but neither was it a town strong for the Theocracy; merely a place, like many another, trying to steer a middle course and come through these times intact, or at the least not too badly bruised to survive.

But it had reckoned without our need and our leader: We must have supplies, and since we could not make it back to Llwynarth without them, we should have to take them wherever they might be found. Talgarth was the only place where we might come by them, and we must take them by force for we did not dare to ask.

It was no fight worthy of the name. After a night's march on the last of our rations, we came under the walls of Talgarth early in the dawn, and Arthur summoned the town to surrender. The place, though well walled, was not garrisoned, and the town mormaors in their flustered panic refused to admit us peaceably. But terrified, half-asleep urrads and their mates and children were no match for Arthur's hungry and hardened battle-hounds: Within the hour the walls, weak toward one quarter, were breached, and we were pouring through the streets like a stream in spate.

Arthur had given strict orders that there was to be no slaughter, nor general sack even but only judicious pillaging, and no blow was to be struck save in self-defense. And I must say that for the first few hours he was obeyed to the letter. He took no part in the action, but stood and watched from a little hill near where we had broken the town walls; I was with him, and Tarian and Kei and some others. Most of the rest of the officers were down in the streets supervising the resupplying of our needs, and it seemed that the chief mormaor (a pragmatic woman) and the town elders had seen the advantage to them in filling those needs; or perhaps it was just that they thought the quicker they gave us what we required, all the quicker still would they be rid of us—and all the better for everyone.

We thought so too: Though the region roundabouts had been carefully scouted beforehand, and Ravens found nowhere nearby, we knew that Madoc Dyffrin, one of Owein's most trusted lieutenants, had a body of horse and foot not too far off. Hence we were more nervous than we might otherwise have been, for we had been betrayed before by bad or incomplete intelligence, and Arthur was in a terror lest that be the case here, and we be taken within walls.

He was not afeared so that any might notice and lose heart, however; only those who knew him best could read the signs. And did—

"Artos, it is as if you look for coming disaster," said Daronwy, having watched him quarter to all airts, as a hunting dog will when seeking to start birds, for perhaps the tenth time in half as many minutes.

"Nay," he said after the smallest of pauses. "But I *do* look not to be surprised if disaster comes."

And so when one of the outpost gallopers came flying up to us with breathless word that Madoc Dyffrin was not safe across the river Saimhor as we had thought and hoped, but two miles off and coming fast, Arthur only laughed and called his officers to him.

"You will never get them off quick enough to be away in time," said Grehan when he had heard the news. "Remember that half of them are new levies, not Companions at all. And not only that, but half of them are half ale-sodden to begin with; and the other half are busy stuffing whatever they can get their hands on, and their hands not able to get it to their mouths fast enough to suit them."

"The Companions?" asked Arthur, flexing his fingers in his old gesture.

"Oh, naught to fear there," said Kei at once. "They will come when you do call them. But the levies—"

"What does my war-leader say?" Arthur seemed a little too calm to be quite true, as he turned to Tarian for her opinion.

"Fly," came her prompt response. "Take the Companions, leave the levies to their fate, and hope for the best." To the shocked look on some faces: "I am a *soldier*, sirs and ladies. . . We can always raise more levies. We cannot easily raise more Companions, and never can we raise another Arthur. Above all else, Artos, you must save yourself, though it means the abandonment of every last one of us.''

"Nay, a charge,'' said some chivalrous idiot. "Death with honor and glory for us all!''

Arthur let them dispute barely a half-minute, and indeed there were few half-minutes to waste.

"No flight, no charge, no abandonment,'' he said, and he spoke in a voice to be obeyed. "We will all of us leave as we came, and the supplies with us that we came for. . . Tarian, do you take some of the Companions and go down into the streets. Beat the levies off their plunder with the flats of your swords if you must, but get them on their feet and get them moving out the west gate. Head round to get the Saimhor between us and Madoc's troops, and into the hills as quick as you can. I with Grehan and Talyn and Kei will cover the retreat with what horse we have.'' In answer to the dark doubtful glances cast his way: "Sirs and ladies,'' he said, with a calm he can never have been feeling, "do as I bid you. Leave the managing to me; the outcome is with dán.''

Had any told me so beforehand I had not believed it, and even after I saw it happen—myself helped to *make* it happen— still it seemed hardly possible. But Arthur whipped his pack off their plunder as easily as a huntsman will whip hounds off their kill: We were on our way out the west gate just as Madoc, astounded and wrathful, came in at the east. When we had leisure to reflect on it later, we laughed until we choked at what must have been Dyffrin's certain confoundment, to have had Arthur Penarvon and so many of his rabble so nearly within grasp, only to have us slope so featly off. I did not envy Madoc, who was a better soldier than that day's work showed him, the explanations he would be making to his master . . .

Just then, however, none of us was laughing: As Grehan had pointed out, many of the levies were too drunk to find their feet, and only the shock of imminent extinction at Madoc's hands found those feet for them. That and the prospect of Arthur's wrath, not to mention the point of Arthur's sword to goad them on where other goads did fail . . .

Whatever got us moving and kept us so, we were stumbling along the hill road in the growing dusk—it was midafternoon by now, the early winter sunset almost upon us—and fear had dispelled our weariness, at least for the moment. Yet the moment might just be enough: Oddly, Madoc seemed reluctant to catch us up, but was content with close pursuit—or perhaps it was the scattershot blasts and flurries of laser flains loosed anyhow to our rear that discouraged him from closing. We did not see his plan at first—well, *we* did not, though Arthur surely did—and though Madoc stuck to our track with grim persistence, when darkness at last closed down we were yet uncaught.

Our road to safety was desperate, though possible: You must think of a bent bow, Madoc coming after us along the line of the string and we marching the bow's curve. Though we had started off together on the same road from Talgarth, our paths soon diverged—as I said, we did not see at once what Madoc was attempting—and if the road we took was less short than his, his was harder.

But as I also said, Madoc was a skilled campaigner—he and Arthur had crossed lances before now, and would again before the end—and this was his ploy: He was trying now not to *catch* us but to get *ahead* of us, to cut off our one sure retreat, the westward passes into the tangled hills. So to that end he was racing ahead with his horse, his foot trudging more slowly to the rear; and by now, we reckoned, he had called up other companies from garrisons to the south of Talgarth, which would come apace, eager to be in at Arthur's downfall.

Arthur, however, had no least intention of being brought down just yet, indeed not at all . . . One tactic there is that a pursuit does not generally expect its quarry to attempt—perhaps because it is a tactic reserved to the mad or the desperate, and by now we were both—and that is that a fleeing force will turn on itself and backtrack. All the pursuer's energies are geared *to* pursuit; it occurs very rarely to his mind that the hunted will cease to flee before him.

Madoc had his forces now flung out beside our route to the west and north; he had as yet none directly behind, not until the reinforcements should arrive from the southern garrisons. So, at Arthur's word—and thank gods we were only a small force, it could scarce have been done with a greater—we doubled in our tracks like a fox dodging under the hounds' noses, reversing direction and staggering back the long painful way we had just come.

By now it was pitch black, and coming on to rain. I and other sorcerers in the company did what we could to help the murk along, with such small touches as we might conjure in weary haste: strange smoky fog and odd things glimpsed through it—tall antlered figures and creatures half horse, half man stalking in the blue-litten mists, gruagachs and glaistigs padding silently in the night. Steel was one thing, and even flains; but alone out there in the rainy dark, pursuing one who was again proving to be so elusive and uncapturable as to be a phantom himself, few indeed of Madoc's forces were willing to face taish or fith-fath or whatever our conjuries might be—and for all their officers' exhortations, fewer still were willing to face Arthur.

So, with desperation and endurance and magic here and there, somehow—to this day I know not how the thing was achieved—we slipped between Madoc and his oncoming reinforcements, and vanished away into the darkness. When our pursuers met at last, and we not caught between them, their bewilderment and rage must have been mirthsome to behold.

But to us it was not yet a matter for mirth: We had marched forty miles to Talgarth, sacked the town, marched twenty miles more, fleeing pursuit and fighting as we did so, and now we were all but dead in our boots. It remained only for us to cover the few miles more to the hills, and at times it seemed even those few miles were more than we should manage.

However, Arthur was resolved that we should not die on our feet, or even off them. I myself was near sleepwalking with fatigue by now—what the ale-swillers must have felt like is perhaps best left to the imagination—and the others were as weary as I. Only Arthur seemed as vital as ever, and I could not think whether I detested him just then more than I admired him. So I thought the evil names only, and chivied the levies, and myself, on as he did bid me.

At last we came to a stretch of ground across which Madoc with his heavier cavalry could not follow, and we faded like the mist-figures I had conjured, into the relative safety of an old overgrown orchard. Even the ever-vigilant Tarian pronounced it secure enough, and here at last Arthur allowed us to collapse and sleep a while.

Five minutes seemed scarce to have passed before he was rousting us like cross hedgepigs from our nests of leaves and moss and sodden cloaks—in truth it had been a good five hours—to press on deeper into the hills while it was yet dark. Only when we were safe again across the Brosna did we stop to pitch a proper camp and have a proper meal out of the spoils of Talgarth carried with us all this way, and a proper sleep to follow.

But as Arthur himself pointed out, at least we now had something out of which meals could be made . . . "A near thing," he admitted privately to Tarian and me later, collapsed with the rest of us. "Still, it did work—but upon my soul, both you, never again do I enter a town save that I have reduced it first."

He was right, and he was prescient, and save for one notable exception he kept to that resolve; but in later years it was this half-mad, wholly desperate, twisty retreat from Talgarth that I was often to hear preferred above his grandest set-piece battles, and was myself most often begged to tell of. The leader who could call off his warriors from sack and plunder was no common commander; the leader who could get them all safe away in the face of superior pursuit—for all that, we did not lose a single levy—was less common still.

But that seemed to be enough of excitement for Arthur just then: We disbanded the levies—sobered and shaken, but still eager to fight; they would return gladly when we had need of them again—and lay up quietly in the hills before heading home to Llwynarth, where Keils Rathen and my Morgan commanded in our absence. Like bears ourselves, we went back to the Bear's Grove, to ride out the months of snow and storm to come, and plan anew for spring.

Chapter 30

And spring followed spring, each one seeing Arthur in command of a little more of Gwynedd. Very soon now Owein could hold back no longer; should be forced to come against us in his own person, instead of doing as he had been doing all these years and sending his minions to face us. True, some of those had been capable enough captains—Madoc Dyffrin, for one, our perpetual nemesis, with whom we had two or three encounters a season; and latterly Sulwenna Keppoch, who was kin to our own Daronwy—but for the most part they had been poor stuff.

Not that our victories had been cheaply won: On the contrary, we had had to fight our hearts out for every skirmish, for if we did not, who knew if we should ever get the chance to fight again? And always we were outnumbered, and more often than otherwise we were outweaponed, and ever we had to march great distances over secret ways before we could even join battle to begin with—while our adversaries had inexhaustible levies, unlimited arms, the luxury of open roads and unchallenged passage over them.

But for all the hinderings and hamperings, we were winning, surely, slowly, steadily, and we knew it. And our enemy knew it too: For his answer came swiftly, and the measure of our triumph was seen in the kind and strength of force sent by Edeyrn to crush us. Indeed, word passed to us by the Hanes had it that the Marbh-draoi was more than faintly displeased with my old master Owein, for allowing the upstart Penarvon and his rebellious riffraff to get so out of hand.

Oh aye, Edeyrn knew Arthur by name now; knew him for Amris's son by birth and Gorlas's by fostering. And no more were the rest of us unknown to the master of Keltia: There were prices set on all our lives now—we used to find a sort of perverse amusement in tracking our fluctuating values, fixed by Owein according to the degree of trouble each of us had caused him most recently. Arthur himself, of course, invariably commanded the highest price, but it was a matter of pride, and something of a contest, for the rest of us to come as near him as we might.

By now Llwynarth had grown too small to hold us: We had expanded the cavern system as far as we dared, but so many of us, and so many key officers, all in one place not only endangered our effort—think of the potential disastrous loss should Ravens have learned our location and struck in force— but overtaxed the local ecosystems as well. So Elen and Betwyr and Ferdia had gone to establish a satellite refuge farther north, while others of the Companions, and even some new conscripts who showed exceptional promise in essential disciplines, had been sent to distant shielings and to Coldgates itself.

And, for all our crowding, some new Companions joined us—new to the Company and to the Bear's Grove, that is, not new to our struggle: my sister Tegau Goldbreast, for one, and with her our brother Cadreth. But we knew that victory was truly riding the winds above us—Malen Ruadh, the Red War-crow herself—when Merlynn Llwyd came to us in Llwynarth; and then, a month or so later, Gweniver.

If I have not spoken overmuch of Gweniver for some pages, it is not because we did not see much of her during these years of secret war. Our meetings were brief, but fairly frequent—particularly in the years since Gwenwynbar's going.

She would descend on Llwynarth for a sevennight, or a month, or a week's-end, and then race back to Coldgates to convey information and impressions to Uthyr. Or else Arthur—though him seldom—or Tarian or I or one of the senior Companions would journey to Coldgates in turn; we had grown bold enough and confident enough of late to use aircars, the more so since Keils had invented a concealment device for them, of the same sort that had worked so well so long on the larger starships and on Sulven itself.

As for Arthur, he had come into his early power; though he would in years to come grow stronger still, no more was he a youth of promise but a man of full achievement, though his greatest achievements lay yet ahead by many years. And we his Companions were devoted to him; we would have moved Agned for him, emptied Glora with a spoon—as it was, we only lived and died for him, and we never doubted, for he gave us no cause to doubt, that he would do as much for us.

But we at least could lose ourselves in our comradeship: For our leader there was no such easy escape. Never for one instant was he out of the blaze of our attention; always he was there, and always his little army was enthralled. It must have been a burden almost beyond bearing, yet he gave no sign of the strain he must surely have felt; he was there to confide in or to hearten, to guide or to command, and in all our time together never did I know him to fail at any of those tasks. Small wonder the Companions adored him, and the common folk upon whose general goodwill and active support we depended came to think of him as but one step less than a god himself.

But in Keltia even the gods are human; and however godlike a mortal may be held by others, in the end he or she is human still, with all a human's flaws and failings. Though he had Grehan and Tarian and me and the rest of the inner circle of Companions to shoulder some of the burden, Arthur knew better than any of us that he must lift the chief part of it himself, else all was in vain.

*   *   *

In the course of our reivings we had most often managed to move too swiftly for Owein's lead-footed garrison soldiers to offer any real threat of pursuit; Ravens were swifter, but still too slow to catch us up.

Now, however, had we picked up a grim shadow, and a vengeful one: Madoc Dyffrin, whom we had so badly embarrassed at Talgarth years before, was close on our heels, doubtless fueled by thoughts of payback to be had for the bit thumb we had shown him, and the fool he had been made to look in his master's eyes. But Arthur did not seem too much concerned, and planned to lose him, as most of those who thought to chase us were lost, deep in the trackless hills.

But this time Madoc was not so easily shaken, and long after we expected to have brushed him from our cloak-tails, he clung there still.

"Soon or late," said Tryffin, "we must turn and stand to him." Having delivered himself of judgment, he blushed, as if all at once aware of the impropriety of his suggesting tactics to his illustrious cousin—who gave no sign one way or another. A comrade of ours long since at Bargodion, Tryffin—son of Ygrawn's brother, Marc'h—had recently rejoined the Company after a protracted absence attending to family business on his homeworld of Kernow, and we were pleased to have him back among us.

"Where think you this stand might be made, then?"

That was Gweniver; she too was with us, and we were perhaps less pleased at that. But there had been no help for it: She had been at Llwynarth, and on hearing that Arthur and a small mobile force were out raiding, she had insisted she be allowed to join us. Keils Rathen, who often commanded in Llwynarth when its lord was away, had tried to persuade her against it; and knowing Keils, and his past heart-history with Gweniver, I do not doubt he considered every means short of forcible restraint, and probably even that.

But oddly enough, Morgan and Merlynn had sided with the Princess; and at last Keils, outranked and outsworded, had capitulated, sending Gweniver after us with Kei ap Rhydir and Elen Llydaw as disapproving escort.

Arthur, to whom Gweniver's question had really been addressed, did not answer her directly, but stepped forward to where the tent flap had been tied back, framing a wedge of gray sky and grayer mountain, and pointed.

''There.''

It need not be said that Arthur, whose eye for ground was extraordinary and all but unerring—in all our campaigns, together and apart, I knew him to choose badly two times only; though let it also be said that those two wrong choosings were mistakes of spectacular proportion—had some place in mind to take a stand very much more definite than his churlish response to Gweniver's inquiry might suggest.

Not that he was entirely displeased with the Tanista's presence: On the contrary, he seemed glad of a chance to show so august and judgmental an observer just how things were done by his Companions and their leader. Though their old antagonism seemed tempered somewhat by years and wisdom, and by mutual respect for each other's undeniable gifts, there remained between Arthur and Gweniver a rivalry almost like to that between two sibs very close in age, competing for some prize or toy or trinket that each desired greatly and would not willingly relinquish to the other. Which comparison was not so far off the mark: Uthyr the High King, uncle to them both, still had not declared either to be his sole and formal heir. Nor *would* he name one above the other, for reasons discussed at length elsewhere in these pages; but they were not to come to know that for a while yet, and so the rivalry continued.

But Gweniver was as determined to show Arthur her own mettle as he was set to prove himself in her eyes . . . Already on this onc foray she had led harrier parties back to jab at Madoc, and had not shirked the work herself, as could be seen by the hurts she had taken—naught grave, though bloody and dramatic enough; all were easily healed with skinfusers, a laser suturing device recently reinvented by the Fianna scientists at Coldgates and fetched down to us at Llwynarth.

So with Madoc Dyffrin coming on unswerving in cold

pursuit, Gweniver was as eager as any Companion, and had more cause than most, to meet him on the battleground of Arthur's choosing, deep in the mountains of central Arvon, in the range known as the Steppings.

And meet him we did—or rather he met us, after first reducing to smoking ruin a little town of perhaps five hundred souls that lay between him and his quarry. It need not have happened—Madoc might have gone round to spare the village folk, as we had done, and met us all the sooner where we waited for him in a cwm, a great curving hollow among the hills—but it was an act typical of Theocracy soldiering, and it served only to put an extra edge to our blades that were sharp enough to start with.

Despite the fact that we were outnumbered as usual, we made more than usually short work of our opponents—the terrible screams and cries we had heard rising from the burning town having much to do with our grim and redoubled zeal—and, in the grip of an anger such as even I had never seen on him before, Arthur gave the order that we should take no prisoners.

I am not proud of what followed, being as guilty as any of punctilious obedience to—and utter agreement with—our leader's cold command. But I am not sorry for it either. Even Gweniver, less used to military necessity than the rest of us, made no protest against her cousin's edict once she beheld the slaughter in the town.

Easy for you, or for any who did not see what we had seen, to condemn our work that day; but I say that if you had been among us, you too had done no less. Five hundred men, women, children, all slain unspeakably, their poor butchered bodies then arranged according to a perverted obscene humor; and all because Madoc Dyffrin thought the town had aided us. We had not even asked for help, knowing too well what should befall our helpers did we lose the encounter; and yet they were made to pay all the same by Madoc and his troops.

So we took their price from him and his.

*   *   *

That night, more than a little troubled, I was walking through the streets that had been a slaughtershed only that morning. After our business with Madoc was concluded, we had spent much of the remainder of the day gathering up the bodies of the townsfolk, to give them decent speeding. Even the enemy carrion had been disposed of: Though our true wish was to leave their corpses for the hill beasts to gnaw, reluctant decency had prevailed, and the bodies had been burned anyhow in a great lowe on the edge of the glen.

Arthur—he who only that morning had been capable of saying to us, "The best of you brings me the most enemy dead"—had paced the silent streets all day, his sword laid aside, a compassionate priest giving ease to the dying, grace to the newly dead, comfort to the few survivors. He had sat for two hours holding a child whose family had been slain before her eyes, and who had escaped only by hiding among their corpses. (And to finish the tale on a happier note, Gweniver brought the little girl back with her to Coldgates, where Ygrawn fostered her to a Ban-draoi family, and later took her into her own service; the child recovered fully, and, a woman grown, is alive and happy this day.)

As for Madoc, he ended with more honor than he merited: When he saw his troops falling beneath our hungry, angry blades, and knew there was no smallest hope of mercy—and he was so right to think it; Arthur would have cut him to pieces, very slowly, had he laid sword on him—seeing all this, Madoc fell by his own hand. Arthur sent his head to Owein, with no note.

So now I was wandering through the dead streets—strange that we never even knew the town's name, nor the valley's where we made our stand; it has been known since that day as Glenanaar, the Valley of the Slaughter—when all at once I heard a whimpering sound coming from beneath a pile of broken, burned stone. Appalled—it sounded to my horror-tuned ear like a child too young or too injured to speak—I was on my knees and shifting bricks before I knew I had even moved. The stones came easily away, and then I saw what had cried so piteously.

A wolfhound puppy no more than four months old, its brindled coat floured with brickdust, ears floppy and unset, paws the size of plates, looked up at me with dark pleading hopeful eyes. I looked back, and that was the end of me . . .

Yet it was not for me, nor even entirely for the puppy's sake, that I lifted the warm, wiggling creature, ecstatic to have found someone to care for it and take it from this blood-smelling, smoke-smelling, terrifyingly unpeopled place, out of its prison in the bricks; and carried it under my cloak to the tent where Arthur had gone at last, after his day's labors of bloodshed and blessing both.

At this late hour he still sat at his field-desk, doing paperwork that could undoubtedly be left to another, or to the morrow; he was alone. When I stepped inside the tent, and opened my cloak, and he and the puppy laid eyes on one another, I knew I had won a better victory than the one over Madoc Dyffrin.

"I shall call him Cabal," said Arthur, when at last the puppy had ceased to lick his face and fingers and, after a prodigious supper of cold pastais, had fallen asleep in his lap. "But a puppy on campaign—"

He gave me a reproachful look, or at least a look that was meant to be so, but the old grin broke through, and my spirits soared to see it; I had been thinking that any look, any reproach, would be better than the ghastly, gaunt-faced, stone-eyed bleakness that had sat all day upon his countenance, and I would have found twenty dogs for him if that was what it took to take that look away.

"Oh, I know how you have missed Luath all this time," I said then. "And I could hardly leave the poor thing there to starve— Any road, he will not be a puppy long, so either find an old cloak for him to sleep on or grow a bigger lap."

I left them then, to scrape up some belated supper for myself—I had not eaten all day, and was famished; or at least my body was—and in the end it was Gweniver who took pity on me and fed me. We did not talk much during the meal, but afterwards, over ale in leathern field-methers, quietly, haltingly, we tried to put the horror into words, to lessen it by naming it. So that when I made my way back to my own tent a few hours later, I felt, not cleansed of the slaying in anger that I had done that day, but reconciled to it.

And yet not so, not on a deeper level: It was Kelts I had killed this day, Kelts who had been trying to kill me; it had been Kelts killing Kelts, being killed by Kelts, all along. And a lord who kills his folk kills himself; a king who murders is a contradiction in terms. Kings give life, protect it, preserve it, serve it, assure it, ennoble it; they do not take it away save by law alone, and law had had no part in what had taken place here. And if I felt so who was after all only another sword-arm in this fight, a kern on the fidchell-board, how much more so must Arthur feel it, who would be in time a king?

But when I looked in on the king that was to be, I found him sleeping the sleep of the utterly exhausted in mind and body, and the wolfhound puppy, the newly named Cabal, snuggled beside him under his cloak. I watched for no more than ten seconds, but the puppy, already protective, must have sensed my presence; suddenly he woke to full alertness with a surprisingly menacing growl. Then, as he saw and scented his rescuer, the growl changed into a small whimper of welcome and recognition; the tail thumped twice—cautiously, so as not to awaken his sleeping master—and then Cabal laid nose again on paws and slept.

Which was more than I could manage: For it was that night, as I lay tossing on the Fian's field bedding of branches and bracken, that I had the first of the dreams that were to trouble me almost nightly for many months to come, some nights twice and thrice over. After what we had seen and done that day, no surprise that I should have the horrors and take it out in dreams; but this dream had a strangeness to it in which horror had no share. It was not a prescient dream, nor one of retrocognition; those I knew well from my Druid training, I should not have mistaken their signs. This dream, though it might well foretell, was profoundly different: It was as if someone cried me warning, from a very long way away.

In the dream I stood on the shoulder of a hill. It was late afternoon of a stormy day, and dark clouds rolled south before a rising wind, while off to my right in the west the sky was scoured and sulphurous. It was another battleground, the air thick with aftermath. Yet somehow I knew that it was no defeat, but victory tempered with, bought at the price of, terrible, staggering loss. The loss had names in it, but I could not hear them; the only thing I did hear, and that not clearly for it reverberated like the voice of the thunder, was one word: 'Cadarachta.'

I woke with a start and a cry, the name still booming in my confused ears; after I had reassured the Fian guard who came running to my inadvertent call that there was no danger, or at least none that she could be of any aid in fighting, I lay down again, and this time I slept sound and true and deep.

But though the next morning I consulted maps and memory alike, and asked everyone I encountered, I could find no place that went by such a name. Perhaps I had misheard; already the name was fading from my inner hearing—Carverick, Caderannoc, Caertrachta? Yet whatever it might have been, I knew I should hear it again, and stand there soon.

We had other business elsewhere, though thank gods none was to prove of the same terrible aspect as Glenanaar, and we did not return to Llwynarth for some months. When at last we did so, we were to find there a message from Owein of unexpected nature.

Not in words this message, but it spoke loudly all the same: his answer to our recent work, and to Glenanaar itself, and to the rather unmistakable message Arthur had sent of Madoc Dyffrin's severed head. And the message Owein sent back was this: He was withdrawing all Theocracy forces from Arvon, Ravens and garrison conscripts alike, thus effectively ceding the province to Arthur, its new and undisputed master.

Though the more cautious souls among us—Tarian, Kei, Betwyr—urged that same virtue on our leader, arguing that Owein but abandoned what he could no longer hold at acceptable cost, Arvon's new master did not take their counsel. The first thing Arthur did when the troops had gone—it took a month or two in all for them to leave—was to proclaim

Uthyr Pendreic as Ard-rígh of Keltia, in right and lawful
succession from Alawn Last-king, and from the Ard-rían
Seirith, and the Ard-rígh Elgan, and the Ard-rían Darowen;
and Ygrawn Tregaron as his Queen.

The first thing *I* had done, on our return, was to fall into
Morgan's arms, and allow her to induce in me forgetfulness
of what I had seen, insensibility to all but her; and then even
to her. Later she had listened with empathy and kindness as I
told her of Glenanaar, and recounted it yet again to Merlynn,
and to my sister Tegau. All of them were warmly sympathetic, and outraged by Madoc's conduct, but all the same
they were a little puzzled that I should be so shaken by what
was merely another encounter; bloodier and more savage than
most, true enough, but still just one more fight in our life of
fighting.

In truth I could not blame them for their shortfall of
understanding: They had not been there, and they could not
know. But I was a little hurt even so; and of course the dream
continued to plague me of the stormy battlefield with the
name I could never recall with my waking mind.

However, soon all such things must be set aside at last; for
hard on the heels of his proclaiming Uthyr King—an open
declaration of war if ever there was one—Arthur called a
council of his close advisors, for now things began to move at
speed.

We stood round the table and stared down in silence at the
map of Gwynedd that Arthur had spread before us. At first
the various lines and scribbles and arrows conveyed but little
to my mind; then my perspective shifted, and I saw the
campaign for the planet laid out plain. And still no one spoke.

It was left to Tarian Douglas to make the assessment—
which was as it should be, for she was Arthur's chief war-
leader—and Arthur himself waited in silent patience for her to
determine.

"By gods!" she said at last. "It is very fine on paper,
Artos, but there is no such thing in the field!" She was

amending the dispositions—erasing and redrawing the scribbly lines—as she spoke. "Look now."

We looked, and wondered. She had pulled our forces far to the west of their original positions, so that now they came round the great massif of Cruach Agned, through the low-lying water-valleys and moorlands thereabouts: Lorn Water, Bruan Moor, the Brosna, the Saimhor, the plain called Lyvennet and the river Velindre.

Arthur was marching troops down from the shielings in his head. "*Can* an army pass that way? It is soft ground, Tari."

"Ours can, and must," replied his war-leader. "Now Owein will think that when we move on Caer Dathyl, as soon we must, we shall come by way of Ravens' Rift and the South Road and bear the heavy cost of such a passage, for in the vastness of his stupidity that is what he himself would do, and he will be seeing no other road. Therefore he will march to meet us at the Rift; but we must lure him westwards before that, to meet us instead on the far side of Agned. And we must time it most carefully too, so that those forces already in the Rift garrisons are kept busy with problems of their own, and cannot break away west to his aid."

"A two-pronged attack—"

"And, Artos, I have a few thoughts as to how that might be managed," said Keils Rathen, his bearded face wreathed in smiles. "One last, and everlasting, game of pig-i'-the-wood for us all . . . Indeed, it is already in train—but let us discuss it amongst ourselves first, you and Tarian and Grehan and some other of the commanders. As for the rest of you, many tasks need doing; go now and do them."

"And as for *you*," said Arthur, catching my cloak as I made to leave the council room, "I have one task in especial. Let us speak of it now."

"I am to go to Coldgates." I glanced down at Morgan with a grave face, then broke into a grin. "To fetch your father—or I should say rather, the Ard-rígh Uthyr—down to Llwynarth."

She threw both arms round my neck. "Ah Talyn, glad I am

it is you to bring him home! He will be pleased too, I know
it . . . I would go with you, but for that my mother is already
on her way here from the eastern shielings, and my sister too
comes down from Erith.''

I felt a jolting shock. ''Marguessan? I did not know she
was to come to Llwynarth.''

''Irian her lord commands levies for my brother; since she
is near her time, he liked not to leave her so far away, and
asked if she might come here. To which Arthur agreed most
willing.''

Would that he had mentioned it to me before he did so . . .
''You do not mind, cariad, that she should come?''

The luminous hazel eyes turned up to meet mine. ''The
meaning being, clearly, that I *should* mind . . . I have not
seen my sister for some years, Talynno, and we were never
close, though we were born of the same birth. If there is
aught to be seen, be sure that I shall See it.'' Morgan changed
the subject with an air of finality. ''But I shall remain for
other reasons as well: There is work here for sorcerers, and
Merlynn and I must command it. Also there is something else
I have in hand.''

''Oh aye?'' I asked, noting that she did not specify the
nature of the magical working, and knowing that I could not
ask. But this other thing it seemed I might safely inquire
about, and I was glad of anything that had naught to do with
Marguessan. ''What then?''

She slipped her arm round my waist as we walked. ''I have
been learning from Keils,'' she began, ''how the pale round
Sulven, that protects Coldgates, is maintained; and how it
was raised to begin with, and how adapted to shield small
craft.''

''Do such matters interest you? Whenever it was explained
to me, I could never see it. The magic of it I could master; it
was the mathematicals destroyed me.''

''Oh, they are not so bad as that . . . I was wondering if
such means can be used only in the concealment of small
things?''

''Such small things as starships and mountains?''

Morgan laughed. "Aye, well, not so small then! Nay, I was thinking—how if a pale could be raised to protect all Keltia?"

I blinked in genuine surprise. "Seven star systems, and all the space between! That would be the mightiest work our people ever made, here or on Earth or in our first home."

"It would, else why should the thought so appeal to me!" Her face grew serious again almost at once, and I saw that, incredibly, this was a thing she had thought much upon. "Consider how safe we should be, Talyn, behind such a shield. None outside would know we were here, no galláin ever again could enter save that we did permit it—"

"Perils in it, too. Such a wall would keep out more than foes."

"You mean it would keep out change, and free commerce of thought and ideas; that we might grow stagnant and selfish behind it, to stand so apart from the galaxy. It might be; but any road, such a wall is itself only a thought just now."

So we laughed, and our converse turned to other matters, and if Morgan fed her great new thought she did so from then on in secret. But we had no other secrets between us: We had been together six years now, to our great joy and Arthur's delight; and though our union was not always harmonious— all is not invariable serenity even between two persons who loved one another as completely as did we—it was ever in harmony, which is not by any means the same thing.

On the morrow I rose betimes, and left for Coldgates with a small company; we went in one of the aircars, for our master now was haste, and we were with Uthyr in the shieling before high twelve had struck.

For all his long exile so patiently borne—or perhaps because of it—Uthyr Pendreic needed very little time to bring his years at Coldgates to an end. He had ever shared with his nephew the belief that swift changes were the best and easiest changes, and now he acted on that belief with a vengeance.

So we rested in Coldgates one night only, after a farewell feast at which the King took loving leave of his longtime companions, and thanked them for their care and protection, and pledged himself to their preferment when he was on the Throne of Scone. He did not scant the moment, for he was much moved by this parting he had never thought to live to make; but he had a king's duties now, and they had duties of their own—some to join Arthur, others to another venture—and goodbyes on both sides though deeply felt were swiftly said.

I had some farewells of my own to make—to people and memories both—and taking a page from Uthyr's book I made them and looked not back again. One last night in Sulven's shadow, then, and in the morning we should ride for Llwynarth, and the battle that would be.

Chapter 31

*T*hus did I leave Coldgates for the last time in the old fashion of secrecy and stealth; and though I knew well that I should see it again—had Seen, indeed, Morgan and me there together one time in the future, an era of peace and joy—my leaving had something of valediction about it all the same.

The mood of sorrowful parting was strengthened as I looked behind me, heading down into the plain below the Spindles, back through the narrow stony pass called the Throat. Today Sulven wore its storms like a battle flag, or a veil of royal mourning: Clouds of blowing snow swirled round the summit, diamonded by the rays of the rising sun. Alongside the path we rode all morning, and in the narrow steep valleys that ran in from every side, streams foamed like milk in their channel-cut gorges. Spring had come to the End-lands, and in the south, where we and so many thousands of others all were bound alike, it was already green and growing.

I was leaving Coldgates with the one last value without which all our labors had been in vain: Uthyr, King of Kelts, rode at my right side. At Arthur's order, we were conveying the Ard-rígh to the battle that would proclaim and set seal to his rightful lordship; and be very sure that all of us felt the honor and the joy of our task equally with the responsibilities.

Some in Llwynarth had argued that we should go in strength,

that the High King should come south so hedged with warriors that Ravens could not think to reach him, and some had
spoken for a fleet of the precious aircars to bring the King and
escort him. But others—and Arthur and Uthyr were foremost
among them—had thought a small, anonymous marchra, riding swiftly and by well-travelled ways, but riding openly,
should be the likeliest surety for the King's safety. As Arthur
had observed, none outside ourselves even knew what Uthyr
looked like—certain it was that Edeyrn and Owein did not
know—and as for the rest of us, though some of us had more
recognizable faces than did others, our everyday aspect
should serve us for disguise—by which he meant our 'cus-
tomized disheveled state. Oh, we were all scrupulously
clean, I hasten to add—no Kelt born will go in filth when
there is a choice, the Kelt and the Bath have a long co-
history—it was just that the campaign's demands had left us
little time or energy to devote to primping up garb and
harness.

Which suited us, and our errand, and our royal charge,
very well indeed: though Arthur could ill spare any of his
Companions, he had sent four of his finest with me—Elphin
my old teacher, Daronwy, Betwyr and Elen—as escort for his
uncle. "Let there be round Uthyr a hand for every skill,"
Arthur had said in making the selection; and among us were
represented every magical and martial and craftly discipline
that Keltia could boast. We were Druid, bard, Ban-draoi,
Fian, pilot, healer, hunter, apothecary, horse-leech, farrier
and more besides—any need the King might have could be
met by one or more of us. From Coldgates also came Marigh
Aberdaron, his Taoiseach, and a few others.

Though caution was the watchword as we rode, we were
also merry; even Uthyr himself was in unaccustomedly ferocious high spirits. That first day I kept a careful eye on him,
as indeed I had been bidden by everyone from Arthur to the
humblest kern in Llwynarth; and often as I stole glances at
him I would meet the glances, also covert, being thrown his
way by Elen, the healer of our riding. Yet Uthyr never looked

other than most hale and happy, and when I questioned Elen
wordlessly she nodded and smiled satisfied approval.

But if we Companions could scarce control our eagerness
and delight that the struggle was at last an open one, and soon
to be decided for good and all, and to our triumph, how much
more so must it have been for Uthyr. His kindred had suffered in hiding for their lives for two hundred years; today he
rode at last to claim before all Keltia their birthright and his,
the Copper Crown itself, and by Arthur's arm to wear it as no
king or queen had worn it since Alawn, to wear it in Edeyrn's
despite. He would have been more than human had he been
able to encompass it with calm detachment; and we would
have been less than human had we demanded that he do so.

As Arthur had prophesied, our journey south was an un-
eventful one. We encountered no Ravens between Coldgates
and Llwynarth—all had been called back to their nests, to
prepare for the coming fight—and few travellers of any sort.
Perhaps rumor of battle had frightened folk from the roads; or
perhaps it was simply that the god of journeys and good
causes, shining Aengus, held his hand above us on the southward road, for never did we lack for shelter or forage or fair
weather, and Uthyr looked younger and stronger with each
passing day.

Still, I could not but ponder on how strangely sure Arthur
had grown of late that we should triumph; he had ever been
confident, but such absolute certainty was not like him. True,
it had all been prophesied long since by Merlynn, and Seen,
however imperfectly, with almost comic regularity by one or
another of us down the years. Yet prophecies have failed of
fruition before now, and even Sight may see amiss; but
though I reminded myself of this daily, sometimes almost
hourly, Arthur's assurance seemed to have passed to me, for
the certainty that countered my doubts was so strong as to
near collapse me with delight, and I would ride grinning like an
idiot with the sheer pleasure of it.

For all his confidence, though—bringing Uthyr from
Coldgates, naming him High King openly, challenging Edeyrn's
rule and hold as they had never been challenged before—

Arthur had not closed his ear entirely to his inner voice of caution; and so he had instructed us to bring Uthyr not to the regions round the great mountain Cruach Agned, where his leaguer was already forming, but to Llwynarth.

Not for that reason alone: Queen Ygrawn was at the Bear's Grove, and Marguessan was with her. Heavy with her first child—Uthyr's first grandchild—the Princess was down from the North, seeking safety while her lord went to the wars in her brother's cause. As for her sister: Morgan tarried at Llwynarth only for me to return there and to greet her father; once Uthyr was safe in our stronghold I would ride to join the others at Agned, and Morgan would ride with me.

Our journey continued peaceful, for which I gave profound and fervent thanks to every god and goddess I could think of—my grateful requitals even now to them all again, and any I may have forgotten that first time in my haste—and a fortnight after leaving the shieling we came to our destination.

To bring the Ard-rígh of Keltia to our own place, through masses of cheering, weeping, shouting Companions and Fians and kerns and other inhabitants of Llwynarth, and those who had gathered there from other shielings, eager for one glimpse before riding to war of the man for whom that war would be made—it is a thing that brings tears to my eyes even to this day. Yet it should have moved me just so had I never had sight of Uthyr Pendreic before that hour; knowing him as I did, and loving him as I had, how much the more did I feel his triumph now.

For triumph it was, and no mistake; no matter that it was yet to be won, that much Keltic blood was about to be shed to uphold Uthyr's right to the Copper Crown—or to continue to deny it him. That would be as it would be: No more was it a matter for men and women, or even for Arthur, to think to determine, but for the lords of dán; and so, of course, it had been determined long since. We had only to play it out, and so we would; but in the meantime there was this interval of dreams that anticipated reality, and we deserved it, for it had been hard earned.

And when Ygrawn came out to meet us, and greeted her husband, and stood with him for the first time publicly as Ard-rígh and Queen of Keltia, our joy knew no bounds; so that I think even Edeyrn, far away on Tara in Ratherne, must have sensed the upwelling of rapture, and the martial resolve that underlay it, and been troubled where he walked. As for Uthyr, he was a man transfigured; he and his Queen and his people were met that day, and had he been cut down in that very moment—and this I know for fact for he did tell me—he would have counted his life well spent in the buying of such an hour.

But the glad tumult died down at last, and we each of us turned to our sober tasks in preparing for the battle to come. Uthyr and Ygrawn went into Llwynarth for some privacy with themselves and those closest to them; yet for all his gladness to be with his Queen and his daughters—Morgan he saw but seldom, and Marguessan he had not seen since her marriage— for all that happiness Uthyr's chiefest preoccupation was with his absent nephew.

He spoke of it to me privily, before I left Llwynarth two days later with Morgan and such of the Companions as had tarried there on Arthur's order and were now bound with us for the battle. And once again, as I had been on the ride south, I was struck by Uthyr's shining aura of force and living energy: He seemed to have thrown off all his old weaknesses and infirmities, and had in that hour such a strength as might have more properly belonged to the Sun Lord Leowyn, his slain brother.

And, thinking this, I did not like what leaped all unwillingly into my mind: Might not this sudden splendor be the last burst of leaf and vigor that a dying oak puts forth, or the blazing brilliance of the woods before the first killing frost, or the song a swan is said to sing before the end? But I turned the thoughts aside, and hailed my much-loved guardian as King.

"Beannacht do Rígh! Pendreic an uachdar!"

A smile of extraordinary sweetness touched Uthyr's face. "And blessing likewise upon those that do hail him so . . . Ah,

Talyn, I tell you now, in those dark days at Coldgates, though I never lost faith that *this* day should come, and better ones still to follow, even so many times there were when that faith did falter.''

"And now, Lord?''

Uthyr put back his head and laughed. "I think faltering is done with! At least it is for my part . . .'' He grew grave again at once. "There are some things I would say, Talyn, and I would say them to you, and not to any other, for many reasons: for that you are the inventor of the Hanes, and growing into such a bard as Plenyth himself would not shame to call cousin; and for that you are beloved of my youngest child, and my dear wife's foster-son, and fostern to my brother's son, and birth-son to a friend I loved; and most of all for that you have been a son to me these many years.''

I took his hand and kissed it, deeply moved. "You are my father, Lord, and Keltia's father; not one of us lifts sword in this quarrel for any other save yourself alone.''

The hand tightened briefly on mine, then was gently withdrawn to rest upon my shoulder; seldom did Uthyr permit in himself, or in others for that matter, such displays of open emotion, and only did so now for that he was as moved as I.

"You will lift your swords in my name,'' he said then, "but you will bring them down in Arthur's; and I am well pleased it should be so. He will be High King after me—nay, do not interrupt, you know it well—and Gweniver will be High Queen; they shall rule together, and their rule is not far distant. This have I long known, and Merlynn has confirmed it: I shall live to see myself High King in truth, and Keltia restored, but I shall not see it long. Therefore I tell you these things, so you may tell Arthur when I cannot.''

"And those things?'' I found myself more than a little disconcerted by Uthyr's revelation that he should perish even in the triumph of his kingship, and wondered briefly if Arthur had Seen this as well.

Uthyr was silent a long time. "My daughter Marguessan and her lord Irian,'' he said at last. "It is a terrible thing, Tal-bach, to speak distrust of one's own child, and I pray that ncver you come to it. But I have not been King so long to pay no heed to a kenning, and something there is in those two that I would bid Arthur be most wary of in future.''

He glanced sidewise at me as if he expected some disagreement or denial; but he would find none for my part. I had been keeping a magical 'eye' on Marguessan these many years now, ever since her attempt to practice distant murder on the folk of that birlinn, back when she was an innocent lass of ten. Somehow I did not think she had changed much since that day, and as for Irian, her husband . . . Well, true it was I had heard only good of him as yet—which made him suspect right there: how devoted he was to his brother-in-law's cause and person, how fine a strategist he was, how skilled a warrior. His kindred had been unimpeachably loyal to the House of Dôn for centuries in exile and many more before; but then so had Gwenwynbar's family, and just see how *she* had turned out . . . Blood was no guarantee anymore; not unless it was spilled, and even then one could be in error.

''I will bid him so, Ard-rígh,'' I said at length. ''Though I pray your mistrust may be mistaken. What more?''

''Only what I need never say to you: that you love and cleave to my other daughter, who shall be your wife, and to your fostern, and to your methryn, as you do now and have ever done before.''

''No command could sit lighter upon me,'' I said smiling, but again I felt running through my bones a cold thread of dread and misgiving, deep beneath the moment's joy. If Uthyr were having genuine presentiments of death—his own death, as he had hinted earlier—then should we perhaps not speak of it straight out? I was Druid priest as well as bard, and though I was not belike so skilled in counsel as were others of my order, I was certainly able to pray with and for folk in the face of death. Any road, death to a Kelt is not the thing of dread and terror I have since learned it can be— sadly, needlessly—to other races. To us it is merely a change of life: When those we love die, we sorrow for ourselves, who are deprived of their bodily company for a time, but for them we feel only joy; and even a little envy, for that they are free, and dwell between lives in the Light.

But looking at Uthyr's face, calm and strong and happy as it was just then, I held my peace, that the moment not be lost; and afterwards I was glad that I had done so.

We rode that day to rejoin Arthur; much of the remaining population of Llwynarth came with us, though a strong guard was left (pride-puffed with their charge and lamenting their stay-at-home status by turns) to protect the King and Queen, and the Princess Marguessan, and the other noncombatants who remained in safety at the Bear's Grove.

Once we were well on our way, I spoke to Morgan of her father's warning to me, not in jest precisely, but more lightly than Uthyr had done, thinking to make as little of it as I might. I was most disconcerted to see her reaction: The planes of her face shifted, the hazel eyes grew clouded, and, as she had been that time in Collimare so long since, she was 'gone' even as she still rode beside me. Then almost at once she was back again, looking somberly at me out of eyes now piercingly clear.

"It is not what I wish to say, Talyn, but I fear my father is correct to fear my sister and her lord." She looked as if she could say more, but would not; then she shook her head and turned her gaze away east, where Arthur awaited us in Agned's shadow.

So it was that I returned to Arthur's side, joining his forces as they began to slip now southward and eastward and northward, meeting in the mountains to the west of Agned, where they should go unseen by spying Ravens and curious townsfolk alike.

I remembered well the land hereabouts, from my passing through with Elphin, on our way to Tinnavardan so many years ago; indeed, I myself had crossed the region on occasion during my time of travel as anruth, picking my way along the valleys of the three main rivers—the Brosna, the Saimhor and the Velindre. That last was the largest of the three, becoming larger still after the others did pour their waters into it, sweeping south and east past Agned in a great loop, then running southwestward to find the sea, down by the coast at the little island of Caer Ys.

Many other watercourses there were as well, some little more than riverlets seeping down from the hills, others sizable streams, all latticing the high upland that lay between the Rough Bounds to the west and Agned's sprawling bulk in the east. Cruach Agned was more a massif than a single great hill: Three-peaked and slope-shouldered, it dominated the landscape of low hills and high moors, and it was two days' march from side to side.

We had staked much upon that distance: For on the far side of Agned, some fifty miles away from where we had set camp, was Ravens' Rift, the chief Theocracy garrison in these parts. Midway between the mountain and the Sea of Glora, the Rift sat across the main road to Caer Dathyl, a menacing gray hulk housing enough Ravens to shadow our entire force. Indeed, more Ravens still had been sent there in the fortnight past, their mission being to bar our passage at whatever cost. Well—our *ostensible* passage: We had no more intention of coming within ten miles of the Rift than we had of walking to Tara. But Owein and his wool-brained advisors thought we had no more of strategy and daring than did they; thought that we should simply stroll down into the Rift's guarded pass, straight and stupidly into their arms. We had plans for the troops at the Rift, right enough; but not the same plans as those.

"They think we cannot deal with all the bog and marshland hereabouts," said Tarian, greeting us with affection and relief when at last we arrived in camp, and plunging at once into a briefing on our military prospects. "And that we must go by way of the Rift because we have no other choice of ground; that is their limited wisdom! In truth," she added, linking one arm through mine and the other through Morgan's and walking us down toward Arthur's tent at the camp's center, "had I any real choice, I too had chosen ground less laced with water upon which to make our stand—but it will serve well enough. By the time they tumble to what we are working on them, it will be too late; but first we must come down from *here* and get ourselves over *there*." She pointed east, to the rolling gray-green moor on the other side of Saimhor. "And by then the vermin at the Rift will have other pressing business with which they must deal."

"Oh aye?" I had not yet heard this part of the battle plan, and should have liked to hear it put forth by one of its chief architects; but we had come by now to Arthur's tent, and halted just beyond the faha that was guarded by two of our Companions. "Even so, Tari, Owein's armies are near halfway here from Caer Dathyl; they must soon swing north to make the Rift. To lure them here instead will take much, and they will come at us hard."

Tarian's grin flashed. "I am counting on it! Else *our* plan fails . . ."

"A risky plan, War-leader," said Morgan, speaking for the first time.

"Only risk will serve these days, Princess . . . But your brother waits on you both within. Go and see and speak with him, while we still have time for talk."

Chapter 32

*T*ime ran short indeed: That next morning after our arrival in camp, Arthur led his forces down from the hills and across the three rivers, with no smallest attempt at concealment or stealth; indeed, his whole purpose just now was that we *should* be seen. And two days after, as obediently as if he had been a sheep and Arthur the herd-dog, came Owein Rheged lumbering up out of the southeast with all his force.

They camped facing us across the expanse of moorland, thinking that by so doing they blocked our further march south; but in truth they had positioned themselves precisely where Arthur wished to have them. In numbers they were our superior, but that we had expected; and the odds were not much longer than those we had fought often enough before.

For a full day there was silence, as Owein's commanders ordered their leaguer and we waited on their doing so; but we knew we should hear from them soon enough. Indeed, the silence broke on the second morning: We had been out among the lines, Arthur and some of the rest of us, when Daronwy, who had been looking out over the ground between the two encampments, suddenly stiffened and straightened.

"Artos, an embassy comes."

But he too had seen, and was already making his way down the slope to where those who rode toward us under the white banner must come. Unbidden, we scurried behind him, for all the world like Cabal after his master and ours: myself, Daronwy, Elen, Betwyr, a few others who like ourselves had no pressing duties just then. The true tasks lay heavy upon the shoulders of Tarian and Keils and Grehan, in their Fian clochan overlooking the plain, where they planned the fight both here and elsewhere.

Arthur halted so abruptly we all but piled into him. From my place just to his left, I ran a glance over the embassy from Owein, and then started violently in my sudden shock: The rider beneath the white flag *was* Owein, just now dismounting to come forward on foot to where we stood waiting.

I could not see Arthur's face, but I could well behold Owein's; and he also mine, for I saw the baleful five-second glance with which he favored me, and I read the astonished thought behind the half-rueful smile: *Mabon Dialedd, indeed!* I made a small bow in civil greeting, but he ignored me from then on, being instead intent on Arthur.

Who studied Owein just as intently for half a minute in expressionless silence; and if you do think that sounds no great time, I invite you to count those moments out for yourself while staring into the eyes of your own worst foe. And then he spoke.

"Owein," said Arthur, "forbid thy Ravens."

Whatever Owein Rheged might have been expecting to hear from the lips of Arthur Penarvon, it surely was not that; and he was plainly taken aback by the surprise of it. But recovering at once—not for naught had he been master of the planet for nigh on thirty years—he replied in kind.

"Arthur," said Owein, "play thy game."

That was all they said to each other, then: Owein mounted and rode back to his camp; Arthur watched him out of sight, then turned on his heel and strode back to the clochan and his war-leaders. But late that night, as we sat around the table in Arthur's tent and pondered what might come from Owein in form of battle in the morning, another message came to Arthur from his enemy's hand.

It was not even a message diptych, the usual medium for

such things, but a more ancient form of communication: a sheet of parchment, folded several times and sealed with Owein's seal.

Arthur received it with apparent lack of interest from the hand of the Fian who brought it, then glanced up to meet a full dozen imploring stares.

He shook his head, a smile of amusement and exasperation both on his face. "It will say little, you know. He and I said all there was to say this afternoon."

"Artos, you exchanged *eight words*," said Betwyr. "Eight only, out of all that might have been said."

Again he shook his head, with less of amusement and more of sadness in the smile now.

"Nay, braud, had we talked from now to Nevermas we had said but little more, and naught more to the point; only swords shall be our discourse now . . . But, to please all you, before you perish of curiosity—"

He broke the seal and read the contents. When he said nothing, I held out my hand, and still without a word he pushed the parchment to me across the table's width. I picked it up and unfolded it, and no more was on the page but this:

'If thou come, and if ever thou come to Tara.' The words were in the High Gaeloch; the sign-manual was bold and clear: *'Edeyrn.'*

I passed the parchment round the table, and the silence in the tent was absolute. When the page came back again to me, I handed it once more to Arthur, who had watched with great interest our faces as one by one we read the Marbh-draoi's message.

"A threat, if you like," I said. "What answer shall you give him?"

Arthur sat up with sudden energy. "This first," he said. "Later, perhaps some other answer. But for now this."

He had been writing a few words on a parchment of his own, and this he now pushed across to me. I looked down at the words that were written there, in the blackest of ink, in Arthur's sprawling scrawl; and the others craned and crowded close to read.

No more was on that page but this:

'And if I go to Tara, and if I go.' The words were in the High Gaeloch; the sign-manual was firm and flowing: *'Arthur.'*

So we left it, that last night before Keltia changed forever: Arthur, having sent his parchment on its way to Edeyrn, thrust the Marbh-draoi's letter under his tunic and inside his leinna, swearing to Morgan and me a private vow to keep it next his heart until the heart of one of them—Edeyrn or Arthur—no longer beat.

Neither Morgan nor Merlynn—who had joined us in camp, bringing the renewed and constant prayers and blessings of Uthyr and Ygrawn, to witness for himself what he had Seen so many years since—much liked this rather dramatic and most uncharacteristic gesture. No more did I, and I could guess the ground of their misgiving: that perhaps some subtle ill-working had been wrought upon the parchment, a scribed rann for evil and hurt against Arthur and his folk, or Arthur alone. Though I did not share their doubts, to set their minds at rest I promised to speak of it to Arthur; but when I did mention it, he laughed and shook his head.

"Nay, that would be too simple for his devious mind! Be assured, the Marbh-draoi has other plans for me; indeed, for all of us . . . There will be a time for such fears; but just now there is naught here, Talyn, but ink and parchment only, and we have far realer things to face this day. So Guenna and Merlynn can rest easy, and do you bid the others easy also, and be so yourself. We will be giving his words a proper answering very soon now."

Indeed, the answer Arthur was preparing to make was beginning to be phrased even now, beyond the door of the tent: Dawn was breaking far off past Agned, though here at the mountain's foot it was yet dark, and with that distant daybreak came the first stab of that other horn of battle with which Owein Rheged would be this day gored. By this hour, the second strike of our two-pronged attack—the forces that Arthur had sent by water, sailing down the length of the Sea of Glora—would be coming to land on the beaches near Ravens' Rift, would be moving inland to engage the Theocracy forces stationed there to bar our passing—or rather, the passing they had been expecting us to make by road. The main battle would of course be ours at Agned, since here it was that Arthur and Owein would cross swords at last; but unless those Rift troops were prevented from marching west to join with Owein, our fight was doomed from the start.

This then was the strategy that Tarian had alluded to on that morning Morgan and I came to camp; that had been planned by Grehan and Keils and Arthur and herself—and it was far more than a diversionary attack. In truth, it had been the original plan for the main attack, and only after Tarian had devised the strategy for battle beneath Agned had the plan been altered. Hellish difficult of implementing as well; not until afterwards did I come to learn how the craft for the sea venture had been built and hidden—some had been concealed at Collimare itself, as it happened—or how the forces to sail them had trained in secret, small groups at a time, in every loyal fishing village on Gwynedd.

The fleet was under the command of Tryffin Tregaron, who had not been engaged on family business those months of absence of Kernow (save in the larger sense of 'family'), but in shipbuilding and fitting and seamanship, at which callings the Kernish are equalled by few and surpassed by none; also my old teacher Scathach, who came of a seafaring line; and—somewhat of a surprise here—Marguessan's husband, Irian Locryn, who knew the Sea of Glora well, as his family's lands bordered its shores. They proved bonny shiplords all three, as would soon be seen.

But though our friends on the sea that morning were much in our hearts and prayers—as were we in theirs—we had matters of our own to attend to; and after perhaps two hours' sleep, Arthur came out of his tent to begin to deal with them.

He looked by no means like a hard-pressed commander about to lead his forces into the fight of all their lives. His red-brown hair bare of any helm, his frame armored for the field in a findruinna lorica, his scarlet cloak whipping out

behind him and the sword Llacharn hanging at his side—
despite the last-minute panics all round him, the shouted
contradictory orders, the sleep he had not gotten, Arthur
looked that day like a man who had come at last within reach
of that which he had long sought, and not about to let it slip
through his grasp.

The ground Arthur had chosen for his first great battle, and
onto which he had so cleverly lured his opponent, was a vast
plain that lay between Agned and the river Saimhor; level if
rough for the most part, at one side it sloped abruptly into a
hollow, masked from the higher ground across which Owein
must come to engage us. To the west, the lattice of streams
and wetlands, which we had crossed two days since, and the
broader barrier of the Saimhor effectively narrowed in Owein's
front and choice of approach, and had the additional advantage of preventing him from trying to turn our right flank. On
the east, the plain ran right up into the outlying spurs of
Agned, and neither we nor Owein could take that way for
escape.

But Arthur's strategy made no allowance for escape: A
deliberately understrength right, pledged to a holding action,
and a center denied, can serve as the pin on which the rest of
the army pivots to smash the enemy's line. It is a daring
tactic, but irresistible when it works—it can crumple an enemy flank like a dead leaf—and we had had occasion to
employ it before now, though never for such high and desperate stakes as these.

"The operative word here being 'desperate,' " Tarian had
dourly observed at the commanders' council the preceding
night. "Well, Artos, you did say you had something new in
mind. What you did not see fit to mention to Keils and
Grehan and me was that the something new was defeat."

But Arthur, not offended in the slightest, had grinned and
made her a half-bow from where he sat at the table's head.

"Now there speaks my cautious war-leader! Nay, Douglas,
look not so; that is just what I do wish to hear from you—and
from Aoibhell, or Rathen, or any other of you here who cares

to play antiadvocate," he had added, glancing over the score or more of us Companions who packed the tent and crowded the table.

"Then I shall do so as well," Kei had said at once. "Artos, it is a most uncertain plan, and I am not sure the armies will not be slow to follow you. Do not forget, this is the first time they have been flown all together at Ravens. The raids and skirmishings we have fought are one thing, but this is the first true battle we shall fight as one force, and takes a deal more leading. Who, for one thing, shall you put on the right to hold this pivot?"

Arthur had given him a quick quizzical look. "You and Betwyr," he had said, smiling as Kei rolled his eyes. "You have been my wheelhorses long time now; never have I had greater need of two stern and steady anchors on whom all the fight shall turn, and maybe all the day depend."

Kei had shaken his head dolefully. "And do you not think to use that silver tongue of yours on me, either—aye, well, who else *but* Betwyr and me?"

And just so had the dispositions been settled: Arthur put those two on the right with several companies, artfully placed to appear a far larger force; and in the center with Ferdia and Elen—a brazen ruse, for it was not a proper center at all but just sufficient to make Owein think the position strongly held—he placed the standard. This was not the vexillum of the Counterinsurgency that flew that day from many lances, but the ancient, forbidden Royal Standard of the House of Dôn, that had not been seen or flown for two hundred years.

"Would that my father might see that," said Morgan, tucking her hair under a helm and slinging on her baldric.

"A brave sight," I agreed. And so was she: It hurt my heart to look at her and know that very soon now she would be beside me in the thick of things; still, better she was at my side than off where I could not see her and know how she did fare. I had told myself this a thousand times that day already, and it made me feel no better now than it had the first time of telling; so to hide my fear and shame I pointed out over the expanses of moor and upland lying before us. "Good ground for a fight; but how is this place called, so that we bards may properly sing of it after?''

Daronwy had come up to us in time to hear my question. ''Blair Catterick it is on the maps,'' she said. ''But that is a new name, and one not fit for song. Of old it was ever known as Cadarachta.''

It was as if she had driven a spear-butt into my ribs: I doubled over, catching my breath in a gasp, reaching out blindly to Morgan as I reeled on my feet.

''Name of Dâna, Talyn, are you hit?'' That was Daronwy, looking wildly around for my nonexistent attacker; finding none, she and Morgan supported me between them until I might stand again upon my own feet.

''Are you well, cariad?'' murmured Morgan.

After a moment I managed a nod, for I dared not trust my voice—I, a bard. Cadarachta: the name I could not remember, that had haunted my dreams and tormented my Sight these many nights. And yet, now I stood here in my own waking self and not in sleep, on the spot I knew so well yet had never stood upon before, I realized that my staggerment just now had not been pain or terror or defeat, though the battle to come might well encompass all those things. That would be as it would be: But the feeling that had near buckled my knees a moment since had been a feeling of joy.

It did not work precisely to Arthur's plan, of course. Such things seldom do, taking on instead a life of their own apart from that which their hopeful initiator has intended for them.

For one thing, Betwyr (of all people!), as a rule the steadiest and solidest of captains, seemed to suffer a fit of momentary madness; instead of holding rocklike as Arthur had commanded, granite for Owein's left to break upon, he became hammer rather than anvil, charging down the slope with his small company, cutting down Owein's warriors like so many cabbages. Oh aye, it was a pretty thing to see, but I thought Arthur was going to throttle him.

In the event it did no great harm, and may have helped, even, by further disordering an attack that had not been oversteady to begin with. For once we did not charge first, but let Owein advance unhindered; then as soon as he was led up far enough, his left already beginning to come apart because of the uncertain ground, Arthur swung the gate on its hinge.

Roaring up out of the hollow where they had lain hidden all this time, our main horse, led by Grehan and Gweniver and Arthur himself, smashed into Owein's right; under the shock, the enemy line stopped, wavering, and then collapsed, shattering like a struck goblet. Indeed, in the panic of the moment, wrong orders were apparently given—or perhaps it was pure panic after all— for instead of wheeling to the charge as was customary practice, Owein's horse turned the wrong way, and began to ride down their own foot.

We shouted to see it, for that confusion was very helpful for us: In the midst of the bloody turmoil I led my own company across to relieve the hard-pressed Kei, who was holding the right all alone after Betwyr's unsanctioned, if successful, charge. Elen Llydaw saw our move, and followed; together we came down on Owein again, scattering what remained of his left front, and Gweniver's horse coming up from behind them put them to unvarnished, and unavailing, flight. They could not flee south or east because of the fighting, could not escape west because of the water and soft ground; but west seemed the way of least peril, and many took it. To their destruction: When they were found, after the battle's end, they had not a mark of the sword upon them; they had all drowned in the streams and the deep pools.

Give Owein the praise, though: He gathered what warriors he could in the face of our unorthodox assault—bewildering to any captain used to more conventional tactics—and held them together by sheer force of voice and will. His purpose was to call them off, collecting them for an ordered retreat, and they began to disengage then, under his order, as best they could; but in the face of a new charge they broke and ran. We chased them nearly to the skirts of Corva Wood; it was said after that one might have walked there from Agned on the bodies of the slain. An exaggeration—I recognized a bard's love for a good line when I heard one—but not so far off the truth for all that; and the losses that day were overwhelmingly Owein's.

It reads quick enough when so set down—the Battle of Cadarachta—a thing of flow and unity, but it was scarce that for us who fought it: The battle lasted from dawn to near sunset, and though it was slaughter beyond all right reason, the slaughter was by no means a continuum. Rather it came in waves, and went again according to a rhythm of its own: You might be fighting for very life the space of an hour, or a quarter that, and then have the equal of that in respite before the tide rolled again to your part of the field.

Perhaps five hours into the fight that tide turned for us in truth: Our forces who had engaged Ravens' Rift, sailing boldly down Glora to meet the enemy on the beaches of the inland sea, had triumphed utterly. The fighting had swirled westward, engulfing the fortress, but after a sharp and bloody encounter, the generalship of my old tutor Scathach and my old friend Tryffin, assisted by Irian, had secured the Rift for us, and the pass it guarded. Word was already being sent to the shielings that the road lay clear to Caer Dathyl.

Or at least it would very soon, once we at Agned had put paid to the tiny detail that was Owein Rheged; though at that moment we did not dream the price should come so high . . .

Through all the day's fighting I had caught glimpses only of Arthur. He seemed to be a flame flickering across the battlefield, never to be grasped at but everywhere at once, Cabal hunting beside him: Indeed, to listen to folk tell it after, he must have been in a score of different places all at once—leading that first great charge to destroy Owein's flank, rallying weary warriors, chasing down foes who fled before him, cutting the Theocracy standard from its bearer's hand, even sword to sword with Owein himself, until the eddy of battle parted them.

Others there were I was just as fretted for, and sought to see—Morgan, thank the Mother, had not been far from my

side nor out of my sight all that day—but now, as the battle
bloomed and spread and spent itself at last, rippling out in all
directions like wind in a wheatfield, I saw enough to reassure
me of the safety of those dearest friends I sought: Gweniver,
flushed and triumphant at the head of her horse; Kei, untired
and methodical; a chagrined but very pleased Betwyr; Tarian
cool and unruffled as ever; Grehan with one arm bound across
his chest; Keils and Elen Llydaw both limping, though I could
see no visible hurt on either; Daronwy exhausted but otherwise hale.

Merlynn I had never lost sight of: He had not borne sword
in the fight, but he had served as warrior even so. Taking up
a stance on a crag of Agned where both sides could see him,
he had stood there unmoving as a dolmen-stone from dawn to
dusk. More than once during the course of the battle I had
looked up from my labors to see him there—no weapon could
reach him, and no enemy had been brave enough to try,
though I think none could have come close—and I had taken
courage, as did many others, from his simple presence.

Yet the one I sought most desperately I could not find
straightway; then at last, as I skirted a shoal of the slain—few
of them our own, praise gods, though in truth all of them
were our own, and there was little to praise in this hateful
conflict save the valor of both sides—I met Arthur coming
slowly toward me on foot, Cabal at his heels looking ferocious indeed for a yearling hound. I sighed and breathed a
silent prayer to see my fostern safe and relatively unscathed—he
had some cuts and slashes such as we all had taken, few came
unmarked from that field—and altered my course to meet
him. But he had already seen me, and Cabal bounded ahead
to leap joyfully upon me, thumping his huge paws down on
my weary shoulders. I staggered a little under his weight, and
at my soft word he dropped again to the ground; but my eyes
had never left the one who came so slowly on behind him.

"Hail master of Gwynedd!" I said when he came up to us.
Then I saw his eyes, and wished I had not spoken so.
"Artos? Is it well?"

He gave a short harsh laugh. "Well enough, for one who

has compassed the death of thousands of his countryfolk . . . Talyn, if ever I take joy in such a sight as this''—his hand traced the miles of slaughter—''you have my leave to send me to join them.''

''Arthur,'' I said gently, pulling all my old tricks of soothing from my smoke-sore throat, ''none thinks you do take joy in this; not now, not ever. It was not you did make this quarrel, though it be you who finish it.''

''Kelts killing Kelts—''

''Aye. I know. But it must be so; it was the only way open to you, and the last way open for us all. Artos—Prince Arthur—today you have won Gwynedd for the Ard-rígh Uthyr Pendreic. That is more than any man or woman in two centuries against the Theocracy has managed to do: to take back a planet, any planet, from the Marbh-draoi by force of arms.''

I saw by his eyes that he knew all this, and saw too that my words that should have comforted had not sufficed; perhaps no words could. But it seemed that I had reached him somewhat, for muttering that I should find what friends of ours I might and come later to his tent, he went away with Cabal over the bloody ground.

I remained there awhile, on the place of my dreaming—the little rise, a shoulder of an outlier of Agned—staring out over that scene I knew so well and yet had not known until this day, this moment: It was all there, the dark clouds, the stormy sunset, the drifts of the dead, the faint shouts as the last of the fight rolled southward. I have come to battle often enough in my time, had seen war before and would again after, but that day stands alone.

Never was field like to Cadarachta: Rivers ran red in the red light; before Agned armies groaned.

Chapter 33

*I*n the end, I did not go straightway to Arthur's tent as I had said I would, or at least as he had bidden me; if I had—well, of all self-tortures, what-ifs are the least satisfactory, being neither honest shame nor true blame.

Coming down from my hill, I was pressed into service by Elen Llydaw to help among the healers. Bards learn a good deal of the healing lore in the course of their training, and Druids too; so that between the two disciplines I myself might have qualified for the healer's white cowl, and I turned a hand with a good will. Friend or foe, it made no differ now; all the wounded were wounded alike, no distinction remaining save that impartial assessment: Can this man, this woman, be healed of the hurts sustained?

But though I said 'impartial' just now, it was by no means a dispassionate assessment, as any will know who has had to make it. At times it seemed there were hardly enough hands among us to heal the hurts those hands were set to. For very many had taken very many more hurts in that terrible fight: warriors, as the old chaunt has it, so sore wounded that birds might have flown through their bodies, never once tipping their feathers with blood.

Already countless hundreds had slipped out through those bloody lattices, their spirits spreading wings of their own to soar; and no healer worth the name would have called those back if he could—not to dwell in maimed cages only for the sake of living, for that is not Kelu's way. So they went to find their freedom, and we were diminished, and they were not forgotten.

But even remembrance was for later—remembrance and rites—for the moment we were still busy with the business of war, and just now it seemed a neverending business indeed.

In the course of my labors I met with many I had not seen all that long and dreadful day: Tegau, my sister, who arrived at Agned with the first eyewitness account of the battle at Ravens' Rift, where she had been second in command to Scathach Aodann aboard the leading ship; Companions from Llwynarth, some of whom I knew well and others of whom I had scant acquaintance save that of face and name. Most astonishing of all, I came across that same apparently indestructible Trevelyan who had ridden his fleet white mare out of Gwaelod before the onrushing wave so many years since. Not only had he escaped Gwaelod's ruin, but he—and his mare! —had survived the destruction of Daars as well, and had lived happily all the decades after. Not to mention surviving this day's work; though his mount at Cadarachta was not that famous mare but her great-great-grandson, who must have been possessed of all his ancestress's speed and heart, for he had preserved both his hide and his rider's unblooded and whole.

But few that day went as unscathed as the bold Trevelyan: I myself lost a sister and brother—Adaon and Rainild—whom I had scarcely known, such had been the Counterinsurgency's demands and needs; Tarian's brother Rohan, Grehan's sister Digna, Kei's beloved Samhra, all had fallen at the Rift. Of our own Companions at Agned, none had been slain though near all were wounded, some sorely, and some like to die even yet. No wonder Arthur's soul was bowed beneath the weight of it . . .

And yet in all this time of evil word we had no word, neither good nor ill, of Owein Rheged. He was not among the slain, for we searched most closely for him, and not with eyes alone; nor was he among the many prisoners taken, and none could give us news of him. Oh, they would have if they could, even against their will, for those most skilled in so doing kenned them hard; but it seemed that he had vanished from the field.

For myself I was not surprised, and supposed simply that he had ingloriously fled when the battle swung to Arthur; but Morgan was strangely troubled, and did not share my thought. When I pressed for her own thought on Owein's absence, she only shook her head, her face taking on that questing look I knew so well on her brother's.

"He is here somewhere, Talyn," she said at last. "But when I reach for him, my othersense closes only on his absence; as if he had been there, but had just then stepped into some pocket of air, or cloaked himself with another's reality."

"A shapeshift?" I asked, interested and alarmed both. "But any sorcerer can see through any ordinary fith-fath or glamourie, and with you and Merlynn and so many others here surely even Owein would not be bold enough to try a greater change. Remember, he is no magician; his power, howsoever great it be, is but borrowed plumes."

But I could get no more from her, and after a few moments and a quick kiss I left her to go on to her other duties, and turned at last, after these many hours of tending to others, to tend a little to myself.

But as I walked away from Morgan, I wondered again at Owein's absence, and after a while a darker, grimmer thought came to me: If we had had no word of Owein, still less had we had word of his master. Edeyrn had made no move, had sent no pronouncement: Yet by now he would surely have heard of Cadarachta, and its twin slaughter at Ravens' Rift; knew by now that Arthur Penarvon—Arthur Pendreic—held all Gwynedd against him. Yet he kept silence.

And that silence out of Tara was already making me profoundly uneasy, as uneasy as I had been made by the lack of Owein. Time to come would show that both fears were well founded; but in the meantime, I could only wonder anew. Why had Edeyrn not chosen to armor his adopted heir's fist? He might have sent wave upon wave of troops, aircraft, even starships against us; might have flown all his dark magic at us like a hawk from his fist—magic of Sidhe and Druid alike, the sorcery of one who was both Ro-sai of the Pheryllt and the son of the Queen of the Sidhe; yet he had not done so—or at least not yet. He seemed to have left Owein to his own resources and to his own fate; perhaps it was a test? If so, then Owein had wretchedly failed. But what would Edeyrn do next?

"If *I* were the Marbh-draoi," said Daronwy consideringly as we walked at last to the bath-tent, free finally—and most eager—to scrub away the mud and blood of Cadarachta, "I should be thinking to make Arthur work as hard as possible for anything he may gain. It is now past the point of Arthur being denied, I think, so Edeyrn will be hoping either to contain or to destroy. Preferably destroy; and if I—I the Marbh-draoi—were unable to manage this alone . . ."

"If?" prompted Betwyr, who walked on my other side; Betwyr whose unsanctioned charge downslope into Owein's left had already become one of the legends of the day, though as yet he had not dared to face Arthur's wrath.

"If I could not do so alone," continued Daronwy, "I should call in those who might help me do so."

I looked at her, startled, and suddenly sure. "You mean from outside? You think he might call in galláin?"

"I think it not unlikely. Many folk fight for hire these days: the Thallo, the Mederai, the Parishen; even the Fomori, come to that. Perhaps it will not be straightway; but I would be more surprised, Talyn, if we did *not* cross swords with galláin before this thing is done."

I was soaking in the steaming bathwater—I think I have mentioned the near-mystical addiction of Kelts to hot water; even the Romans thought us excessively fond of bathing, and they were by no means an uncleanly people—luxuriating in the way it unstrung muscles too long tensed, washing away the battle grime, and perhaps other soil more ingrained than that, when the messenger came for me. And when she had delivered herself of her charge—even before the words were full spoke—I was out of the bath with a great *huish* of water, pulling on the clean garb I had brought without even taking time to dry myself off.

For the news she had been sent to tell me was this: Uthyr Ard-rígh had come to the leaguer, and Ygrawn the Queen with him; and I had been summoned to the King's tent to hear a thing that he would say.

Uthyr had come to the camp upon the Saimhor heavily guarded from Llwynarth, to see for himself the victory that his nephew's arm had given him. But that was not his sole reason, nor even his chief reason for coming; and so it was that I was witness to a scene I had sooner *not* witnessed. I had rather faced ten battalions of Ravens, and I armed with but a table-sgian, than face what awaited me in that tent; and what came after . . . But the King required my presence, and so I was there.

Nor was I there alone: Ygrawn, of course, was already there, and embraced me fiercely, all her fear and relief apparent in the strength of her clasped arms round me. Over in a corner of the tent, Merlynn sat quietly, down at last from the crag where he had watched our battle; only the gleam in his eye falling on me gave me greeting—but it was enough. And Morgan, who met me with a wink and a kiss.

Others there were in the tent, whom I had not thought to see: a tall man I did not know by sight, but who was, as Ygrawn informed me, the new Chief Brehon, Alun Cameron; and a woman I knew well, Marigh Aberdaron, Uthyr's longtime Taoiseach.

And from her seat near her uncle's side, Gweniver smiled up at me. She looked so fair that night, glad and high-hearted; weary as were we all with battle's strain and battle's horror, but still sword-sharp. I do not recall how she was clad, but her long black hair was still braided up in the mionn, only a few loose tendrils come undone to soften the planes of her face.

All this I took in at a moment's glance: Uthyr had swept me into his arms, his delight at seeing me even greater than his Queen's, and now he kissed me on either cheek as my own father would have done, with a murmured word for my ear alone of his love and pride, and his joy to see me safe. I returned his embrace and his loving words as the son he had always avowed me, then stepped back and drew myself up, giving formal salute to the High King of Keltia from his loyal liegeman.

Just as I looked about for the one person I had thought surely to see, the tent door opened and he came in. Arthur went arrow-straight to his uncle—I am sure he saw no one else just then, not even his mother—and, hand on sword-hilt, went to one knee before his King.

Uthyr raised him at once, looked on him in silence for perhaps ten seconds—and even I, clear on the other side of the tent, had to lower my eyes before the look in the King's— then embraced him, not as he had embraced me, with exuberance, or as I later heard he had hugged Gweniver, with tenderness and tears, but with a kind of fierce wordless vehemence I had never seen in him before; nor in anyone, for that matter—it is the kind of emotion born of an infrequent moment, combining love and terror and relief and pride. Arthur looked back at his uncle, and though I could not see his face I saw his shoulders tremble.

Then the mood broke, Uthyr calling out for winc or ale to celebrate; Arthur turning then to his mother and to me, the others talking together of the day's events. Only Merlynn maintained his silent watchfulness; though what he watched for I could not imagine, and, strangely, feared to try.

When all of us held full methers, and the tent doors closed at last, Uthyr nodded once, and we seated ourselves in obedience to his wish. But he himself remained standing, Ygrawn in a field-chair at his right hand, Morgan on his left, and Arthur and Gweniver side by side before him.

I myself was over against the tent wall, next to the still-silent Merlynn; though I had ventured a mental inquiry, my old teacher had chosen not to reply—Ailithir yet lived, it seemed—and with a sigh I turned expectantly toward the King.

And Uthyr looked that night every inch a king: Healthily flushed, bright-eyed, clad openly now in the colors and embroidered device of the House of Dôn, he stood before us as our ruler, and he spoke to us as our friend.

"I have bidden all you here this night," he began, "to tell you a thing I think most of you may know already, or have guessed at. This day I am High King of Keltia in openness, not merely in name; and though it may take long before I am Ard-rígh in truth, over a Keltia free of the scourge it has borne these two centuries past, tonight I take action for that future, and I name my successor to follow me in formal naming."

Gweniver's head came up at that, and Arthur lowered his. I saw Ygrawn's violet glance move from one to the other of them, then it slanted over to meet my own. And all this time it seemed that no one breathed in that tent; even the camp outside seemed hushed.

Uthyr could restrain himself no longer. "Now in the presence of this company to witness it, Merlynn Archdruid"—I startled at the unexpected title, but kept still—"to bless it, Alun Cameron Lord Chief Brehon of Keltia to sanction it, Marigh Aberdaron Taoiseach of Keltia to confirm it, do I name Gweniver Pendreic ferch Leowyn and Arthur Pendreic ap Amris, latterly known as Arthur Penarvon ap Gorlas, to be co-heirs to Keltia; jointly to rule when time comes for it as High Queen and High King equally, Ard-rígh and Ard rían together. So say I, Uthyr King of Kelts."

The silence was profound; even though I daresay most of those who heard this ringing pronouncement had known beforehand what the King should say, and most of the others had suspected, still it came as a shock—even to me—to hear it declared.

But two there were to whom it came as a greater shock even than that, two who had had absolutely *no* knowledge, *no* suspicions, and those were the two it concerned most nearly: Arthur and Gweniver themselves.

At his uncle's pronouncing Gweniver's name, Arthur had relaxed in his chair; when Uthyr had gone on to declare him as co-heir, Ard-rígh to be, Arthur's face had flushed red as fire, and he would not lift his eyes to the King's. But Gweniver stared at her uncle, and I thought as I looked on her that I had never seen so pale a face or so tight-drawn a mouth.

"Gwennach, I am sorry," said Uthyr then, in a voice so gentle I felt tears come hot to my eyes. "But it is the best and only way for you both, and for all Keltia."

"Highness, it is truly best," said Marigh, slipping adroitly in before any other could speak. "I say this as Taoiseach, and as your uncle's honored friend and servant who would be yours also, and the Prince's, in the years ahead."

Gweniver gave her barely a glance, still intent on her uncle. "Why is it then I have a feeling there is more to come? Let you drop the other boot, Lord, before the echo of the first has faded."

Uthyr glanced down at Ygrawn, who slipped her hand into his but did not look up.

"Well then," he said, and now he looked at Gweniver alone, "it is likewise ordered that you two shall wed. For the good of the succession, and since there is no lawful way that either of you can take the throne in the other's despite. Your heirs would then be unquestioned heirs of the line of Dôn, and the law be satisfied. This is my will, Gwennach," he added in a gentler voice, "but it is also my wish; and it is my hope, devoutly, that it will likewise come to be yours."

Neither word nor move from Arthur or Gweniver; but I sat back a little in my chair, blowing out my breath in a silent whistle. Of all those in the tent, perhaps only Merlynn and I, and doubtless Ygrawn, had known the King's full intent, and I—presumably Merlynn also—was most interested to see how this second part of Uthyr's intention did work upon the others. Alun Cameron's face bore a small smile, as if this were something he should have seen coming but had not; Marigh Aberdaron, initially astonished, had mastered her sur-

prise almost at once, and was now almost visibly running
over the options and reasons in her most beautifully logical
mind.

And what of Morgan, who was after all Uthyr's own
daughter? Not to mention Marguessan, who as Uthyr's *elder*
daughter might be forgiven for thinking some heirship rights
due to her—and to the child about to be born to her . . . I
could not see Morgan's face from where I sat, but I did not
need to see her: Reaching out with my mind, I found hers
reaching at the same instant for mine, and sensed only a cool
amusement at the idea I hesitantly suggested. *I, or Marguessan,
as Ard-rían? Talyn, sometimes you can be so very stupid . . .*
But the scorn was lovingly and teasingly expressed, and I sent
back sheepish agreement in answer. Our communication was
interrupted as Gweniver rose abruptly to her feet; she threw
Arthur one burning look—which he missed, having still his
glance bent upon his hands—and then faced her uncle.

"And if I do not agree to this?" she snapped. "This
compact was made behind my back and without my knowledge; without the knowing of most of those here, if the surprise I
see and sense is any true indicator. How if I say no?"

"Be Ard-rían, then," said Uthyr wearily. "Take the throne
alone, and welcome to it—if you think you can hold Keltia
together *and* draw the folk to follow you only *and* command
the fight against the Marbh-draoi. You will lose, Gwennach;
and we will be the lesser for it, and the folk will suffer for it
most of all, and more than you."

Her resistance to the thing had not lessened one scrappet;
but at the King's word of how the people would pay for her
refusing, Gweniver's resolve faltered a little. And not to be
wondered at: She was a princess born and bred, to her the
folk were everything; she would do on their behalf what she
would never do on her own. Even, it appeared, marry
Arthur . . .

"We have never had such a thing—a joint sovereignty—in
Keltia," she said then, uncannily echoing my words long
since to Merlynn.

"We have never had such times in Keltia," I countered,

judging it my moment to speak. "You are unquestionably to be Ard-rían, lady, by law of succession and right of descent; but Arthur is unquestionably to be Ard-rígh by law of arms and right of conquest, and by a different mode of reckoning succession. And Keltia has never failed to honor a claim of either sort. The only solution—for you, for Arthur, for us all—is as the Ard-rígh does bid you."

The battle that had been that day was not plainer fought than the war now to be beheld raging on Gweniver's face. And all this time Arthur sat in his chair beside her and never said a word and never moved at all. If he had, I think he would have lost Keltia and Gweniver together, right there, right then. As it was . . . but he had ever known how to wait, one of the most difficult learnings there is. Some never learn—myself perhaps among those—and some take longer than others, but do learn most well in the end—and Gweniver ferch Leowyn was surely among *those*.

All at once Gweniver smiled—a bitter smile, but a real one—and capitulated.

"Then I do submit me to the will of the Ard-rígh. How says the Prince of the Name? Shall he take up his father's place?"

Arthur flushed, then paled again, then rose to stand beside the Princess, his hand clenched around the great seal ring he wore on his left hand: the seal of Amris Pendreic, Prince of Dôn.

"My father—as you know well, lady—was never King of Kelts as should have been; as yours was. But I say in his name that I too submit me to the will of the Ard-rígh; and if it is likewise your will, we shall wed and rule as Uthyr King of Kelts has said."

For one moment more Gweniver held out mutinous and counter; then she held out her hand in silence, and in silence Arthur took it, and in silence they both did reverence before the King.

That was not the last of it that night: After Arthur and Gweniver had sworn between Uthyr's hands, taking the oath together as Tanist and Tanista to uphold the Ard-tiarnas of Keltia, there were documents produced by Alun Cameron and Marigh Aberdaron for the two co-heirs to sign, and then all of us present set our own hands thereto as witnesses.

Gweniver left the tent as soon as she might decently do so, alone and hastily; Morgan—with a quizzical glance at me that might have been either exasperation or rare understanding, and most like was both—went out after her, to offer what cheer or consolation she might. The more likely to be accepted because of the source—Gweniver was sincerely and deeply attached to Morgan, and that not least because she knew her cousin, in spite of being the reigning King's child, had not the smallest tiniest design on queenship. Nor, to the best of my knowing, had Morgan ever had such design: Her ambitions, high enough, lay with magic and not with majesty. Now her sister Marguessan— But my reflections were interrupted by Arthur's hand on my shoulder.

"Come, braud; I would walk a while, and would not walk alone." The tent had emptied by now of all save us two and the King and Queen; we made our goodnights lovingly if swiftly, and left them—doubtless they were glad to be private at last, to discuss the day's victory, and this night's victory as well.

Outside, the camp was quiet, settling down for the night. We walked with no clear destination in mind, just wandered through the camp shoulder to shoulder, in silence for the most part, Arthur mechanically taking the salutes of the Fian guards we passed. After perhaps half an hour's walk, round and about, we found ourselves near to that little hill from which I had that afternoon looked southward over the land my visions had shown me. That region was dark now, all the south was dark; but turning back again we could see that all else was strewn with the sparks of quartz-hearths, and the warm glow of the little field-lamps that hung in hundreds of tents.

"I had not thought to wed again," said Arthur abruptly. "And clearly she had not thought to wed *me*—for which I scarce do blame her. We have not been the most loving of cousins over the years, nor the dearest of friends; as to anything more, or deeper—''

"She *will* wed you, Artos," I said.

I saw his head nod against the little lights. "Aye, for it is duty. And duty will see me wed to her—as you and the King did say, there is no other choice. She will make a fine Ard-rían."

"And you a great Ard-rígh—perhaps the greatest."

His laugh was bleak and bitter. "Certainly the most fated! And yet do you remember, Talynno, when we were lads at Daars, how I longed for just such a dán—now it seems that I shall have it, will I or nill I. All if the Marbh-draoi falls, that is . . . at the moment I am not even able to lay hands on his heir and creature, the execrable Owein—who this day, even I am bound to say, fought more creditably than I did think to see. But I shall slay him all the same."

I held my tongue, for I knew what he was thinking, and it was not to do with Owein, but with the mother of Owein's heir: Gwenwynbar, and the boy Malgan who might or might not be Arthur's son. *One fight at a time, braud,* I said silently, mind to mind, and heard his answering laugh of agreement.

"Let us go back now," he said then aloud. "I would change my garb, and bathe, and sleep at least a few hours; also I left Cabal tied up in my tent so that he might not follow us, and now I must take him out for a run before we sleep. I would look in again on the King and my mother, too," he added. "It was more tiring, I think, for him waiting at Llwynarth for word of the fight than for us who actually fought."

"Bid them good rest from me also," I said, then caught his cloak, for there was a great swath of red-brown, still damp, along the side of his tunic, visible now in the glare as we passed a torch-pole, that I had not noticed before; the rusty color matched his hair.

"A scratch, literally," he said smiling, seeing my horrified look. "One of the fighting-cats whose Raven master I had killed—Cabal dispatched the beast, but not before it had dug in its claws. Almost as sharp a scratcher as that ill-tempered little kitten my mother used to keep . . . Give you good night, braud.''

I watched him walk away, then took another path through the campment, for I was utterly wide-awake, juddery with that kind of energy that comes of overtiredness, and had not a hope of sleep until I had walked my mood out a little. So, though I thought with longing of my bed, and of Morgan already asleep—I could sense her calm dreamlessness even through my unsettled humor—I hitched my cloak around me to keep out the spring chill and headed back toward the lights.

After perhaps another half hour I began to grow tired, and turned my steps to take me back to the tent I shared with Morgan. As I crossed the path that led up to Uthyr's tent, my dull brain registered Arthur passing perhaps twenty yards ahead of me. It was not until a hundred paces later that the thought struck me: Cabal had not been with him. And then a further thought, and this one struck to the heart: As Arthur—or the man I had thought to be Arthur—had passed in front of me, the light from a quartz-hearth had fallen on him, and there had been no bloodstain on his tunic.

The thought takes too long to recount: By now I was flying back to Uthyr's tent as if Arawn's death-hounds, those red-eared, white-coated, four-footed terrors, were upon my heels.

Because now I knew why we had not been able to find Owein Rheged.

It was a longer distance back to the King's tent than I had realized; but I covered it like a hunted hare, shouting as I went for warriors to follow me, praying against the dawning certainty rising within me that my fears were all unfounded.

At last I reached the little hill on which stood Uthyr's tent. All looked peaceful from without: The lights still shone within, though there were no guards outside, and that too gave new wings to my fears and feet alike. Then I saw the guards, lying huddled just outside the light thrown by the torches; and in that same moment of seeing, and knowing they were dead, I threw open the flap of Uthyr's tent.

I have heard that a warrior receiving a mortal wound, or a charioteer driving headlong into an unavoidable collision, or a rider being thrown at a wall, will all say alike, if they live to speak of it after, that it seemed the moment was endless: that they could count the spokes on the oncoming chariot wheels, could have reached up to seize the flying spear, could have counted every stone of the fence, so stretched and slow-moving did time suddenly become.

And I felt it now, save that it was more as if time had *stopped*, for me and for all of us: For what I saw, as I stood frozen on the threshold of the tent, could have stopped time forever.

Uthyr lay crumpled on the floor of the tent, the arms of Dôn on his tunic reddening as I watched. Ygrawn I could not see at all. But what held my gaze and near stole away my reason was what I saw not ten feet in front of me: Arthur, locked in mortal combat with—himself.

Two Arthurs were blade to blade before me, fighting in silence and in savagery: And even as I watched in anguish and horror, even as Fian guards came pounding up behind me, even as I stepped forward—instinctively, and unarmed as I was—with some mad thought of halting the fight, even as all this the two Arthurs—one of whom was Arthur in truth and the other Owein Rheged—cut each other down, falling to lie beside the fallen King on the blood-washed floor of the tent.

(Here ends *The Hawk's Gray Feather*, the first book in *The Tales of Arthur* sequence of THE KELTIAD. The second book is called *The Oak Above the Kings*.)

Appendices

Glossary

adhalta: pupil, student; used in the vocative

aer: sung satirical verse

Aes Sidhe: (pron. *eyes-shee*) the Shining Ones; a race of possibly divine or immortal beings; their king is Nudd ap Llyr

afanc: large, savage carnivore native to the planet Gwynedd

aircar: small personal transport vehicle used on Keltic worlds; at the time in question, almost unheard-of

Airts: the four magical directions to which sacred circles are oriented: East, South, West and North

aisling: waking, wishful dream; daydream

alanna: "child," "little one"; Erinnach endearment

Alasdair Mór: the historical personage known as Alexander the Great

amhic: "my son"; used in the vocative

anama-chara: "soul-friend"; term for those close and strong friends limited to one or two in a person's life

an-da-shalla: "The Second Sight"; Keltic talent of precognition (also **Sight** or **Seeing**)

Anfa: "Storm"; byname for Athyn Cahanagh, Ard-rían of Keltia

annat: place of formal public worship or contemplation; indoors, as opposed to nemetons (q.v.); usually attached to institutions such as convents or monasteries, but frequently found in private homes as well

annerch: formal embrace given by monarch to liegeman or liegewoman

anruth: bard who travels and plays for hire, unattached to any household

an uachdar: lit., "uppermost"; in salutations (e.g., *Pendreic an uachdar!*) usually translated as "Long live _____!"

aonach: formal gathering, assembly or fair

ap: "son of"

Ard-rían, Ard-rígh: "High Queen," "High King"; title of the Keltic sovereign

Ard-tiarnas: "High Dominion"; generic term for supreme rulership over Keltia

arva-draoi: "Druid's Fence"; magical spell of hindering

Arvor: chief planet of the Brytaned system

athra: "father"; a formal style

athra-chéile: "father-in-law"; lit., "mate-father" (**mathra-chéile,** "mother-in-law")

athro: "teacher," "master"

Awen: (usually, **Holy** or **Sacred Awen**) lit., the Muse or sacred poetic gift of inspiration; as used by bards, the personified creative spirit

bach: (also **-bach,** added as suffix to male names) denotes affection; used to all ages and stations and can be translated as "lad" (fem., **fach** or **-fach,** "lass")

balister: laser crossbow

ban-charach: lit., "the loved woman"; term for a woman formally and legally associated with a man (**far-charach,** man so associated with a woman; **céile-charach,** "loved mate," term for either partner or the partnership itself)

Ban-draoi: lit., "woman-druid"; Keltic order of priestess-sorceresses in the service of the Ban-dia, the Mother Goddess

bansha: female spirit, often red-cloaked, that sings and wails before a death in many ruling Erinnach families; often seen as a wild rider in the air or over water

bards: Keltic order of poets, chaunters and loremasters

beannacht: "blessing"; used as salutation of greeting and farewell

Beltain: festival of the beginning of summer, celebrated on 1 May

birlinn: elegant, galley-type ship, usually both oared and masted

bodach: term of opprobrium or commiseration, depending on circumstances; roughly, "bastard"

bonnive: young pig, piglet

borraun: wood-framed, tambourine-shaped goatskin drum, played by hand or with a small flat wooden drumstick

braud: "brother"

brehons: Keltic lawgivers and judges

Broinn-na-draoichta: "Magic's Womb," chief hallow of the Ban-draoi order; a sacred cavern located beneath their college at Scartanore

brugh: fortified manor house, usually belonging to one of the gentry or nobility; in cities, a town-palace of great elegance and size

bruidean: inn or waystation, maintained by local authorities, where any traveller of whatever rank or resources is entitled by law to claim free hospitality

Buarach: "stall-rope"; binding-spell used by sorcerers to restrain an unfit person from the use of magic

caer: fortress, stronghold

Caerdroia: capital city of Keltia, on the throneworld of Tara

cait-sith: faerie panthers, gold-furred and the size of a foal, kept as pets by the Sidhe

caltraps: three-spiked iron balls, tossed into the path of horses in battle to bring them down with their riders

Camcheachta: constellation of the Plough

cantred: political division of planets in the Kymric system, roughly equivalent to county or shire; province

cantrip: very small, simple spell or minor magic

Caomai: constellation of the Armed King (Orion)

caredd, pl. **careddau:** "heart," "dear one"; used to family and friends

cariad: "heart," "beloved"; used to a lover
cariadol: "heart," "little love"; used to a child
castaun: chestnut; also, the red-brown color of a chestnut
céadchosach: "hundred-foot"; centipede
ceili: (pron. *kay-lee*) a dancing-party or ball; any sort of revelry
clarsa: Keltic musical instrument similar to harpsichord
cleggan: vicious biting insect that buzzes annoyingly
cliamhan: relation by marriage; generic term that applies to
    any indirect kinship (wife's niece's husband's father,
    sister's husband's mother, and the like)
cliath: journeyman bard
clinker-built: of boats or ships, construction technique in
    which planks are laid to overlap downwards and sternwards
clochan: dome- or yurt-like structure used by the Fianna in
    the field
Companions: also, **the Circle;** those who are known to his-
    tory as Arthur Ard-rígh's earliest and closest supporters;
    latterly raised to knighthood
cu-sith: faerie hounds, green-furred and golden-eyed
cwm: (pron. *coom*) hollow; a natural amphitheatre found
    in hilly lands

dán: "doom"; fated karma
Dânai: the Folk of the Goddess Dâna (also **Danaans**); the
    original Kelts
deosil: righthandwise or sunwise (on a ship, the starboard side)
dermasealer: skinfuser; medical tool used to repair flesh
    lacerations by means of laser sutures
dichtal: bardic finger-language, often used as secret code
Dobhar and Iar-Dobhar: the lands of Water and Beyond-
    Water; magical planes attained to by sorcerers in trance
dolmen: sacred pillar-stone
Domina: in the Ban-draoi order, title of a high priestess
Druids: magical order of Keltic sorcerer-priests in the service
    of the Ollathair, the Lord-father
dubhachas: "gloom"; melancholy characterized by cause-
    less depression and inexpressible longing for unname-
    able things

dúchas: lordship or holding; usually carries a title with it

duergar: in Kernish folklore, an evil elemental or place-spirit

dún: a stronghold of the Sidhe (also **liss** or **rath**)

earthfasting: a simple magic, often the first a child will learn, whereby the practitioner causes the victim to be rooted to the ground, unable even to lift a foot until released

faha: courtyard or enclosed space in a castle complex or encampment

Fáinne: "The Ring"; the six system viceroys and vicereines of Keltia; instituted by St. Brendan and abolished by Edeyrn, the council was re-established by Arthur

falair: winged horse whose species is native to the Erinna system

far-a-tigh: man householder (*ban-a-tigh,* woman householder)

far-eolas: "man of knowledge"; title bestowed on an especially learned teacher (*ban-eolas,* woman teacher)

farl: quarter of loaf of bread or bannock

far-labhartha: tonguetalker's model of person or beast, which is made to appear to speak (**tonguetalker:** ventriloquist)

ferch: "daughter of"

Fianna: Keltic order of military supremacy; officer class

fidchell: chess-style board game (**kern:** equivalent piece to a pawn)

fidil: four-stringed musical instrument played with a bow

findruinna: superhard, silvery metal used in swords, armor and the like

Fionnasa: feast of the god Fionn, celebrated on 29 September

fíor-eolas: truthsense, ability to discern truth from falsehood; can be learned or-inborn

fireflaw: lightning-bolt

fith-fath: spell of shapeshifting or glamourie; magical illusion

flain: laser arrow fired from balister

Fomori: ancient enemies of the Keltic people

fostern: relation by fosterage; foster-brother or foster-sister

galláin: "foreigners"; sing., **gall** (fem., **gallwyn**); generic term for all humanoid non-Kelts and often used for non-humanoids as well

galloglass: Keltic foot-soldier

garron: breed of small, sturdy horses, 13–14 hands high, usually gray or dun in color

gauran: plow-beast similar to ox or bullock

glaistig: on the planet Scota, a legendary demon or hag-creature

glaive: (from Erinnach, *claideamh*) lightsword; laser weapon used throughout Keltia

glib: hair above forehead; bangs or forelock fringe

goleor: "in great numbers, an overabundance"; Englic word *galore* is derived from it

graal: shallow, two-handled cup or dish, usually made of precious metal and decorated with jewels and carving

grianán: "sun-place"; solar, private chamber

grieshoch: embers; low-smoldering fire

gruagach: long-haired female spirit associated with woods or hills

gúna: generic name for various styles of long robe or gown

gwlan: fine, strong wool-linen weave, used for everyday apparel

Gwynfyd: the Circle of Perfection; eternal afterlife to be attained to only after many cycles of rebirth

hai atton: "heigh to us"; the horn-cry that rallies an army

Hail: the Eagle-people; winged race native to the planet Galathay, with an average lifespan of more than a thousand years

hanes: (pron. *hah-ness*) "secret," "tale," "reporting" (**Hanes Taliesin,** the bardic code devised by Taliesin ap Gwyddno while yet a student of his craft)

hedge-school: informal, unstructured places of learning, run by journeyman bards, which came into being under the Theocracy so that children might be secretly taught true knowledge

Hu Mawr: Hu the Mighty; father of the gods in the Kymric pantheon

immram: "voyage", pl. **immrama**; the great migrations from Earth to Keltia; also, initiatory trance of Druid and Ban-draoi training sequences

inceptor: third and highest degree of Druid aspirants

inghearrad: intaglio carving; anything incised or engraved

Inion Rían na Reanna: constellation of the Daughter of the Queen of the Stars

jurisconsult: brehon engaged in law-court cases

keeraun: country-boy; any unsophisticated lad

keeve: beaker or barrel

Kelu: "The Crown"; the One High God above all gods, held by Kelts to be both Father God and Mother Goddess, or neither, or beyond such distinctions altogether; cannot be known in earthly life, though frequently prayed to as *Artzan Janco*, "Shepherd of Heaven," and *Yr Mawreth,* "The Highest"

kenning: telepathic technique originally developed (and now used almost exclusively) by Ban-draoi and Druids

kern: Keltic starfleet crew-member; uncommissioned warrior

laeth-fraoch: "hero-light"; the exceptionally visible aura that surrounds an individual of advanced development

lai: unit of distance measurement, equal to approximately one-half mile

lasathair: "half-father"; stepfather

leinna: long, full-sleeved shirt worn under a tunic

lennaun: lover without benefit of formal arrangement

lily-oak: common lilac

Llacharn: "Flamebright"; the sword that Arthur took from the stone on the island of Collimare

llan: retreat-place; cell or enclosure for religious anchorite

Llenaur: lit., "golden cloak"; The Lady of Heaven's Mantle, Keltic name for the Milky Way

lochan: small lake or mountain tarn

Lughnasa: feast of the god Lugh, celebrated on 1 August; by custom, marks first sexual encounter for most young Kelts (the celebratory rite known as **Teltown**)

maenor: hereditary dwelling-place, usually a family seat, in the countryside or city

maeth (also **-maeth**): "foster-father"

maigen: "sanctuary"; border, fixed by law and its extent acccording to rank, that surrounds a noble's lands, within which that lord is responsible for the peace and safety of all folk and their goods

Malen: Kymric goddess of war (usually **Malen Ruadh, Red Malen**)

mamaith: child's word for "mother"; equivalent to Englic "mama" or "mommy"

Marbh-draoi: "Death-druid"; universal byname for Edeyrn ap Rhûn

Master (Scotan and Erinnach); title of heir to clann name (as **Master of Douglas**); **Mistress** for woman heir

mathra: "mother"; a formal style

mathra-chairde: "heart-mother"; style of deepest affection, generally used to foster-mother, nurse or teacher

Mathr'achtaran: "Reverend Mother"; former mode of address used to the head priestess of the Ban-draoi order

m'chara: "my friend"; used in the vocative

mether: four-cornered drinking-vessel, usually made of wood or pottery

methryn: "foster-mother"

Mihangel: Kymric god of battle, known as the Prince of Warriors; legend says that he will command the forces of Light at the battle of Cymynedd, which will decide the fate of the universe between good and evil

mionn: braided hairstyle worn by Fians in battle, so that no enemy can seize them by the hair

mormaor: civic official, usually the chief elected governor of a town or settlement

nathair: generic term for any of various poisonous snakes of the adder type

neladoracht: cloud divination; sorcerers' technique for seeing visions

nemeton: ceremonial stone circle or henge

Nevermas: a time that never comes

nicksticks: divination by pattern of thrown twigs or carved wooden sticks

ollave: master-bard; by extension, anyone with supreme command of any art or science

Olwen White-track: in Keltic legend, a queen's daughter of such power and holiness that white snowflowers sprang up before and behind her as she walked

pastai: small handmeal; turnover consisting of a pastry crust filled with meat or vegetables or both

Pen-bardd: "Chiefest of Bards"; ancient title given to two bards only in all Keltic history—Plenyth ap Alun, founder of the bardic order, and Taliesin ap Gwyddno, its greatest exemplar

petty place: by tradition, the first professional position won by a newly fledged bard, warrior or craftsman

Pheryllt: class of master-Druids who serve as instructors in the order's schools and colleges

piast: large amphibious water-beast found in deepwater lakes on the planets Erinna and Scota; the species was known to Terrans as the Loch Ness Monster

pig-i'-the-wood: children's game in which those in a "safe" place are lured out by those who are "it"

pirn: spindle, thread-winder

pishogue: small magic, cantrip

quaich: low, wide, double-handled drinking-vessel

rann: chanted verse stanza used in magic; spell of any sort

Ravens: Edeyrn's enforcers, used as terror-police

rechtair: steward in royal, noble or wealthy households

rígh-domhna: members of any of the Keltic royal families, as reckoned from a common ancestor, any of whom may (theoretically, at least) be elected to the Sovereignty

ríogh-bardan: "royal bard"; bard in personal employ of the monarch or the monarch's heir

riomhall: magical circle used for ritual or protective purposes

Rocabarra: in Keltic legend, a great gray rock in the seas of Scota; cursed by a Druid to sink beneath the waves, it has risen twice, and its third rising will signal the end of the world

Ro-sai: "Great Teacher"; chief of the **Pheryllt** (q.v.)

saining: rite of Keltic baptism, administered anywhere from seven days to a year and a day after a child's birth

saltar: style of literary composition

Samhain: (pron. *Sah-win*) festival of the beginning of winter and start of the Keltic New Year, celebrated on 31 October (Great Samhain) and continuing until 11 November (Little Samhain)

saulth: ghost or apparition

scaldings: volcanic vents or fumaroles; pools of bubbling sulphurous mud in seismically active areas

scriptal: style of literary composition

sea-bear: sudden tidal surge or wave; groundswell

Seachtanna: the Seven Tests of Druidic initiation

seastone: the gem aquamarine

sgian: small black-handled knife universally worn in Keltia, usually in boot-top (**table-sgian:** knife used at meals, duller and longer-bladed)

shakla: chocolate-tasting beverage brewed with water from the berries of the brown ash; drunk throughout Keltia as a caffeine-based stimulant

shieling: mountain cavern where herds are stabled against the weather

sith-silk: very fine, very costly silk fabric

Six Nations: the six star systems of Keltia (excluding the Throneworld system of Tara); in order of their founding, Erinna, Kymry, Scota, Kernow, Vannin, Brytaned (Arvor)

sizar: first degree of Druid aspirants

snaim-draoi: "Druid's Knot"; technique of magical binding

Solas Sidhe: "The Faery Fire"; natural phenomenon similar to the will-o'-the-wisp but occurring over rocky ground, usually seen in the spring and the fall

sophister: second degree of Druid aspirants

Speiring: "The Asking"; rite of Druidic initiation

spireling: severe windstorm, hurricane (**húracán**)

stravaiging: idle wandering about, rampaging

strawcross: harvest knot traditionally woven by reapers to celebrate the completion of gathering in the crops; pulled to pieces in a ceremony the following spring

streppoch: term of opprobrium; roughly, "bitch"

Sunstanding: the summer or winter solstice

taish: magical projection of a person's own face or form

talpa: blind, blunt-snouted digger animal native to the planet Kernow

Tanist, Tanista: designated heir of line to the Keltic throne

Taoiseach: the Prime Minister of Keltia

tasyk: child's word for "father"; equivalent to Englic "daddy"

telyn: Kymric lap-harp

thrawn: stubborn, unreasonably perverse

Three Cuts: tiny ceremonial nicks made on one's wrist during rites of saining, fostering and marriage, to obtain a drop or two of blood for ritual purposes

Three Shouts: in Keltic legend, given by the Highest God Kelu before the universe was created, at the utterance of which the universe's three circles—Annwn, Abred (or Hollfyd), and Gwynfyd—came into being

tinna-galach: "bright-fire"; the will-o'-the-wisp, occurring over marshy ground; especially noted for its appearances in the great marshlands of Gwenn-Estrad, on the planet Arvor

tirr: cloaking effect, part magical, part mechanical in nature, used to conceal ships, buildings and the like; does not work on living things

torc: massive neck ornament worn by Kelts of rank; heavy, open-ended circle usually of gold or silver

traha: "arrogance"; wanton pride, hubris

Turusachan: the royal palace at Caerdroia; by extension, the entire central government; also, the plateau area above the city of Caerdroia where the governmental buildings are located

ulagaun: the common woods owl

Ulkessar: the historical personage known as Julius Caesar

urrad: townsman, usually landless; lowest Keltic social class

usqueba: "water of life"; also **usqua**; whiskey, generally unblended

Vallican: Kymric dialect, most frequently used in the westlands of the planet Gwynedd

widdershins: lefthandwise or antisunwise; counterclock-wise

Characters

Amris Pendreic, Prince of Dôn; late Tanist of Keltia; eldest son of Darowen Ard-rían and King Gwain; brother to Leowyn and Uthyr; far-charach to Ygrawn Tregaron; father to Arthur

Arthur Pendreic, known also as **Arthur Penarvon**; Prince of the Name of Dôn; son of Amris and Ygrawn; adopted son of Gorlas Penarvon; nephew to Leowyn and Uthyr; foster-brother to Taliesin Glyndour; later Ard-rígh of Keltia by joint rule with Gweniver his second wife

Benesek, house bard to Gwyddno Glyndour; first teacher to Taliesin

Berain, Fian warrior in Ygrawn's service at Daars and Coldgates

Betwyr ap Benoic, Companion; friend to Arthur

Birogue of the Mountain, a lady of the Sidhe

Daronwy ferch Anwas, Companion; heir to the Lord of Endellion; friend to Arthur

Edeyrn Archdruid, known also as **the Marbh-draoi**; magical dictator-usurper now ruling Keltia

Elen Llydaw, Companion; daughter of the Duchess of Arvor; friend to Arthur

Elphin Carannoc, Companion; ollave; chief teacher to Taliesin

Ferdia mac Kenver, Companion; friend to Arthur

Grehan Aoibhell, Companion; the Master of Thomond (heir to the Prince of Thomond); friend and warlord to Arthur

Gorlas Penarvon, Lord of Daars; first husband to Ygrawn Tregaron; adopted father to Arthur

Gweniver Pendreic, Tanista of Keltia; only child of Leowyn Ard-rígh and Queen Seren; niece to Amris and Uthyr; cousin to Arthur; later Ard-rían of Keltia by joint rule with Arthur her husband

Gwenwynbar; daughter of Gerwin, Lord of Plymon, and Tamise Rospaen; first wife to Arthur; mother of Malgan

Gwyddno Glyndour, Lord of Gwaelod; husband to Medeni ferch Elain; father to Taliesin, Tegau, *et al.*; murdered by Edeyrn

Halwynna, nurse to Taliesin; wife to Benesek

Ildana Parogan, Mathr'achtaran (Reverend Mother) of the Ban-draoi order; teacher to Ygrawn and Gweniver

Kei ap Rhydir, Companion; friend to Arthur

Keils Rathen, Companion; warlord to Uthyr Ard-rígh and to Arthur; lover of Gweniver

Leowyn Pendreic, High King of Keltia; second son of Darowen Ard-rían and King Gwain; husband to Seren of Galloway; father to Gweniver

Maderil Gabric, Chief Bard of Keltia

Madoc Dyffrin, Theocracy general; in service of Owein Rheged

Malgan ap Owein; son of Gwenwynbar, reputed son of Owein Rheged

Marguessan Pendreic, Princess of Keltia, Duchess of Eildon; elder daughter of Uthyr Ard-rígh and Queen Ygrawn; cousin and half-sister to Arthur; wife to Irian Locryn

Marigh Aberdaron, Taoiseach of Keltia in Uthyr's service

Medeni ferch Elain, Lady of Gwaelod; wife to Gwyddno; mother of Taliesin

Merlynn Llwyd, known also as **Ailithir**; Druid; teacher to Arthur and Taliesin

Morguenna Pendreic, known as **Morgan**; Princess of Keltia, Duchess of Ys; Companion; younger daughter of Uthyr Ard-rígh and Queen Ygrawn; cousin and half-sister to Arthur; wife to Taliesin

Owein Rheged, Lord of Gwynedd; Edeyrn's regent over the planet Gwynedd; second husband to Gwenwynbar; reputed father of Malgan

Perran of Vangor, alleged spy for Owein Rheged

Pyrs Vechan, Lord of Ruabon; vassal to Owein Rheged

Scathach Aodann, Companion; Fian general; teacher to Arthur and Taliesin

Taliesin Glyndour ap Gwyddno, narrator; Companion; youngest son of Gwyddno and Medeni; foster-brother to Arthur; husband to Morguenna Pendreic

Tarian Douglas, Companion; the Mistress of Douglas (heir to the Prince of Scots); friend and warlord to Arthur

Tegau Glyndour, known as **Tegau Goldbreast**; Companion; eldest daughter of Gwyddno and Medeni; sister to Taliesin

Tryffin Tregaron, Companion; son of Marc'h Duke of Kernow; nephew to Ygrawn; cousin and friend to Arthur

Uthyr Pendreic, High King of Keltia; youngest son of Darowen Ard-rían and King Gwain; second husband to Ygrawn Tregaron; father to Marguessan and Morguenna; uncle to Arthur and Gweniver

Ygrawn Tregaron; daughter of Bregon Duke of Kernow, sister to Marc'h Duke of Kernow; ban-charach to Amris

Pendreic; wife to Gorlas Penarvon; wife and Queen to Uthyr Pendreic; mother of Arthur (by Amris) and Marguessan and Morguenna (by Uthyr)

Taliesin is pronounced tal-YES-in, not tally-essin (nor the more exotic, and equally erroneous, tal-uh-SEEN).

Marguessan is pronounced as spelled; *Morguenna* is pronounced mor-GWEN-a.

Tegau is pronounced TEG-eye.

THE ROYAL HOUSE OF DÓN: Rulers of the Druid Interregnum (Theocracy) and the Dóniaid Restoration

ALAWN Last-king† = Breila Douglas†

Garin† = Athonwy† Brahan† Cador† *SEIRITH = Rhys† of Gwent

(Dukes of Kernow)

Farrand† Keira†

Eilian†

*ELGAN = Suanach ní Ruairc

(Lords of Daars)

Gorlas Penarvon†
(2)

*DAROWEN = Gwain of Kells

Bregon Tregaron = Keresen Harllech

*UTHYR = Ygrawn = Talliesin Glyndour
(3)

Geraint (Gerrans)

Senara = Marc'h   Ygrawn ≠ Amris†   *LEOWYN† = Seren of Galloway   Irian Locryn = Marguessan   Morgan
(1)

Mordryth Gwain Galeron

Isyld ≠ Tryffin   Gwenwynbar = ARTHUR = GWENIVER   Arwenna

Loherin   Malgan   ARAWN

Capitals denote monarchs of Keltia.
*rulers in exile
≠ céile-charach union
† slain by Edeyrn

The Books of The Keltiad

The Tales of Brendan
*The Rock beyond the Billow
*The Song of Amergin
*The Deer's Cry

The Tales of Arthur
The Hawk's Gray Feather
 *The Oak Above the Kings
*The Hedge of Mist

The Tales of Aeron
The Silver Branch
The Copper Crown
The Throne of Scone

The Tales of Gwydion
*The Shield of Fire
*The Sword of Light
*The Cloak of Gold

*forthcoming